D0453972

Penguin Books
Selected Stories

Mary Lavin was born in Massachusetts, and came to Ireland
when she was ten years of age. She has lived there ever since
and now divides her time between her home in County Meath
and Dublin. She is married to Michael McDonald Scott, an
Australian. She was awarded a D.Litt. *honoris causa* by
University College, Dublin, in 1968. Mary Lavin has twice been
awarded a Guggenheim fellowship and has won many prizes
including the James Tait Black Memorial Prize. She is now
considered one of the most gifted living short-story writers and
the reception of each new volume has continued to strengthen
her reputation. Her stories have frequently appeared in the *New
Yorker* and her most recent collections are *The Shrine and Other
Stories* (1977) and *Stories of Mary Lavin, Vol.III* (1978).

Mary Lavin

Selected Stories

Penguin Books

Penguin Books Ltd, Harmondsworth, Middlesex, England
Penguin Books, 40 West 23rd Street, New York, New York 10010, U.S.A.
Penguin Books Australia Ltd, Ringwood, Victoria, Australia
Penguin Books Canada Ltd, 2801 John Street, Markham, Ontario, Canada L3R 1B4
Penguin Books (N.Z.) Ltd, 182–190 Wairau Road, Auckland 10, New Zealand

First published in Great Britain in two volumes by Constable & Co., 1964, 1974
This collection first published in Penguin Books 1981
Reprinted 1984

Printed and bound in Great Britain by
Cox & Wyman Ltd, Reading
Phototypeset in Monophoto Palatino
by Filmtype Services Limited, Scarborough

Contents

Preface

When Penguin invited me to make my own selection for this volume it seemed to me that the choice should be as representative as possible of the whole body of my work in the field of the short story. But, as I have written well over one hundred stories in magazines and in the eleven volumes already published, it was quite clear that a very rigid method of selection would have to be imposed.

After much casting about I hit on the simple solution of taking one story from each volume and, to simplify the choice further, making it the title story in each case. This presented one small difficulty: my first book did not have a title story but only a general one, *Tales from Bective Bridge*, so the choice was made at random. The method, of course, had a certain disadvantage in that titles of volumes of short stories are often chosen by the publisher for reasons other than merit but still in their own way valid. Counterbalancing this, however, I saw a very positive advantage: readers would not be presented with a bookful of stories with which they might already be too familiar from their inclusion in innumerable anthologies.

I hope, therefore, that this method of selection will in fact be found representative of the work to which I have devoted myself almost exclusively for the past forty years.

Mary Lavin
February 1981

Lilacs

'That dunghill isn't doing anyone any harm, and it's not going out of where it is as long as I'm in this house,' Phelim Mulloy said to his wife Ros, but he threw an angry look at his elder daughter Kate who was standing by the kitchen window with her back turned to them both.

'Oh Phelim,' Ros said softly. 'If only it could be moved some-where else besides under the window of the room where we eat our bit of food.'

'Didn't you just say a minute ago people can smell it from the other end of the town? If that's the case I don't see what would be the good in shifting it from one side of the yard to the other.'

Kate could stand no more. 'What I don't see is the need in us dealing in dung at all!'

'There you are! What did I tell you!' Phelim said, 'I knew all along that was what was in the back of your minds, both of you! And the one inside there too,' he added, nodding his head at the closed door of one of the rooms off the kitchen. 'All you want, the three of you, is to get rid of the dung altogether. Why on earth can't women speak out – and say what they mean. That's a thing always puzzled me.'

'Leave Stacy out of this, Phelim,' said Ros, but she spoke quietly. 'Stacy has one of her headaches.'

'I know she has,' said Phelim. 'And I know something else. I know I'm supposed to think it's the smell of the dung gave it to her. Isn't that so?'

'Ah Phelim, that's not what I meant at all. I only thought you might wake her with your shouting. She could be asleep.'

'Asleep is it? It's a real miracle any of you can get a wink of sleep, day or night, with the smell of that poor harmless heap of dung out there, that's bringing good money to this house week after week.' He had lowered his voice, but when he turned and looked at Kate it rose again without his noticing. 'It paid for your education at a fancy boarding school – and for your sister's too. It paid for your notions of learning to play the piano, *and* the violin, both of which instruments is rotting away inside in the parlour and not a squeak of a tune ever I heard out of the one or the other of them since the day they came into the house.'

'We may as well spare our breath, Mother,' Kate said. 'He won't give in, now or ever. That's my belief.'

'That's the truest word that's ever come out of your mouth,' Phelim said to her, and stomping across the kitchen he opened the door that led into the yard and went out, leaving the door wide open. Immediately the faint odour of stale manure that hung in the air was enriched by a smell from a load of hot steaming manure that had just been tipped into a huge dunghill from a farm cart that was the first of a line of carts waiting their turn to unload. Ros sighed and went to close the door, but Kate got ahead of her and banged it shut, before going back to the window and taking up her stand there. After a nervous glance at the door of the bedroom that her daughters shared, Ros, too, went over to the window and both women stared out.

An empty cart was clattering out of the yard and Phelim was leading in another from which, as it went over the spud-stone of the gate, a clod or two of dung fell out on the cobbles. The dunghill was nearly filled, and liquid from it was running down the sides of the trough to form pools through which Phelim waded unconcernedly as he forked back the stuff on top to make room for more.

'That's the last load,' Ros said.

'For this week, you mean,' Kate said. 'Your trouble is you're too soft with him, Mother. You'll have to be harder on him. You'll have to keep at him night and day. That is to say if you care anything at all about me and Stacy.'

'Ah Kate. Can't you see there's no use? Can't you see he's set in his ways?'

'All I can see is the way we're being disgraced,' Kate said angrily. 'Last night, at the concert in the Parish Hall, just before the curtain went up I heard the wife of that man who bought the bakehouse telling the person beside her that they couldn't open a window since they came here with a queer smell that was coming from somewhere, and asking the other person if she knew what it could be. I nearly died of shame, Mother. I really did. I couldn't catch what answer she got, but after the first item was over, and I could glance back, I saw it was Mamie Murtagh she was sitting beside. And you can guess what that one would be likely to have said! My whole pleasure in the evening was spoiled.'

'You take things too much to heart, Kate,' Ros said sadly. 'There's Stacy inside there, and it's my belief she wouldn't mind us dealing in dung at all if it wasn't for the smell of it. Only the other day she was remarking that if he'd even clear a small space under the windows we might plant something there that would smell nice. "Just think, Mother," she said. "Just think if it was a smell of lilac that was coming in to us every time we opened a door or a window."'

'Don't talk to me about Stacy,' Kate said crossly. 'She has lilac on the brain, if you ask me. She never stops talking about it. What did she ever do to try and improve our situation?'

'Ah now Kate, as you know, Stacy is very timid.'

'All the more reason Father would listen to her, if she'd speak to him. He may not let on to it, but he'd do anything for her.'

Ros nodded.

'All the same she'd never speak to him. Stacy would never have the heart to cross anyone.'

'She wouldn't need to say much. Didn't you hear him, today, saying he supposed it was the smell of the dung was giving her her headaches? You let that pass, but I wouldn't – only I know he won't take any more from me, although it's me has to listen to her moaning and groaning from the minute the first cart rattles into the yard. How is it that it's always on a Wednesday she has a headache? And it's been the same since the first Wednesday we came home from the convent.' With that last thrust Kate ran into the bedroom and came out with a raincoat. 'I'm going out for a walk,' she said, 'and I won't come back until the smell of that stuff has died down a bit. You can tell my father that, too, if he's looking for me.'

'Wait a minute, Kate. Was Stacy asleep?' Ros asked.

'I don't know and I don't care. She was lying with her face pressed to the wall, like always.'

When Kate went out, Ros took down the tea-caddy from the dresser and put a few pinches of tea from it into an earthenware pot on the hob of the big open fire. Then, tilting the kettle that hung from a crane over the flames, she wet the tea, and pouring out a cup she carried it over to the window and set it to cool on the sill while she went on watching Phelim.

He was a hard man when you went against him, she thought, a man who'd never let himself be thwarted. He was always the same. That being so, there wasn't much sense in nagging him, she thought, but Kate would never be made to see that. Kate was stubborn too.

The last of the carts had gone, and after shutting the gate Phelim had taken a yard-brush and was sweeping up the dung that had been spilled. When he'd made a heap of it, he got a shovel and gathered it up and flung it up on the dunghill. But whether he did it to tidy the yard or not to waste the dung, Ros didn't know. The loose bits of dung he'd flung up on the top of the trough had dried out, and the bits of straw that were stuck to it had dried out too. They gleamed bright and yellow in a ray of watery sunlight that had suddenly shone forth.

Now that Kate was gone, Ros began to feel less bitter against Phelim. Like herself, he was getting old. She was sorry they had upset him. And while she was looking at him, he laid the yard-brush against the wall of one of the sheds and put his hand to his back. He'd been doing that a lot lately. She didn't like to see him doing it. She went across to the door and opened it.

'There's hot tea in the pot on the hob, Phelim,' she called out. 'Come in and have a cup.' Then seeing he was coming, she went over and gently opened the bedroom door. 'Stacy, would you be able for a cup of tea?' she asked, leaning in over the big feather-bed.

Stacy sat up at once.

'What did he say? Is it going to be moved?' she asked eagerly.

'Ssh, Stacy,' Ros whispered, and then as Stacy heard her father's steps in the kitchen she looked startled.

'Did he hear me?' she asked anxiously.

'No,' said Ros, and she went over and drew the curtains to let in the daylight. 'How is your poor head, Stacy?'

Stacy leaned toward Ros so she could be heard when she whispered. 'Did you have a word with him, Mother?'

'Yes,' said Ros.

'Did he agree?' Stacy whispered.

'No.'

Stacy closed her eyes.

'I hope he wasn't upset?' she said.

Ros stroked her daughter's limp hair. 'Don't you worry anyway, Stacy,' she said. 'He'll get over it. He's been outside sweeping the yard and I think maybe he has forgotten we raised the matter at all. Anyway, Kate has gone for a walk and I called him in for a cup of tea. Are you sure you won't let me bring you in a nice hot cup to sip here in the bed?'

'I think I'd prefer to get up and have it outside, as long as you're really sure father is not upset.'

Ros drew a strand of Stacy's hair back from her damp forehead. 'You're a good girl, Stacy, a good, kind creature,' she said. 'You may feel better when you're on your feet. I can promise you there will be no more arguing for the time being anyway. I'm sorry I crossed him at all.'

It was to Stacy Ros turned, a few weeks later, when Phelim was taken bad in the middle of the night with a sharp pain in the small of his back that the women weren't able to ease, and after the doctor came and stayed with him until the early hours of the morning, the doctor didn't seem able to do much either. Before Phelim could be got to hospital, he died.

'Oh Stacy, Stacy,' Ros cried, throwing herself into her younger daughter's arms. 'Why did I cross him over that old dunghill?'

'Don't fret, Mother,' Stacy begged. 'I never heard you cross him over anything else as long as I can remember. You were always good and kind to him, calling him in out of the yard every other minute for a cup of tea. Morning, noon and night I'd hear your voice, and the mornings the carts came with the dung you'd call him in oftener than ever. I used to hear you when I'd be lying inside with one of my headaches.'

Ros was not to be so easily consoled.

'What thanks is due to a woman for giving a man a cup of hot tea on a bitter cold day? He was the best man ever lived. Oh why did I cross him?'

'Ah Mother, it wasn't only on cold days you were good to him but on summer days too – on every and all kind of days. Isn't that so, Kate?' Stacy said, appealing to Kate.

'You did everything you could to please him, Mother,' Kate said, but seeing this made no impression on her mother she turned to Stacy. 'That's more than could be said about him,' she muttered.

But Ros heard her.

'Say no more, you,' she said. 'You were the one was always at me to torment him. Oh why did I listen to you? Why did I cross him?'

'Because you were in the right. That's why!' Kate said.

'Was I?' Ros said.

Phelim was laid out in the parlour, and all through the night Ros and her daughters sat up in the room with the corpse. The neighbours that came to the house stayed up all night too, but they sat in the kitchen, and kept the fire going and made tea from time to time. Kate and Stacy stared sadly at their dead father stretched out in his shroud, and they mourned him as the man they had known all their lives, a heavy man with a red face whom they had seldom seen out of his big rubber boots caked with muck.

Ros mourned that Phelim too. But she mourned many another Phelim besides. She mourned the Phelim who, up to a little while before, never put a coat on him going out in the raw, cold air, nor covered his head even in the rain. Of course his hair was as thick as thatch! But most of all, she mourned the Phelim whose hair had not yet grown coarse but was soft and smooth as silk, like it was the time he led her in off the road and up a little lane near the chapel one Sunday when he was walking her home from Mass. That was the time when he used to call her by the old name. When, she wondered, when did he stop calling her Rose? Or was it herself gave herself the new name? Perhaps it was someone else altogether, someone outside the family? Just a neighbour maybe? No matter! Ros was a good name anyway, wherever it came from. It was a good name and a suitable name for an old woman. It would have been only foolishness to go on calling her Rose after she faded and dried up like an old twig. Ros looked down at her bony hands and her tears fell on them. But they were tears for Phelim. 'Rose,' he said that day in the lane. 'Rose, I've been thinking about ways to make money. And do you know what I found out? There's a pile of money to be made out of dung.' Rose thought he was joking. 'It's true,' he said. 'The people in the town – especially women – would give any money for a bagful of it for their gardens. And only a few miles out from the town there are farmers going mad to get rid of it, with it piling up day after day and cluttering up their farmyards until they can hardly get in and out their own doors! Now, I was thinking, if I got hold of a horse and cart and went out and brought back a few loads of that dung, and if my father would let me store it for a while in our yard, I could maybe sell it to the people in the town.'

'Like the doctor's wife,' Rose said, knowing the doctor's wife was mad about roses. The doctor's wife had been seen going out into the street with a shovel to bring back a shovelful of horse manure.

'That's right. People like her! And after a while the farmers might deliver the loads to me. I might even pay them a few shillings a load, if I was getting a good price for it. Then if I made as much money as I think I might, maybe soon I'd be able to get a place of my own where I'd have room to store enough to make it a worthwhile business.' To Rose it seemed an odd sort of way to make money, but Phelim was only eighteen then and probably he wanted to have a few pounds in his pocket while he was waiting for something better. 'I'm going to ask my father about the storage today,' he said, 'and in the afternoon I'm going to get hold of a cart and go out the country and see how I get on.'

'Is that so?' Rose said, for want of knowing what else to say.

'It is,' said Phelim. 'And do you know the place I have in mind to buy if I make enough money? I'd buy that place we often looked at, you and me when we were out walking, that place on the outskirts of the town, with a big yard and two big sheds that only need a bit of fixing, to be ideal for my purposes.

'I think so,' Rose said. 'Isn't there an old cottage there all smothered with ivy?'

'That's the very place. Do you remember we peeped in the windows one day last Summer. There's no one living there.'

'No wonder,' Rose said.

'Listen to me, Rose. After I'd done up the sheds,' Phelim said, 'I could fix up the cottage too, and make a nice job of it. That's another thing I wanted to ask you, Rose. How would you like to live in that cottage – after I'd done it up, I mean – with me, I mean?' he added when he saw he'd startled her. 'Well Rose, what have you to say to that?'

She bent her head to hide her blushes, and looked down at her small thin-soled shoes that she only wore on a Sunday. Rose didn't know what to say.

'Well?' said Phelim.

'There's a very dirty smell off dung,' she said at last in a whisper.

'It only smells strong when it's fresh,' Phelim said, 'And maybe you could plant flowers to take away the smell?'

She kept looking down at her shoes.

'They'd have to be flowers with a strong scent out of them!' she said – but already she was thinking of how strongly sweet rocket and mignonette perfumed the air of an evening after rain.

'You could plant all the flowers you liked, you'd have nothing else to do the day long,' he said. How innocent he was, for all that he was thinking of making big money, and taking a wife. She looked up at him. His skin was as fair and smooth as her own. He was the best looking fellow for miles around. Girls far prettier than her would have been glad to be led up a lane by him, just for a bit of a lark, let alone a proposal – a proposal of marriage. 'Well, Rose?' he said, and now there were blushes coming and going in his cheeks too, blotching his face the way the wind blotches a lake when there's a storm coming. And she knew him well enough, even in those days, to be sure he wouldn't stand for anyone putting between him and what he was bent on doing. 'You must know, Rose Magarry, that there's a lot in the way people look at a thing. When I was a young lad, driving along the country roads in my father's trap, I used to love looking down at the gold rings of dung dried out by the sun, as they flashed past underneath the horses' hooves.'

Rose felt like laughing, but she knew he was deadly serious. He wasn't like anybody else in the world she'd ever known. Who else would say a thing like that? It was like poetry. The sun was spilling down on them and in the hedges little pink dog roses were swaying in a soft breeze.

'Alright, so,' she said. 'I will.'

'You will? Oh, Rose! Kiss me so!' he said.

'Not here Phelim!' she cried. People were still coming out of the chapel yard and some of them were looking up the lane.

'Rose Magarry, if you're going to marry me, you must face up to people and never be ashamed of anything I do,' he said, and when she still hung back he put out his hand and tilted up her chin. 'If you don't kiss me right here and now, Rose, I'll have no more to do with you.'

She kissed him then.

And now, at his wake, the candle flames were wavering around his coffin the way the dog roses wavered that day in the Summer breeze.

Ros shed tears for those little dog roses. She shed tears for the roses in her own cheeks in those days. And she shed tears for the soft young kissing lips of Phelim. Her tears fell quietly, but it seemed to Kate and Stacy that, like rain in windless weather, they would never cease.

When the white light of morning came at last, the neighbours got up and went home to do a few chores of their own and be ready for the funeral. Kate and Stacy got ready too, and made Ros ready. Ros didn't look much different in black from what she always looked. Neither did Stacy. But Kate looked well in black. It toned down her high colour.

After the funeral Kate led her mother home. Stacy had already been taken home by neighbours, because she fainted when the coffin was being lowered into the ground. She was lying down when they came home. The women who brought Stacy home and one or two other women who had stayed behind after the coffin was carried out, to put the furniture back in place, gave a meal to the family, but these women made sure to leave as soon as possible to let the Mulloys get used to their loss. When the women had gone Stacy got up and came out to join Ros and Kate. A strong smell of guttered-out candles hung in the air and a faint scent of lilies lingered on too.

'Oh Kate! Smell!' Stacy cried, drawing in as deep a breath as her thin chest allowed.

'For Heaven's sake, don't talk about smells or you'll have our mother wailing again and going on about having crossed him over the dunghill,' Kate said in a sharp whisper.

But Ros didn't need any reminders to make her wail.

'Oh Phelim, Phelim, why did I cross you?' she wailed. 'Wasn't I the bad old woman to go against you over a heap of dung that, if I looked at things rightly, wasn't bad at all after it dried out a bit. It was mostly only yellow straw.'

'Take no heed of her,' Kate counselled Stacy. 'Go inside you with our new hats and coats, and hang them up in our room with a sheet draped over them. Black nap is a caution for collecting dust.' To Ros she spoke kindly, but firmly. 'You've got to give over this moaning, Mother,' she said. 'You're only tormenting yourself. Why wouldn't you let him see how we felt about the dung?'

Ros stopped moaning long enough to look sadly out the window. 'It was out of the dung he made his first few shillings,' she said.

'That may be! But how long ago was that? He made plenty of money other ways as time went on. There was no need in keeping on the dung and humiliating us. He only did it out of obstinacy.' As Stacy came back after hanging up their black clothes, Kate appealed to her. 'Isn't that so, Stacy?'

Stacy drew another thin breath.

'It doesn't smell too bad today, does it?' she said. 'I suppose the scent of the flowers drove it out.'

'Well, the house won't always be filled with lilies,' Kate said irritably. 'In any case, Stacy, it's not the smell concerns me. What concerns me is the way people look at us when they hear how our money is made.'

Ros stopped moaning again for another minute. 'It's no cause for shame. It's honest dealing, and that's more than can be said for the dealings of others in this town. You shouldn't heed people's talk, Kate.'

'Well, I like that!' she said. 'May I ask what you know, Mother, about how people talk. Certain kinds of people I mean. Good class people! It's easily seen you were never away at boarding school like Stacy and me, or else you'd know what it feels like to have to admit our money was made out of horse manure and cow dung!'

'I don't see what great call there was on you to tell them!' Ros said.

'Stacy! Stacy! Did you hear that?' Kate cried.

Stacy put her hand to her head. She was getting confused. There was some truth in what Kate had said, and she felt obliged to side with her, but first she ran over and threw herself down at her mother's knees.

'We didn't tell them at first, Mother,' she said, hoping to make Ros feel better. 'We told them our father dealt in fertilizer, but one of the girls looked up the word in a dictionary and found out it was only a fancy name for manure.

It was astonishing to Kate and Stacy how Ros took that. She not only stopped wailing but she began to laugh.

'Your father would have been amused to hear that,' she said.

'Well, it wasn't funny for us,' Kate said.

Ros stopped laughing, but the trace of a small bleak smile remained on her face.

'It wasn't everyone had your father's sense of humour,' she said.

'It wasn't everyone had his obstinacy either!' Kate said.

'You're right there, Kate,' Ros said simply. 'Isn't that why I feel so bad? When we knew how stubborn he was, weren't we the stupid women to be always trying to best him? We only succeeded in making him miserable.'

Kate and Stacy looked at each other.

'How about another cup of tea, Mother? I'll bring it over here to you beside the fire,' Stacy said, and although her mother made no reply she made the tea and brought over a cup. Ros took the cup but handed back the saucer.

'Leave that back on the table,' she said, and holding the cup in her two hands she went over to the window, although the light was fading fast.

'It only smells bad on hot muggy days,' she said.

Kate gave a loud sniff. 'Don't forget Summer is coming,' she said.

For a moment it seemed Ros had not heard, then she gave a sigh.

'It is and it isn't,' she said. 'I often think that in the January of the year it's as true to say we have put the Summer behind us as it is to say it's ahead!' Then she glanced at a calendar on the wall. 'Is tomorrow Wednesday?' she asked, and an anxious expression overcame the sorrowful look on her face. Wednesday was the day the farmers delivered the dung.

'Mother! You don't think the farmers will be unmannerly enough to come banging on the gate tomorrow, and us after having a death in the family?' Kate said in a shocked voice.

'Death never interfered with business yet, as far as I know,' Ros said coldly. 'And the farmers are kind folk. I saw a lot of them at the funeral. They might think it all the more reason to come. Knowing my man is taken from me.'

'Mother!' This time Kate was more than shocked, she was outraged. 'You're not thinking, by any chance, of keeping on dealing with them – of keeping on dealing in dung?'

Ros looked her daughter straight in the face.

'I'm thinking of one thing and one thing only,' she said. 'I'm thinking of your father and him young one day, and the next day, you might say, him stretched on the bed inside with the neighbours washing him for his burial.' Then she began to moan again.

'If you keep this up you'll be laid alongside him one of these days,' Kate said.

'Leave me be!' Ros said. 'I'm not doing any harm to myself by thinking about him. I like thinking about him.'

'He lived to a good age, Mother. Don't forget that,' Kate said.

'I suppose that's what you'll be saying about me one of these days,' Ros said, but she didn't seem as upset as she had been. She turned to Stacy. 'It seems only like yesterday, Stacy, that I was sitting up beside him on the cart, right behind the horse's tail, with my white blouse on me and my gold chain that he gave me bouncing about on my front, and us both watching the road flashing past under the horse's hooves, bright with gold rings of dung.'

Kate raised her eyebrows. But Stacy gave a sob. And that night, when she and Kate were in bed, just before she faced in to the wall, Stacy gave another sob.

'Oh Kate, it's not a good sign when people begin to go back over the past, is it?'

'Are you speaking about Mother?'

'I am. And did you see how bad she looked when you brought her home from the grave?'

'I did,' said Kate. 'It may be true what I said to her. If she isn't careful we may be laying her alongside poor father before long.'

'Oh Kate. How could you say such a thing?' Stacy burst into tears. 'Oh Kate. Oh Kate, why did we make her cross father about the dunghill? I know how she feels. I keep reproaching myself for all the hard things I used to think about him when I'd be lying here in bed with one of my headaches.'

'Well, you certainly never came out with them!' Kate said. 'You left it to me to say them for you! Not that I'm going to reproach myself about anything! There was no need in him keeping that dunghill. He only did it out of pig-headedness. And now, if you'll only let me, I'm going to sleep.'

Kate was just dropping off when Stacy leant up on her elbow.

'You don't really think they will come in the morning, do you – Kate – the carts I mean – like our mother said?'

'Of course not,' Kate said.

'But if they do?'

'Oh go to sleep Stacy, for Heaven's sake. There's no need facing things until they happen. And stop fidgeting! You're twitching the blankets off me. Move over.'

Stacy faced back to the wall and lay still. She didn't think she'd be able to sleep, but when she did, it seemed as if she'd only been asleep one minute when she woke to find the night had ended. The hard, white light of day was pressing on her eyelids. It's a new day for them, she thought, but not for their poor father. Father laid away in the cold clay. Stacy shivered and drew up her feet that were touching the icy iron rail at the foot of the bed. It must have been the cold wakened her. Opening her eyes she saw, through a chink between the curtains, that the crinkled edges of the big corrugated sheds glittered with frost. If only – she thought – if only it was Summer. She longed for the time when warm winds would go daffing through the trees, and when in the gardens to which they delivered fertilizer, the tight hard beads of lilac buds would soon loop out into soft pear-shaped bosoms of blossoms. And then, gentle as those thoughts, another thought came into Stacy's mind, and she wondered whether their father, sleeping under the close, green sods, might mind now if they got rid of the dunghill. Indeed it seemed the dunghill was as good as gone, now that father himself was gone. Curling up in the warm blankets Stacy was preparing to sleep again, when there was a loud knocking on the yard-gates and the sound of a horse shaking its harness. She raised her head off the pillow, and as she did, she heard the gate in the yard slap back against the wall and there was a rattle of iron-shod wheels travelling in across the cobbles.

'Kate! Kate!' she screamed, shaking her. 'I thought Father was leading in a load of manure.'

'Oh shut up, Stacy. You're dreaming – or else raving,' Kate muttered from the depths of the blankets that she had pulled closer around her. But suddenly she sat up. And then, to Stacy's astonishment, she threw back the bedclothes altogether, right across the footrail of the bed, and ran across the floor and pressed her face to the window pane. 'I might have known this would happen!' she cried. 'For all her lamenting and wailings, she knows what she's doing. Come and look!' Out in the yard Ros was leading in the first of the carts, and calling out to the drivers of the other carts waiting their turn to come in. She was not wearing her black clothes, but her ordinary everyday coat, the colour of the earth and the earth's decaying refuse. In the raw cold air, the manure in the cart she was leading was still giving off, unevenly, the fog of its hot breath.

'Get dressed, Stacy. We'll go down together!' Kate ordered and grabbed her clothes and dressed.

When they were both dressed, with Kate leading, the sisters went into the kitchen. The yard door was open and a powerful stench was making its way inside. The last cart was by then unloaded, and Ros soon came back into the kitchen and began to warm her hands by the big fire already roaring up the chimney. She had left the door open but Kate went over and banged it shut.

'Well?' said Ros.

'Well?' Kate said after her, only louder.

Stacy sat down at once and began to cry. The other two women took no notice of her, as they faced each other across the kitchen.

'Say whatever it is you have to say, Kate,' Ros said.

'You know what I have to say,' said Kate.

'Don't say it so! Save your breath!' Ros said, and she went as if to go out into the yard again, but Stacy got up and ran and put her arms around her.

'Mother, you always agreed with us! You always said it would be nice if – '

Ros put up a hand and silenced her.

'Listen to me, both of you,' she said. 'I had no right agreeing with anyone but your father,' she said. 'It was to him I gave my word. It was him I had a right to stand behind. He always said there was no shame in making money anyway it could be made, as long as it was made honestly. And another thing he said was that money was money, whether it was in gold coins or in dung. And that was true for him. Did you, either of you, hear what the priest said yesterday in the cemetery? "God help all poor widows." That's what he said. And he set me thinking. Did it never occur to you that it might not be easy for us, three women with no man about the place, to keep going, to put food on the table and keep a fire on the hearth, to say nothing at all about finery and fal-lals.'

'That last remark is meant for me I suppose,' Kate said, but the frown that came on her face seemed to come more from worry than anger. 'By the way, Mother,' she said. 'You never told us whether you had a word with the solicitor when he came with his condolences? Did you by any chance find out how father's affairs stood?'

'I did,' Ros said. But that was all she said as she went out into the yard again and took up the yard-brush. She had left the door open but Stacy ran over and closed it gently.

'She's twice as stubborn as ever father was,' Kate said. 'There's going to be no change around here as long as she's alive.'

Stacy's face clouded. 'All the same, Kate, she's sure to let us clear a small corner and put in a few shrubs and things,' she said timidly.

'Lilacs, I suppose!' Kate said, with an unmistakable sneer, which however Stacy did not see.

'Think of the scent of them coming in the window,' she said.

'Stacy, you are a fool!' Kate cried. 'At least I can see that our mother has more important things on her mind than lilac bushes. I wonder what information she got from Jasper Kane? I thought her very secretive. I would have thought he'd have had a word with me, as the eldest daughter.'

'Oh, Kate.' Stacy's eyes filled with tears again. 'I never thought

about it before, but when poor mother –' she hesitated, then after a
gulp she went on – 'when poor mother goes to join father, you and I
will be all alone in the world with no one to look after us.'

'Stop whimpering, Stacy,' Kate said sharply. 'We've got to start
living our own lives, sooner or later.' Going over to a small
ornamental mirror on the wall over the fireplace, she looked into it
and patted her hair. Stacy stared at her in surprise, because unless
you stood well back from it you could only see the tip of your nose in
that little mirror. But Kate was not looking at herself. She was
looking out into the yard, which was reflected in the mirror, in
which she could see their mother going around sweeping up stray
bits of straw and dirt to bring them over and throw them on top of
the dunghill. Then Kate turned around. 'We don't need to worry too
much about that woman. She'll hardly follow father for many a long
day! That woman is as strong as a tree.'

But Ros was not cut out to be a widow. If Phelim had been taken
from her before the dog roses had faded in the hedges that first
Summer of their lives together, she could hardly have mourned him
more bitterly than she did when an old woman, tossing and turning
sleeplessly in their big brass bed.

Kate and Stacy did their best to ease her work in the house. But
there was one thing Kate was determined they would not do, and
that was give any help on the Wednesday mornings when the farm
carts arrived with their load. Nor would they help her to bag it for
the townspeople, although as Phelim had long ago foreseen, the
townspeople were often glad enough to bag it for themselves, or
wheel it away in barrowfuls. On Wednesday morning when the
rapping came at the gates at dawn, Kate and Stacy stayed in bed and
did not get up, but Stacy was wide awake and lay listening to the
noises outside. And sometimes she scrambled out of bed across Kate
and went to the window.

'Kate?' Stacy would say almost every day.

'What?'

'Perhaps I ought to step out to the kitchen and see the fire is kept
up. She'll be very cold when she comes in.'

'You'll do nothing of the kind I hope! We must stick to our
agreement. Get back into bed.'

'She has only her old coat on her and it's very thin, Kate.'

Before answering her, Kate might raise herself up on one elbow
and hump the blankets up with her so that when she sank back they
were pegged down.

'By all the noise she's making out there I'd say she'd keep up her
circulation no matter if she was in nothing but her shift.'

'That work is too heavy for her, Kate. She shouldn't be doing it at all.'

'And who is to blame for that? Get back to bed, like I told you, and don't let her see you're looking out. She'd like nothing better than that.'

'But she's not looking this way Kate. She couldn't see me.'

'That's what you think! Let me tell you, that woman has eyes in the back of her head.'

Stacy giggled nervously at that. It was what their mother herself used to tell them when they were small.

Then suddenly she stopped giggling and ran back and threw herself across the foot of the bed and began to sob.

After moving her feet to one side, Kate listened for a few seconds to the sobbing. Then she humped up her other shoulder and pegged the blankets under her on the other side.

'What ails you now?' she asked then.

'Oh Kate, you made me think of when we were children, and she used to stand up so tall and straight and with her gold chain and locket bobbing about on her chest.' Stacy gave another sob. 'Now she's so thin and bent the chain is dangling down to her waist.'

Kate sat up with a start. 'She's not wearing that chain and locket now, out in the yard, is she? Gold is worth a lot more now than it was when father bought her that.'

Stacy went over to the window and looked out again. 'No, she's not wearing it.'

'I should hope not!' Kate said. 'I saw it on her at the funeral but I forgot about it afterwards in the commotion.'

'She took it off when we came back,' Stacy said. 'She put it away in father's black box and locked the box.'

'Well, that's one good thing she did anyway,' Kate said. 'She oughtn't to wear it at all.'

'Oh Kate!' Stacy looked at her.

'What?' Kate asked, staring back.

Stacy didn't know what she wanted to say. She couldn't put it into words. She had always thought Kate and herself were alike, that they had the same way of looking at things, but lately she was not so sure of this. They were both getting older of course, and some people were not as even-tempered as others. Not that she thought herself a paragon, but being so prone to headaches she had to let a lot of things pass that she didn't agree with – like a thing Kate said recently about the time when they were away at school. Their mother had asked how many years ago it was, and while Stacy was trying to count up the years, Kate answered at once.

'Only a few years ago,' she said. That wasn't true but perhaps it only seemed like that to Kate.

Gradually, as time passed, Stacy too, like Kate, used to put the blankets over her head so as not to hear the knocking at the gate, and the rattle of the cart wheels, or at least to deaden the noise of it. She just lay thinking. Kate had once asked her what went through her head when she'd be lying saying nothing.

'This and that,' she'd said. She really didn't think about anything in particular. Sometimes she'd imagine what it would be like if they cleared a small space in the yard and planted things. She knew of course that if they put in a lilac bush it would be small for a long time and would not bear flowers for ages. It would be mostly leaves, and leaves only, for years, or so she'd read somewhere. Yet she always imagined it would be a fully grown lilac they'd have outside the window. Once she imagined something absolutely ridiculous. She was lying half awake and half asleep, and she thought they had transplanted a large full grown lilac, a lilac that had more flowers than leaves, something you never see. And then, as she was half-dozing, the tree got so big and strong its roots pushed under the wall and pushed up through the floorboards – bending the nails and sending splinters of wood flying in all directions. And its branches were so laden down with blossom, so weighted down, that one big pointed bosom of bloom almost touched her face. But suddenly the branch broke with a crack and Stacy was wide awake again. Then the sound that woke her came again, only now she knew what it was – a knocking on the gate outside, only louder than usual, and after it came a voice calling out. She gave Kate a shake.

'Do you hear that, Kate? Mother must have slept it out.'

'Let's hope she did,' Kate said. 'It might teach her a lesson – it might make her see she's not as fit and able as she thinks.'

'But what about the farmers?'

'Who cares about them,' Kate said. '*I* don't! Do you?'

When the knocking came again a third time, and a fourth time, Stacy shook Kate again.

'Kate! I wouldn't mind going down and opening the gate,' she said.

'You? In your nightdress?' Kate needed to say no more. Stacy cowered down under the blankets in her shame. All of a sudden she sat up again.

'There wouldn't be anything wrong with mother, would there?' she cried. This time, without heeding Kate, Stacy climbed out over her to get to the floor. 'I won't go out to the yard, I promise, I'll just go and wake mother,' she cried. She ran out of the room.

'Come back and shut that door,' Kate called after her. Stacy mustn't have heard. 'Stacy! Come back and shut this door,' Kate shouted.

Stacy still didn't come back.

'Stacy!' Kate yelled. 'Stacy?'

Then she sat up.

'Is there something wrong?' she asked. Getting no answer now either, she got up herself.

Stacy was in their mother's room, lying in a heap on the floor. As Kate said afterwards, she hardly needed to look to know their mother was dead, because Stacy always flopped down in a faint the moment she came up against something unpleasant. And the next day, in the cemetery, when the prayers were over and the grave-diggers took up their shovels, Stacy passed out again and had to be brought home by two of the neighbours, leaving Kate to stand and listen to the stones and the clay rumbling down on the coffin.

'You're a nice one, Stacy! Leaving me to stand listening to that awful sound.'

'But I heard it, Kate,' Stacy protested. 'I did! Then my head began to reel, and I got confused. The next thing I knew I was on the ground looking up at the blue sky and thinking the noise was the sound of the horses going clip-clap along the road.'

Kate stared at her.

'Are you mad? What horses?'

'Oh Kate, don't you remember? The horses mother was always talking about. She was always telling us how, when she and father were young, she used to sit beside him on a plank across the cart and watch the road flashing by under the horse's hooves, glittering with bright gold rings of dung?'

Kate, however, wasn't listening.

'That reminds me. Isn't tomorrow Wednesday?' she said. 'Which of us is going to get up and let in the farm carts?' When Stacy stared vacantly, Kate stamped her foot. 'Don't look so stupid, Stacy! They came the day after father was buried, why wouldn't they come tomorrow? Mother herself said it was their way of showing – showing that as far as they were concerned the death wouldn't make any difference.'

'Oh Kate. How do you think they'll take it when you tell them – '

'Tell them what? Really Stacy, you *are* a fool. Tomorrow is no day to tell them anything. We'll have to take it easy – wait and see how we stand, before we talk about making changes.'

Kate was so capable. Stacy was filled with admiration for her. She would not have minded in the least getting up to open the gate, but she never would be able to face a discussion of the future. Kate was able for everything, and realizing this, Stacy permitted herself a small feeling of excitement at the thought of them making their own plans and standing on their own two feet.

'I'll get up and light the fire and bring you a cup of tea in bed before you have to get up, Kate,' she said.

Kate shrugged her shoulders. 'If I know you, Stacy, you'll have one of your headaches,' Kate said.

Stacy said nothing. She was resolved to get up, headache or no headache. On the quiet she set an old alarm clock she found in the kitchen. But the alarm bell was broken, and the first thing Stacy heard next morning was the rapping on the gate. When she went to scramble out, to her surprise Kate was already gone from the room. And when Stacy threw her clothes on and ran out to the kitchen, the fire was roaring up the chimney, and a cup with a trace of sugar and tea leaves in the bottom of it was on the window-sill. The teapot was on the hob but it had been made a long time and it was cold. She made herself another pot and took it over to sip it by the window, looking out.

Kate was in the yard, directing the carts and laughing and talking with the men. Kate certainly had a way with her and no mistake. When it would come to telling the farmers that they needn't deliver any more dung, they wouldn't be offended.

One big tall farmer, with red hair and whiskers, was the last to leave, and he and Kate stood talking at the gate so long Stacy wondered if, after all, Kate mightn't be discussing their future dealings with him. She hoped she wouldn't catch cold. She had put a few more sods of turf on the fire.

'Do you want to set the chimney on fire?' Kate asked when she came in. Stacy didn't let herself get upset though. Kate was carrying all the responsibility now, and it was bound to make her edgy.

'I saw you talking to one of the men,' said she. 'I was wondering if perhaps you were giving him a hint of our plans and sounding him out?'

'I was sounding him out alright,' Kate said, and she smiled. 'You see, Stacy, I've been thinking that we might come up with a new plan. You mightn't like it at first, but you may come round when I make you see it in the right light. Sit down and I'll tell you.' Stacy sat down. Kate stayed standing. 'I've been looking into the ledgers, and I would never have believed there was so much money coming in from the dung. So, I've been thinking that, instead of getting rid of it, we ought to try and take in more, twice or three times more, and make twice or three times as much money. No! No! Sit down again,

Stacy. Hear me out. My plan would be that we'd move out of here, and use this cottage for storage – the sheds are not big enough. We could move into a more suitable house, larger and with a garden maybe – '

When Stacy said nothing Kate looked sharply at her. It wouldn't have surprised her if Stacy had flopped off in another faint, but she was only sitting dumbly looking into the fire. 'It's only a suggestion,' Kate said, feeling her way more carefully. 'You never heed anything, Stacy, but when I go out for my walks I take note of things I see – and there's a plot of ground for sale out a bit the road, but not too far from here all the same, and it's for sale – I've made enquiries. Now if we were to try and buy that it wouldn't cost much to build a bungalow. I've made enquiries about the cost of that too, and it seems – '

But Stacy had found her tongue. 'I don't want to move out of here, Kate,' she cried. 'This is where we were born, where my mother and father – ' She began to cry. 'Oh Kate! I never want to leave here. Never! Never!'

Kate could hardly speak with fury.

'Stay here so!' she said. 'But don't expect me to stay with you. I'm getting out of here at the first chance I get to go. And let me tell you something else. That dunghill isn't stirring out of where it is until I've a decent dowry out of it. Cry away now to your heart's content for all I care.' Going over to their bedroom Kate went in and banged the door behind her.

Stacy stopped crying and stared at the closed door. Her head had begun to throb and she would have liked to lie down, but after the early hour Kate had risen she had probably gone back to bed. No. Kate was up and moving about the room. There was great activity going on. Stacy felt so much better. She knew Kate. Kate had never been one to say she was sorry for anything she said or did, but that need not mean she didn't feel sorry. She was giving their room a good turn-out. Perhaps this was her way of working off her annoyance and at the same time show she was sorry for losing her temper. Stacy sat back, thinking her thoughts, and waited for Kate to come out. She didn't have long to wait. In about five minutes the knob of the bedroom door rattled. 'Open this door for me, Stacy! My arms are full. I can't turn the handle,' Kate called and Stacy was glad to see she sounded in excellent form, and as if all was forgotten. For the second time in twenty-four hours Stacy felt a small surge of excitement, as Kate came out her arms piled skyhigh with dresses and hats and a couple of cardboard boxes, covered with wallpaper, in which they kept their gloves and handkerchiefs. It was to be a real spring cleaning! They hadn't done one in years. She hadn't noticed it before but the wallpaper on the boxes was yellowed with age and the flowery pattern faded. They might paste on new wallpaper? And seeing that Kate, naturally, had only her own things she went to run and get hers, but first she ran back to clear a space on the table so Kate could put her things down.

But Kate was heading across the kitchen to their mother's room.

'There's no sense in having a room idle, is there?' she said, disappearing into it. 'I'm moving in here.'

There was no further mention of the dunghill that day, nor indeed that week. Stacy felt a bit lonely at first in the room they had shared since childhood. But it had its advantages. It had been a bit stuffy sleeping on the inside. And she didn't have so many headaches, but that could possibly be attributed to Kate's suggestion that she ignore them.

Every Wednesday Kate was up at the crack of dawn to let the carts unload. As their father had also foreseen, they were now paying the farmers for the manure, but only a small sum, because they were still glad to get rid of it. And the townspeople on the other hand were paying five times more. Kate had made no bones about raising her prices. The only time there was a reference to the future was when Kate announced that she didn't like keeping cash in the house, and that she was going to start banking some of their takings. The rest could be put as usual in the black box, which was almost the only thing that had never been taken out of their mother's room. A lot of other things were thrown out.

Kate and Stacy got on as well as ever, it seemed to Stacy, but there were often long stretches of silence in the house because Kate was never as talkative as their mother. After nightfall they often sat by a dying fire, only waiting for it to go out, before getting up and going to bed. All things considered, Kate was right to have moved into the other room, and Stacy began to enjoy having a room of her own. She had salvaged a few of her mother's things that Kate had thrown out and she liked looking at them. If Kate knew she never said anything. Kate never came into their room anymore.

Then one evening when Con O'Toole – the big whiskery farmer with whom Kate had been talking the first day she took over the running of things – when Con started dropping in to see how they were getting on, Stacy was particularly glad to have a room of her own. She liked Con. She really did. But the smell of his pipe brought on her headaches again. The smell of his tobacco never quite left the house, and it even pursued her in through the keyhole after she had left him and Kate together, because of course it was Kate Con came to see.

'Can you stand the smell of his pipe?' she asked Kate one morning. 'It's worse than the smell of the dung!' She only said it by way of a joke, but Kate, who had taken out the black box and was going through the papers in it, a thing she did regularly now, shut the lid of the box and frowned.

'I thought we agreed on saying fertilizer instead of that word you just used.'

'Oh but that was long ago, when we were in boarding school,' Stacy stammered.

'I beg your pardon! It was agreed we'd be more particular about how we referred to our business when we were in the company of other people – or at least that was my understanding! Take Con O'Toole for instance. He may deliver dung here but he never gives it that name – at least not in front of me. The house he lives in may be thatched and have a mud wall, but that's because his old mother is alive and he can't get her to agree to knocking it down and building a new house, which of course they can afford – I was astonished at the amount of land he owns. Come Stacy, you must understand that I am not urging him to make any changes. So please don't mention this conversation to him. I'll tell him myself when I judge the time to be right. Then I'll make him see the need for building a new house. He needn't knock down the old one either. He can leave the old woman in it for what time is left her. But as I say, I'll bide my time. I might even wait until after we are married.'

That was the first Stacy heard of Kate's intended marriage, but after that first reference there was talk of nothing else, right up to the fine blowy morning when Kate was hoisted up into Con O'Toole's new motor-car, in a peacock blue outfit, with their mother's gold chain bumping up and down on her bosom.

Stacy was almost squeezed to death in the doorway as the guests all stood there to wave goodbye to the happy couple. There had been far more guests than either she or Kate had bargained on because the O'Tooles had so many relations, and they all brought their children, and – to boot – Kate's old mother-in-law brought along a few of her own cronies as well. But there was enough food, and plenty of port wine.

It was a fine wedding. And Stacy didn't mind the mess that was made of the house. Such a mess! Crumbs scattered over the carpet in the parlour and driven into it by people's feet! Bottle tops all over the kitchen floor! Port wine and lemonade stains soaked into the tablecloth! It was going to take time to get the place to rights again. Stacy was almost looking forward to getting it to rights again because she had decided to make a few changes in the arrangement of the furniture – small changes, only involving chairs and ornaments. But she intended attacking it that evening after the guests left. However, when the bridal couple drove off with a hiss of steam rising out of the radiator of the car, the guests flocked back into the house and didn't go until there wasn't a morsel left to eat, or a single drop left to refill the decanters. One thing did upset Stacy and that was when she saw the way the beautiful wedding cake on which the icing had been as hard and white as plaster had been attacked by someone who didn't know how to cut a cake. The cake had been laid waste, and the children that hadn't already fallen asleep on the sofas were stuffing themselves with the last crumbs. Stacy herself hadn't as much as a taste of that cake, and she'd intended keeping at least one tier aside for some future time. Ah well. It was nice to think everyone had had a good time, she thought, as she closed the door on the last of the O'Tooles, who had greatly outnumbered their own friends. Jasper Kane, their father's solicitor, had been their principal guest. He had not in fact left yet, but he was getting ready to leave.

'It will be very lonely for you now, Miss Stacy,' he said. 'You ought to get some person in to keep you company – at least for the nights.'

It was very kind of him to be so concerned. Stacy expressed her gratitude freely, and reassured him that she was quite looking forward to being, as it were, her own mistress. She felt obliged to add, hastily, that she'd miss Kate, although to be strictly truthful, she didn't think she'd miss her as much as she would have thought before Con O'Toole had put in his appearance.

'Well, well. I'm glad to hear you say that, Miss Stacy,' Jasper Kane said, as he prepared to leave. 'I expect you'll drop in to my office at your convenience. I understand your sister took care of the business, but I'm sure you'll be just as competent when you get the hang of things.' Then, for a staid man like him, he got almost playful. 'I'll be very curious to see what changes you'll make,' he said, and she saw his eye fall on a red plush sofa that Kate had bought after Con started calling, and which Stacy thought was hideous. She gave him a conspiratorial smile. But she didn't want him to think she wasn't serious.

'I intend to make changes outside as well, Mr Kane,' she said, gravely. 'And the very first thing I'm going to do is plant a few lilac trees.'

Jasper Kane looked surprised.

'Oh? Where?' he asked and although it was dark outside, he went to the window and tried to see out.

'Where else but where the dunghill has always been? Stacy said, and just to hear herself speaking with such authority made her almost lightheaded.

Jasper Kane remained staring out into the darkness. Then he turned around and asked a simple question.

'But what will you live on, Miss Stacy?'

The Long Ago

Everyone was kind to Hallie. You'd be surprised at the number of young people in the town who visited her, and went for walks with her, and did little messages on her behalf. But, although she was always nice to them and offered them tea when they called, there were only two people in the town whose company Hallie really enjoyed. One was Ella Fallon, who used to be Ella White. The other was Dolly Feeny, who used to be Dolly Frewen. For Dolly and Ella and Hallie had all been girls together, and they had a great many memories in common. Their main bond was that Dolly and Ella had been in Hallie's confidence in the days long ago when all three of them were young, and Dolly knew for a fact, what other people took to be gossip, that in happier circumstances – and if it had not been for the intervention of a certain person – Hallie too would have been married like them, and have a home of her own. Dolly and Ella had read every note that had passed between Hallie and Dominie Sinnot. And they knew it was Dominie who had given Hallie the brooch which she always wore; a gold brooch with the word 'Dearest' written on it in seed pearls. They both stoutly maintained that Dominie had once as good as told them, although not in so many words, that he would never marry any other girl but Hallie.

Ah well, that was all long ago, and Dominie at the time was only a law student, apprenticed to old Jasper Kane. And being young and innocent Dominie perhaps had not realized that an ageing solicitor would hardly make an offer of partnership to a penniless young apprentice unless there was more to the offer than met the eye. There was a string to it. And the string was Blossom – Jasper's only daughter.

Hallie never blamed Dominie, when he married Blossom, but she felt it no injustice to Blossom that a small spark of the truth should be kept alive and tended, particularly when poor Dominie lived so short a time.

'He would be alive today if it was you he married, Hallie!' Dolly said, one day, and Ella agreed. They were a great comfort to Hallie.

She felt she could speak her heart to them at any time. And indeed, shortly after Dominie's death, when an awkward situation developed with Blossom, Ella and Dolly took a firm stand in Hallie's defence. Why shouldn't she visit Dominie Sinnot's grave if she wanted? they cried. They knew all about the dream she'd had – three nights in a row – a dream in which Dominie had come to her, and in which he seemed to be trying to convey some message that she did not at first understand, until quite suddenly one day she guessed what he wanted. He wanted her to visit his grave! And promptly that very evening she went down to the cemetery and knelt beside the mound. She not only said a few prayers for him. She shed a few tears for him as well. And after that she went down to the cemetery every evening.

Those moments kneeling by Dominie's grave were the happiest moments of Hallie's day. But even those moments were sometimes spoiled by the appearance of Blossom draped to the waist in widow's weeds, and when Blossom arrived Hallie, of course, had to get up off her knees and move away. In fact she had to pretend she was visiting her own family plot – as if, like everyone else in the town, Blossom didn't know quite well that Hallie's parents had been laid to rest in the burial grounds of the old Friary before it was closed. No one had been buried in the Friary for at least a decade.

The situation could have been difficult for Blossom too, if matters had not settled themselves unexpectedly. Because a short time after Dominie's death Blossom married again. And unlike Dominie, her second husband was a big, assertive fellow who would not let Blossom out of his sight. She was always hanging from his arm. And since the main gates of the cemetery were kept locked except on the days of funerals, and the side gates were so narrow two people could not go through linked, Blossom soon gave up visiting the grave. She ordered a headstone to be erected, and never went near the cemetery again. The grave was all Hallie's after that.

Hallie soon had the grave a regular showpiece. A yew tree she planted back of the headstone did remarkably well. A box hedge she put inside the curbstone did not do quite so well, but Hallie took it up and put down a small privet hedge. People thought this behaviour a bit odd. There were raised eyebrows. And one or two unkind remarks were carried back to Hallie. But with Dolly and Ella to take her part she rose superior to all criticism.

'Don't mind what people say, Hallie,' Dolly urged. 'As for the Kanes – their consciences can't be too clear about the way you were treated.'

Those were the kind of remarks Hallie treasured.

The year that Hallie decided to buy a plot for herself in the new cemetery right beside the plot in which Dominie lay, people felt that she was going altogether too far. But again, Ella and Dolly took her part.

'We know how you feel,' Ella said. 'If things had gone as they should, we know where your coffin would go by rights – down into the same grave with Dominie!'

'I thought over it for a long time,' Hallie assured her friends, 'and I would not have bought the plot if Blossom had stayed a widow.'

After that particular conversation, however, Dolly and Ella felt sadder for her than ever.

'She doesn't seem to realize that Blossom will have to be buried with Dominie anyway, whether she likes it or not,' Dolly said. 'A wife is buried with her first husband no matter how many times she marries.'

'I hope nobody will tell her that,' Ella said kindly. 'Let her have what small comforts she can get.'

Ella was always softer hearted towards Hallie than Dolly was, because, as far as these things can be known, it seemed that Ella was happier in her marriage than Dolly. Not that Dolly was dissatisfied; Sam Feeny was a man in a million. He was making money fast. He was buying up property hand over fist. And Dolly would have an easy life of it some day, although, for the moment, she had to fall in with his ideas about economy and thrift. The marriage was not the love-match of Ella and Oliver. Dolly had married Sam for security. And so it was a terrible blow to her when Sam was brought down with pneumonia one day and – putting up hardly any fight – was dead three days from the day he took bad.

Strange to say, it was to Hallie that Dolly turned. It was Hallie who held her together and gave her strength on the day of the funeral. No one would ever have imagined that an inexperienced spinster could have acted so tactfully, but it was she who, after the coffin had been got downstairs, put her arms around Dolly and persuaded her to control herself enough to go to the cemetery.

'Think of me,' Hallie said. 'When Dominie died I had to stand at the back of the crowd, like a stranger. It's different for you. You'll be standing at the lip of the grave, knowing no one has a better right to stand there.'

Dolly recovered her composure at once.

'Poor Hallie,' she said. 'I never realized how you must have suffered that day.' Her mind was taken off her own trouble for a few minutes. 'Do you know, Hallie,' she said, 'I had forgotten until this minute, but now I distinctly remember that when Dominie's coffin was being lowered into the clay, Blossom was looking across the grave at the man she is married to today! He had only just come to town. I'm certain she was wondering who he was and already sizing him up! There were tears in her eyes, but there was curiosity in them as well.' At the thought of Blossom's infidelity to Dominie, Dolly had braced up, and seen where her own duty lay. 'Give me my hat,' she said. 'I mustn't keep the hearse waiting. Sam was always on time wherever he went. I won't delay him now.'

Hallie was proud of the way Dolly behaved at the graveside. People were more impressed by her silence than they would have been by any amount of sobbing and screaming. Her behaviour was certainly most edifying by comparison with Blossom, whose screams could have been heard a mile away when the first sod thudded down on Dominie's coffin. Indeed Ella was astonished at Dolly's calm – and told her so. 'I don't know how you did it, Dolly. I'd have broken down, I'd have thrown myself into the grave if it was Oliver – God forbid that the like should happen,' she added tactlessly, and she hastily made the sign of the Cross. Dolly and Hallie exchanged glances. There are times when the silent heart grieves deepest, they seemed to say, each to the other.

After Sam's death it was Ella who was the odd one out, as Dolly and Hallie saw more and more of each other. Not that Dolly had much time to spare. She had two children and they took up a good part of her time. As well as that Sam's affairs were not in as good order as might have been expected – or desired – and his widow was in and out of old Jasper Kane's office every other day. There was even talk of a lawsuit. Nevertheless, it was undeniable that she had more free time than formerly, and it became an almost regular thing for Hallie and herself to go for a walk every evening after supper – just as they used to do in the long ago. No one could have known what those walks meant to Hallie. The thought of them bore her up through the long day, in a house that was empty and dark and cold, for nothing she did – no fire she lit, no light she burned – could bring back the warmth and brightness of the time when she was young. Young! Her faded face, and her faded hair, and her thin body that had dried up without giving out any of its sweetness, had been a bitter sight to her in her mirror for many a day. But somehow her ageing appearance did not trouble her as much after she took up her old companionship with Dolly. The days went quicker when there was something she could look forward to in the evenings. True, she, Dolly, and Ella had occasionally taken a walk together, even after the other two were married, but it was a different thing altogether to look forward to a walk every evening – regularly. It was, she told herself, just like long ago. And as she and Dolly strolled along the country roads in the soft twilight it sometimes seemed to Hallie that they were indeed back in that long ago. Walking idly along, sometimes softly humming a tune together in part time, it was so like when they were young! The evening skies were the same as ever, darkening away to the east, with a gleam still lingering in the branches of the western trees. There were bats striking through the dark air in fits and starts. There was the sweet sound of a little stream, that ran alongside the road, hidden by a high hedge from behind which came the sound of cattle moving noisily in the rushy bottom. The same. The same. All around them the countryside was the same. The night sky was the same. And deep, deep down under the changed shape of their bodies, weren't they – she and Dolly – the same Hallie and Dolly of long ago?

More and more of the past was dragged back into their conversation as they walked and talked in the twilight.

'Do you remember the first day Ella put up her hair?' Hallie said one evening.

'Do I!' Dolly said. 'It was a Sunday! In the chapel at last Mass! It fell down when she was genuflecting. I thought she'd die of embarrassment.'

'So did I,' Hallie said, and she laughed heartily, seeing Ella again in her mind's eye as clearly as she saw her that day – thin as a rod, with her toppling heap of pale hair, standing all confused halfway up the centre aisle, her cheeks flaming, not knowing whether to stoop and pick up her hairpins, or get into a pew as if nothing had happened, letting her hair hang down her back as it always had. She squeezed Dolly's arm. 'Do you remember the day you first put up your own hair, Dolly?' she said.

'Will I ever forget it!' Dolly smiled as she thought of the day when she herself stood in her bedroom looking into the spotted mirror that reflected a saucy seventeen-year-old, her mouth filled with hairpins and a pile of chestnut hair caught on top of her head, while the rest of her hair rambled over her shoulder. She gave Hallie's arm a squeeze. 'I'll never forget the day *you* put up your hair, Hallie,' she said generously. 'And I know there was someone else who never forgot it either.'

'Who?' breathed Hallie, her heart fluttering. As if she needed to be told! Oh that day! Oh! Oh! Such a day. A Sunday too of course. She'd let her hair loose from its braids and piled it up on the top of her head, but all the way down the street to the chapel she was trembling with apprehension in case it might fall down like Ella's. And when she went into the chapel, although she did not turn her head to look in his direction, she knew that Dominie was kneeling just inside the door. And she knew he would be staring at her. If *her* hair had fallen down then what would she have done?

'Oh, what would I have done, Dolly, if my hair had come undone?' she cried. 'At least Ella knew Oliver wasn't in the chapel the day hers fell down. He was laid up with a cold. How lucky she was: just think how awful it would have been for her if he had been there!'

'Oh, I don't suppose it would have mattered very much,' Dolly said, indifferently. She was willing to talk endlessly about those days long ago, but she could not re-live them. And sometimes she wished Ella were with them. But Ella seldom got out in the evening. The children had to be put to bed, and after that she was usually tired. Dolly sighed. She understood why Ella did not want to come with them, whereas Hallie never understood. Hallie was always bemoaning Ella's absence, and regretting she was not with them. She got quite censorious at times. 'Ella ought to get out in the evenings, if only for half an hour. Just for a change. Just for the fresh air.' She wouldn't listen to any excuses from Dolly. 'You have children too, Dolly!' she said.

'My girls are older than Ella's little people,' Dolly said. 'And anyway girls are able to do a lot for themselves.'

'Why doesn't she come out after she's put them to bed?'

'But that's the only time she has alone with Oliver,' Dolly blurted out at last, although she had regrets at once. Hallie unlinked her arm.

'I should think she'd have seen enough of him by now,' she said.

That annoyed Dolly. It was all she could do not to say something mean – to let Hallie see, for once and for all, that there was a big difference between a married woman and a spinster, and even a widow was not the same as a woman who had never had a man in the house at all!

But as soon as these bitter words came into Dolly's mind she suppressed them. After all, it wasn't fair to regard Hallie as an old maid. She had been the prettiest of the three of them, and she had a nicer disposition. If Dominie Sinnot had not been a worthless weakling, Hallie would have been married before either her or Ella. If it came to that, Hallie could have married someone else, even after Dominie married Blossom, if she hadn't remained so absurdly wrapped up in him. It really wasn't fair to call her an old maid.

'Don't walk so fast, Hallie,' she said. 'My shoe is hurting me.' She was trying to pretend that it was she who lagged back, and not Hallie who had gone on ahead in a huff. 'Isn't it chilly?' she added, as they drew abreast again, making this as an excuse for drawing Hallie's arm through hers again. And then, deliberately, she herself tried to feel critical of Ella. Ella should be more considerate. It was not very tactful of her to keep talking about Oliver all the time, considering poor Sam, and where *he* was now, poor soul. Ella and Oliver may have been nearer to each other in age than she and Sam, but that didn't necessarily mean their marriage was any happier. Love wasn't everything! But try as she might to turn against Ella, Dolly found herself echoing Hallie's regret that she was not with them on their evening walks. For one thing, the past to Ella – as to her – was a misty place, in which it was nice to let their minds wander, but which they knew they could never re-enter, whereas Hallie had never left it.

But they had reached the crossroads at which they usually turned back. Beyond this the road ran between tall trees, lonely and dark, and on the left somewhere – they weren't quite sure where – a man had once been done to death by thieves, or so they had always been told. One night in the long ago Ella had insisted that they should go further. It was a moonlit night, full of light and shadow.

'Oh, come on. Let's go down the ghosty road,' Ella urged. 'Come on.' But they wouldn't go. She, Hallie, claimed to have a stone in her shoe, and Dolly flatly refused to go a step further, saying she was too scared.

'All right, go home!' Ella said. 'I'll go by myself!' And away she went, with her sprightly gait, down the lonely road that was lit only in the centre where the moon played down through the branches of the trees, but dark and gloomy to either side where tangles of undergrowth cast their shadows. On Ella went, firm and straight, and fearless! And there they stood, feeling foolish at the thought that they, who were two years older than Ella, had less spirit than she. But a few seconds after Ella had gone out of sight around the first bend of the road, they heard her calling to them and, next thing, she came flying back, her skirt held up with both hands and her silk stockings flashing. 'Run, run!' she cried as she caught up with them, but they only laughed, because they knew that she had fancied her courage so great, her imagination had had to supply terrors to equal it. And ever after, when they came to that crossroads they used to tease her about that night. 'How about going on another few yards?' they used to say, just to rattle her. Even after Ella married, Hallie tried to keep up the joke. 'If we had Ella with us we might go a bit further,' she'd say when they reached that point.

It was the kind of remark Hallie was always making – a remark that concentrated so much of the past in its essence, and Dolly didn't object as long as she didn't elaborate on it too much. But she always did. 'I wonder if Ella really saw something that night or if her imagination ran away with her?' she asked this very evening as she and Dolly stood at the crossroads and looked down the ghostly road. 'What do you think Dolly?' she said. 'We must remember to ask her next time we see her.' Unfortunately at that moment Dolly had been thinking of something quite different she herself wanted to ask Ella – a practical question about the future. She was having trouble filling in some forms that came in the post, relating to Sam's insurance policy and she was wondering if Ella could help her with them. She didn't reply to Hallie.

'What are you thinking about, Dolly?' Hallie asked peevishly, having seen that she was preoccupied.

'I was just wondering if Oliver has his life insured,' Dolly said.

Hallie turned her head away. She wasn't interested.

However, if Hallie was not interested in what Dolly said that night, she had reason next day to recall Dolly's words. She ran down the street and knocked on her door.

'Wasn't it queer you should speak of Oliver the other night?' she said, breathless from running.

'Why? What did I say anyway?' Dolly asked.

'Oh, don't you remember?' Hallie was impatient. 'You were wondering if he had his life insured.'

'Well? What was queer about that?'

'But haven't you heard?' Hallie cried. 'He's ill.'

Dolly had an unpleasant feeling that Hallie was overstraining the coincidence.

'I don't see anything queer about that. What's the matter with him anyway? I suppose he has a cold? He's hardly likely to give anyone the benefit of his insurance!'

Hallie drew an enormous breath. 'Oh, but it's not a cold, Dolly. It's more than that. The doctor doesn't know what's the matter with him. Yes! He's had the doctor. And a nurse. And there's talk of getting a night nurse. Ella is nearly out of her mind.'

Dolly was still reluctant to believe it was serious, but she began to feel uncomfortable about having made that remark about the insurance policy. She was determined Hallie must be exaggerating Oliver's condition.

'Oh, I wouldn't mind Ella,' she said scathingly. 'Look at me. I was nearly out of my mind when Sam got ill.' She had no sooner mentioned poor Sam, however, than she saw the look on Hallie's face, and her own face fell, thinking of where Sam had finished up.

'Well,' she said crossly. 'If he is bad, we'd better go up there at once. Ella is no person for dealing with an emergency. Think of that houseful of children! Think of the turmoil! Oh! if anything should happen! Hurry! Hurry!' She grabbed her coat and together they hurried up the street to Ella's.

When they got to Ella's house Hallie and Dolly found they were not the only ones who thought it their duty to be there. It was Ella's mother who opened the door. She showed them into the parlour – a room that was rarely used and in which they had hardly ever before set foot. And on their way into the room they had to stand aside to let Ella's sister-in-law pass out with a tray. The parlour was crowded. And in the middle was Ella, sitting down like a visitor.

'Oh, Hallie! Oh, Dolly!' When she saw them, Ella's face lit up, and she tried to get to her feet but several people urged her back into her chair. She sat back again docile as a child. They saw that her poor face was as white as a sheet, and that she looked as if she did not know where she was or what she was supposed to do. It was someone else who provided them with chairs, and when the sister-in-law returned a few minutes later with fresh cups of tea, as she proffered them tea she pressed upon them also the information that Oliver's condition was grave. The crisis was expected any minute.

Hallie and Dolly felt awkward. They had come to help. To take charge of the children. To see that everything possible was being done for Oliver. And instead of that they were being treated like visitors. In other parts of the house they could hear people charging themselves with the tasks they had intended to undertake.

'Is the doctor with him?' Dolly asked, reluctant to stay in the background.

'The doctor has been here twice already,' Ella's mother said. 'He's upstairs with him now.' Then she glanced at the clock and frowned. 'He ought to be brought down for a cup of tea,' she said and she turned away importantly, pausing only to whisper something to a cousin of Ella's sitting near the door, who promptly rose and followed her out of the parlour, closing the door.

'Can't we do something?' Dolly whispered to Hallie. 'Did you say there was a nurse?'

'I believe so,' Hallie said, 'but I don't know if she's a proper nurse.'

'What do you mean by that?'

'She's a cousin of Oliver's. They say she has some kind of a nursing diploma.' She needed to say no more.

'A nursing diploma!' Dolly exclaimed contemptuously, but she had to lower her voice hastily because at that moment the so-called nurse put her head around the corner of the door, looking for someone who was not there. Then she went out again, and she too closed the door after her. But Dolly and Hallie had seen that although she wore a nurse's cap all right and a white coat, the coat was too short and under it showed a gaudy dress with a flowery pattern. But what they objected to most was that her long legs were covered with flashy flesh-coloured stockings, and stuck into small fashionable shoes with high heels.

'I don't think much of her,' Dolly said. 'Someone ought to send down for the district nurse.' She stood up.

But just then the young nurse appeared again. This time she tiptoed over and whispered to the women on either side of Ella, who immediately began to assist Ella to her feet. Indeed this assistance was given with such vigour that, almost before Hallie and Dolly knew what had happened, Ella had been whisked from the room.

'The crisis!' Everyone whispered the same word at the same time, so the whisper ran around the parlour like a breeze. 'The crisis!'

Up to then most people had been talking quietly, but now, subdued, they sat silent, straining to interpret the sounds from above. But where, formerly, there had been an occasional soft footfall, and the sound of an occasional voice, there was now absolute silence.

The silence lasted a long time. And the longer it lasted the more oppressive it became, until those who had occasion to move – to cross their legs, or open their handbags – did so with exaggerated care and self-consciousness. Once during this vigil, there was a short diversion when a child was heard outside in the passage, asking a question in a shrill voice. In the parlour several people started to their feet in dismay. But the child's voice stopped in the middle of a word, and then heavy footsteps were heard again, hurrying away. The child had obviously been snatched up and carried out of earshot. After that such stillness settled over the room, Hallie and Dolly were weighted down by it. On Dolly it lay so heavily her indignation could do no more than smoulder. But Hallie found it easy enough to yield to silence. Wasn't she used to it? One by one her thoughts began to drift away to their usual strolling ground: the past.

First she thought about Oliver, and of how strong and hearty he was long ago. It was sad to think of him, now, flat on his back, and helpless with strange women whispering and tiptoeing around him. Even the resentment she had borne against him for being best man at Dominie's wedding began to wear away. After all, he could hardly have refused. He had nothing against Blossom either, she supposed. He would have been best man for Dominie no matter who Dominie married. Poor Oliver! Was he really going to die? Did he know he was so low? When Dominie was dying, it was said he didn't know it. Even when they had brought the priest to him he thought the priest had just dropped in for a friendly chat. And he was unconscious when he was anointed. Would it have made any difference to her, she wondered, if Dominie had known he was dying? Would he have sent her any message? Suddenly a startling thought entered her mind. Perhaps Dominie had sent her a message. Perhaps Blossom had kept it from her. But at this point she pulled herself up. It was by never putting the strain of incredulity upon it that she had kept intact through the years the thin web of her romance. She had no doubt whatever that Dominie's last thoughts had been of her, but to think that he had expressed them would have been straining things too much.

Her mind returned to Oliver. Was he conscious, she wondered? Did he know that Ella was beside him? Not for anything in the world would Hallie want to deprive Ella of anything that might solace her in her sorrow, but if it should happen that Oliver was too far gone to recognize her at the end, then it was to her, Hallie, that Ella could turn. She would understand. After all, Sam had been fully conscious right up to the end. Hadn't his last words to Dolly been something about an insurance policy? Yes, it was to her, and not to Dolly, Ella would turn.

Hallie felt very close to Ella at that moment. After all they had both felt, at the time of Dolly's marriage, that there was something a bit too practical about Dolly's choice. Dolly had picked out Sam. There had not been the instantaneous, mutual attraction between them that there had been between Ella and Oliver, and between her and Dominie. She had never forgotten something Ella said the night before her wedding.

'Oliver will never have much money, Hallie,' she said. 'I'll never have things nice, the way I planned.'

'That doesn't matter,' Hallie had confidently answered.

Ella had pressed her hand. 'I knew you'd say that, Hallie,' she said. 'You and Dominie wouldn't have cared about money either.'

That was why it had hurt so bitterly, after Dominie married Blossom, to have to stand in the chapel and smile and smile when Ella and Oliver were married. That wound had never healed. It was strange, but even now when she'd sigh and say to Dolly that it would have been like long ago if Ella was with them she knew in her heart it wasn't really true. Things wouldn't have been the same.

Because Ella would never have stopped talking about Oliver all the time. And it hurt. It hurt.

But now Oliver was ill and Hallie knew she mustn't bear resentment against him. He was ill, and maybe dying.

Just then the nurse threw open the parlour door again. 'Where are the children?' she demanded to know. 'I thought they were here.' When she saw they were not in the parlour she withdrew her head, and shut the door with a slam. Those in the parlour exchanged glances.

'The children are wanted to say goodbye to him. He must be sinking fast.'

A woman who was only distantly related to Oliver threw up her hands and burst into tears.

'Hush, hush!' the woman beside her murmured, not to silence her but to direct her grief into more suitable channels. 'Poor Oliver is not the one to be pitied,' they cried. 'He's going to a better world. But think of his poor young widow. Think of her! Poor Ella!' And everyone in the room broke into the same refrain. 'Poor Ella. Poor Ella.' What in the world would she do now, with those young children and no father to look after them? 'Poor Ella.'

'Poor Ella. Where was she? She shouldn't be up there till the very end. Poor Ella. Had she any arrangements made? And the children. Where were they? They ought to be taken to a neighbour's, otherwise they'd be under everyone's feet!'

Everyone was aware of things to be done, and eager to undertake those tasks. No one could be expected to remain shut up in a small front parlour, when now, all over the house, in the kitchen and in the passages, there were people running back and forth, and running up and down the stairs, and people dragging articles of furniture across the floors. For the suspense was over. Oliver was sinking fast. The death rattle had been heard in his throat. Not a minute was to be wasted if everything was to be ready when death imposed a final and absolute decorum. Dolly, certainly, could not sit in the parlour a minute longer. She got up and ran out.

Hallie found herself alone at last. She had no urge to join in the tumult. Looking around her, she began indifferently to gather up cups and saucers and pile them on a tray, but she left the tray down on a side-table inside the door and sat down again, herself, by the dying fire. Poor Ella. It was strange to think that all three of them – Dolly, Ella and herself – had been left alone within so short a time. Dominie was only seven years dead – Sam less than a year. And now Oliver. She sighed. In various ways all three of them had been preyed upon by the years that once, far off on the horizon, had appeared like beautiful birds of paradise, laden with sweetness. The tears came into her eyes. She had been the first to feel Time's bitter beak and claw. She had been torn apart even before Dominie died. And, after he died, it was still a long time before the others suffered anything like what she had gone through.

But now they were all three alike again in their grief and loss as they had once been alike in their hopes and dreams. Never, never would she have admitted it before, but now she faced it, that in her heart she had always resented the happiness the other two had known, and she had missed. And that was why when she and Dolly talked about their girlhood, it had secretly made her heart ache to think of Ella, snug and warm between the four walls of her home, occupying herself by attending to the needs of her children, and satisfying the demands made on her by Oliver, her husband.

Oliver's demands upon Ella had always been very obvious. Whenever Hallie met her she was never able to stop and talk to them for more than a minute or two. 'I must get back. I have to iron Oliver's shirt!' she'd say. Or some such nonsense. Even after Mass on Sundays he'd be waiting impatiently for her outside the chapel gate, and she'd be in a hurry to join him. 'I must fly,' she'd say. 'I mustn't keep him waiting.'

But now Ella too would be lonely. Now she would be glad enough to go out walking with Dolly and herself of an evening. And whereas she used to put the present before the past, now she too would begin to put the past before the present. She would be willing and even eager to talk about when they were young. Those golden days. That leafy springtime.

For a moment as Hallie sat there in the stuffy parlour it seemed to her that the leafy boughs of youth and springtime were about to form a bower about her, when, abruptly she was recalled to her whereabouts by a piercing scream. Oliver was gone!

Poor Ella. It was all over.

The next minute there were voices in the passage, among which Hallie distinguished the voice of Dolly, who had clearly taken command.

'Bring her into the parlour,' Dolly was saying. 'And keep her there.' Then the door opened and Dolly and Ella's mother appeared in the doorway with Ella between them. Ella was struggling to free herself, but over her head the others spoke authoritatively to each other – entirely disregarding her. 'Keep her in here,' Dolly ordered. 'Don't let her upstairs again. It's no place for her now. Is there any brandy in the house? She should be given a sip of it, whether she likes it or not.'

Hallie stood up. She was dazed and disconcerted. And indeed Dolly herself, who thought they were showing Ella into an empty room, was just as taken aback. 'Oh, are you here?' she said, surprised.

But to Ella it seemed the most natural thing in the world to see Hallie standing there.

'Oh Hallie!' she cried, and where until then she had hung back protesting she now rushed forward and threw out her arms. 'Oh Hallie! He's dead. Oliver is dead. He's gone from me.'

Hallie came to life at that, and her arms flew out to enlace with Ella's. This was how they had always flung themselves upon each other in their tempests of girlish grief.

'Oh Hallie, Hallie, what will I do?' Ella cried, as she clung to her. And where she had been deaf to the others, she seemed willing and eager to listen to Hallie. Behind Ella's back Dolly made signs to Hallie. 'See if you can calm her,' she said out loud, feeling justified perhaps in disregarding Ella since Ella had buried her face in Hallie's bosom.

Hallie realized she was the centre of attention. They were all waiting for her to speak. And after a minute, Ella, too, raised her head and looked up at her with swollen eyes.

'Oh, Hallie, Hallie! What will become of me? How will I live without him?' she cried.

All at once Hallie knew what to say. 'Oh Ellie darling,' she cried and she pressed her close. 'Hush – hush. Time heals everything.' Then her voice grew softer and more persuasive. 'While you were all upstairs,' she said, almost crooning the words, 'I was sitting here thinking how lovely it would be when you, Dolly and I would be together again like we used to be. Like long ago.'

But almost before she finished, Ella broke away from her, and began to scream again and to struggle to get out of the room again. Her mother had to take hold of her and try to pacify her.

'Don't mind her, Ella. She didn't mean it,' she said. 'She didn't know what she was saying.'

What was the matter? What had she said? Hallie looked around for Dolly, but Dolly was staring at her with eyes that would take the heat out of the sun.

'Have you gone out of your mind, Hallie?' Dolly said. Hallie got more confused. 'What did I say?' she cried. But Dolly pushed her to one side, and dropping down on her knees she put her arms around Ella, and whispered something into her ear. Ella stopped screaming at once.

Hallie stared at them. She hadn't heard what Dolly whispered, but her eyes fastened on the hands of her friends, that were tightly clasped. And on their hands she saw their wedding rings. She knew then what Dolly had said.

The Becker Wives

When Ernest, the third of the Beckers to marry, chose a girl with no more to recommend her than the normal attributes of health, respectability and certain superficial good looks, the other two – James and Henrietta – felt they could at last ignore Theobald and his nonsense. Theobald had been a bit young to proffer advice to them, but Ernest had had the full benefit of their youngest brother's counsel and warnings. Yet Ernest had gone his own way too: Julia, the new bride, was no more remarkable than James's wife Charlotte. Both had had to earn their living while in the single state, and neither had brought anything into the family by way of dowry beyond the small amount they had put aside in a savings bank during the period of their engagements, engagements that in both cases had been long enough for the Beckers to ascertain all particulars that could possibly be expected to have a bearing on their suitability for marriage and child-bearing.

'And those, mind you, are the things that count,' James said to Samuel, now the only unmarried Becker – except Theobald. 'Of course every man is entitled to make his own choice,' he added with a touch of patronage, because no matter how Theobald might lump the two wives together, the fact remained that Ernest had taken Julia from behind the counter of the shop where he bought his morning paper, whereas his Charlotte had been a stenographer in the firm of Croker and Croker, a firm that might justifiably consider itself a serious rival to the firm of Becker and Becker. But Theobald ignored such niceties of classification. In his eyes both of his brothers' wives came from the wrong side of the river, as he put it, and neither of them differed much – in anything but their sex – from Robert, the husband of Henrietta. Robert had been just a lading-clerk whom James had met in the course of business, but since it had never been certain that Henrietta would secure a husband of any kind, the rest of the family – except Theobald of course – thought she'd done right to jump at him. Theobald had even expected *her* to make a good marriage. But once Robert had been raised from the status of a clerk to that of husband, it had been a relatively small matter to absorb him into the Becker business.

The Beckers were corn merchants. They carried on their trade in a moderate-sized premise on the quays, and they lived on the premise. But if anyone were foolish enough to entertain doubts about the scale and importance of the business conducted on the ground floor, he had only to be given a glimpse of the comfort and luxury of the upper storeys, to be disabused of his error. The Beckers believed in the solid comforts, and the business paid for them amply.

Old Bartholomew Becker, father of the present members of the firm, had built up a sizeable trade by the good old principles of constant application and prudent transaction. Then, having made room in the firm for each of his three older sons, one after another, and having put his youngest son Theobald into the Law to ensure that the family interests would be fully safeguarded, the old man took to his big brass-bound bed – a bed solemnified by a canopy of red velvet, and made easy of ascent by a tier of mahogany steps clipped to the side rail – and died. He died at exactly the moment most opportune for the business to be brought abreast of the times by a little judicious innovation.

In his last moments, old Bartholomew had gathered his sons around him in the high-ceilinged bedroom in which he had begot them, and ordering them to prop him upright, had given them one final injunction: to marry, and try to see that their sister married too.

The unmarried state had been abhorrent to old Bartholomew. He had held it to be not only dangerous to a man's soul, but destructive to his business as well. In short, to old Bartholomew, marriage represented safety and security. To his own early marriage with Anna, the daughter of his head salesman, he attributed the greater part of his success. He had married Anna when he was twenty-two and she was eighteen. And the dowry she brought with her was Content. By centring her young husband's desires within the four walls of the house on the quayside, Anna had contributed more than she knew to the success of the firm. For, when other young men of that day, associates and rivals, were out till all hours in pursuit of pleasure and the satisfaction of their desires, Bartholomew Becker was to be found in his countinghouse, working at his ledgers, secure in the knowledge that the object of his desires was tucked away upstairs in their great brass bed. And as the years went on, the thought of his big soft Anna more often than not heavy with child, sitting up pretending to read, but in reality yawning and listening for his step on the stairs, had in it just the right blend of desire and promise of fulfilment that enabled him to keep at the ledgers and not go up to her until he'd got through them. In this way he made more and more money for her. Anna might not take credit for every penny Bartholomew made, but she was undoubtedly responsible for those extra pence, earned while other men slept or revelled, that made all the difference between a firm like Beckers and other firms in the same trade. It was inevitable, of course, that the more money Anna inspired her husband to amass, the more her beauty became smothered in the luxury with which he surrounded her. Yet, on his death-bed, his memory being more accurate than his eyesight, it was of Anna's young beauty that he spoke. And reminding her of their own happiness, he laid on her a last injunction to be good to his sons' wives. He made no mention of how she should conduct herself towards a son-in-law, no doubt fearing it unlikely such a person would put in an appearance. Anna gave the dying man an unconditional promise.

Theobald therefore had his mother to contend with as well as his brothers when he objected to each of his sisters-in-law as they came on the scene.

'Have you forgotten your father's last words, Theobald?' Anna pleaded, each time. 'How can you take this absurd attitude? What is to be said against this marriage?'

'What is to be said in its favour?' Theobald snapped back.

And on the occasion of Ernest's engagement, when Theobald had put this infuriating question for the third time, his mother had been goaded into giving him an almost unseemly answer.

'After all,' she said, 'the same could have been said about your father's marriage to me!'

That, of course, was the whole point of Theobald's argument, although he could not very well say so to Anna. Surely he and his brothers ought to do better than their father: to go a step further, as it were, not stay in the same rut. It was one thing for old Bartholomew, at the outset of his career, to give himself the comfort of marrying a girl of his own class, but it was another thing altogether for his sons, whom he had established securely on the road towards success, to turn around and marry wives who were no better than their mother.

'No better than Mother!' Henrietta was outraged. She could hardly credit her ears. She had the highest regard for Charlotte and Julia, but a sister-in-law was a sister-in-law, and the implication that either of them could be put on the same plane as her mother was unthinkable. 'No better than Mother!' she repeated, her voice shrill with vexation. 'As if they could be compared with her for one moment. I'm shocked that you could be so disrespectful, Theobald.'

But Theobald was always twisting people's words.

'So you do agree with me, Henrietta?' he said.

'I do not,' Henrietta shouted, 'but you know very well that both James and Ernest would be the first to admit that no matter how nice Charlotte and Julia are they could never hold a candle to Mother. They've said as much, many many times, and you've heard them.'

It was true.

On his wedding day James had stood up, and putting his arm around his bride's waist and causing her to blush furiously, he had addressed his family and friends.

'If Charlotte is half as good a wife as Mother, I'll be a fortunate man,' he said.

And Ernest, on *his* wedding day, had said exactly the same, giving James a chance to reiterate his sentiments.

'My very words,' James said, and all three wives, Anna, and the two young ones, Charlotte and Julia, had reddened, and all three together in chorus had disclaimed the compliment, although old Anna had chuckled and nodded her head towards the big ormolu sideboard, laden with bottles of wine and spirits and great glittering magnums of champagne, from the excellent cellar laid down by old Bartholomew.

'I never heed compliments paid to me at a wedding,' old Anna said. They all could see though that she was pleased and happy. But just then, happening to catch a glimpse of her youngest son between the red carnations and fronds of maidenhair fern that sprayed out from the silver-bracketed epergne in the centre of the bridal table, Anna leant back in her chair, and lowered her voice for a word with James who was passing behind her with a bottle of Veuve Cliquot that he didn't care to trust to any hands but his own. 'For goodness' sake, fill up Theobald's glass,' she said. 'It makes me nervous just to look at him, sitting there with that face on!'

For Theobald sat sober and glum between Henrietta and Samuel, where he had stubbornly placed himself, thereby entirely altering the arrangement of the table, and causing the bride's elder sister and her maiden aunt to be seated side by side. Theobald had flatly refused to sit between them, and it had been considered unwise to press the matter.

'I would have made him sit where he was told,' Charlotte said to James, when he came back to her side after pouring the champagne and she had ascertained what Anna had whispered to him. 'Theobald is odd, but he'd hardly be impolite to strangers.'

'I don't know about that,' James said morosely. 'Don't forget the way he behaved at our wedding. He wasn't very polite to – ' James stopped short. He'd been about to say 'your people' but he altered the words quickly to 'our guests'.

'Oh, that was different,' Charlotte said. 'That was the first wedding in the family.'

James wasn't listening though. He was trying to read the expression on Theobald's face as, just then, his youngest brother turned and spoke to Henrietta. Henrietta frowned. What was the confounded fellow saying *now*?

It was just as well James could not hear. Theobald was on his hobby horse. 'The joke of it is, Henrietta,' he said, 'that for all their protestations to the contrary, both James and Ernest would get the shock of their lives if anyone saw the smallest similarity between their wives and our dear mother.'

'Well, there are differences of appearance, of course,' Henrietta said crisply. 'No one denies that.' She always felt that in every criticism of her sister-in-law there was an implied criticism of Robert, and she was annoyed, but on this occasion she was ill at ease as well in case Theobald would be overheard. He hadn't taken the trouble to lower his voice.

'My dear Henrietta,' he exclaimed. 'You would hardly expect our brothers' wives to wear spectacles and elastic stockings on their wedding day and take size forty-eight corsets, would you? Give them a little time. For my own part I'd like to think my wife would have something more to depend upon for attraction than slim ankles and a narrow waist.'

Yet, even Theobald could hardly have foreseen the rapidity with which his sisters-in-law lost their youthful figures. The punctual pregnancy of Julia coinciding with the somewhat delayed pregnancy of Charlotte made both women look prematurely heavy, and there was something about their figures that made it seem they would never again snap back to their original shape. Indeed, since both of them thought it advisable to conceal their condition under massive fur coats, soon there wasn't a great deal – unless you were at close quarters – to distinguish one from the other of the three Becker wives.

After their confinements, of course, Charlotte and Julia regained some of their differentiating qualities, but even then, due to having followed the advice of Anna and adopted such old-fashioned maxims as 'eating for two' and putting up their feet at every possible chance, neither their ankles nor their waists would ever be slender again. Now, too, Charlotte and Julia felt entitled to accept freely the fur capes, fur tippets, and fleece-lined boots that they had been a bit diffident of demanding when they were dowerless brides. Indeed as the years went on, they came to regard these things more in relation to the effect they made upon each other than to the effect upon their own figures, so that when finally Anna passed to her last reward, and the fallals and fripperies she had won in happy conjugal contest with Bartholomew were dispersed among her three daughters, it seemed at times that instead of passing from the scene Anna had been but divided in three, to dwell with her sons anew. And nowhere was their resemblance to Anna as noticeable as when, in accordance with a custom first started by Bartholomew, and strictly kept up by James, the Beckers went out for an evening meal in a good restaurant. But whereas formerly Anna had sat at the head of the table, comfortable and heavy in furs and jewellery, there were now three replicas of her seated on three sides of the table.

Henrietta, Charlotte, and Julia. There they sat, all three of them, all fat, heavy, and furred, yet like Anna, all emanating, in spite of the money lavished on them, such an air of ordinariness and mediocrity that Theobald, when duty compelled him to be of the party, squirmed in his seat all the time, and rolled bread into pellets from nervousness and embarrassment. Yet he had to attend these family functions. One had to put a face on things, as he explained to Samuel, who came nearest to sharing his views. After all, although it was for the benefit of the family that old Bartholomew had made a lawyer out of his youngest son, Theobald was not without a return of benefit. His practice was mainly dependent on family connections and he just couldn't afford to ignore family ceremonial. But it went against the grain. Indeed, ever since he was a mere youth of sixteen or seventeen Theobald had nurtured strange notions of pride and ambition, and when to these had been added intellectual snobbery and professional stuffiness, it became a positive ordeal for him to have to endure the Becker parties. In Anna's time, a small spark of filial devotion had made them bearable. Without her it was all he could do to force himself to go through with them. But once at the party, however, he could at least make an effort to keep control of the situations that sometimes arose. With a little tact it was possible to gloss over the limitations of the others.

'Not there, Henrietta!' Just in time he'd put his hand under his sister's elbow and shepherd them all to a quiet corner of the restaurant, whereas left to themselves they would have made straight for a table in the centre of the room. 'How about over there?' he'd murmur, and guide them towards a table in a corner behind a pillar, or a pot of ferns.

It was not that he was ashamed of them. There was nothing of which to be ashamed. Indeed, the Beckers were the most respectably dressed people in the restaurant, and they were certainly better mannered than most. Moreover, one and all they possessed robust palates that almost made up for their hit-and-miss pronunciation of the items on the menu. And James, who as the eldest was always the official host, was more than liberal with tips to the waiters. Nevertheless, Theobald was ill at ease and cordially detested every minute of the meal.

'Are you suffering from nerves, Theobald?' Henrietta asked one evening, frowning at the disgusting pellets of bread all round his plate. She was the one who was most piqued at being led to an out-of-the-way table. 'I don't know why you had us sit here. The table isn't large enough in the first place, and in the second place we can hardly hear ourselves thinking, we're so near the orchestra.'

The table was in a rather dark corner, behind a potted palm, and it was indeed so near the orchestra that James had to point out with his finger the various choices from the menu, in order to come to an understanding with the waiter.

'I wanted to sit over there,' Henrietta said, indicating an undoubtedly larger and better placed table, but just then the orchestra reached a lightly scored passage, and overhearing his sister, James looked up from the menu.

'Would you like to change tables, Henrietta?' he asked. 'It's not too late yet: I haven't given the order.'

Theobald shrank back into his chair at the mere thought of the fuss that would accompany the move. Charlotte and Julia were already gathering up their wraps and their handbags and scraping back their chairs. His left eye had begun to twitch, and the back of his neck had begun to redden uncomfortably.

'Aren't we all right here?' he cried. 'Why should we make ourselves conspicuous?' In spite of herself, Henrietta felt sorry for him.

'Oh, we may as well stay here, James,' she said, settling back into her chair again and throwing her fur stole over the arm of it. 'We can't satisfy everyone, although I must say I don't know what Theobald is talking about when he says we'd make ourselves noticeable, because I for one can't see that anyone is taking the least notice of us!'

There was a thin, high note of irritability in his sister's voice that made Theobald more embarrassed than ever. Under the table he crossed and uncrossed his long legs, and took out his handkerchief twice in the course of one minute, as he tried in vain to disassociate himself from them all. The paradox of his sister's words suddenly came home to him. She'd put her finger on what was wrong with them. His discomfort came precisely from the fact that there was no one looking at them. They were the only people in the whole restaurant who were totally inconspicuous. Around them, at every other table, he saw people who were in one way or another distinguished. And those whom he did not recognize looked interesting, too. The women stood out partly because of their appearance, but mostly because of their manner which was in all cases imperious. The men were distinguished by some quality, which although a bit obscure to Theobald, made itself strongly felt by the waiters and where the Beckers often had a wait of ten or even twenty minutes between courses, these men had only to click their fingers to have every waiter in the room at their beck and call. As well as that, most people seemed to know each other. They were constantly calling across to each other, and exchanging gossip from table to table.

Yes, it was true for Henrietta. No one was taking the slightest notice of the Beckers. In that noisy, unselfconscious gathering, the Beckers were conspicuous only by being so very inconspicuous. It was mainly because they liked to stare at other people that the Beckers went out to dinner. Theobald looked around the table at the womenfolk, at his family. There they sat, stolid and silent, their mouths moving as they chewed their food, but their eyes immobile as they stared at someone or other who had caught their fancy at another table. There was little or no conversation among them, such as there was being confined to supply each other's wants in matters of sauces or condiments.

As for the men, Theobald looked at his brothers. They too were unable to keep their eyes upon their own plates, and following the gaze of their wives, their gaze too wandered over the other diners. They had a little more to say to each other than their women, but the flow of their conversation was impeded by having to converse with each other across the intervening bulks of their wives.

Theobald bit his lip in vexation and began to drink his soup with abandon. He felt more critical of them than usual. Was it for this they had dragged him out of his comfortable apartment – to stare at strangers? He was mortified for himself, and still more mortified for them. Such an admission of inferiority! And why should they feel inferior? So far as money was concerned, weren't they in as sound a position as anyone in the city? And as for ability – well, money like theirs wasn't made nowadays by pinheads or duffers. James was probably the most astute business man you'd meet in a day's march. There was no earthly reason why his family should play second fiddle to anyone in the room.

'Look here!' Theobald roused himself. As long as he was of the party, he might as well try to put some spirit into it. He leant across the table. 'I heard an amusing thing today at the Courts,' he said, determined to draw the attention of his family back to some common focus. To help his own concentration he fastened his eyes on a big plated cruet-stand on the table. His story might gather up their scattered attention and make it seem that they were interested in each other, that they had come here to enjoy each other's company, to have a good meal, or even to listen to the music: anything, anything but expose themselves by gaping at other people. 'I said I heard an amusing thing at the Courts this morning,' he repeated, because his remark had passed unheard or unheeded the first time, the gaze of all the Beckers having at that moment gone towards a prominent actor who had just seated himself at an adjoining table. But Theobald's simple ruse seemed doomed to failure. Only James appeared to be listening.

'I didn't think the Courts were sitting yet,' James said. 'I didn't know the Long Vacation was over.' In Theobald's story he displayed no interest at all. He had done no more than, as it were, listlessly lift his fork to pick out a small morsel of familiar food before pushing aside the rest of what was offered.

Theobald did not know for a moment whether to be amused or annoyed. It might perhaps be an idea to try and make a joke of their inattention. If only he could rouse them to one good genuine laugh, he'd be satisfied. If only he could gather them for once into a self-absorbed group! But how? Just then, however, to his surprise he found Charlotte had been attending to what James had said.

'Of course the Courts are sitting,' she said, and the glance she gave her husband had an exasperated glint. Theobald was about to metaphorically link arms with her and enlist her as a supporter, when she leant forward to reprimand her husband. 'How could you be so stupid, James? Didn't you see the Chief Justice and his wife in the foyer when we were coming in here tonight? You know they wouldn't be back in town unless the Supreme Court was sitting.' But after another scathing glance she turned the other way, and this time leaning across Theobald, she caught Henrietta's sleeve and gave it a tug. 'They're sitting at a table to the right of the door, Henrietta, if you'd like to see them. She has a magnificent ring on her finger. I can see it from here. And that's their daughter in the velvet cloak. What do you think of her? She's supposed to be pretty.'

Theobald's story was not mentioned any more that evening by anyone, least of all by himself, and he had the further mortification of knowing that it was due to his abortive attempt to tell it that Henrietta and James, the least curious of the Beckers, and the least given to gossip, were craning their necks all during the meal to see the Chief Justice's wife and daughter. As if they were a different race of beings! Some species of superior animal which they – the Beckers – were kindly permitted to observe.

And those were exactly the words he used, later that night, when he and Samuel were walking home. Being unmarried, they were the only two of the Becker men who were at liberty to walk home from these gatherings. James and Ernest, and Henrietta's husband, had to hire cabs to convey their wives to their abodes.

Samuel and Theobald were in rooms, but not of course in the same locality – Samuel thinking it advisable to reside near the business, and Theobald feeling that for the sake of his practice he had to live further out in a more fashionable area, although he admitted that at times it was inconvenient.

'A good address is essential to a man in my position,' he said. It irritated him that he had to explain this so often to the others. Samuel was the only one who understood. He had even made mention once or twice of doing likewise. For the present, however, Samuel was alright where he was. As bachelor's quarters his rooms were quite comfortable.

The two brothers walked along the streets talking without great interest, but with a certain affection, and looking down as they walked at the pavement vanishing under their feet, except when, intermittently in the patches of pale light from the street lamps they raised their heads and appeared to look at each other, giving the impression that they were attending to what was being said.

Samuel had enjoyed his dinner. He was also enjoying the walk home. The streets late at night had an air of unreality that appealed to him. Like limelight the moon shone greenly down making the lighted windows of the houses appear artificial, as if they were squares of celluloid, illuminated only for the sake of illusion. He hoped Theobald wouldn't insist on dragging him back to reality. But he might have known better.

'Did you see them tonight, Samuel? Did you see them staring at the Chief Justice and his wife? Did you see the way they were turning around in their chairs?'

'I didn't notice particularly,' Samuel said. He still hoped to hold himself aloof. High up in a window on the other side of the street a light went out. What was going on up in that room? What unknown people were intent on what unknown purposes? Vague curiosity stirred in him.

Theobald was relentless. 'What do you mean?' he fumed. 'You were as bad as anyone yourself.'

Samuel reluctantly lowered his eyes and looked at his brother and sighed.

'What harm is it to look at people?' he asked mildly.

Theobald came to a stand. 'You know the answer to that as well as I do, Samuel,' he said. 'You know it marks people off at once as coming from a certain class, to stare at anyone who has raised himself the least bit above the common level. It's tantamount to acknowledging one's own inferiority, and I for one won't do that.' All Theobald's pent-up vexation of the evening threatened to break over the head of the defenceless Samuel. 'How is it no one ever stares at us when we go into these places? Isn't there a single one of us distinguished enough in some way to attract a little attention from others instead of our always being attracted to them?'

Samuel did not reply, not knowing whether it was wiser to reply or to remain silent. Theobald's words might be no more than a protracted exclamation, and a reply might provoke an argument. As they walked on a few more paces in silence it seemed as if he had followed the wisest course. But when they were passing under another lamp-post Theobald stood again.

'I'll never get used to it,' he cried.

This time Samuel was genuinely caught. 'To what?' he asked, taken by surprise.

But it was only the same old pill in another coating.

'To the poor marriages they made,' Theobald said, and of course he was talking about James and Ernest. Samuel sighed. He was into the thick of it. 'It makes me sad every time I think of them,' Theobald went on. 'I don't feel so bad about Henrietta, but I hate to think of the chances our brothers let slip – with their positions and their looks, and above all, with their money. Think of the opportunities they had. They might have made excellent marriages. Instead of that – what did they do?' Unable to find words caustic enough to answer his own question, Theobald made a noise in his throat to indicate the greatest of contempt. Then he put out his hand and patted Samuel on the shoulder. 'The only hope we have rests in you, old man,' he said.

Except for the fact that Theobald was younger than him, which gave an unpleasant sense of patronage to his brother's words and gestures, Samuel felt flattered. He immediately paid more heed than the Beckers normally paid to Theobald. This did not mean he approved of Theobald's nonsense. He was just vaguely titillated by his brother's confidence in him, though there was something about his brother's attitude that he still didn't like.

'When your time comes, Samuel,' Theobald said, 'I hope you'll do a bit better for yourself than the others. I hope you'll have some aspiration towards a better social level.'

That was it. *That* was the undertone Samuel disliked. He had not been able to put his finger on it before. All this talk about lifting themselves up to a higher level implied a criticism of their present level which was decidedly disagreeable to him.

'Look here, Theobald,' he said. They were passing under yet another lamp-post but it was he this time who came to a stand. 'I don't know what you're talking about, and I don't know what levels *you* want to reach, but personally I don't think there is anyone in this city, whatever his position, with whom *I* am unacquainted. Why only this morning I was talking to Sir Joshua Lundon over a cup of coffee and –'

Samuel was trying to speak casually, but as he uttered the baronet's name his voice rose to a higher and thinner note, and his eyes bulged slightly with the strain of trying to appear indifferent. He drew back a pace or two on the pretext of clearing his throat behind a large grey silk handkerchief heavily monogrammed in purple silk to match the silk clocks that ran up the outer sides of his grey lisle socks: he was the most elegant of the Beckers. But he was smart enough to know that the only time their younger brother's views were acceptable to any of them was when the fellow managed to get hold of one of them separately – as now – because while they were all unable to apply his counsels and criticisms to themselves, they came within reasonable distance of agreeing with him when discussing each other.

And, of course, in the present case Samuel felt sure there could not possibly be any personal application intended. Unless Theobald was using the past of the others as a future warning to him, who, though he might have the elegance, had few other attributes of the real dyed-in-the-wool bachelor. Samuel indeed entirely lacked the stamina of the successful bachelor, and at the time of this late night walk with Theobald, he was almost at the end of his tether. So he was at one and the same time drawn towards the dangerous topic of matrimony and anxious to skirt it. He felt, however, that his reference to the baronet had been particularly clever, because it might serve to draw Theobald out in his views without leaving him, Samuel, open to direct examination. Yet when he saw the look that came on Theobald's face, he had an uneasy feeling that he had made a false move, and he was about to be out-flanked.

'Yes,' he said nervously, repeating his words, as if having taken up a poor position he felt it was best to dig himself in – 'Yes, Sir Joshua Lundon. He came over and sat down at my table. We had a most interesting talk.'

But whereas on the first occasion he had looked at Theobald as much as to say 'What do you think of that?' he now looked at him as much as to ask 'What can you say against that?'

Theobald, however, had another most irritating habit, learned no doubt from his profession. He kept people in suspense before replying to their simplest remarks, thereby giving his own words a disturbing preponderance.

'My dear Samuel,' he said at last, 'I have no doubt but that you have often sat down with people as notable – and I hope a lot more interesting – than old Sir Joshua. One meets all kinds of people in public places.'

Under Samuel's heavy chin a blush began to spread. That was a confounded insinuation. No doubt it was another trick of the trade. No Becker had ever been bred to such cute ways. Not that he, Samuel, couldn't summon up certain wiles if needed and beat the damn fellow at his own game. He knew very well what was implied. And he'd give an answer in the same wrapping.

'Curious – that's just what Sir Joshua was saying to me only today,' he said, as casually as possible. 'He was remarking on that very thing – the promiscuity of persons one meets with when one ventures into public places. "As a matter of fact, Becker," he said to me, "I'm always delighted to see you, or someone like you, with whom one can suitably sit down when one is forced to come into this kind of place"'

As he spoke, Samuel's confidence returned, and he felt there was no small skill in the way he parried the lawyer's thrust. He even felt for an instant that the Old Man could as readily have sent him, Samuel, for the Bar as the younger brother. Now, of course, after a number of years, training told, but if it came to native wit and natural aptitude he believed he would be prepared to cross swords with Theobald any day. Why, Theobald was as good as eating his words. Listen to him!

'I didn't think you knew the baronet so well,' Theobald was saying. And in spite of Samuel's efforts to twitch it away, a look of gratification stole over his face. This was almost an apology. He felt he could afford now to be magnanimous about the whole thing.

'Oh, yes, yes. I've known him a long time,' he said. 'I'd like you to meet him – I must arrange something some day. You might come and have a meal with me in the city?' He looked at his younger brother. The fellow appeared to be thoroughly deflated. Oh, how Samuel wished that James or Ernest could see him. 'Yes,' he said, intent on enjoying his position, 'as a matter of fact I have had it in mind for some time to make you two acquainted. The baronet might be of some assistance to you. And I think he'd be glad of a chance to do me a favour because I don't mind telling you I have obliged him in a number of ways over the years.'

'Thank you, Samuel,' Theobald said, and Samuel could hardly credit the look of humility that he thought he saw on the other's face. But all at once he felt a twinge of uneasiness. Surely there was an excessive quiet in the tone of Theobald's voice? Yes, undoubtedly there was. And what was he saying? However suave it sounded Samuel was on the alert.

But Theobald was only thanking him.

'Thank you, Samuel,' he'd said. 'I'd like that very much indeed.' Then he paused. 'I have often thought that Lady Lundon looked more intelligent than the old man. I'd be most interested in making her acquaintance. For when shall we arrange?'

For one moment Samuel measured eyes with Theobald and thought of taking refuge in dissimulation, saying that he would drop him a line when he had arranged something. But at the thought of the calculating way he had been led into this conversational trap, his temper so got the better of him that dissimulation was impossible. A feeling of positive hatred for Theobald rose within him, and he felt a vein begin to pulse in his forehead, and his jaw to twitch involuntarily. He was only too well aware of these distressing indications of ill temper, and his awareness did nothing to ease them.

The young cur, he apostrophized. He was well suited to the Law. A fox to the snout. He himself could do nothing but bark out the truth.

'If it's Lady Lundon you want to meet you can get someone else to introduce you,' he said sourly. 'I only know the old man.'

This, of course, was what Theobald was waiting to hear. He met the explanation with one simple word.

'Ah!' he said. Just that, no more. 'Ah!' The vein in Samuel's temple throbbed more violently, but Theobald put out his hand and patted him on the shoulder. 'Take it easy, Samuel,' he said. 'I'm sorry for baiting you, but it gets to be a habit with us fellows at the Courts, I'm afraid.'

As he patted his brother approvingly, however, Theobald looked anxiously at him. How the chap shook when he got agitated! But when Samuel relaxed again into his usual complacency, Theobald abruptly withdrew his hand. 'You did rather ask for it though, old fellow,' he said.

They had reached the street in which Samuel resided and had slackened pace to lengthen the time at their disposal, for in spite of a customary invitation to do so, it was not a practice for the brothers to accept hospitality from each other on such occasions. Tonight, however, Theobald wanted a little more time with Samuel to say something important he thought ought to be said.

'For heaven's sake let's drop the pretence, Samuel,' he cried. 'Don't try to pull the wool over my eyes with your social contacts in public places. Of course, you don't know Lady Lundon, or anyone like her if it comes to that, and if you did you'd keep your mouth shut about it or the rest of the family would be living vicariously on your relationship.' Dropping his normal tone, Theobald affected a thin, high and wholly unnatural tone, instantly recognizable to his brother as the voice of their sister-in-law Julia. 'Oh, Lady Lundon,' he mimicked. 'Oh yes. Oh yes. I haven't met her myself yet, personally, but she's a great friend of Samuel's. I believe she is a charming person – simply charming – and most unassuming. I understand she is a very friendly person, and so simple – just like anyone else in fact.'

Theobold as he imitated her was so like Ernest's wife that Samuel had to smile in spite of himself. And some of his resentment left him.

'Isn't that true?' Theobald asked, although he had not actually formulated a question.

'Well – up to a point I suppose it's true,' Samuel said, knowing what Theobald meant.

'Of course, you understand I have nothing against them,' Theobald said, and in spite of a certain ambiguity in his use of the pronoun, it was possible to tell by the derogatory tone of his voice that Theobald was referring to his sisters-in-law. 'In fact,' he said more explicitly, 'Julia is a very decent sort really. Those socks she knit for me last winter look as if they'll never wear out, although the colour is a bit drastic, but all the same she meant well and poor Charlotte isn't a bad sort either. It's only a pity James and Ernest didn't do a little bit better for themselves.'

Samuel couldn't let this pass.

'They're happy!' he protested weakly.

'Happy! Well, I should hope so!' Theobald said with a flash of contempt. 'That's all they considered at the time, their own comfort and pleasure. If they'd been let down about that I wouldn't know what to say. But happy or not, I still maintain, and will do so till my dying day, that it's a pity their wives hadn't a little more to recommend them.'

'It is certainly regrettable that not one of them – Robert included – had a single penny to bring into the business,' Samuel said with a sudden burst of animation.

'There you are!' Theobald was delighted by Samuel's agreement, although as a matter of fact he himself had not been thinking of his in-laws' lack of money when he'd spoken of their limitations. But it was so encouraging to have someone agree that they did have limitations he let this pass. 'There you are!' he repeated. 'Why, it's ludicrous to think we tolerated it – that no one said "boo" at the time. In proper levels of society there is some kind of control in these matters: not that I approve altogether of too much interference. In fact interference ought not to be necessary if a family is brought up to an understanding of its obligations, its duties.' He frowned. 'I must, of course, say in defence of James and Ernest that we ourselves were not brought up to have that understanding, but –' He stopped and looked Samuel straight in the eye.' – but how is it, then, that you and I came to have the proper outlook?'

Whatever disparity might still have been between the two brothers was blasted away by this shattering bolt of flattery.

'Oh well,' Samuel said modestly, 'people can't all be alike, I suppose.'

'I suppose not,' Theobald agreed, but more curtly, and he turned aside in case he would laugh out loud at the foolish look on Samuel's face, although it was not indeed a laughing matter, and he felt he was to be congratulated on the evening's conversation. If he had been too late to do anything about the marriages of his older brothers, he believed that at least he had made an impression on Samuel.

There were as a matter of fact two special reasons why Theobald was glad to think he had influenced Samuel. The first was that he had sensed for some time past that the citadel of Samuel's celibacy would not continue to stand much longer, and that he had spoken just in the nick of time. The second reason was that he himself had begun to engage his mind with plans of his own in a certain interesting direction, and he did not want to have any more mediocre connections to have to drag out into the light.

'Well, goodnight, Samuel,' he said abruptly.

They had reached the foot of the steps that led up to the old Georgian house where Samuel still resided in single dignity. Taking a last look at him, Theobald congratulated himself again on having said his say so determinedly. Then having watched his brother admit himself into the house he started to saunter on his way, giving himself up, with more ease of mind than he had done for some time, to the joys of contemplating his own plans – plans which, by the way, he told himself, he would shortly have to divulge to the family.

Before, however, Theobald had time to divulge anything to anyone, Samuel's capitulation had taken place.

' – and I was guided a great deal by you, Theobald, in making my choice,' Samuel said, turning to his younger brother with a special courtesy after he had made the announcement of his forthcoming marriage to the rest of the family. 'I was greatly impressed by that conversation we had the other evening.'

'Did you hear that, Theobald?' Henrietta cried, her face purple with excitement. All the Beckers – bar Theobald – loved weddings. There was nothing they enjoyed more, unless perhaps christenings. 'Did you hear that? Samuel says he was largely guided by you in picking his bride.'

'Is that so?' Theobald said morosely. 'Well, all I can say is that he wasn't guided very far!'

'Theobald! What do you *mean*?' Henrietta cried, but she didn't wait for him to answer. 'Really, there is no understanding you at all,' she said. And indeed it seemed that there was not, because unlike the rest of them Samuel was marrying money. He was in fact marrying a great deal of money. He was uniting himself to Honoria, only daughter of the elder Croker of the firm of Croker and Croker, which was the only other firm of corn merchants in the city which might be said to be in any way comparable in size and importance with the firm of Becker and Becker. Although, as James had quietly expressed himself, there was not much point in making speculations as to the relative importance of the two firms since now undoubtedly there would be an amalgamation between them, Honoria being the sole heiress to Croker and Croker.

'Perhaps you didn't understand that, Theobald?' Henrietta said, willing to give him another chance to alter his extraordinary attitude.

But Theobald understood. He understood everything. He shook his head sadly. It was the rest of them that did not understand. To them it seemed that Samuel had scored over him in a way that would protect them for evermore from what they regarded as his notions.

'This will silence Theobald for good and all,' James had said earlier in the day, when as the head of the family he had been given an intimation of what Samuel planned before it was announced to the others.

'Did he get any hint of it at all?' Charlotte had asked eagerly, when it was whispered to her. 'I'd give anything to be there when he's told.'

That was what they all wanted to know – what Theobald would say.

What would Theobald say? What would Theobald do? The question went from lip to lip all that day as one after another the

Beckers passed on a hint to each other of the felicitous step Samuel was taking. Julia alone refrained from this eager questioning because Theobald, she maintained, would have nothing to say now. Samuel had cut the ground from under his feet.

And that was exactly what Samuel himself felt he had done.

'He may not come out with it,' Samuel said, 'but I'd dearly like to know what's in his mind.'

And although Samuel got a shock when he was told what Theobald *had* come out with, he did not let his younger brother's words rankle because he felt that in cases like this one always had to make allowances for a certain amount of jealousy.

Only when he was alone with Honoria did Samuel allow himself to brood over Theobald's reaction.

'Theobald is your youngest brother, isn't he?' Honoria asked. To an only child the Becker family seemed at times bewilderingly large. 'I heard something or other about him, I think,' she said, 'but I can't remember exactly what it was – Anyway I'm dying to meet him.'

'You'll shortly be meeting them all, my dear,' Samuel said. 'James is giving a dinner for that purpose I understand.' Then suddenly remembering the last dinner party James had given, and his walk through the empty streets afterwards with Theobald, he frowned. 'I hope James will agree to giving it in his own house,' he said. 'It would be more suitable than in a restaurant, don't you think?'

'Oh, I don't know so much about that,' Honoria said, and she seemed disappointed. 'I love eating out,' she said. 'I love looking at the other people. Father and I go out for dinner occasionally, just for that alone – to look at people. We went out last evening and, Samuel, you'd never guess who was sitting at the next table to us – Father knows him slightly – Sir Joshua Lundon. Father whispered who he was to me. And Lady Lundon was with him. Oh Samuel, she was so nice. Just as simple as could be! She ordered the simplest food too, just like you or me, or anybody else.'

Where had Samuel heard that before? Familiar and unpleasant echoes sounded in his brain. Had he himself not said something like this to Theobald recently and been promptly and severely shown his error?

'It would be more suitable for us to meet in James's house,' he said, and he resolved to insist on it.

When Samuel mentioned the matter to James, James agreed – if reluctantly.

'Very well,' he said. 'I'll tell Charlotte and we'll arrange for some night next week. All right?'

It was more than all right. It was perfect. For once the whole family was in accord in its preference for the betrothal celebrations to be as private as possible. For once their attention was focused fully on themselves. There was not one member of the family but wanted to witness Theobald's reaction to the wealthy bride-to-be. Their interest was centred on their own affairs for another reason too. Was there not a growing rumour that Theobald himself was about to introduce a new member into the family? And might it not be possible that in the intimacy of Samuel's party there could be further disclosures made? The hearts of the Becker women beat faster at the thought. The girl that was good enough for Theobald! How they longed to see her.

Who was she? What would she be like? Above all, would she live up to Theobald's own lofty notions? Not one single member of the family but was sorely tempted to hope she would not. And this, from no more unworthy motive than the common one of self-preservation. It would be such an ease to everyone if Theobald's mouth could be shut once and for ever.

And as the rumour grew this ungenerous feeling grew with it until finally the nearest any of his sisters and brothers could go to letting themselves believe Theobald's principles were inviolable was to disbelieve the rumour entirely.

'It can't be true,' Henrietta declared flatly on the morning of the day James and Charlotte were giving their little dinner for Samuel and Honoria. 'I don't believe it!'

'Well, I do!' Charlotte said. 'And so does Julia.'

'What about you, Robert? What do you think?' Henrietta asked, because Robert had come along with her to James's place to see if they could give a hand in the last-minute preparations.

'I must say I'm inclined to believe the rumours,' Robert said with a grin he couldn't seem to control.

'Why don't you ask Theobald straight out, Henrietta? Charlotte said slyly.

'That's just what I intend doing,' Henrietta said. 'I'll make a point of asking him the very next opportunity – that is to say the very next time I'm alone with him.'

It was therefore rather unfortunate for Henrietta that a few minutes later, having volunteered to collect a few pot plants in town for Charlotte and having left Robert behind to attend to some hitch in the lighting arrangements, who should she run into – right outside Charlotte's door – right under the windows in fact – but her younger brother. There was nothing to do but take a rush at him.

'Is it true, Theobald?' she demanded, and she actually put out her arm to bar his way as if she feared he might bolt off.

'Is what true?' Theobald asked coldly and looked at her even more coldly. 'Are you feeling all right, Henrietta?'

For the life of her Henrietta could not bring herself to speak any plainer, but feeling forced to say something she took refuge behind further obscurity.

'Well, if it *is* true,' she said, 'all I can say is I hope you'll do as well for yourself as Samuel.'

Then, telling herself she had done what she proclaimed she would do, Henrietta threw a triumphant glance up at the windows of the house behind her, feeling pretty sure that Charlotte would be watching them from behind the curtains. She was so carried away by a sense of her own courage she wished Charlotte could have heard her, as well as seen her.

It was perhaps no harm that her sister-in-law had not heard, because Theobald did not seem to understand what she'd been driving at. Or did he? Really, he was impossible. No one could ever tell what he was thinking. Henrietta stared at him to try and figure out what was in the back of his mind. But the next minute she stepped back in alarm. Theobald's face had begun to work as if he was going to have a fit.

'What's the matter, Theobald?' she cried.

'The matter!' Theobald, although he had calmed down again, still looked very peculiar. 'Pray tell me, Henrietta,' he said then, 'in what way you consider our brother Samuel has done so well for himself?'

Henrietta simply did not know what to make of him. Who were they talking about anyway? Him or Samuel? She'd been under the impression that she was unearthing information about *him*.

'Well,' she said, taken aback, 'Honoria has plenty of money.'

'Money!' Theobald positively sneered at the word. 'What does money matter? To Samuel anyway! What does he want with any more than he has already? Money, my dear Henrietta, is not the only thing in this world.'

Was it not? Henrietta allowed herself to have mental reservations in the matter, but for the moment she was concerned with a less general aspect of what was being revealed. Very quickly she came to a decision. If there was any truth in the rumours about Theobald, well then it looked very much as if *his* intended was penniless. But Theobald was still ranting on about Samuel.

'I never thought he'd be so short-sighted,' he said. 'He's making a worse mistake than any of you.'

Henrietta had swallowed too many of these jibes to object to one more, and anyway she was just beginning to think she might draw him out a bit after all.

'How is that?' she asked faintly.

'Oh, can't you see!' Theobald cried impatiently. 'What difference does it make to Samuel whether he has thirty thousand or fifty thousand. It isn't more money Samuel needs: it's less. And that applies to all of us.'

'Less?' The daughter of the Beckers felt faint at the suggestion.

'Exactly,' Theobald said. 'I thought Samuel would have had the wit to forget about money for once and try and acquire some of the things of which this family stands in such sore need.'

'And what are they?' Henrietta gaped.

Theobald fixed her with a cold eye.

'Social position for one thing, and distinction for another; preferably the latter. But instead of that Samuel turns up with this mediocre Croker person. As I said before, he's made a worse mistake than any of you. What did the rest of you do? – Well, to put it bluntly you did no worse than keep within, whereas Samuel has widened, the circle of our mediocrity.'

In his vexation Theobald made several extravagant gestures, that to Henrietta appeared most unseemly in the street, but when his arms fell suddenly to his sides she felt still more uneasy about him.

'Tell me,' he said in a low despairing voice, 'I expect this girl has a horde of relatives? How many of them do you think there will be at James's tonight?'

'Only her father, I think,' Henrietta said quickly, 'and maybe an old aunt, but the aunt is deaf.' The question had made her very anxious. 'Why?'

'Because,' Theobald said, 'I was thinking that if there weren't too many Crokers there, tonight might be as good a time as any for the family to meet my Flora.'

'Flora?' Henrietta said stupidly, and then with a rush of blood to the head, she realized that this Flora, whoever she was, must be the living embodiment of the very rumours she had been trying to run to earth. 'Why, Theobald,' she cried, 'is her name Flora? I mean is it true? What I mean to say is we heard a rumour but –'

'That's all right, Henrietta,' Theobald said, cutting her short, and he allowed her to find and briefly hold the hand she was vaguely feeling for, as her words stumbled and tumbled over each other. Her muttered incoherence was painful to him, and it was painful too for him to have to watch what he took to be her embarrassment, knowing that Flora would call it gaucherie.

But Theobald was wrong, for although Henrietta was confused, her confusion came, not from embarrassment, but from trying to do two things at the one time: to talk, and to think. She was thinking furiously. Apparently whatever attributes this Flora of his might possess, she, Henrietta, must be right in assuming that untold wealth was not one of them. Flora certainly couldn't claim to be the heiress that Honoria was. How far therefore was it wise – she was thinking in terms of worldly wisdom, of course – to make use of the party given in honour of Honoria to introduce into the family another prospective bride who could, money apart, if Theobald's prognostications were true, put poor Honoria's nose out of joint? Was it even fair? And above all, was she, Henrietta, to be the only one to know of the bombshell that her young brother was planning to throw into their midst that night? If so, the responsibility was just too much for one pair of shoulders. Should she tell him so? Decidedly she would have to tell him.

These were the thoughts that were running through her head while actually she was shaking his hand in felicitation.

'Of course I'm longing to meet her, Theobald,' she said, when she regained her hand. 'I'm just wondering if tonight is the proper occasion for introducing her to us?'

'Why not?' Theobald said. 'She has to meet you sometime.'

Memories of certain scathing remarks Theobald had made about Robert still rankled with Henrietta, and they bred a sudden vicious hope in her mind. Was he ashamed of this Flora?

But she was quickly and in fact rudely shown how wrong she was. It was not of Flora Theobald was ashamed.

'I'll have to get it over some time or another,' he said. 'It's something that will have to be faced sooner or later, and anyhow I'm sure Flora will make allowances. It is always people like her who are most understanding when it comes to the shortcomings of others.'

Henrietta swallowed quickly, and took a deep breath. Was it possible Theobald had accomplished the feat he expected of himself? She swallowed again. All the more reason, then, to protect poor Honoria from the hazards of a comparison.

'All the same, Theobald,' she said firmly, 'I think it wouldn't be nice – for your Flora, I mean – to introduce her to us casually like that. I think we ought to wait and talk to James and get him to name a definite evening for the purpose. It's nice to be formal about these things don't you think?'

She spoke so primly Theobald threw back his head and gave a loud guffaw.

'Formal? Is it Flora? Easily seen you don't know her. My dear Henrietta – don't you think for a moment that she's the kind of person who'd sit down to one of our vulgar spreads. Why, I don't believe Flora knows such orgies exist. After all, they *are* purely middle-class functions. As a matter of fact when I was telling her about this evening's party I must confess that I more or less conveyed that we ourselves didn't ordinarily go in for this kind of gathering. I'm afraid I told a white lie – I rather gave the impression that we were going through with it mainly to please the Crokers, who were a bit old-fashioned. I sort of suggested that for us it was going to be quite an ordeal. So I'd be glad, Henrietta' – this time it was he who reached for her hand – 'if you'd help me out a bit and play up that suggestion?'

'Well –' Henrietta said slowly, 'if you insist on bringing her, I suppose I can't show you up for a liar. But it will be very hard to do it convincingly.'

'I know that,' said Theobald dryly.

Henrietta wasn't sure what he meant, and she didn't at all like his tone, but she felt she more or less had him at a disadvantage.

'We must warn the others, Theobald,' she said.

'On no account must that be done, Henrietta,' Theobald cried. His voice rose urgently and he glanced over Henrietta's head towards the windows of the house in case the wind might have carried their words in that direction. 'I don't want anyone to know about it, only you and me and Flora. I want to take everyone by surprise. Indeed those were the only conditions under which I could make Flora consent to come. She wouldn't come under any other.'

'But, Theobald!' Henrietta protested once more. She felt her responsibility in the matter come down on her with an insuperable weight. 'I'll have to tell James. And I'll have to tell Charlotte. We might get away with keeping it from the others, but we'll have to tell them. You can't possibly expect to land an extra person down on them without notice – and for that matter – you can't let Flora arrive and find no place set for her! There mightn't even be enough chairs!' Henrietta was as embarrassed as if she were the hostess and Theobald's bombshell was about to fall on *her* dinner table.

Theobald only laughed. 'Don't worry about that, Henrietta,' he said. 'We're only going to look in on you for a minute or two towards the end of the meal. We're not going to stay. We're not to be counted as far as place setting and that are concerned.' He looked sternly at her. 'I thought I made it plain to you that Flora wouldn't understand sitting down to the big gorges that James and Charlotte provide.' He gave another laugh, a different sort: a pleased laugh. 'Flora doesn't eat as much as a bird.'

A bird? All the time they'd been talking, Henrietta had been trying unsuccessfully to visualize the appearance of this person. Flora. Now, all at once, with Theobald's mention of her birdly appetite,

Henrietta's imagination rose with a beat of wings, and before her mind's eye flew gaudy images of brightly plumed creatures of the air. They made her quite dizzy, those images, until they merged at last into one final image of a little creature, volatile as a lark, a summer warbler, a creature so light and airy that it hardly rested on the ground at all. Perhaps not a lark – a chaffinch, maybe? A minute little creature with yellowy golden hair.

'Oh, is it wise, Theobald?' she cried again. 'Is it wise under the circumstances?'

'What circumstances?' Theobald asked obtusely, but then as he saw Henrietta redden he understood. 'Oh, you needn't worry on that score either. Flora's life is too rich, too filled with variety, to notice that at all. I assure you she isn't the kind of person to take in little details.'

'Little details!' Henrietta reddened, this time with annoyance. There was only one detail and she wouldn't call it little. You wouldn't have to stare very hard to be aware of it. One of the circumstances to which she had alluded was the fact that she was pregnant again, and beginning to be more than a little remarkable. The other circumstances were the pregnancies of her two sisters-in-law, both of whom were in the same condition, only more advanced. A nice time, she thought, to bring to the house a giddy little bird like this Flora. Because now Henrietta's conception of Flora's appearance had hardened like cement.

'You don't understand, Theobald,' she said stiffly. 'It could be embarrassing for an unmarried young woman.'

'Nonsense!' Theobald said. 'But if so, what about embarrassing Honoria?'

'Oh, it's different for Honoria,' Henrietta replied, although immediately after she'd spoken, it occurred to her that she hadn't been very kind to Samuel's intended. Honoria's plump, well-fed figure was furred and beribboned as much as any matron in token of her independent means, and there wouldn't be anything like the same embarrassment for her that there could be for a birdy bride-like creature with a name like Flora. Why Honoria might as well have been a matron already.

'Oh, it's altogether different for Honoria,' she said, trying to make emphasis do for explanation. It was not a matter one could explain to a man: least of all a man like Theobald who was so lacking in understanding.

Lacking in understanding Theobald certainly appeared to be that day.

'I think you're absurd, Henrietta,' he said. 'I can only attribute it to

your condition. I'm sorry I mentioned the matter. Please forget it.'
Raising his hat, her brother was about to move away.

Henrietta was speechless. This made things worse. She did not
know whether he was going to carry out his intention or not. It was
impossible to remain in such uncertainty.

'Theobald!' she called.

Theobald, upon being called, turned with forced politeness.

'Does that mean you are not going to bring her?' Henrietta asked.

'It does not!' Theobald stopped. 'I'm not going to miss an
opportunity like this for killing two stones with the one – I mean two
birds with the one *stone*. Good morning, Henrietta.' This time he
quite definitely walked away.

Henrietta stared after him, more upset than ever. Her brother
usually affected such a slow and deliberate manner of speech there
was seldom danger of a verbal mishap such as he had just suffered.
Henrietta shook her head. He must be out of his mind about this
Flora, she thought, and she shivered. To think of having to meet and
entertain a person capable of turning the head of a man like
Theobald!

All during that morning as Henrietta tried to do Charlotte's
messages for her, she continued to experience unpleasant shivers of
apprehension, and several times when Theobald's slip of the tongue
came to her mind, she had a sensation of the ground going from
under her. But at bottom Henrietta was a sound and sensible
woman. By the time she'd done the messages and got back to James's
house she had made up her mind – Theobald's injunctions apart.
She'd say nothing at all about the impending surprise. For, unlikely
as it seemed that Theobald would play a joke, the thought had
occurred to her that he might be having her on. And if that were the
case, what a fool she'd make of herself in the eyes of the others.
Henrietta deposited with Charlotte the flowers, the frills for the
cutlets, and an extra carton of fresh cream, and departed with
Robert, taking with her the secret about Flora.

It was really only later that evening when she took her place at
Charlotte's beautifully appointed table where she'd been seated
between Honoria's father and Ernest that the burden of her guilty
knowledge began to tell.

'Are you feeling all right, Henrietta?' Charlotte asked on at least
two occasions, once during the soup, and once during the fish,
when Henrietta, thinking she'd heard a footfall on the stairs, began
to perspire across her forehead.

Oh, why hadn't she told someone – if only Robert? She looked
across the table at him in desperation. Could she, even now, convey

her fears to him? But Robert was not attending to Julia on his left, much less to Henrietta across the board, because Robert was nervous of swallowing small fish bones. He made it a rule never to talk when eating fish.

The fish, however, had gone the way of the soup and there was no sign of Theobald, and soon the dinner was mid-way through its courses at least with regard to the number of dishes consumed, although considering the rich nature of these first dishes it might perhaps be said to be nearing an end. The guests having, as it were, successfully crossed the biggest of the fences, were coming into the straight, and would no doubt gather speed now for the gallop home. In other words, having consumed the turtle soup, the curled whiting, the crown of roast young pork (accompanied by mounds of mashed potatoes, little heaps of brussels sprouts and a ladle or two of apple sauce), might be expected to make quicker progress through the green salad, the peach melba, the anchovy on toast, the coffee, and the crème de menthe. Still no sign of Theobald! He must arrive soon if he expected them to be still at the table as Henrietta understood him to have intended.

In spite of her irritation with him, Henrietta found herself trying to go slow with her peach melba, until feeling Charlotte's eye upon her, and fearing her sister-in-law might think there was something wrong with the dessert, she had to act like everybody else and gobble it up.

In a trice the anchovies were being passed. In a trice their remains were being removed, and the cheese and crackers were being carried on stage.

It was then, just as the crunch of crackers made hearing difficult, that Henrietta once more fancied she heard sounds indicative of Theobald's arrival. A cab had stopped in the street below, right outside James's door. It must be Theobald. Henrietta told herself that she might have known that a person like Flora would have insisted on arriving by cab. She put down her cracker and listened. Yes, there were voices in the hall. There was laughing. She looked around the table. Did no one else hear? Apparently not. Henrietta's heart stood still. Then, all at once, with a belated access of loyalty she came to a decision: she'd have to let the others know what was about to befall them: she must prepare them for the shock.

'Excuse me. Forgive me for interrupting,' she cried, breaking in upon what, unfortunately, was the first time the whole evening that Honoria had essayed to display the confidence to which her position entitled her by telling a story. Realizing how unfortunate her interruption was, Henrietta felt she had no option but to continue.

'I must tell you all something,' she went on desperately. 'I knew it since morning, but he wanted it to be a surprise.'

Normally, having a rather squeaky voice, Henrietta might not have made herself heard if she tried to address the whole table, but as everyone was giving punctilious attention to the story Honoria was trying to tell, every single word of what Henrietta had to say fell on upright ears.

'What's that?' several of the Beckers cried, speaking all together, and looking first at Henrietta and then at each other.

James alone kept his head.

'Who wanted what to be a surprise?' he asked, almost shouting at Henrietta.

'Theobald, of course,' Henrietta said impatiently, because surely the others had ears as well as herself and ought to be able to recognize Theobald's laugh, rare as it was, and he had just given a hearty laugh on the stairs. 'Theobald, of course, who else?' she said, permitting herself this tick-off, before she fastened her own eyes on the dining-room door.

'Theobald?' James seemed to affect some diminution of interest at the sound of his brother's name. Indeed a curious frigidity had fallen on the company in general, because if Theobald had not come this would have been the first occasion that a member of the Becker family had voluntarily absented himself from a family celebration. And although on this occasion Theobald had been formally excused, there was an underground feeling of dissatisfaction with him.

'Theobald?' Honoria's deaf aunt asked loudly, addressing herself to no one in particular.

'Oh, he's another brother,' Honoria replied impatiently.

'Is it the one you dislike so much?' Honoria's father asked, and as the Beckers all seemed to be at hounds and hares, he didn't feel it necessary to lower his voice all that much. Charlotte, in fact, was the only one to hear and as hostess felt obliged to cover up for her brother, Theobald.

'It's nice that he's been able to join us after all,' she said. Truth will out, however, and she added an unfortunate rider. 'I can't believe that whatever appointment he said he had would have kept him busy all day *and* all evening. I'm glad he has decided to look in on us even for a few minutes!'

'But that – ' Henrietta cried, addressing herself to Charlotte first and foremost, and then the whole family – 'that is just what I wanted to tell you. He is coming! It was to be a surprise!' In her excitement she rose in her chair. 'And now he's here with her!'

'With *her*? With *whom*?' they all cried.

'Flora!' Henrietta almost screamed the name. 'Flora was to be the surprise.'

'Flora?' James gave a startled look at Henrietta. 'Are you out of your mind, Henrietta?' he cried, because at the sound of the name a vague memory stirred in him and gaudy and tinsel images pirouetted before his mind's eye. Hadn't there been an operetta in his youth called *The Flora Doras*? What on earth was coming over Henrietta, he wondered? Flora? Flora? 'What are you talking about?' he demanded.

It was all Henrietta could do to refrain from saying that Flora was a bird. But suddenly she recalled Theobald's slip of the tongue about killing two stones with the one bird, and whatever about his fiancée, it seemed to her that when, at that moment the dining-room door was flung open by Theobald, all the seated Beckers, and all their seated guests, seemed to have been turned into stone.

And the bird?

Henrietta stared. Perched on Theobald's arm, or rather hanging from it by one small hand, was the little chaffinch-type of thing she had expected to see.

Flora was small. She was exceedingly small. She was fine-boned as well, so that, as with a bird, you felt if you pressed her too hard she would be crushed. But in spite of her smallness, like a bird she was exquisitely proportioned, and her clothes, that were an assortment of light colours, seemed to cling to her like feathers, a part of her being, a part moreover of which she herself was entirely unconscious. She accepted her clothes as the birds their feathers: an inevitable raiment.

Indeed Flora appeared to be entirely unconscious of her person. She was hardly into the room before her bright eyes darted from one face to another, her own small pointed face eager with interest in them. It was a birdlike face, thin and sharp, and since her chin was slightly undershot, she gave the impression that like a bird her head was tilted at right angles to her little body. She was evidently very curious about them all, but unlike the curiosity of the Beckers that strove to conceal itself, her curiosity had taken open possession of her. It almost seemed that the excited beating of her heart was causing her frail frame to vibrate and tremble, and that she would simply have to find some outlet: beat her wings, flutter her feathers, or clutch at her perch and burst into song, song so rapturous the perch too would sway up and down.

Theobald, however, was not that kind of perch, and no tremor of Flora's excitement shook the arm to which she clung. Theobald was intent on making his entry.

'Well, everybody?' he said, and with his free hand he possessively clamped to his arm Flora's little hand with its long varnished fingernails. 'Hello, Samuel. Hello, Honoria. I want you all to meet another future Becker bride.'

Had the Beckers been totally unprepared for this shock there is no knowing how the seated table would have reacted, but Henrietta had, as it were, broken the fall for them. And so when Theobald looked around for evidence of surprise, all he saw was stupefaction. The faces that stared at Flora and himself seemed to stare at them out of a coma.

'Well?' he repeated, a little half-heartedly. 'Aren't you going to welcome us?'

At this, James, who had been the most stunned of all, upon being given a dig in the ribs by Julia, got awkwardly to his feet.

'We are unfortunately nearly finished dinner,' he said, looking around the table, 'but we are just going to have coffee.' He ventured his first real look at Flora – 'Perhaps you'd care for a cup?'

Ah! That was better. Good old James! The Beckers relaxed and began to breathe again.

'Where will they sit?' Julia asked, and she went to move her chair to one side. Not that there was much room for movement round the massive mahogany table because it was already so crowded. It was doubtful if a single extra chair, much less two, could be squeezed in at any point. And since, to add to the difficulty, everyone at the table was following Julia's example and trying to make room for the newcomers, there was soon complete confusion. As Julia moved her chair to the right, Henrietta at the same moment was trying to move hers to the left, and on Henrietta's other side Ernest, moving right, was clashing with Charlotte, moving left.

'They look as if they are playing some game,' Flora said to Theobald in a whisper, but a whisper which Charlotte to her intense mortification overheard while she was leaning forward to try and catch the attention of that stupid, stupid James, as she crossly apostrophized him in her mind. Giving up discretion, Charlotte shouted at him.

'Why don't we have coffee in the other room?'

'Just a minute!'

To everyone's surprise the voice that sang out was as sweet and melodious as a bar of music. It was Flora's.

'Please don't move, any of you!' she cried. 'Please, please stay as you are. We've had dinner. Just ignore us.'

There was such poised authority in Flora's voice that one or two of the Beckers who had stood up, sat down again immediately. In fact only James remained standing, and he did so from uncertainty about his duties as host. But Charlotte gratefully seized on Flora's words.

'Don't tease them, James,' she said, and she turned to Theobald. 'If you're sure you've had your dinner, why don't you both go into the drawing-room while we finish our coffee. You can show Flora the albums while you're waiting.'

But as she made the suggestion, Charlotte knew it was not a very good one. Yet what was the alternative? They couldn't be let stand there. Really this was an outrageous thing for Theobald to have done. To bring a strange girl in on top of them like this, and take them at such a disadvantage, particularly when – as Charlotte couldn't fail to see – there was something so distinctive about the girl, something unusual, something indeed downright remarkable.

All at once, irrelevant though it might seem, Charlotte was shot through with bitter regret that she had not had the dining-room redecorated last month as she had intended. But enough of that! What was to be done with the pair now – they didn't seem to be moving off into the drawing-room?

During her brief reverie, however, Charlotte had missed something. Flora had smiled, and Flora's smile was not something to be missed. It was what the Beckers were always to remember about her – her sudden, luminous smile. And on that first occasion that it shone out, it transformed their awkwardness into gaiety. Flora had saved the situation.

'You simply mustn't move!' she cried. 'Such a charming group as you make.' Then, from the purely exclamatory, her voice changed to the intimately conversational as she turned to Theobald. 'Isn't it a wonder photographers never seem to think of posing people around a table this way?' With a charming gesture she indicated the group before her, and smiled again. This time Charlotte didn't miss the smile, and she too, like the rest of the Beckers, felt warmed by it, as by yellow sunlight. 'Oh,' Flora cried, 'oh how I wish *I* was a photographer.' Then suddenly she did the funniest thing. 'Let's pretend that I *am* one,' she cried, and bending down her head in the drollest way, just as if she had a tripod in front of her, and letting her yellow hair fall down over her face like a shutter curtain, she made a circle with her fingers and held them up to her eyes to act as a lens for her make-believe camera. 'I think I can get you all in,' she said, turning her head from side to side to get them in better focus. 'Keep still, everyone. Look at the dickie-bird. And smile! Smile!' Then, when she had them all smiling, she reached down her hand and squeezed the imaginary rubber bulb that controlled the shutter.

It was the most unexpected thing that could possibly have

happened. It was exactly as if she was a real photographer. The Beckers had unconsciously stiffened into the unnatural and rigid postures of people being taken by the camera. Then, when the girl straightened up and pushed back her hair, the group came to life again. Realizing how ridiculous they must have looked, Julia laughed. Then they all laughed, even the parlour-maid, even Honoria, who looked as if she didn't often do so. Above all, Theobald laughed. He was delighted with himself. He looked proudly at his fiancée. She'd be able for any situation.

'Isn't she wonderful?' he said to Charlotte.

But they must be introduced to her.

'Come, Flora,' he said, starting to lead her round the table, beginning, of course, with the head of the house. 'This is James,' he said, and in no way constrained now, he laid his hand on his older brother's shoulder.

In the hilarious mood that had developed, no one really expected Flora to put out her hand and utter conventional commonplaces. They watched her eagerly.

'James?' Flora said, and there was a pert little note in her voice that made some of the family titter. Then, to the accompaniment of general laughter, she circled her eyes with her fingers again and bent once more over her make-believe camera and took a head-and-shoulders portrait of James.

It was quite a few minutes before anyone could speak, they were laughing so much, and James himself, although he was startled for a second, soon saw what the funny girl was up to, and he too gave way to the merriment.

'I hope I didn't break the camera, my dear?' he said.

Theobald's pride in Flora was infectious. It even infected stuffy old James. He was charmed by her.

Flora herself didn't smile. She was doing something to her camera. And her serious expression convulsed the group. She straightened again.

'I must take one of each of you,' she said, and she turned to her next subject. 'Who are you? You're Julia, aren't you?' she asked, while she was adjusting the lens. 'Just a minute please. Try not to move.' From the intent way she was looking at her it seemed Julia was a difficult subject, which fortunately Julia found flattering. 'Smile!' Flora ordered suddenly. But when Julia laughed as the bulb was being squeezed, the photographer was quite annoyed. 'You moved,' she said severely. 'Your picture will be blurred.' She turned around. 'Who's next?'

It was Samuel, and she had to speak sternly to him too. 'I can't take you, you know, while you're grinning like that! Please try to keep still. Look at the dickie-bird!' When she'd taken him she didn't seem altogether satisfied, and she took another shot. 'You're Samuel, aren't you?' she said. 'You're a bad subject I'm afraid, but with a bit of luck it may come out quite well.' She moved her apparatus further along. Her sobriety was the best part of the fun.

'Who have I now?' she asked. It was Henrietta. 'You're very photogenic,' she said to the delighted Henrietta. 'Your face is so angular. Turn your head a little to one side, if you please. Yes – I think a profile would be best in your case.'

It was side-splitting. Never in their lives had the Beckers met anyone remotely like this.

'Well, what do you think of her?' Theobald asked James in an undertone. 'This performance is nothing! She's a sort of genius really. You've no idea how people stare at her everywhere we go. Of course, she's well known anyway; she comes from a very old family, but that doesn't account for all the attention she attracts. It's because she's so amazing. There is nothing she cannot do.' He laughed. 'And nothing she won't attempt too, if she takes it into her head. She's very accomplished. You should hear her play the piano. And she paints. You should see her water colours. She's going to hold an exhibition one of these days. And I believe she has tried her hand at poetry too, if you don't mind! Some publisher has approached her with a view to bringing out a little volume. Oh, there's no end to her gifts. But I always tell her that her real talent is for acting. You've just seen for yourself! And she's a wonderful mimic. You should see her impersonations!'

'Well, if that was any indication!' Samuel said admiringly, coming up to the other two just then, because the party had loosened up and one or two people were going around with Flora pretending to be her assistants, helping to move her equipment and pose those yet to be taken.

They were just about to photograph Honoria's father, and at the expression on the father's face even Honoria burst out laughing, although up to now her laughter had only been following suit.

'Look at my father's face. Please, please,' she begged, and she was laughing so much she had to hold her sides to keep from shaking the whole table.

'That girl is a born actress,' Samuel said, happy to be able to give free rein to his admiration because up to then he'd had some misgivings about offending Honoria, having noticed that her merriment had been somewhat more subdued than that of his family.

Now he could let himself go and enjoy this extraordinarily exciting young woman who unbelievably – thanks to that dry stick Theobald – was about to become one of them.

Samuel ventured a good look at Flora. This he had avoided doing previously, as it didn't seem generous to do so with Honoria present. And he was surprised at a boyish quality about her, because unconsciously, and perhaps because of her name, his first impression had been of quite extravagant girlishness. In fact before he'd met her at all, from the first instant he'd heard the name Flora, it had brought a vision to his mind of a nymph in a misty white dress, with bare feet and cloudy yellow hair, who in a flowering meadow skipped about, gathering flower heads and entwining them in a garland. It was a bit of a shock to see she was wearing a trim black suit and that her small black shoes had buckles, not bows. There was just one thing about her that was flowery though: her perfume. Honoria never wore perfume. Samuel wished she would. It was captivating.

Captivating was the word; all the Beckers were captivated. Flora was not in their midst more than a few minutes before they had all succumbed to her charm. As Ernest expressed it afterwards when he and Julia were going home, there was only one thing that bothered him and that was to think that such a fascinating person should be tying herself up to a bore like Theobald.

'He is a bore, Julia, you know, with all his theories and principles.'

'He has put them into practice, though,' Julia said, 'you must admit that. I'll confess something now, Ernest: it was always my belief he'd make a fool of himself in the long run. People who are too particular always do. I felt certain he'd make a disastrous marriage. I really did.'

Ernest would have liked to confess that he too had often thought the same, but at that moment he felt so well disposed towards his young brother that he hedged.

'Theobald hasn't made many mistakes in his day,' he said.

'That's what I mean!' Julia cried. 'It's that kind of person who makes the worst mistake of all in the end.'

But Ernest wasn't listening. He was thinking about his brother. So there had been something behind his nonsense. He wasn't such a blower after all. Ernest felt subdued. He wondered if Flora had money? The jewellery she was wearing must have cost something. He tried to recall it in greater detail, but as he did he got confused. Had she jewellery on at all? He was puzzled. It didn't seem possible that someone as observant as he prided himself on being could be uncertain about a significant detail. Ernest was so perplexed his wife had to repeat herself twice before she got his attention.

'What is the matter with you, Ernest? Are you deaf? I said her fake photography was the cleverest thing I've seen in years.'

'Oh yes, yes. She certainly is a bit of an actress.'

'More than a bit I'd say!' Julia replied, but there was something in the tone of her voice that made Ernest look at her out of the corner of his eye.

'What do you mean by that?'

'Oh nothing,' Julia said lightly. 'Only I thought once or twice that she carried it just a bit too far. I'd say she doesn't believe in hiding her light under a bushel. And quite honestly, I thought she went into the realms of absurdity altogether when we were saying good-bye on the steps.'

'Why? I didn't notice.'

'Oh, you must have heard what she said to James? He was shaking hands with her, when with a deadly straight face, she said she'd let him have the proofs of the photographs as soon as ever she had them developed.'

But in spite of the small trace of censoriousness with which she had started to relate the incident, Julia couldn't help laughing herself at the recollection. 'James's face was a scream,' she said, 'and that wasn't all! When James got her meaning at last and started to laugh, she really carried the thing to extremes. She put on an injured air, as if her dignity had been offended, and took Theobald's arm and went off down the steps without another word. Oh, it was really funny. I don't believe one person in ten thousand would have been able to go away like that without dropping the pretence at *some* point.'

'There is no doubt about it,' Ernest said, 'Theobald is right. There is a touch of genius about her. Now that you mention it, I think I did notice that she was carrying the thing a bit far at the end of the evening. I saw her pretending to pack up her photographic equipment, and when Theobald gave her his arm, she made as if she was changing it to her other hand. As a matter of fact Theobald didn't twig it at all: he's a bit slow sometimes in spite of his high opinion of himself. I saw the joke immediately. And I let her see I did. ''Why don't you let Theobald carry it for you?'' I said, and went as if to assist her myself. ''That's all right,'' she said. ''I can manage.'' And she smiled. Good lord, that smile!'

'Oh, she's something new in our lives and no mistake,' Julia said, but seeing that they had reached their own street and were approaching their own door, she waited until Ernest had turned the key and admitted them before she gave him a little jab.

'I still can't help thinking it's a pity Theobald has had the satisfaction of knowing he's done so much better for himself than the rest of you.'

This just about expressed the reaction of all the Beckers. Not one of them but could see the distinction and talents possessed by his intended, yet not one but felt that in the long run these would only add to his conceit.

Never mind though. Their wedding would be the next thing. They had that to look forward to anyway. When would it be?

The wedding would take place quite soon. Flora didn't believe in long engagements, it seemed, a fact which might have elicited some cynical remarks were it not that the family all agreed. Theobald wasn't half good enough for her, and the quicker he made sure of her the better.

James kept his head, though, and pointed out that family protocol demanded that Samuel's wedding be first. He glanced at Flora's hand; Theobald had not got the engagement ring yet.

But, it appeared, that was another thing Flora didn't believe in – engagement rings. And this the Becker women found completely baffling.

'She says the feel of a ring on her finger makes her fidgety,' Charlotte reported.

'She'll have to wear a wedding ring, won't she?' Julia said.

'I wouldn't be too sure of that either,' Charlotte said. 'I heard her saying they look dowdy.'

Charlotte and Julia looked down at their own thick bands of gold, guarded by big solitaires set in massive claws. They used to be so proud of them, but now at every minute they found their notions of things suffering a jolt. And soon the jolting was as good as continuous.

First of all Theobald broke it to them that he was not going to buy a house. He and Flora were going to live in apartments. It now appeared Flora could not saddle herself with a house. She was at that particular time engaged in bringing out her book of poems, and she had a responsibility to her publisher. Afterwards they might consider the possibility of a house; but not until afterwards.

'That may be all very well now,' James said, 'but it could be awkward later on.'

The others nodded. They knew what he meant.

'Although, mind you, I wouldn't be surprised – ' Henrietta said, beginning to say something, but stopping. She had recollected the presence among them of Honoria, who although only one month married might take offence. Afterwards she had a private word with Charlotte.

'Of course,' she said to Charlotte, 'it would not matter so much in

Flora's case, she is so gifted in other directions. And I don't believe Theobald would mind as much as another man – he'd have such a lot of compensations.'

Flora's gifts were indeed many. A few weeks before the wedding her book of poems came out, and although frankly the Beckers were unable to understand two words of it, their pride in her was even greater than Theobald's. Samuel was particularly pleased. He made it his business to go down to the club every day to see if there were any reviews of the book.

'She should have had it illustrated,' he maintained every time the book was mentioned. 'She should bring out an illustrated edition.'

Samuel in fact went one further than them all at times in his admiration for her, and actually took a censorious attitude towards poor Theobald. 'That fellow doesn't realize a man has responsibilities towards a woman like Flora,' he muttered. 'He should take her around more. There was an exhibition of modern paintings last week in Charleville House. I read about it in the paper. But I bet Theobald knew nothing about it. I hope she didn't have to go without an escort, because I'm sure it's the kind of thing she wouldn't want to miss.'

And there and then he promised himself that when she was his sister-in-law, he'd make a point of remedying Theobald's deficiencies in such matters. He was beginning to suspect that Theobald, for all his talk, did not really have a very deep feeling for the Arts. He, Samuel, might not understand a great deal about art, and with one thing and another he hadn't had much time for it, but he intended to do something about it. And now, with the added security of Honoria's dowry he might even venture to buy a few pictures; start a small private collection perhaps. If bought wisely, pictures could be a profitable investment he'd heard. And in this sphere Flora's advice would probably be invaluable. He'd make a start at once; go to a few galleries, make a few enquiries. If Flora were with him he'd feel safe. Yes, they'd make a few tentative expeditions.

The prospect of entering the realm of art in the company of Flora was a particularly pleasant one for Samuel just then, because he would soon be temporarily deprived of Honoria's company. A few weeks after Henrietta's tactful regard for her feelings on a certain subject, Honoria had given evidence that such tact was superfluous. But he must not let his enthusiasm run away with him. The proprieties had to be considered. Oh well! The wedding was just around the corner.

Meanwhile there was the question of the wedding presents.

Presents were a main concern with the Beckers. Every occasion for

making an exchange of gifts was eagerly seized on by them, weddings of course being the best occasions of all. The giving and
receiving of presents had always been a way of expressing emotions
which nervous reticence made it impossible to express in any other
way. Presents were a silent symbol of their family solidarity. They
spoke loud to the Beckers, and in a language they understood. Thus,
when the James Beckers went to visit the Ernest Beckers it always
gave them a feeling of family unity to drink coffee after dinner from
the Crown Derby service they themselves had given the couple on
their wedding day. The Ernest Beckers in turn felt something
identical when having spent an evening with James and Charlotte,
they were obliged to acquaint themselves with the time by consult-
ing the big ormolu clock of which they were the donors on a recent
anniversary of the marriage of their host and hostess. And both the
James Beckers and the Ernest Beckers found it pleasurable, when
visiting Henrietta and Robert, to be given tea from an old Georgian
silver service, the tray of which had been the gift of one and the
service itself of the other, both bought separately, as it happened,
but matching exactly due to the tact and intelligence of the very
reliable antique dealer from whom the Beckers had bought all their
furniture, porcelain and silver since time began.

The Becker men, and Henrietta, of course, had grown up in an
aura of good sound taste, and it hadn't taken the Becker wives long
to learn from them. It hadn't taken them long to profit by good
example and to realize the stigma that attached itself to the brand-
new furniture that in their single state they used to admire in the
shop windows of Grafton Street. Just exactly what the stigma was
they were not certain, but nevertheless they weren't long in resolv-
ing at all costs to avoid having it attach itself to anything belonging
to them. They rapidly reduced their disturbing new knowledge to
the working formula that nothing was worth buying that was less
than a hundred years old.

It was therefore the biggest jolt of all for the Becker wives to learn
that Flora had other ideas about furniture and decoration. Flora, or
so she declared, would not tolerate anything in her home that
wasn't as fresh as paint. They were not only startled; they were
dumbfounded. This was clearly not another case of their own former
ignorance, when they had been unable to distinguish between the
merely old and the antique and had contemptuously classed both as
second-hand. Not that they often dwelt on those days. Sometimes,
however, they had to entertain friends from those early days,
friends who had made less fortunate marriages – and who were
inclined to voice surprise that they, the Becker wives, having

married money, did not have newer furniture, and then, smugly, Julia and Charlotte would put these people right. And if they failed to convince their friends they contented themselves by thinking to what zenith their own taste had soared.

Yet here was Flora making positively heretical statements, not only about tables and chairs, but about glass and table-ware and even jewellery. And with her it was clear they were up against something different from their own early lack of knowledge. There was more behind her prejudice than there had been behind their former ignorance, no matter what the surface similarities. It was most bewildering, and a disturbing thought entered their minds – was there perhaps another world more esoteric even than the world of antiques? A world of which they yet knew nothing? Oh, but how willing and eager they were to learn!

Flora had a phrase and they grasped at it. *The antiques of tomorrow*. That was what the new bride intended to have in her apartment, and for weeks prior to the wedding her conversation abounded in the names of joiners and cabinet-makers, designers, brass-workers and handlers of gold leaf, craftsmen of whom neither James nor Ernest had ever heard, living in streets not even Robert knew existed, peculiar lanes, dead ends, and back alleys. It was odd. It was distinctly odd. And although the James Beckers and Henrietta and Robert too made valiant efforts to catch and memorize the names of some of these obscure craftsmen, and track them down to their haunts, they found it exceedingly hard to believe that any value could be set upon the shapeless and colourless articles they were seriously offering for sale.

Samuel was the only one with an ounce of real courage, and one day he instructed Honoria not to hesitate any longer, but go out and buy, as their present for Flora, a large canvas on which there was inscribed a name he had definitely heard Flora mention, although, apart from the signature, there was nothing else intelligible to him on the canvas.

After Samuel had purchased the painting and Flora had been quite pleased with it, some of the others took courage. Ernest and Julia bought an etching, and Henrietta a most uncomfortable modern chair. But they never got the same feeling of pride in these presents that they formerly used to get buying things for each other. They could not feel either that they would get the same pleasure when dining with the Theobalds that they got when dining with each other, that is to say the feeling of pride in their own selective judgment. There would be little or nothing of themselves in their gifts, and they had had no fun in buying them. Of course they had to allow that they might not see very much of these presents after they left their hands, because they might not be very prominently displayed by the Theobalds, or even displayed at all. Not that they would resent this, recognizing that the fault could be in themselves: they might not have really mastered all the nuances of the new brand of good taste.

In consequence Flora became vested with still greater charm. Only Samuel claimed to come anywhere near understanding her. He had in fact confided to Henrietta that in some ways he had a greater affinity with her than Theobald. And when he was requested to be the best man at their wedding, he felt it was a tribute to this affinity and that Flora was behind the request.

'My height is about right, I dare say,' he said deprecatingly when talking to James. 'I expect they have to look into that kind of thing at a large fashionable wedding where there will be newsmen galore and photographers.'

'Will there be a lot of photographers?' James asked. He really was stupid at times, Samuel thought, in spite of his business capabilities.

'Don't you know there will!' Samuel said curtly, 'with a bride like that!'

'I suppose you're right,' James said, and he began to feel nervous at the prospect of such publicity. But his nervousness was quickly superseded by a feeling of family pride. Theobald's acquisition of Flora was the best thing that had happened to the Beckers for a long time.

Everywhere she went Flora attracted attention. Shades of the days when Theobald had sighed over the nonentity of his family! Now, wherever they went – that is to say if Flora was with them – they were followed at every step by glances of admiration or curiosity. And if they happened to take a meal out in a public restaurant, which they did not do so often nowadays, far from worrying Theobald by staring around the room, it was almost absurd the way the Beckers fastened their eyes on Flora and kept them on her. They certainly had a common focus now, as indeed did everyone in the room. The funny part of it was that it began to look as if in this regard Theobald could have had too much of a good thing. To the amusement of his brothers and sister it seemed at times that he rather wished he could hide Flora's light under a bushel.

'I think he's jealous,' Flora herself said jokingly in his hearing to Samuel the day she and Theobald came home from their honeymoon, when he and some of the others called at the apartment to pay their respects to the happy pair.

'That is absurd,' Theobald replied, disclaiming such unworthy motives. He'd only been trying to put some small curb on a wife who didn't really seem to know when to stop. It wasn't everyone who could appreciate her high-flying acts and antics. At the hotel where they'd been staying when they were away she had been unique. To the other guests her energy, her fire, her undiminishable vitality had made her seem like someone from another planet. Her wit, her sallies, her vivid word-pictures had left them breathless. As for her impersonations, these had left everyone, including himself, exhausted.

'You have no idea, Flora, the effect you had upon those people,' he said, trying to speak a little crossly to her because it really had been embarrassing. He turned to the others. 'She was like a flame playing over them incessantly, withering the life out of them.'

'A flame?' Flora had heard him. 'Oh, how lovely!' she cried. She ran over and gave him a kiss. 'That's the nicest thing you've ever said to me, Theobald.' She closed her eyes and a frail smile played over her face, a reflection perhaps of some inward thought that caused her also to sway slightly from side to side and then, after a minute, to tremble.

Watching her Samuel saw that she had begun to glow, to grow more vivid and more vital. Under the influence of the compliment she seemed to vibrate as if a strange new force ran through her. The flesh and blood Flora had vanished, and where her feet had rested a flame struggled in the air.

But that was absurd, he thought. He was getting over-imaginative and he would have been a bit worried about himself only Theobald just then got very cross with her.

'I know what you're up to, Flora. Stop it,' Theobald said. 'See! She's at it again,' he said, turning to Samuel. 'Trying to imagine what it's like to be a flame!'

Samuel sighed with relief. It had not been his imagination then. He was greatly reassured and pleased, too. It just showed how alive he was to Flora's moods. No longer alarmed, he looked at her appraisingly. It was hard to see why Theobald was so put out. What a dull dog he was!

'It was this way all the time at the hotel,' Theobald said. 'You'd only to mention something and Flora would start to personify it.' He took her arm and shook it, rather violently. 'Stop it, Flora.'

As if drenched with cold water, the flame that was Flora died down. Theobald looked ridiculously relieved. He laughed uncomfortably. 'I wish you wouldn't encourage her, Samuel,' he said, because Samuel was complimenting her.

'You have a great gift, my dear,' his brother was saying as he pressed her hand.

'Now, Theobald! Do you hear that?' Flora cried. She turned confidingly to Samuel. 'I wish Theobald had your appreciation of things. Why! he was even annoyed with my little green dragon.'

In spite of himself Theobald had to laugh at her this time. He didn't approve greatly, but there was something irresistible about the casual, intimate way Flora spoke of these imaginative creations of hers.

'What green dragon? Is this something new?' Samuel asked.

'A green dragon?' At the other end of the room Henrietta had overheard and given a little fictitious scream as she hurried over to them. 'What are you talking about?' she cried, and in a minute everyone was clamouring for an explanation.

The green dragon was evidently one of Flora's most successful performances, and the one she had put on most frequently at the hotel. The affair of the photography on the first day they met her had been impromptu, but the green dragon was apparently part of a steady repertoire.

'Oh, do it for us. Do it! Please, Flora,' several of her new relatives cried, speaking all together.

'I don't *do* it,' Flora said. 'I *see* it.'

They did not understand.

'It's really very clever.' Theobald was softening. 'I have to admit that. It's absurd of her to say I was annoyed about it. It was only that I thought she put on the act too often. And that strangers wouldn't understand anyway. They were a dull lot on the whole in that hotel!'

Samuel appealed to his new sister-in-law.

'I beg you, Flora, please remove the imputed stigma that we are no better than that dull lot. May we please see the green dragon?'

Theobald nodded his consent. He even tried to make it easier for his family to enter into the spirit of the thing.

'It's quite a simple trick, basically,' he explained. 'Flora just stands up and looks in front of her and claims she sees it – sitting on the table or on a chair – anywhere in fact. That's all there is to it, but the way she stares at it you'd swear it was there. Her way of looking at it is so convincing. And she puts on such a comical expression.'

'Oh, it sounds most amusing,' Henrietta said. 'Please, Flora, please.'

'Please what?' Flora asked, and truly her expression was masterly at that moment. No one could have been more serious. That was the core of her genius: that she could keep her face straight when everyone else was doubled up with laughter. They were all sure that she was going to oblige with the entertainment. There was a look of expectancy on every face.

But Theobald, who was able to read Flora's face a little better now than before they were married, saw an obstinacy in it that the others didn't see. For a moment he had the feeling that he used to have years earlier, when Henrietta was a girl – a big awkward girl – who when asked to perform on the piano used to wear away the whole evening with wearisome refusals that were part vanity, part hysteria. There wasn't going to be that kind of stupid scene now, was there? He looked uneasily at his wife. But he'd misjudged her. Turning suddenly she looked around at one of the small gilt chairs that were so fragile the Beckers were afraid to sit on them, and then at the curious marble table that they found so hard to consider suitable for a meal, and when finally she looked at Henrietta it was with the faintest trace of contempt.

'I'm sorry I can't show it to you,' she said. 'I don't see it anywhere. It must have gone into the garden.'

Such roguishness, but at the same time such a graceful way to refuse. It was almost as good as putting on the act. Everyone was looking around the room, and Samuel stepped over to the window and looked out. The green dragon's absence was almost as positive as his presence would have been. Theobald saw that his family could almost visualize the little creature. All his own pride in Flora came back. He didn't mind how she showed off in the bosom of the family. And this wasn't just showing off. She had handled the situation very neatly. She hadn't felt like performing and she'd got out of it with tact. That of course was the reason her little charades were always so successful: she did not attempt them unless she felt the compulsion, or the inspiration, or whatever you fancied calling it.

Then, as if to corroborate her husband and just as the others were taking their leave and were about to go, the wives secure in their warm wraps and James and Ernest with their mufflers already round their necks, Flora, who had come to the door with Theobald to see them off, peered suddenly out of the open doorway into the dark street.

'Ah, there he is!' she cried. 'I'm glad he came back before you left. See him?'

'See who?' some of the slower ones asked, staring out.

'The green dragon, of course – who else?' Flora said, affecting impatience as she bent down and held out her arms. 'Come here, my pet,' she said, and she made a feint of catching something that had, as it were, leapt through the air at her bidding and was now cuddled against her.

'Well, isn't that the most amazing thing you could see in a month of Sundays,' James said. 'You'd swear she had something in her arms.'

'Isn't he a darling?' Flora said. 'Look! He likes me to tickle him behind his ear.'

'Oh please, please, Flora.' The Becker ladies begged for mercy. They had already laughed so much they couldn't bear to watch any more. But Flora went on. It was exactly – oh but exactly – as if she had a little animal in her arms, cuddling it and talking to it and tickling it, in much the same way that they themselves – some of them anyway – Robert perhaps? – might play with a kitten or puppy; except – and this was important – except that Flora's fingers moved delicately, guardedly, as if her pet had some prohibitive quality, such as a scaly skin.

'Genius. Sheer genius,' Samuel said.

Even James rose to the occasion with another rare flash of wit.

'Take him inside, my dear,' he said. 'Good night, good night. We'll find our way ourselves. Don't stand out here in the night air. *The little fellow might catch cold.*'

The little fellow! He meant the little dragon. James had never been known to make such a good joke. It showed how he responded to his new sister-in-law.

There was a further peal of laughter, and shaking with merriment the women had difficulty finding their feet on the steps. Theobald stared after them. Had the Beckers ever before laughed out loud like that in the street? A change had certainly come over them. And this was only the beginning. With Flora around, new and surprising things would be happening every hour.

Some days, with no more than a few hours' warning, the Theobald Beckers would invite the whole family to join them at the theatre, and all because Flora, when she went out to buy fish, had booked a whole row of seats for the theatre, and it would take every available Becker to fill them if Theobald's money was not to be thrown upon the waters.

Another time it would be a picnic in the country. Theobald would have to make a hurried round of calls to gather the James Beckers or the Ernests or the Samuels or Henrietta and Robert to fill the seats on a side-car that Flora had seen outside the Shelbourne Hotel and couldn't resist hiring. And if any of them felt it made them too remarkable to be seen sitting up on an old-fashioned vehicle, no matter, the next week it could be a char-à-banc. Forward in time or back in time, it made no difference to Flora as long as she could escape from the tedium and boredom of the present, just as it didn't matter to her whether it was Henrietta or Honoria she was imperso-nating as long as she stepped out of her own personality and became another being. When this desire for change came over her nothing was allowed to come between her and making the change. Often in the middle of a conversation, a sentence, a word, she had been known to spring to her feet and turn a picture face to the wall.

'I couldn't stand it a single minute longer,' she'd explain. In her own apartment this didn't matter so much, of course, but Julia felt it was going a bit far when she did it in Charlotte's to a water colour which, as a matter of fact, Julia herself had given to James and Charlotte. Another day it was a vase to which she took exception and put out of sight.

'It may be only a little affectation,' Charlotte said, when she and Julia were discussing the matter later.

'That's no excuse,' Julia said. She was still the only one of the Beckers who had not completely capitulated to Flora's charm.

'Julia is jealous if you ask me,' Honoria said to Charlotte when Charlotte told her about Julia's attitude. 'She's just plain jealous because Flora has got such good taste. I think Flora was quite right about the vase. It was hideous,' she added, feeling no disrespect in speaking her mind about the vase because it was she who had given it to Charlotte. 'As a matter of fact,' she went on, looking around her own lavishly furnished drawing-room, 'I'm always nervous when her eye falls on those china dogs my aunt gave me.' She stood up, moved heavily over to the mantelpiece and took down the dogs. Holding them out from her, as if they had the mange, she rang the bell for the servant.

'Throw these out, please,' she said to the astonished maid, 'and this too,' she added as an afterthought, reaching up and taking down a water colour that was over the mantelpiece. 'And if I were you, Charlotte,' she said, 'I'd take your condition into consideration and get rid of that Buddha James gave you last year. It can't be good for you at present to have to stare it in the face – well, to have to stare at it anyway – every time you sit down in your own drawing-room.'

'But what could I do with it?' Charlotte asked, although after seeing Honoria's treatment of the china dogs she could guess what her sister-in-law would say. Honoria did not go in for short measures.

Honoria's vandalism was of course a lot easier to take than Julia's and Charlotte's, neither of whom had brought a penny of dowry into the family, and when they too began to throw things out their husbands were more critical. The only good that could be said for taking such drastic steps was that they were influenced by Flora. That and the fact that their rooms looked unquestionably better without the old junk. Into all their homes, as into their lives, more air had come, more colour, more light. Even Henrietta made changes, and Charlotte finally did throw out the Buddha, or rather she gave it to the washer woman.

Charlotte's washerwoman was what was called a 'character'. She was one of the people that Flora could imitate to the life. If there was a dull moment in a conversation, or even a lull, Flora was liable to say something in a voice utterly unlike her own.

'Charlotte's washerwoman!' four or five people would shout out at once, as if it was a guessing game. There was never any need to tell them who was being impersonated, yet Flora's appearance hadn't altered in any way. Of course there were times when she took more trouble, pulled her hair over her face and dragged her clothes half off to make herself look disorderly. When she did that you'd swear it *was* the washerwoman: she even looked like her.

Flora really enjoyed impersonating people but she liked them to recognize at once who it was she was representing. And it was surprising how irritable she could become if anyone guessed wrongly.

'No! How could you be so stupid!' she said crossly to poor James one evening when he took her to be doing Henrietta. 'I'm Charlotte,' she said. 'Are you blind? Didn't you see me bending when I came in the door?' For Charlotte being unusually tall had a nervous tendency to dip her head when she came through the doorway although there was no danger of hitting her head in her own home where the rooms were spacious and high-ceilinged.

'But you weren't Charlotte when you were coming into the room!' James said a bit argumentatively, Samuel thought, because looking at Flora now anyone could see she was holding herself exactly like Charlotte.

Flora herself gave James a deadly look.

'Charlotte I was born,' she said, 'and Charlotte I will remain!'

There was a peal of laughter at this which James did not quite understand, not having been of the company on the previous evening when, in answer to a suggestion from Flora that she should call herself Lottie, Charlotte had taken umbrage, and uttered almost the same words in identically that tone.

'Charlotte I was born and Charlotte I will remain until I die!' Flora was Charlotte to the life.

There were, however, times when Flora's impersonations were a bit too subtle for anyone to guess. These were times when avoiding the obvious landmarks of voice and gesture, she ventured into the interpretation of some inner characteristic, some quality normally hidden in the other person. There were even times when regardless of an audience, almost it seemed indifferent to one, undesirous of one, for some purely creative satisfaction she could be observed trying to project herself into another person. That, Samuel thought, was the mark of the real artist. He had caught her at this on a number of occasions. He'd see her stare at someone, and then after a minute her lovely agate eyes would alter and fill with curiosity, a curiosity which would grow stronger, would make her eyes deeper and their light more inward. It was really awe-inspiring then to see how her whole face would change, and her eyes would lose their lustre, their vivacity, their depth, but above all, their luminous glow and take on instead an actual physical resemblance to the eyes of the person at whom Flora had been staring. He had seen her lovely eyes grow narrow, and the lids come down obliquely as into them crept the chilly, supercilious expression that was habitual to Julia. He had seen them empty of all depth and stare outward with the naive and childish expression of Honoria. He had seen them become so cold and shallow they seemed to have changed colour like the sea over sand, and he knew Flora was being Theobald.

It was becoming Samuel's biggest pleasure to watch his new sister-in-law in the act of departing from her own body and entering that of someone else. But he was careful to guard her secret for her, and even when he saw the transformation coming, he'd bend one part of himself to the task of diverting the attention of the family, while the other part of him he'd give over to furtively watching her and sharing in her adventure. Only when he was in doubt as to who she was taking off, would he venture to intrude his curiosity upon her. He'd go up to her then, quietly, and bending down understandingly, he'd whisper a name in her ear.

'Charlotte?'

If he was right Flora would look up and smile. If he was wrong – but this rarely happened – although she was not able to conceal her annoyance, she never failed to make a witty answer, correcting his error in some original or comical way.

'What's the matter with you?' she would ask. 'Are you blind? That's Charlotte over there!'

Samuel, however, was seldom wrong. Even when one evening in the very act of raising a glass of claret to her lips at a small party given in a restaurant by the Ernest Beckers, he saw Flora pause and look into her glass for a second before she drank, in that instant, although there had been neither word nor gesture to fasten upon, he knew Flora had become Theobald – Theobald arresting the flow of his consciousness, becoming aware of himself, trying to catch himself as it were, in the act of living. That evening Samuel could not forbear leaning across the table to her.

'Theobald?' he whispered.

For a moment Flora seemed startled. Then she nodded, but curtly, and at once for some reason – possibly to cover embarrassment – she answered out loud, and her voice was impatient. 'What do you want?' she said.

Samuel was always very understanding. He made allowances. She was probably afraid the others would discover her secret game. He resolved not to intrude on her in that way again. And when a few days later he did, it was only under the compulsion of unbearable curiosity, because not for the world would he want to forfeit her friendship. He was becoming more and more dependent on it, particularly of late, because Honoria, although in no way noticeable yet, had already taken to staying home in the evenings and having Charlotte or Henrietta come over to sit with her. Very considerately she refused to keep Samuel tied to the house. One or two nights a week at least she insisted he go out, and if it weren't for having Theobald and Flora, where would he spend those evenings? Certainly not with James or Ernest. And to put oneself voluntarily into Robert's company would, of course, have been ludicrous. So to Flora's he went, every evening Honoria could spare him.

Then came one particular evening. Samuel had had dinner at home, but after dinner walked over to the Theobald Beckers to spend a short while with them before retiring. It was a summer evening and the lamps were not lit when the servant admitted him. The master, she said, was dining at the club that evening, but the mistress was in the drawing-room. Would she announce him, or would he go in to her?

Samuel went across the hall and opened the dining-room door. For a moment he thought there was no one at all in the room. It was only faintly lit by the paling daylight and the furniture had begun to confound itself with its own long shadows on the wall. Beyond the window the trees in the garden were still visible. Samuel was staring at the black branches when he saw Flora.

She was standing by the side of the window, leaning back against the white woodwork to which her back was closely pressed, her shoulder blades drawn downward, and her face tilted upward more than usual. She seemed to be staring through the upper panes of the glass, and when he moved nearer, Samuel saw the thin spikes of the first stars. She was like the bowsprit of an ancient ship, he thought, and as sightless – at any rate sightless so far as he was concerned. She was unaware of him until he came close – or so it seemed, although he did not think it possible she had not heard him when he first entered. But then, when he'd come close and seen the rigidity of her body and the intensity of her expression, he was paralysed with embarrassment. He did not dare to break in upon her, but stood silent too, afraid to breathe. He felt as if he was in the presence of someone he had never known, and he began to tremble and his face to twitch in a way it had not done for a long time.

This was not Theobald's wife. This was someone else. But who? It was someone Samuel had never seen before. He pulled himself together. It was, of course, quite possible that it was some former acquaintance of hers. Or it could even be some person who did not exist at all except in her imagination, someone who borrowed life from her as characters in a book borrow life from their creator. If novelists and dramatists could invent people, well then, why not Flora? She must write, he thought. A play perhaps? She must! She must! She must! Breathing more than speaking it, he whispered the question that tormented him.

'Who is it?' he whispered. 'Who are you now?'

First Theobald's wife shuddered. Then she turned, and her eyes were sad and wearied. Samuel felt a catch at his heart. Was there something wrong? But her voice was normal enough when she spoke.

'Why Samuel! What a strange thing to ask! I'm Flora, of course, who else?'

Who else indeed? Who else would have made such an answer?

Yes, it was Flora: but if ever a person was caught in the act of self-impersonation, that person was Theobald's wife, for in that tense, motionless figure which a moment before had been unaware of his presence, he realized that Flora had concentrated her whole personality. And the essence of that personality was so salt-bitter that a salt-sadness came into his heart too.

'I understand,' he said quickly. 'I won't intrude.' Turning away swiftly he went out of the house.

Yet, the next evening Flora was as gay as ever. If possible she was more hilarious, in higher spirits, and more irrepressible than they'd ever seen her. Except for Julia, the Beckers were all enthralled.

'Irresponsible is what I'd call her, not just irrepressible,' Julia said when during the course of the evening Flora had twice mimicked Theobald when he was out of the room. 'If he ever finds out he'll never forgive her.'

'Oh, he won't find out,' Charlotte said. She'd hate to have missed that particular take-off: it was the one she enjoyed the best of the lot. 'It was so amusing,' she said, laughing again at the thought of it. 'She only stood with her back to us but there was something about her that would make you swear she was Theobald.'

'All the same,' Julia carped, 'I think it is disloyal of her, and what, is more, I think some of her other impersonations are coarse.'

'Coarse? Julia!' Charlotte was astonished at the viciousness of the accusation.

'Well,' Julia said, determined to be even more explicit, 'I suppose I oughtn't to mind as long as Honoria herself doesn't seem to care.'

'Oh that!' Charlotte was relieved and she laughed again. It was, perhaps, a bit coarse, but at the same time it was comical to watch a little scrap of a thing like Flora imitating – and with such success – a big lump like Honoria, particularly in view of Honoria's increased size. 'Anyway, Honoria enjoys it as much as any of us,' she said, defending Flora further. Charlotte, being the most insipid of the Beckers except for her height, had up to then been relatively safe from Flora's mimicry, and so, next after Samuel, she had the keenest appreciation of it. But it was true that Honoria took the imitations in surprisingly good part, considering how often she was the victim.

In fact, where, at the beginning of her relationship with the Beckers, Flora had been continually calling upon them to witness that she was now Henrietta, now Charlotte, now James, now Julia, now Ernest, and now perhaps one of the servants, or a tradesman with whom they were all familiar, of late she had confined herself to making Honoria the butt of her humour. She had merely to smile in a certain way, or go up to Samuel and pick a bit of fluff off his sleeve, or do no more than take out her handkerchief and blow her nose, and everybody screamed.

'Look at Honoria!' they'd cry.

Once or twice Flora carried things so far as to answer for the real Honoria when Samuel came into the room and called his wife.

'I'm here, Samuel,' she said. 'What do you want?' And once when Honoria answered at the same time, Flora was so funny, so amusing. She turned on the real Honoria and gave her a chilling look, calling *her* Flora.

'Please, Flora,' she said. 'Please give up these childish impersonations.' As if it was Honoria who had been pretending!

It was side-splitting.

And in spite of Julia's misgivings, when summer came and at Flora's instigation the Beckers made a big family party and rented a villa on the coast, it was enlivening for them all in the monotony of their rural surroundings to have her with them, up to her pranks and antics.

'I realize all that,' Julia said, when this was pointed out to her, 'but I still say she shouldn't pick on Honoria. If I were you, Samuel, I'd put an end to it quick, now that Honoria is so near to her time.'

'Oh but surely,' Charlotte interrupted, and she was about to say that Flora would have too great a delicacy to continue making fun of Honoria much longer, until at that very moment she saw Theobald's wife going over to Samuel, and she was walking with a most peculiar gait. Julia saw her too.

'Look at her now!' Julia cried. 'What did I tell you! It's disgusting. It's shameless. Poor Honoria: it's so unfair! Her first baby, too!'

It being the third time that her own figure had become somewhat grotesque – and the fourth time for Charlotte – she felt they could be supposed less sensitive than Honoria who was pregnant for the first time. 'I'm going to put a stop to it at once,' she said, and she went straight over to Flora. 'Look here, Flora, what do you think you're doing?' she asked in a harsh tone.

But Flora answered so sweetly Julia was momentarily disarmed.

'Please don't call me by the wrong name, Julia,' Flora said sweetly. 'Can't you see I'm not Flora: I'm Honoria. How can you mix us up, particularly now?'

In spite of himself Samuel chuckled. Julia turned on him. 'What is wrong with you?' she cried. 'Why do you think it so funny?' Then she shrugged her shoulders. 'If that's the attitude you intend to take, I may as well mind my own business.'

It was on the tip of Samuel's tongue to say 'Please do,' but instead he smiled falsely and turned to the rest of the company.

'How about some music, ladies?' he asked, and only after he'd spoken did he realize how rarely it was they played the piano since Flora had come among them with her diverting ways. 'Well, how about some music?' he repeated, although he was surprised at his duplicity because Julia was the musician of the family, and his suggestion might appease her. But before Julia had time to lift the piano-lid Flora had snatched at the suggestion and converted it to her own use.

'I'll play,' she said, still speaking with the voice of Honoria. 'I'll play the tune Samuel likes best!' she cried, and the next minute she was seated on the piano stool playing the only tune that Honoria's memory had managed to retain from all the long and expensive music lessons that had formed the largest part of her education.

Flora played Honoria's tune. She played it and replayed it. And she might as well have been Honoria, so faithfully did she reproduce all the little twists of the wrist, turns of the waist and nods of the head by which Honoria had learned to make up for the deficiencies of her musical talent.

'Well?' Charlotte whispered to Henrietta. 'That seems harmless enough.'

'Do you think so?' Julia hissed, cutting in on them. 'Well, if you think that, please look at the way she is sitting on the piano stool.'

True enough, Flora was sitting peculiarly. Charlotte and Henrietta both had to admit there was something awkward about it. She was sitting at least a foot further away from the keyboard than was either necessary or normal.

'It's disgusting! I've said so before,' Julia said, 'I'll say it again.' She glanced around her to make sure the women were alone. 'I hope the men don't notice,' she said. 'It's making a mockery of mother-hood.' And having glanced pertinently at the waist-line of the other two, she indicated her own loosely slung garments. 'It's all due to jealousy, I hope you realize that. Flora is jealous of all of us, but particularly of Honoria because they were married so nearly the same time.'

Whatever malice underlay these words however miscarried of its effect because both Charlotte and Henrietta suffered a sudden suffusion of pity for Theobald's poor little bride.

'Oh, poor, poor Flora,' they cried, and both together they looked in her direction. 'Perhaps –?' they began eagerly, but Flora's waist was as slim as ever, and her figure gave a complete denial to their kindly hopes for her. Julia hadn't bothered to look at Flora at all.

'Quite the contrary,' she said, then she lowered her voice. 'And if I'm any judge of these things, *that* will be the fly in Theobald's ointment.'

'Oh!' Charlotte exclaimed. 'You don't think so, really, do you? It would be such a pity.' Her thoughts raced to the nursery upstairs where her big pale baby lay sucking its thumb. 'Why, I've heard of dozens of cases where there was no sign of anything for much, much longer than this, and yet there was success before the end!'

But two days later, it was Charlotte herself who had to bring up the subject again.

'Are you sure, Julia?' she asked. 'Are you sure there couldn't be some possibility of mistake in what you said yesterday?'

'Why?' Julia said coldly.

'Because,' Charlotte said, 'I couldn't help noticing how she acted at supper last night.' No need now to name names. 'She used to love pickled onions, you know that? Well, last night she didn't have any. Wouldn't touch them in fact! And it was the same with the apple sauce. She used to love that too. I couldn't help thinking it odd after what you were saying because I myself couldn't bear anything with the slightest flavour of onion in it when I was expecting, and I couldn't touch apple sauce. It used to give me the most appalling heartburn. But that wasn't all. During supper – the whole time in fact – she sat – well she sat a foot out from the table just like when she was playing the piano. It may be that the thing has got on my nerves, but as well as everything else, I thought she was *walking* queerly after supper when she and I went for a short stroll in the garden. The stroll was at *her* suggestion, mind you, which I thought odd – and here's another thing! – I hope you won't think me coarse to mention it, but I couldn't help noticing that she never buttons her coat, not properly anyway: she lets it hang out loosely from her. Now why on earth is that, do you think?'

'Why do you think?' Julia asked. But she was only leading Charlotte on for a fall.

'Well,' Charlotte said, 'I was wondering if there was any possibility that you could be wrong, and that she might be going to have a baby after all?'

This was what Julia had anticipated, and she was ready for it.

'In that case,' she said acidly, 'isn't it odd that it's thinner Flora is getting, not stouter?'

For a moment Charlotte was defeated. Then she came to the fore again. 'Some women do get thin in the early stages.'

'Is that so?' Julia was more than doubtful. 'Then tell me, in a case like that does the woman have to sit a full foot out from the table? Does she have to wear her coat unbuttoned? And above all, does she have to walk like Flora walks?' For Flora had certainly taken to a most peculiar gait. 'No,' said Julia, answering her own questions so emphatically that Charlotte was silenced. 'I tell you, I'm tired of your talk of impersonations. It's not impersonation. It's mockery. Flora is making a mockery out of poor defenceless Honoria.'

'Oh for goodness' sake, Julia,' Charlotte cried. 'Are you losing your sense of humour? Anyway, if what you say is true, why would Flora be doing it when she's alone?'

'What on earth do you mean, Charlotte?'

Julia's startled look made Charlotte falter.

'Well, I wasn't going to mention it,' she said, 'but the evening before we came down here, I called in to Theobald's with a message from James, and I was shown into the drawing-room, and for an instant I thought I was alone there until suddenly I saw there was someone else there after all. Oh, Julia, I know it sounds a bit daft – the lamps weren't lit – but for a minute I was positive it was Honoria. I nearly said the name. But it was Flora. She was walking up and down her own drawing-room floor, and if you only saw the way her hips were swaying. Why, even Samuel would have been forgiven if he mistook her for his wife. And when the maid had carried in the lamps and after I knew it was Flora, I still couldn't take my eyes off her, because I could still have sworn she was twice the size she'd appeared when I first came in the door. I've often heard of optical illusions, but I never thought I'd experience one!'

Julia said nothing for a minute.

'It seems to me,' she said then slowly, 'that we are all experiencing them these days. Ernest was saying only this morning that James had commented on the resemblance between Flora and Honoria.

Resemblance! Did you ever hear anything more absurd?'

'It does seem a bit absurd, doesn't it?' Charlotte said. 'On the other hand, I must say I did think once or twice that Flora was beginning to have a look of Honoria. I'm interested to hear James noticed it. I wonder if any of the others did?'

When discreet enquiries were made in the course of that same afternoon, Henrietta too thought she had noticed a slight resemblance.

'I thought it was only my imagination,' she declared, 'and I didn't like to mention it to anyone in case it might be put down to my condition. I'd hate anyone to think I was getting nervy or hysterical, or beginning to get fancies.'

That, however, was just exactly what was happening to all the Beckers, and especially to the Becker wives.

'It's all Flora's fault,' Julia said.

'Isn't it strange, though, that Honoria doesn't appear to notice?' Charlotte said.

'Oh, that's part of her nature,' Henrietta said, 'but all the same it's my belief she's more upset than we think. I came across her by surprise the other day and I could have sworn she had been crying.'

'Crying?' The other two women started up in matronly concern.

'A fit of crying would be the worst thing in the world for her at the present time. It could be the cause of anything!' With this far from lucid statement Julia stood up. 'I'm going to speak to Samuel again,' she said.

Charlotte felt her knees tremble. Samuel was Flora's stoutest champion. She'd have thought it would be more difficult to approach him than Theobald, and to approach Theobald of course was unthinkable.

Samuel, however, was no match for Julia. When he tried to pooh-pooh her complaints, she went for him with fire in her eyes.

'Samuel Becker,' she cried. 'Are you going to put Flora before Honoria? I'm telling you that for some reason or other, Theobald's wife is deliberately trying to make your wife look ridiculous, and what is more, Honoria is beginning to notice.'

Samuel's face was white and drawn. He made one last effort to evade the issue.

'It's not deliberate,' he said speaking lowly. 'If Flora is giving offence I am certain she is unconscious of it.'

So he was willing to admit offence was given. Julia relaxed somewhat.

'Consciously or unconsciously,' she said, 'it has got to stop, and stop immediately. Today! Did you know that Honoria has been

having fits of crying lately? And what do you think is the cause of
that? Above all, may I ask what effect you suppose this state of mind
will have on your unborn child?'

Samuel's face went whiter.

'Where is Flora now?' he asked. 'I'll speak to her.'

Flora was not far away. She was in the breakfast room sitting by
the window, sewing. As a matter of fact Charlotte and Julia thought
Samuel could hardly have gone farther than the end of the passage
when he was back again, but they knew at once by his face that
something had happened.

'What's the matter?' Charlotte cried. Then a sudden inexplicable
fear came over her and she shouted for James.

'James, James!' she called, relieved to remember that he was
sitting on a garden seat just under the open window, reading in the
sunshine.

'What in heaven's name do you want, Charlotte?' James said,
starting up and leaning in across the window-sill, but instantly he
too felt there was something wrong. 'Ernest! Robert!' he cried,
seeing the two men walking along a gravel path to one side of the
villa. Then, without waiting to go around to the door, stiff as he was,
he put his leg over the window ledge and joined the women at once.
'Oh, you're here too, Samuel,' he said with relief.

But whatever had upset Samuel he was now fuming at the fuss
that was being made. 'What is the matter with you people?' He
turned to Julia. 'I only wanted to speak to you, Julia,' he said. 'I
don't understand – what is the meaning of this commotion?' Yet
when Ernest and Robert hurried in he couldn't help deriving some
comfort from the proximity of so many Beckers. 'There's nothing
wrong,' he said. 'I only wanted to have a word with Julia – or
Charlotte – or Henrietta.' He hesitated. 'I wanted one of them to step
to the door of the other room with me.' He hesitated again. 'It's
Flora.'

Charlotte put her hand to her heart. 'Is there something the matter
with her?' she cried.

'Oh no – at least I don't think so,' Samuel said, 'but I was a bit
worried because she didn't answer when I spoke to her. She was
sewing, and when I called her she just went on drawing the needle
in and out and didn't even turn her head.'

'She didn't hear you: that's all,' James said, with an elderly frown.
He'd given his knee a knock on the window ledge. It was vexatious.
'Was it to tell us she was deaf you brought us in from the sunshine? I
thought the place was on fire.' He was turning to go out again when
Samuel put out his hand and laid it on his older brother's arm.

'Wait a minute, James. The odd thing is that I know she heard me.' He turned back to the women: they were more understanding. 'I know she did. I called her by name, not once, but twice or three times, and yet she went on sewing. And the last time I called she was putting the thread between her teeth to break it, and I could see by the way she paused that she was listening. Then, ignoring me, she bit the thread and broke it and bent her head again.'

It wasn't much – but it was decidedly odd.

'What is she sewing anyway?' James asked suddenly. 'She's at it all the time.'

'Oh, for goodness' sake, James,' Charlotte said, 'what does it matter what she's sewing!' It was so like James to fasten on something trivial. She turned back to Samuel. 'Why didn't you go over to her?'

It was only after Samuel answered that they all began to feel anxious.

'I thought one of you women should do that,' he said. 'That's why I came back for one of you.' He looked at Julia. 'I thought you might be best, Julia.'

'Me?' In spite of being the most aggressive earlier on in her assertions that something ought to be done, Julia was most reluctant to put herself forward now. 'Will you come with me, Charlotte?'

'I will of course,' Charlotte said readily enough, but she made a sign to the men. 'Please stay near at hand,' she said. Then she addressed herself to Samuel in particular, and her voice was very kind. 'We'll leave the door open,' she said, 'and you can stand outside and listen.'

'But be quiet,' Julia warned, because James was still inclined to protest that they were making a fuss about nothing. 'Where is Theobald?' they could hear him ask. 'Why isn't he here? Why didn't someone fetch him along? If there's anything wrong it's his business more than it's ours.'

Afterwards everyone remembered what James had said, but they all felt it was fortunate that Theobald was not there. For Flora gave Julia and Charlotte a very different reception from the one she had given Samuel. Being prepared for similar treatment, they were paralysed with fright when she sprang to her feet the instant they called her name. They'd only called once, and as casually as possible.

'Flora?' they'd said timidly. 'Flora?'

But the name had hardly left their lips when Flora sprang up. Lithe as a cat, she swung herself around, and gripped the back of the chair in which she had been sitting. Her sewing had fallen to the floor. Her eyes were blazing.

'What is the matter with you all?' she demanded. 'Have you gone mad? Why are you coming in here and calling me names?' And then, as if she saw – or in some way divined – that the rest of the family was there too, huddled together outside the door, she shook her fist in their direction. Julia and Charlotte drew together, and didn't advance any further. 'Tell me this, Julia Becker, or you, Charlotte Becker!' Flora cried. 'Is it a joke? Because, if it is, you'd better stop it at once. You must know by now that one thing I detest is being called names.'

'But I never called you names, Flora,' Julia cried.

'None of us did, Flora,' Charlotte said.

They seemed to have only made things worse, however. Flora's face became convulsed.

'There you go again,' she cried, and she nodded towards the hallway where the others were rooted to the ground. With her long thin finger she pointed out through the window that looked on the garden. 'As for that one,' she said, 'that wretched creature out there: if someone doesn't stop her from driving me mad, I won't answer for what will become of her.'

They looked.

Out in the sun, on a stone bench, not too far from the house but just beyond earshot of what had gone on within it, Julia saw that Honoria was taking her mid-day rest with her eyes shut and a newspaper over her face to keep her skin from getting too red.

Sensing that behind her the others had come close, Julia called out to them.

'You'd better come in altogether,' she said.

Flora swung around. 'Yes, come in. All of you,' she cried. 'Let's have this out. And make her come in too,' she added, nodding back over her shoulder to indicate the figure at the end of the garden.

James was the first to enter the room.

'Now, now,' he said placatingly, 'there's no need to disturb Honoria. If we have had some little disturbance among ourselves, there is no need to drag poor Honoria into it. It's best for her to be kept as quiet as possible under the circumstances.'

Something in James's words seemed to sting Flora into another ungovernable fury. There was moisture gathering on her forehead and more alarmingly at the corners of her mouth –

'Honoria?' she echoed. 'Under the circumstances? So you are all playing the same game.' She caught at the neck of her dress and tore it open. 'Very well. I warned you. I won't stand it. It was bad enough when it was only her that was tormenting me' – she pointed again at the unsuspecting Honoria. 'I pretended not to take any notice. But if you're all at it, I can't stand it. I can't and I won't!' She clapped her hands over her ears, and tears sprang into her eyes.

'But what are we doing?' Charlotte cried. 'We don't know what you're talking about, Flora!'

'Flora! Flora! Flora!' The girl was almost beside herself. 'You *do* want to drive me mad. You do! You do!' Her eyes ran over the faces one by one, and then she scanned them all as a group in a wild sweeping glance. 'It's a shame for you!' she said. 'You ought at least to consider my condition.'

From where he stood at the back of the group, looking down at the carpet, Samuel started violently and looked up.

'Yes – a shame,' Flora repeated. 'If people only knew how I'm treated.' She wrung her hands. 'Oh, how terrible – I have no one to help me.' Suddenly she placed her hands on her small flat abdomen. 'It's not myself I'm thinking about – it's the child!'

At that the Beckers, all except Charlotte, went rigid. Charlotte laughed hysterically.

'Oh, it's only an impersonation,' she shrilled, but even as she spoke her blood ran cold. Flora's tears had dried as quickly as they'd rushed forth.

'If it's only an impersonation,' she cried, 'then it's time an end was put to it!' She ran over to the window. 'Look at her now. Look at the brazen creature. At this very moment she's out there making a mockery of me. Oh, how can she do it? How can she be so coarse? How can you all see her at it day after day and not be revolted? Don't you notice the way she sits at the table? Don't you notice the way she wears her clothes, not fastening the buttons?' Suddenly she stooped and picked up the piece of material she had been sewing. 'She even went to my work-basket and took out this and pretended it was hers.'

The frightened gaze of the Becker women fell on a small white flannel chemise that was only half-finished. But as she held it up the sight of it made Flora wail. 'I wouldn't mind if she were a normal woman,' she cried, 'a woman that might have a child of her own some day, but look at her, with her hips like a scissors, and her chest like a cardboard doll! *She'll* never have a child. It's just that she's jealous; jealous of me. That's what it is!'

For one moment Flora's face became radiant, glorified, and then the light died out and it was once more haggard and harassed and aged-looking. 'Oh, I can't stand it,' she said in a voice that was now small and whimpering. She put her hand up to her head as if it ached. 'She's got me so confused.' Then, as if she was taking them into her confidence, she tried to steady her voice. 'I'm fighting against it,' she told them. 'See!' Fumbling among the laces on the front of her dress she pulled out a crumpled piece of paper. 'When she says something to put me astray I look at this paper. It has my name written on it. Oh, I won't let her get the better of me. She won't drive *me* mad!'

Urgently, frantically, she pushed the paper into James's hand, then before he had time to uncrumple it, she pulled it back and shoved it into another hand and then into another and another. But all any of them could see was a blur of wretchedly bad handwriting. Snatching it back she stuffed it back into her bodice. And now the look on her face was crafty.

'You see, I'm able for her,' she said. 'I'm able for all of you.' She spread out her fingers and again placed them over her boyish body. 'I have to think of my child,' she said. And it was the change in her voice that was hardest to bear: it had become wondrously gentle again.

'Oh my God!' Charlotte said, muffling her cry with her handkerchief. Next minute she was sobbing convulsively and James had to call on Samuel and Ernest.

'Get her out of here quick,' he ordered.

Flora, however, had not understood it was Charlotte he meant.

'Get who out of here?' she screamed, starting up like a hare. 'No one is going to lay a hand on me.'

'Hush, hush, he wasn't talking about you, my dear,' Samuel said, and he endeavoured to take her hand.

'Are you sure?' Flora's eyes filled first with suspicion and then with fear, and finally with something else, indefinable to the Beckers. They stared at their brother Samuel, who had pushed James aside and seemed to have taken over command of the situation. Flora too recognized that Samuel had put himself in authority. She caught at his lapels. 'That's what she wants, you know – to have me sent away.' She let go the front of his jacket and seizing his hands she clutched them so that the skin went thin on her knuckles and the bone showed through. 'You'll help me, won't you?' she pleaded. 'You're the only one I trust. You won't let her drive me mad, will you, like she's been driven mad herself. That's it, you see. No one knows but me and I didn't tell anyone before now. But I knew it all the time. She's mad. Mad! She was really always mad. Her family was mad – all of them. Her father died in a madhouse. She didn't tell that to Theobald, I bet? She didn't tell it to any of you. But I found out and that's why she had this set against me. She wants to make me mad too. But she won't. None of you will. You can keep on calling me Flora all you like. Flora! Go on! Call it to me, Flora! Flora! Flora! I won't listen. I'll stick my fingers in my ears so I won't hear.' With a wild distracted gesture Theobald's wife pulled her hands away from Samuel's again and went to stick her fingers in her ears, but halfway through the gesture her hands dropped to her sides. 'Where is my piece of paper?' she cried and again she fumbled and found it once more. 'As long as I have my name written down on this bit of paper no one will succeed in getting me mixed up,' she said. Then, having stared at the piece of paper and soundlessly moved her lips two or three times as if memorizing something, she stowed it away again, and rammed her fingers into her ears as far as they'd go.

'She'll pierce her ear-drums,' James said. And as if Flora had gone out of the room the Beckers' tongues were loosened.

'What happened to her?' That was what they all wanted to know.

But Samuel raised his hand and it looked as if he'd scourge them. 'Oh, you fools!' he yelled. 'Get out of here, all of you. Leave this to me.' There was such a look on his face that Robert was already backing out of the room.

'Are you sure it's all right for you to stay alone with her?' James asked from the doorway.

'Oh, James, what do you mean?' Charlotte cried. 'You don't mean – ?' But she didn't dare finish the sentence.

James's meaning was made clear, however, before the door shut. They saw Samuel put his arm around Flora's thin shoulders, and his words sent a chill through their hearts.

'Hush, Honoria. Hush, hush,' Samuel was saying. To Flora!

'Please, Honoria – please hush!'

Then the door shut them out.

'Oh God in heaven,' Charlotte said, and burst into tears again.

'What on earth will we do with her?' Julia asked.

'How was it we didn't find this out before now?' That was what puzzled Henrietta.

'I kept telling you all that something was wrong,' Julia said, 'but none of you wanted to believe me.'

'What good would it have done if we had listened to you?' Henrietta said tartly. 'Sooner or later – what difference does it make – the disgrace is the same.'

'Disgrace? Oh, how can you speak about it like that?' Charlotte stopped crying out loud but tears ran silently down her face. 'How can you use such a word! It's all so terribly sad.'

'And there's Theobald to think about!' James said suddenly. 'What about him? Where is he? When will he be back? And who is going to break this to him?' But knowing it would probably be up to him to do it, he sank down on a chair in the hall and began to mop his forehead with the handkerchief out of his breast pocket that was normally only for show. 'This is only the beginning,' he said.

But inside the room with Flora this was not what Samuel was thinking as he held her hands tightly in his, and tried to keep her calm by lending himself to her delusion, calling her Honoria over and over again. It was all over. That's what Samuel was thinking.

'Hush, Honoria. Hush, hush,' he said. They would have to send for Theobald. They would have to get a doctor and make arrangements to have her taken away somewhere – for a time at least – to try and restore the balance of her poor jangled mind. It might not be for ever, or even for very long, but all the same Samuel knew that the terrible, terrible sadness that had settled on his heart would lie upon it for ever.

It was all over; the fun and the gaiety. Their brief journey into another world had been rudely cut short. They had merely glimpsed from afar a strange and exciting vista, but they had established no foothold in that far place. And the bright enchanting creature that had opened that vista to them had been but a flitting spirit never meant to mix with the likes of them.

Across Flora's shoulder he looked out the window into the garden. The children of Charlotte and Julia and Henrietta had come back from a walk with their nanny and were playing under a tree: a heavy-set little girl, and two stodgy boys. And on the grass Charlotte's fat baby sat sucking its thumb. Beckers to the bone, all of them. And the child that his wife Honoria was carrying would be like them, as like as peas in a pea-pod.

His eyes came back to rest on Flora. The tempest of her passion had died down.

'You'll be all right in a little while, my dear. Try to rest. Try to forget everything. Rest on me – ' he paused '– rest on me, Honoria.'

But when Flora's sobbing finally ceased and, exhausted, she rested against him, her weight was so slight he started. It was as if she had begun to dissolve once more into the wraith-like creature of light that had first flashed on them all in its airy brilliance on the night of his own betrothal party; a spirit which they in their presumption had come to regard – so erroneously – as one of themselves, just another of the Becker wives, like Julia or Charlotte, or the real Honoria.

A Single Lady

Apart from anything else he wasn't that kind of man; the reverse indeed; distant, cool in his manner. And as for his manner towards the servants, in her mother's time at least he used to treat them as if they were made of wood; as if they had no feelings whatever. Latterly, of course, things had changed so much that they both had to alter their attitude towards them. And when it came to having only the one wretched creature for all the drudgery of the great barrack of a house, there had been times when she herself had felt it necessary to be familiar. But even then, even when she had made concession after concession, it was a long time before he unbent to any degree. Was it any wonder, then, that she discredited people's hints and insinuations. At least in the beginning! What daughter in the world would have given any credence to them. And yet the remarks continued to be made.

Oh, but it all seemed so unreal; so impossible. At his age! Why! if he had any inclinations of that sort he could have satisfied them long ago in a manner compatible with his position. There had been nothing in the past fourteen years to prevent him from remarrying if he wished to do so. Up to quite recently he had kept his appearance fairly well, and with that and his first wife's fortune he stood a fairly good chance of marrying some person of suitability. Even five years ago he cut a passable figure. But this! This! Who could blame her for having refused credence to this! Her father – and a common servant! If she were even that! but a wretched little slut. Yes! What was the use of denying it. Had she not, right from the start, been repulsed at the idea of having to have such a poor type of creature in the house. Isabel shuddered. Hadn't she been disgusted by the food? Hadn't she been afraid to look too closely at anything the creature handled? And as for the creature's room, in spite of the fact that she knew it was her duty to do so, she had never once gone into it. She knew so well what it would be like: smelly and close, the windows never opened, and the bedclothes bundled about like rags. A servant indeed. Too good a word for her!

To think that she, Isabel, was responsible for bringing the creature into the house! But what could she do? She was in such a quandary when poor old Mary Ellen was taken ill.

Such a quandary: for a moment a curiously soft, even stupid, expression came over Isabel's thin features, as she tried to recall how it had come about that she had hired the creature in the first place. Then her face sharpened again. It was for his sake; for her father's sake. It was out of consideration for him that she had done it. She didn't want him to suffer any inconvenience while she was endeavouring to find the proper kind of person. That, of course, had been her intention: to look around for a suitable person. And although she had to admit that after a day or two she had drifted into accepting the situation, it might not have been so easy to get anyone better. That was what she said to him when he had been so aghast at letting the like of her into the house.

'Only as a stop-gap, Father! Just to give me time to look around for someone proper.'

'But am I to understand that you are letting this person sleep here?' he demanded. 'Where are you going to put her? What room do you intend her to occupy? What bedclothes will you give her? And what condition will the room be in when you get a proper girl? Have you thought of that?'

He felt that at the very least the creature should come by the day and go home at night.

Isabel smiled bitterly.

It had been in order that he would have his early morning cup of tea that she had insisted on having the girl live with them. If she had only had her own comfort to consider it would have been a different matter. She wouldn't mind if she had had to go without her breakfast until the middle of the morning. Indeed, it was often the middle of the morning now before this impudent slut made any effort to give her anything. It was one excuse after another. First it was her father's early tea. Well, that was all right. But after that it was his shaving water. The kettle had to be filled again for that. And when that kettle was boiled there was certain to be another demand upon it.

'Is the kettle boiled yet for my tea?' One or two mornings, from sheer hunger and cold, she had to come down the passage and humiliate herself to the creature.

She never got any satisfaction.

'It's boiled all right. But what about the milking-pans?'

It seemed as if there was always an opportunity for the creature to appear in the right, and for her, the mistress, to appear in the wrong. The milking-pans had to be scalded. The herd could not be kept waiting about all morning in the kitchen. She knew that. But at the same time she knew that if it wasn't the milking-pans it would be something else! She was always being relegated to the kettle after the next!

And the cleverness of the creature. She was careful never to go too far. After the taunt came the sop.

'I'll fill it up again for you, Miss. You must be starving. It won't be a minute coming to the boil.'

Oh, the cleverness; the slyness. Next thing she'd do would be to jab a poker between the bars of the grate and rattle it until she had filled the kitchen with smoke and ashes, and shaken down all the red embers into the ash-pit. 'That is to say if any kettle could be got to boil on this fire.' That was her method; to taunt and placate, to placate and taunt; making things unpleasant all the time, but careful never to go beyond a certain limit. When there was hardly a spark of red left in the grate, she'd become agreeable enough. 'Wait a minute now, Miss. It's nearly out, but I'll bring it up again with a few sprigs of kindling.' But the sprigs were certain to be wet, or there would be too few of them. As likely as not it would be another hour after that before she got her tea. And such tea!

Once or twice she had thoughts of getting some kind of a small oil-burner and making her own tea in the breakfast-room, but she decided that it would look too much like giving up her authority in the house.

Her authority! Two hard-pressed tears came into Isabel's eyes and fell on to her white blouse, making the starch limp in spots. Authority was a thing of the past. What authority had she, for instance, in the kitchen? She hardly dared go into it. If she had any say at all would it be in the condition in which it was? Would the floor be coated with grease? Would the walls be yellowed with smoke? And would the tea towels be as they were?

Isabel thought miserably of the dirty grey dishcloths, always wet and slimy, and disgusting to handle. They were never put out on the clothes line. They were always hanging wetly over the backs of the chairs. Authority! The word was a joke.

For a long time Isabel sat in the badly-lit room that used to be so bright and gay when her mother had it for her boudoir, and as she sat sadly reflecting there, she stared into the fireplace, where a fair enough fire blazed between the unblackened bars of the grate, under the neglected and discoloured mantelpiece.

Oh, the neglect! The neglect everywhere, she thought. That mantelpiece used to be so white and glossy.

And to think that she didn't dare to say a word about it. She sat forward. How, how did this state of affairs come about? A frown of concentration came between her eyes. Why had she not seen how things were shaping? Why had she let them go so far? Why had she not put down her foot? But as she looked down at it, her narrow foot with the pointed shoe looked a weak and inadequate symbol of the power with which she was to have put down Annie Bowles.

Isabel felt her helplessness could hardly have been so great in the beginning. Surely there must have been some point at which she might have made a stand against the creature?

Just then, faintly, so faintly in fact it was remarkable that her ears should catch it, there was a sound from the kitchen; the sound of a wicker chair creaking.

Isabel tightened in every muscle. There! There was a point at which she could have made a stand. To think that she had said nothing when the wicker chairs were taken down from the bedrooms and brought into the kitchen to be warped and put out of shape by the heat and the damp. And not only one, but two. To think she had allowed the creature to bring down a second one. Oh, she was blind indeed.

At the thought of that second wicker chair, Isabel's hands began to tremble. When it came to the bringing down of that second chair things had come to a nice pass. It was no wonder that people had begun to talk. It was no wonder there had been whispers and hints. The only wonder was that she had been so slow to suspect anything.

Why, why, why had she not seen how the land lay? Against this, however, there was always the same answer. How could she have believed such a thing of her own father? Even now, at this moment, when she should have been accustomed to it, it was still almost unbelievable to her that he was down there in the kitchen, probably sitting on one of those wicker chairs, opposite the creature, looking at her, and making those foolish eyes at her.

There! Faintly, from the far region of the kitchen, came another dry creak of a wicker chair. She knew it; he was sitting down. She could fancy him lifting his long leg to cross it over its fellow. The osiers creaked again. How loudly this time the creaking sounded in the silence.

That was another thing that had baffled her at first; the silence. Even when she had begun to notice one or two things she did not like, even after she had become aware that he was always shuffling down the passage to the kitchen, even after she had taken note of how long he stayed down there, she had been foolishly reassured by that silence. Now, of course, she dreaded it. Now it confused her, put her nerves on edge, like the untidiness and dirt of the girl.

For there had been a time when that, too, she had regarded in a different light. If, she argued, the creature had designs upon him, the least one would expect would be that she would wash her face and keep her clothes together. Isabel smiled forlornly. For days she had fed on this gloomy hope. But as with the silence, she had come to feel there was something flauntingly evil in the disarray of her outer person. Those dirty greasy rags she wore; that ravelled red cardigan pulled across her bust with a safety pin; and those cracked old boots, with her feet showing through them! Had she no respect for how she looked; no shame; no modesty? Modesty? When Isabel went into the kitchen one night wasn't she busy with a needle and thread, there in front of the fire, patching and dragging together some filthy garment that was spread out on her lap. And when in spite of her distaste she had looked more closely at the thing, what was it but a filthy old corset; a corset!

At the thought of such indelicacy a feeling of bewilderment came over Isabel. What was the meaning of it? She flinched from the answer. But as if against her will she was being forced to face some issue, at that moment there came again from the kitchen the sound of the wicker chair creaking and protesting.

Protesting against what? What were they doing? Could it be possible that – ? Her mind for a moment gathered itself together and seemed ready to face whatever lay behind those questions, but as quickly again it shrank back from even a half-thought of such a revolting nature.

Not that she was so innocent! As if she was accused of ignorance, Isabel sat suddenly bolt upright. As a matter of fact, it had always been one of the things she resented most vehemently, the suggestion that a woman should be regarded as in any way ignorant of certain matters just because she was single.

Nothing exasperated her more than the way young married women regarded certain matters as sacrosanct, matters that large-minded people would not hesitate to discuss openly and frankly. In her own university days there was nothing, absolutely nothing, that was not discussed freely, and as often as not in mixed company as well. And then she was only in her twenties, whereas now, at forty, it seemed as if people supposed she knew nothing when it came to talking about certain things. Why! even this wretched slut in the kitchen had a curious look on her face at times, as if she too imagined that she had some hidden knowledge; some secret wisdom.

Isabel trembled with irritation, but after a minute she became calmer. She made a deliberate effort to be tolerant. For some people it was intellectually impossible to apprehend the nature of life. For them knowledge was only soluble in experience. It was so different for her with her university education, and her highly developed intellect.

Isabel felt the better for having recalled her own worldliness. Even this aberration of her father's, she thought, even this was nothing new. It was common enough for men of a certain age to display certain tendencies. It was common enough for them to be subject to peculiar physical disturbances. For a period they might even become unaccountable for their behaviour. It was nature manifesting itself as their bodies became subconsciously aware of the approach of senility and impotence! That was it. There was nothing so dark or hidden about it. The climacteric; that was all.

Reassured somewhat, Isabel began to apply her wisdom to her sores. Yes, even on their last visit to the city she noticed the way he stared at young girls in the street, and on the tram cars, and once or twice in a restaurant when the waitress was giving him his change she fancied – Oh, but that was hardly fair. It was so difficult to take anything from another person's hand without one's fingers touching. And even if he had held the waitresses' hands, or made those foolish eyes at them, she wouldn't really have minded if it stopped at that; she would have put up with it.

Isabel sighed. She had been prepared to put up with so much! All at once another aspect of her misery came over her.

'After all the sacrifices I made for him!' and although those sacrifices were vague and unspecified, the thought of them filled her with new misery, and she stared dismally down at her feet. Abruptly then she stuck out one foot. Her feet hadn't always been as thin and narrow as that! She hadn't always worn such narrow, pointed shoes. The tears started into her eyes again. The dowdy habits of spinsterhood had crept insidiously upon her. But was it to be wondered at: living as she did in this bleak isolated place, never meeting anyone, never having anyone call. That, too, she had done for his sake; never leaving the place, never going away for a visit, however short, and never on any account staying away for the night. Not one night had she been away from the place in twelve solid years. They had gone away together, of course, upon little excursions. But that was not the same thing.

And yet, as she thought of those trips to London, to Southport, and once even to Ostend, her tears scalded her face. If only those times would come again how little she would count all the other sacrifices she had made. They used to be so happy. Only a year ago they had gone to London. It was less than two years since they had been in Ostend. And only a few months ago he was talking of another trip. What had happened since then? How had things altered? What had come over him that he had changed so much?

Desperately Isabel tried to go back over the past to discover an answer to those agonized questions. Had it been her fault in any way? Could she have done anything to prevent things from taking the course they had taken? But her mind had no sooner fastened upon this last question than it grasped avidly at another. Could she do anything even now?

If she could make him come away with her – now – for a few weeks, it might break the spell that was over him. But she knew her hopes were idle. That creature wouldn't let him go. She had a hold over him: some hideous hold over him.

Oh! if only she could get rid of her!

Fallaciously Isabel fed herself with another desperate hope. Why didn't she? Supposing she stood up and walked down the passage and ordered her out of the house this minute?

So powerfully for a moment did she imagine herself bursting into the kitchen, Isabel sprang to her feet and began to walk up and down the floor. She put her hands to her face, it must be ablaze; and her eyes!

But as she strode across the floor for the fourth time Isabel caught sight of herself in the mottled and foggy mirror over the mantel-piece. She came to a stand. Where were the flaming cheeks, and the righteous, angry eyes? In the cold glass she saw only the same pale, harassed face with which she was daily familiar.

That face wouldn't help her much. She stared into the glass. It was hard to believe that the angry hurt of her heart should show so little. She sat down. There was one other thing she could do: go away and leave them to their own devices.

This latter step, drastic as it was, did not excite her greatly, however, for the simple reason that it wasn't the first time that such a thought had come into her head. Months ago this way of evasion had occurred to her, but it had seemed a cowardly and selfish step to take. Now it seemed there was nothing else to do.

Disconsolately Isabel looked around her. She hadn't the first idea of how to set about her departure. Where would she go? That, she supposed, was the first thing to settle. And then the question of money; that was another thing to be settled. In fact that, she supposed, should come before anything else. Briskly she went over to her desk and took out a sheet of paper on which to make the necessary calculations, but her feet lagged and her hands moved uncertainly among her papers, because, with a chill, she was beginning to realize that here, too, the spectre of defeat would rise to confront her. She would have to speak to her father. It would be necessary for him to arrange about her investments, to convert them into money. There could be no question of leaving without his consent. Or could there? She tried to concentrate. There were those papers she had signed a few years ago. What had become of them?

He had taken them away, hadn't he? Yes, he had locked them up somewhere, probably in the tin box he kept under his bed. She supposed she would have to have those papers to take to the bank if matters were to be arranged properly. If she had those papers it might be possible to let her have some money, there and then, on account. That would simplify matters. Dully, however, she felt that things could not be simplified so easily. Why had he taken the papers away? Why had he made her sign them in the first place? And what had she signed? Naturally she had not bothered to read them. If it had been a stranger who had asked her to sign something she would have been more prudent: more cautious. But her father! She tried to be sanguine, but gloomy forebodings settled upon her. It might not be so easy to settle matters. And she was so ignorant of financial affairs. It was a mistake; she saw that now. If she could only concentrate. She forced herself to do so. There had been two occasions when she had signed something. And her father had said something. What was it? What could it have been? Something about temporary accommodation, whatever that might be. Well, Isabel shrugged her shoulders, if, as she must suppose had happened, she had signed something which gave him a use of part, or even all of her money, that would undoubtedly entail a delay.

Then too, if he was irritated with her, as he might easily be, he could probably drag out the transactions. He could probably put her in an awkward position.

Isabel stared at the fire. It was getting low. In her lap her hands had fallen flaccidly apart. A frightened look came into her eyes. Supposing he was vindictive towards her? Supposing – she could hardly bear to think of it – but supposing that creature had a say in the matter? – supposing –

Oh! – Isabel's lids closed over her eyes and she was overpowered by a feeling of weakness, but after a few moments she pulled herself together. Perhaps she was worked up over nothing. After all, her father was her father. He might lose his head. He might make a laughing-stock of himself over this creature, but when it came to touching her money; hers! Isabel's! his daughter's! When it came to that! Isabel was ashamed to think that she had allowed even a shadow of distrust to fall across her mind. How could she have entertained such a thought for a moment? Nature was nature. Blood was thicker than water. Yet fast as those clichés flocked to her aid, a gnawing fear had fastened upon her and she could not shake it from her.

Hadn't he acted very oddly on the only occasion she had thrown out a remark upon the matter? She had merely made some remark about investments in general. She wasn't even thinking of her own investments, but she noticed at once the way he evaded the subject. Indeed, a peculiar glitter had come into his eyes, and a look, at first defensive, then prohibitive, as if warning her not to say anything further!

Thinking of that warning glitter, Isabel's heart, that had risen to no purpose so often, and fallen again, seemed finally to turn over. All the self-pity, all the repugnance, all the humiliation and all the wounded vanity she had suffered in the past twelve months was suddenly set at nothing, and the possibility of her own financial embarrassment was all that concerned her.

Oh, what had she done? Why had she been such a fool? Such a stupid, blind fool!

Another thought flashed into her mind, making her more miserable still. What would her mother say if she could see what a fool she had been; her mother who had so expressly bequeathed the money to her in her own right. The bewildered look came over her face again.

But as she rocked herself from side to side, there began to stir in her mind a vague memory of something her mother had once told her, when she was only a young girl, hardly listening indeed, hardly paying attention at all. It was a story about some servant girl that her mother had heard about long ago, but it seemed to have made an impression upon her. Was this what it was? In spite of her preoccupation with her own distress, Isabel's mind kept turning upon the old story. This girl was working in the house of a small farmer. Yes, that was right, and there was an old man living in the same neighbourhood, a kind of farmer too, she supposed, but he had a couple of hundred acres, and a big ramshackle three-storey house. The old fellow had been married twice and buried both of his wives. He was nearly seventy, bent almost double, and he was bow-legged into the bargain. But he had plenty of money. And the girl knew it.

Isabel sat upright. It was all coming back to her. But why should it come to her mind now? Why, indeed, had Mother told it to her in the first place? To what purpose had she told it? Supposing that she in her turn were to tell it to her father?

Suddenly Isabel's mind was illuminated with a great flash. Supposing her mother, long ago, had perceived some merit in that story: some merit as a parable? For that was just what it seemed to be: a parable.

If I were to tell it to him, she thought with excitement, what would he think of it? What would he say? It would at least let him see that I knew what was going on behind my back. It would at least give him something to ponder upon.

And supposing she told it to the other creature? What effect would it have upon her? It would at least let her see that people weren't as blind as she took them to be all the time!

Isabel sprang to her feet again. Supposing she went down to the kitchen this minute and told them both together.

Would she?

Like an answer, there came from the kitchen a subdued sound of chuckling. That settled it. The next moment she was midway down the dark passage, groping her way with her hands.

'Who is this?'

It was her father who called out. Isabel shuddered. There was something detestable in the false note she detected in his voice, the more so since she could almost have sworn that he called out in order to cover some other sound for which her ear strained in vain as she stumbled down the passage.

But when she went into the kitchen, she felt foolish when she saw how innocently the old man was sitting with his feet up on the range. She felt an impulse of pity towards him. He looked so old; almost feeble, she thought.

Then suddenly she saw that he was in his stocking feet, and at the sight of his grey socks she felt her annoyance return. And when he opened his mouth she immediately caught the false note in his voice again.

'Oh, it's you, my dear! Did you let your fire go down?' He had hastily taken his feet down from the top of the stove when she came into the room and stuck them into his shoes. He put his hands on the arms of his chair, too, as if he was about to stand up, but casting a glance at the range he sank back in his seat while he reached for a sod of turf from the basket beside the chair. 'Not that our fire is so good,' he said. He looked across at the creature. 'What were we thinking about,' he said, 'to let our fire go so low?'

We! Ours!

Isabel stared at him with a cold hard stare, but he was busy poking the fire.

'Will you sit down, my dear?' he said then, setting about getting up again.

Sit down; in that chair; on that filthy cushion? Sit down opposite that slut? Isabel pressed her lips together and looked for the first time at Annie Bowles.

Annie Bowles, as a matter of fact, seemed to be almost asleep. She didn't appear to have moved a muscle since Isabel came into the kitchen, but sat, staring into the fire, her big face red with heat, and

her big calves, that bulged out of her broken boots, so rosy-marbled
from the fire that only an imbecile would continue to sit so close to
the heat.

Isabel looked steadily at the gawky creature. Why she looked like
a gom! She looked back to her father. Was he doting? A half-wit
peasant, and a doting old man. If she wasn't able to pit her wits
against these two!

'No, thank you, Father!' She leant back against the edge of the
table. 'I'm all right here.' She turned to the other creature. 'That's all
right!' she said, making a deprecating gesture. 'Stay where you are!'
she said. This, she felt, was a very tactful remark. It was not
unfriendly, but it had the right element of patronage, because it
went without saying that the ignorant lump hadn't made any effort
to budge out of her chair.

All the same, after a moment, Isabel felt foolish standing there
while the others sat, and so she sat up on the edge of the table.
Compared with that sluggish lump in the wicker chair, she felt that
there was something keen and alert about sitting on the edge of the
table. She felt more confident; and felt altogether more capable of
dealing with the situation.

There was only one obstacle; how to start?

'Oh!'

It was the first syllable the creature had uttered, and at the same
time she drew back her feet with a start from the fire. For, as a sod
fell from the grate, a shower of starry sparks had scattered into the
air, glittering for a moment and then vanishing; but in their
momentary voyage, travelling a fiery path towards Annie Bowles.
'Oh!' she cried again, 'oh!' and she drew back her chair still more.

The occupant of the second wicker chair, on the other hand, sat
forward. To him the scattering of sparks was a welcome distraction
from a situation that threatened to become awkward.

'Ah-ha!' he said, a roguish note in his voice that set Isabel's teeth
on edge. 'Ah-ha, Annie, there's money coming to you!'

Was he mad? Isabel had forgotten this old superstition, but
suddenly she remembered it. And then almost immediately she
saw her chance of using it for her own ends.

'Money coming to you, Annie?' she said quickly. 'I hope it will
bring you luck. Not like a girl I head about!'

Her exclamation was so sudden, her voice so decisive, that the
other two looked up with a surprise that approximated to interest.

'Yes,' she said maliciously, throwing a glance at her father,
'Mother told me the story.' But immediately she tried to disguise her
malice. 'I forgot all about it until this minute,' she said nervously,
falsely, 'I don't know what put it into my head!' Her voice was rapid,

reckless. She laughed too, nervously and hysterically. All the same she knew what she was doing, and the way they were looking at her, stupidly and puzzled, was a help. Why! her father looked stupefied. As for Annie Bowles, she looked no more than a half-wit. There she sat, her legs apart, and her mouth open. 'Do you want to hear the story?' said Isabel brightly and briskly, but they had no chance to reply before she began it, turning from one to the other, but mostly towards her father.

'Not a bad kind of girl at all,' she said, 'came from a respectable home, I believe.' Here Isabel turned and threw a word, direct, to the servant girl. 'As a matter of fact her name was Annie too, as well as I remember,' she said. 'She was attractive, too, I suppose,' she said grudgingly, as her eyes lingered upon the real Annie, 'in a dumpy kind of way, I mean; with a big red face and big red cheeks.' Isabel stared harder at the real Annie, and, as if her imagination was feeding and fattening upon her, she piled detail on detail. 'Her neck was big and soft,' she said, 'I suppose some people might find that attractive, but it looks too much like goitre for me.' Isabel shuddered and turned back to her father. She had begun to forget that her story was supposed to be hearsay. 'Anyway, she was big and strong, and I suppose there would have been plenty of young fellows of her own class willing enough to marry her and provide her bread and butter.' Here Isabel stopped and stared first at her father and then at the girl; they were both listening, although her father's interest was reluctant, and as if he was on his guard against something. 'But,' said Isabel relentlessly, 'it wasn't bread and butter she wanted!'

There was silence for a moment.

'Well, what did she want?' said the man at last.

All at once Isabel felt weak. She had come to the awkward part of the story. The next word, and unless he was a fool her father would have guessed her motive in telling the story. Out of the corner of her eye she felt that the old man was staring at her with a peculiar look.

'I'll tell you what she wanted,' she said, 'but first of all I must tell you there was an old fellow living outside the village,' jerkily she got out her words. She didn't dare to look at either of them now, but out of the corner of her eye she fancied her father was still staring peculiarly at her. 'He was about eighty,' she said, hoping to lessen the likeness between him and the old farmer. 'An old bachelor!' she lied. She was getting more and more nervous and not daring to raise her eyes she fastened them on his shoes. They were so well-cared and polished, so youngly fashioned, so dapper, indeed, for a man of his age, that looking at them Isabel suffered a curious sensation. She felt that his age had fallen away from him, and that he was the spruce and dapper man he had been when she was a child: the father before whom she had always been so cowed and docile. She stared at the shoes and her heart began to beat violently. What wrath was she drawing down upon her foolish head? Where her thin black hair was parted in the middle she suddenly felt as if the skin was as fragile as silk. She wanted to put up her hand to it, and protect it. She even began to imagine that a pulse at that point was opening and shutting like the fontenelle in a new-born child.

But after a moment of staring dully at those dapper patent leather shoes her eye travelled upwards a few inches. Pah! Beyond the neat toecaps the shoes were unlatched, over them the old man's worsted socks were rumpled and untidy, while between the socks and the end of his trousers, his felted underwear showed. And she remembered the indignity in which she had surprised him with his stockinged feet on the range.

'The old fool!' she said, suddenly out loud, meaning at one and the same time the old man in front of her and the old fool in the story. 'The old fool,' she repeated. 'He could have married hundreds of times, but he never seemed to take any notice of any girl until he put his eye on this creature – this girl I was telling you about. I don't know how he first came into contact with her, but it wasn't long until the whole locality was talking about them. He was always finding opportunities for walking past the house where she worked, and when she went into the town he always managed to be in the town at the same time. Then he began to wait for her on the road, and walk home beside her. And after that the gossip started! But the old fellow didn't seem to mind. He didn't seem to care what people said, which was surprising, because he was a man who prided himself on his position, prided himself on his reputation and dignity. There was never anything' – Isabel hesitated – 'never anything –' she hesitated again. Ever since she had first given credence to the hints and whispers about this affair, there was one word above all others she longed to throw in his face; one word she wanted to hear herself utter, but before the enormity of such an utterance her spirit had failed. But now, now was her opportunity – 'nothing lecherous about him!' she said, and she sat rigid as death.

There was a lifetime of silence to be lived through in the instant after the enormous word had fallen upon them all. And then, as she began to feel the throb in her head once more, Isabel got another curious sensation. She got the sensation that the others had not been listening to her at all. But how could that be? A moment before the old man's eyes had burned through her. Isabel was baffled. She lost her place in the story.

But they must have been listening after all because her father was able to prompt her.

'Well,' he said deliberately, but looking queerly at her, 'what did they say about him?'

'They said he was doting!' she said crudely, cruelly.

But her father only laughed. After a moment he spoke again.

'What did they say about her – about Annie?' he asked, and there was something shocking in his having the name right.

'They knew her kind,' she said shortly, 'and anyway, she made no secret of what she had in mind. Even in the start when people gave her a sly dig about the old fellow, she always had the same answer. "How badly off I'd be," she said, "if I had his money." '

There! She was beginning to touch him on the raw.

'The old fool,' she said again, exulting in the appellation. 'He thought she was marrying him for love. For love!' Isabel's voice rose. 'For love!' she said. 'Could you imagine anything more laughable!' She turned her head to look from one of them to the other, but just then again she got the same curious sensation as before that their attention had escaped her. She looked sharply at them. Did she imagine it or had they crossed glances quickly, furtively, under her very eyes? A vague feeling of misgiving came over her, and she began to doubt the wisdom of having begun such a story at all. As long as she had begun it, though, she had to end it. And the end was what mattered.

'They were the laughing-stock of the countryside,' she said. In her excitement once more she forgot that her story was supposed to be hearsay. 'You should see the way he looked at her,' she said. 'You should see him making sheep's eyes at her, and the killing part of it was he had hardly enough sight in his eyes to put one foot in front of the other.'

At this point, unexpectedly, Annie Bowles tittered.

Isabel looked sharply at her.

What made her laugh? She glanced back at her father. He was looking at Annie, but he looked back quickly.

'By all accounts he needed a wife,' he said.

Oh, so that was his attitude. Isabel drew herself up. Wait till he heard more.

'He got a nice one!' she said. 'Do you want to know what she said the night before the wedding? Well, I'll tell you. The house was full of people and she passed near someone in time to hear them saying something about the old fellow. "She'll bury him inside a year!" That's what she overheard. But wait a minute, what do you suppose she said?' Isabel looked straight ahead of her. 'She only gave a laugh. "I won't have to bury the money," she said.'

There! Did he hear that?

Isabel looked at her father. He heard her all right. He wasn't looking at the creature now; he was looking at her.

'How long did he live?' he said.

Isabel hesitated. She could say what she liked. She could make out that he paid for his passion: that he was dead in a few months! But some dissatisfaction with the effect she was making upon the man made her turn towards the other creature.

'He lived for sixteen years,' she said, her voice thick with satisfaction. 'He lived long enough to turn her from a young girl into a dull middle-aged woman, worn out from minding him, and lifting him from the bed to the fire, and from the fire to the bed, to say nothing of the way her heart was scalded with his jealousy and his doting. That's how long he lived,' she said.

But as she looked to see the effect of her words on Annie Bowles, she was in time, unmistakably, to see them look at each other, and she knew that some meaning was passed between them in that look.

Isabel's heart faltered. What had gone wrong with her parable? It had only furthered them in their badness.

'Well!' Ignoring her, her father leaned forward towards Annie Bowles. 'Well,' he said provocatively, 'she got the money, didn't she? She got what she wanted?'

He was asking Annie Bowles. And Annie Bowles had an answer. She gave it at first only with her eyes, and a ribald look at the old man. Then she tossed her head.

'Well!' she countered. 'He got what he wanted too, didn't he?'

And there and then, under her eyes, there passed between them another of those looks that she used to imagine only when she sat alone in the little boudoir, those looks so heavy with intimations beyond her understanding.

Isabel looked from one of them to the other, but it was no longer possible to see them separately. Something seemed to hold them bound together as one.

Oh, the ugliness; oh, the badness! Isabel pressed her lips together. She didn't want them to see what they had done to her. She got to her feet. She might as well go to bed and leave them to their devices.

'Good night,' she said abruptly and awkwardly. But they hadn't heard her. She went to the door but at the door she looked back at them. And she was struck by the brightness and glitter of her father's eyes. They burned upon Annie Bowles. And Annie Bowles? Isabel looked at her, but Annie's back was turned. She could not see her face, yet she knew the light that lit her eyes. And ugly or not, evil or not, Isabel knew its meaning was not discoverable to her.

A Likely Story

Once upon a time there was a widow who had one son. He was her only son: her only joy. His name was Packy. Packy and the widow lived in a cottage in the shadow of the old abbey of Bective. The village of Bective was opposite, on the other side of the river Boyne.

Do you know Bective? Like a bird in the nest, it presses close to the soft green mound of the river bank, its handful of houses no more significant by day than the sheep that dot the far fields. But at night, when all its little lamps are lit, house by house, it is marked out on the hillside as clearly as the Great Bear is marked out in the sky. And on a still night it throws its shape in glitter on the water.

Many a time, when the widow lit her own lamp, Packy would go to the door, and stand on the threshold looking across the river at the lights on the other side, and at their reflection floating on the water, and it made him sigh to think that not a single spangle of that golden pattern was cast by their window panes. Too many thistles, and too many nettles, and too much rank untrodden grasses rose up in front of their cottage for its light ever to reach the water.

But the widow gave his sighs no hearing.

'It's bad enough to have one eyesore,' she said, 'without you wanting it doubled in the river!'

She was sorely ashamed of the cottage. When she was a bride, its walls were as white as the plumage of the swans that sailed below it on the Boyne, and its thatch struck a golden note in the green scene. But now its walls were a sorry colour; its thatch so rotten it had to be covered with sheets of iron, soon rusty as the docks that seeded up to the doorstep.

'If your father was alive he wouldn't have let the place get into this state,' she told Packy every other day of his life. And this too made him sigh. It was a sad thing for a woman when there was no man about a house to keep it from falling down.

So, when the rain dinned on the tin roof, and the wind came through the broken panes, and when the smoke lost its foothold in the chimney and fell down again into the kitchen, like a sack of potatoes, he used to wish that he was a man. One day he threw his arms around his mother's middle.

'Don't you wish I was a man, Mother,' he cried, 'so I could fix up the cottage for you?'

But the widow gave him a curious look.

'I think I'd liefer have you the way you are, son,' she said. She was so proud of him, every minute of the day, she couldn't imagine him being any better the next minute. He was a fine stump of a lad. He was as strong as a bush, and his eyes were as bright as the track of a snail. As for his cheeks, they were ruddy as the haws. And his hair had the same gloss as the gloss on the wing of a blackbird.

'Yes, I'd liefer have you the way you are, son,' she said again, but she was pleased with him. She looked around at the smoky walls, and the broken panes stopped with old newspapers. 'What would you do to it, I wonder – if you *were* a man?'

Her question put Packy at a bit of a loss. Time and again he'd heard her say that all the money in the world wouldn't put the place to rights.

'Perhaps I'd build a new cottage!' he said cockily.

'What's that?' cried the widow. But she'd heard him all right, and she clapped her hands like a girl, and a glow came into her cheeks that you'd only expect to see in the cheeks of a girl. 'I believe you would!' she cried, and she ran to the door and looked out. 'Where would you build it, son? Up here on the hill, or down in the village? Would you have it thatched, or would you have it slated?'

'Slated, of course,' said Packy decisively, 'unless you'd prefer tiles?'

The widow looked at him in astonishment. Only the Council cottages had tiles.

'Would there be much of a differ in the price?' she asked timidly.

'Tiles would cost a bit more I think,' Packy hazarded. 'And they mightn't be worth the differ.'

A shadow fell on the widow's joy.

'Ah well,' she said. 'No matter! If we couldn't do everything well I'd just as soon not build at all! I wouldn't want to give it to say that it was a shoddy job.'

There would be nothing shoddy about it though.

'I was only thinking,' said Packy, 'that it might be better to put the money into comfort than into show. We might get a range in the kitchen for what we'd save on the tiles!'

'A range?' cried the widow. Never, never, would she have presumed to think that she, who had stooped over a hob for forty years, would ever have a big black range to stand in front of and poke with a poker. But all the same she felt that it might be as well not to let Packy see she was surprised. Better to let him think she took a range for granted. So instead of showing surprise she looked at him slyly out of the corner of her eye. 'What about a pump?' she said. 'A pump in the yard?' But she saw at once by the way his face fell that she'd gone a bit too far. The Council houses hadn't as much as a mention of a pump.

'I thought maybe it would be good enough if we built near the pump in the village,' Packy said uneasily.

'Sure of course it would be good enough, son,' she conceded quickly. After all, a pump in the yard was only a dream within a dream. But she would have given a lot to stand at the window and see her neighbours passing on their way to the pump in the village, and better still to see them passing back again, their arms dragging out of them with the weight of the bucket, while all she'd have to do would be to walk out into her own yard for a little tinful any time she wanted. It would make up for all the hardship she'd ever suffered. Oh, she'd give a lot to have a pump in her own yard!

And looking at her face, Packy would have given a lot to gratify her with a pump.

'I wonder would it cost a lot of money?' he asked.

'Ah, I'm afraid it would, son,' said the widow, dolefully. Then all at once she clapped her hands. 'What about the money we'll get for this place when the new cottage is built? Couldn't we use that money to put down a pump?'

Packy stared blankly at her. Up to that moment he had altogether forgotten that building a new cottage would mean leaving the old one. To him, the little cottage never seemed as bad as it did to the widow. He had listened, it is true, to her daily litany of its defects, but out of politeness only. Never had he seen it with her eyes, but always with his own. According to her, its tin roof was an eyesore, but he liked to hear the raindrops falling on it clear and sweet. According to her the windows were too low, and they didn't let in enough light by day, but in bed at night he could stare straight up at the stars without raising his head from the pillow. And that was a great thing surely! According to her, the cow shed was too close to the house, but if he woke in the middle of the night, he liked to hear Bessie, the old cow, pulling at her tyings, and on cold winter nights it comforted him to find that the fierce night air was not strong enough to kill the warm smell that came from her byre.

There was one wintry night and he thought he'd die before morning, like the poor thrushes that at times fell down out of the air, too stiff to fly, but when he thought of Bessie and the way the old cow's breath kept the byre warm, he cupped his own two hands around his mouth and breathed into them, and soon he too began to feel warm and comfortable. To him, that night it seemed that together, he and the old cow, with their living breath were stronger than their enemies, the elements. Oh, say what you liked, a cow was great company. And as far as he was concerned, the nearer she was to the house the better. So too with many other things that the widow thought were faults in the little house; as often as not to Packy they were things in its favour. Indeed, it would want to be a wonderful place that would seem nicer and homelier to him than the cottage where he was born. After all, his Mother came to it only by chance, but he came to it as a snail comes to its shell.

'Oh, Mother!' he cried, 'maybe we oughtn't to part with the old cottage till we see first if we're going to like the new one!'

To hear the sad note in his voice you'd think the day of the flitting was upon them. The widow had to laugh.

'Is that the way with you, son? You're getting sorry you made such big promises! Ah, never mind. It'll be a long time yet before you're fit to build a house for any woman, and when that time does come, I don't suppose it will be for your old mother you'll be building it.'

But her meaning was so lost on him.

'And for who else?' he cried.

But the widow turned away and as she did she caught sight of the clock.

'Look at the time! You're going to be late for school. And I have to cut your lunch yet,' she said crossly. Bustling up from the bench she seized the big cake of soda bread that she had baked and set to cool on the kitchen window-sill before he was out of bed that morning. 'Will this be enough for you?' she cried, cleaving the knife down through the bread and mortaring together two big slices with a slab of yellow butter. Then, as he stuffed the bread into his satchel and ran out of the door, she ran after him. 'Hurry home, son,' she called out, leaning far over the gate to watch him go up the road.

Hardly ever did he go out of the house that she didn't watch him out of sight, and hardly ever did he come home that she wasn't there again, waiting to get the first glimpse of him. And all the time between his going and his coming, her heart was in her mouth wondering if he was safe and sound. For this reason she was often a bit edgy with him when he did come home, especially if he was a few minutes late as he was sometimes when he fell in with his friends the Tubridys.

The widow was death on the Tubridys, although nobody, least of all herself, could say why this should be so. Perhaps it was that, although she often said the whole three Tubridys – Christy and Donny and poor little Marty – all sewn up together wouldn't put a patch on her Packy, still – maybe – it annoyed her to see them trotting along behind Rose Tubridy on the way to Mass of a Sunday while she had only the one set of feet running to keep up with her.

'Well! What nonsense did the Tubridys put into your head today?' she'd call out as soon as he came within earshot.

'Oh, wait till you hear, Mother!' he'd cry, and before he got to the gate at all, he'd begin to tell all he heard that day.

One day he was very excited.

'What do you know, Mother! There is a big pot of gold buried beyond in the old abbey! Christy Tubridy is after telling me about it. He didn't know anything about it either until last night when his father told him while they were all sitting around the fire. He said he'd have got it himself long ago, only every time he put the spade into the ground, a big white cock appeared on the top of the old abbey and flapped its wings at him, and crowed three times! He had to let go the spade and run for his life! What do you think of that, Mother?'

But the widow didn't give him much hearing.

'A likely story!' she said. 'What harm would an innocent old cock have done him? Him of all people: that ought to be well used to the sound of cocks and hens, with the dungheap right under the window of the house. It's a wonder he wasn't deafened long ago with cocks crowing right into his ear! Oh, it would take more than an old cock to scare that man! And furthermore, let me tell you that if there was something to be got for nothing in this world, the devil himself wouldn't knock a feather out of him till he got it. You mark my words, son, if there was as much as a farthing buried in the old abbey, by now old Tubridy would have scratched up the whole place looking for it. He wouldn't have left one stone standing on another. He'd have done a better job on it than Cromwell! A pot of gold, indeed! A likely story!'

'I suppose you're right,' said Packy, and he left down the spade that he had grabbed up to go digging for the gold.

'Don't be so ready to believe everything you hear!' said his mother.

But barely a day later he came running home again to tell something else he had heard.

'Mother! Mother! Do you know the heap of old stones at the bottom of the hill in Claddy graveyard, where there was an old church one time? Well, last night Christy Tubridy's father told him that when they were building that church long ago they never meant to build it there at all, but at the top of the hill, only the morning after they brought up the first load of stones and gravel, where did they find it all but down at the bottom of the hill! Nobody knew how it got there, but they had to spend the day bringing it all up again. And what do you suppose? The morning after when they came to work, there were all the stones and the gravel down at the bottom once more. And the same thing happened the day after that again and on every day after for seven days! But on the seventh day they knew that it must be the work of the Shee. The Shee didn't want a church built on that hill at all. There was no use going against them, so they built it down in the hollow.'

But the widow didn't give him any hearing this time either.

'A likely story!' she said. 'It's my opinion that the workmen that carried those stones up the hill by day, were the same that carried them down-hill at night. I don't suppose the men that were going in those days liked work any better than the men that are going nowadays, and it's likely they decided it would pay them better to put in a few hours overtime taking down the stones, than be lugging them up there for an eternity – as they would be in those days with not many implements. The Shee indeed! How well no one thought of sitting up one night to see who was doing the good work? Oh no. Well they knew it wasn't the Shee! But it suited them to let on to it. The Shee indeed! If that hill belongs to the Shee – which I very much doubt – what harm would it do them to have a church built on it? Isn't it *inside* the hills the Shee live? What do they care what happens outside on the hillside? A likely story! I wonder when are you going to stop heeding those Tubridys and their nonsense?'

Never, it seemed, for the very next day he came running down the road as if he'd never get inside the gate quick enough to tell another story.

'Oh Mother!' he cried, jumping across the puddles at the door. 'Are you sure I'm yours? I mean, are you sure that I belong to you – that I'm not a changeling? Because Christy Tubridy told me that their Marty is one! I always thought he was their real brother, didn't you? Well, he's not! One day, when he was a baby, their mother was hanging out the clothes to dry on the bushes, and she had him in a basket on the ground beside her, but when she was finished hanging up the clothes she looked into the basket, and it wasn't her own baby at all that was in it but another one altogether that she'd never seen before, all wizened up, with a cute little face on him like a little old man. It was the Shee that came and stole her baby, and put the other crabby fellow in place of him. The Tubridys were terribly annoyed, but they couldn't do anything about it, and they had to rear up Marty like he was their own.'

But this time the widow gave him no hearing at all.

'A likely story!' she cried. 'A likely story indeed! Oh, isn't it remarkable the lengths people will go to to make excuses for themselves. That poor child, Marty Tubridy, was never anything but a crabby thing. He's a Tubridy, all right. Isn't he the dead spit of his old grandfather that's only dead this ten years? I remember him well. So they want to let on he's a changeling? God give them wit. The Shee indeed! The Shee are no more ready than any other kind of people to do themselves a bad turn, and if they make it a habit to steal human children – which I very much doubt – I'd say they'd be on the watch for some child a bit better favoured than one of those poor Tubridys. Now, if it was *you* they put their eye on, son, that would be a different matter, because – even if it's me that says it – you were the sonsiest baby anyone ever saw. Not indeed that I ever left you lying about in a basket under the bushes! It would want to be someone smart that would have stolen you! I never once took my eyes off you from the first minute I clapped them on to you, till you were big enough to look after yourself – which I suppose you are now? Or are you? Sometimes I doubt it when you come home to me stuffed with nonsense! Changeling indeed! A likely story.'

But as a matter of fact it would have been hard to find a story that would not be a likely story to the widow. The gusts of her wisdom blew so fiercely about the cottage that after a while Packy began to feel that it wasn't worth while opening his own mouth at all so quickly did his mother rend his words into rags. And when, one spring, he began to fancy every time he went out of doors that there was someone beckoning to him, and calling him by name, he said nothing at all about it to his mother. For of course he could be mistaken. It was mostly in the evenings that the fancies came to him, and the mist that rose up from the river and wandered over the fields often took odd shapes. There were even days when it never wholly lifted, and like bits of white wool torn from the backs of the sheep as they scrambled through briars and bushes, or rubbed up against barbed wire, the mist lay about the ground in unexpected hollows. It lay in the hollows that are to be found in old pasture that once was broken by the plough, and on the shallow ridges where the fallow meets the ley. Ah yes! It was easy enough then to mistake it for a white hand lifted, or a face turned for an instant towards you, and then turned swiftly aside.

It is said however that a person will get used to anything, and after a while Packy got used to his fancies. He got used to them, but he was less eager than usual to go out and wander in the fields and woods, above all after the sun went below the tops of the trees. And the widow soon noticed this. It wasn't like him to hang about the cottage after school.

What was the matter, she wondered? Did something ail him?

'Where are the Tubridys these days, son?' she asked at last. 'God knows they're here often enough when they're not wanted. It's a wonder you wouldn't like to go off with them for a ramble in the woods.'

She went to the door and looked out. It was the month of May, the very first day of it. But Packy didn't stir from the fire. Nor the next day either. Nor the next. Nor the next.

'That fire won't burn any brighter for you to be hatching it,' said the widow at last.

That was true, thought Packy, for it was a poor fire surely. He looked at it with remorse. It was nearly out. There was nothing on the hearth but a handful of twigs that were more like the makings of a jackdaw's nest than the making of a fire. It was like a tinker's fire, no sooner kindled than crackled away in a shower of sparks. He looked at his mother. He knew what was wrong. She had no one to depend on for firing now that he never went out for he never came back without a big armful of branches from the neighbouring demesne. He looked at her hands. They were all scratched and scored from plucking the bushes.

'Oh, Mother,' he cried in true contrition, 'tomorrow on my way home from school I'll go into the woods, no matter what, and get you an armful of branches!'

But the next day – and in broad sunlight too – his fancies were worse than ever.

Just as the bell rang to call in the scholars from play, what did Packy see, around the corner of the schoolhouse, but a finger beckoning: beckoning to him! It turned out to be only the flickering of a shadow cast on the wall by an old hawthorn tree beyond the gable, but all the same it unsettled him. And when school was over he made sure to keep in the middle of the little drove of scholars that went his way home.

For there is no loneliness like the loneliness of the roads of Meath, with the big, high hedges rising up to either side of you, so that you can't even see the cattle in the fields, but only hear them inside wading in the deep grass and pulling at the brittle young briars in the hedge. Closed in between those high hedges, the road often seems endless to those who trudge along it, up hill and down, for although to the men who make ordinance maps the undulations of the land may seem no greater than the gentle undulations of the birds rising and dipping in the air above it, yet to those who go always on foot – the herd after his flock, the scholar with his satchel on his back – it has as many ripples as a sheet in the wind, and not only that, but it often seems to ripple in such a way that the rises are always in front, and the dips always behind.

It was that way with Packy anyway.

Oh, how good it would be at home: first to catch a glimpse of the little rusty roof, and then to run in at the gate and feel the splatters of the mud on his knees as he'd dash through the puddles in front of the door.

It was not till he got to Connells Cross that he remembered his promise about the fire-wood. Oh sorely, sorely was he tempted to break that promise, but after one last look at the far tin roof that had just come into view above the hedge he let the little flock of scholars go forward without him. Then, with a sad look after them he climbed up on the wall of the demesne and jumped down on the other side. Immediately, under his feet twigs and branches cracked like glass, and for a minute he was tempted to gather an armful although he knew well they were only larch and pine. But he put the base temptation from him. Try to light a fire with larch? Wasn't it larch carpenters put in the stairs of a house so the people could get down it safely if the house took fire! And pine? Wasn't it a dangerous timber always spitting out sparks that would burn holes the size of buttons in the leg of your trousers! Oh no; he'd have to do better than that; he'd have to get beech or ash or sycamore or oak. And to get them he'd have to go deep into the woods to where the trees were as old as the Christian world. He'd have to go as far as the little cemetery of Claddy. There, among the tottering tombstones and the fallen masonry of the ancient church, there was always a litter of dead branches, and what was more, every branch was crotched over with grey lichen to make it easier to see against the dark mould of the earth.

Like all cemeteries, the cemetery of Claddy was a lonely place, and to get to it he would have to cross the hill that Christy Tubridy said belonged to Shee, but he remembered that his mother had heaped scorn on that kind of talk. All the same, when he came to the small pathway that led up to the hill, he faltered, because it was so overgrown with laurel it was more like a tunnel than a path. Away at the far end of the tunnel, though, there was a glade and there the light lay white and beautiful on the bark of the trees. Shutting his eyes, Packy dashed into the leafy tunnel and didn't open them until he was out of it. But when he did open them he had to blink, because, just as the sky would soon sparkle with stars, so, everywhere, under his feet the dark earth sparkled with white windflowers. Who could be afraid in such a place?

As for the branches: the ground was strewn with them. Ah! there was a good one! There was a fine dry one! And there was one would burn for an hour!

But it didn't pay to be too hasty. That last was a branch of blackthorn and it gave him a nasty prick – 'Ouch,' it hurt. Letting fall his bundle, Packy stuck his finger into his mouth, but the thorn had gone deep and he couldn't suck it out. He'd have to stoup his finger in hot water, or get his mother to put a poultice of bread and water on it. He'd better not forget either, he told himself, because there was poison in thorns. Christy Tubridy knew a man who . . . At the thought of the Tubridys, though, Packy grew uneasy. All the stories they had ever told him again crowded back into his mind. Supposing those stories were true? Supposing the Shee really did still wander about the world? Supposing they did steal away human children?

Suddenly his heart began to beat so fast it felt like it was only inside his shirt it was instead of inside his skin. And the next minute, leaving his bundle of twigs where it lay, he made for the green pathway up which he had come, meaning to fling himself down it as if it were a hole in the ground.

And that is what he would have done only that – right beside him – sitting on the stump of a tree, he caught sight of a gentleman! A stranger it is true, but a gentleman. At least, Packy took him to be that – a gentleman from the Big House, perhaps? Now although Packy was glad he was not alone, he was afraid the gentleman might be cross with him for trespassing. But not at all. The gentleman was very affable.

'There's a fine dry limb of a tree!' he said, pointing to a bough of ash that Packy had overlooked.

He spoke so civilly that Packy ventured a close look at him.

Was he a man at all, he wondered? The clothes on him were as fine as silk, and a most surprising colour: green. As for his shoes, they were so fine his muscles rippled under the leather like the muscles of a finely bred horse ripple under his skin. There was something a bit odd about him.

'Thank you, sir,' said Packy cautiously and he bent and picked up the branch.

'Don't mention it: I assure you it's a pleasure to assist you, Packy.' In surprise Packy stared. The gentleman knew his name!

'Yes, Packy, I know your name – and all about you,' said the little gentleman smiling. 'In fact I have been endeavouring all the week to have a word with you – alone, that is to say – but I found it impossible to attract your attention – until now!'

Packy started. So he wasn't mistaken after all when he fancied that someone was beckoning to him, and raising a hand.

'Was it you, sir?' he cried in amazement. 'I thought it was only the mist. Tell me, sir – were you at it again today?' he cried. The little gentleman nodded. 'Well doesn't that beat all!' said Packy. 'I thought it was a branch of hawthorn swaying in the wind.'

The gentleman bowed.

'I'm complimented. A beautiful tree; always a favourite of mine, especially a lone bush of it in the middle of a green field. But to come to practical matters. I suppose you're wondering what I wanted to see you about. Well, let me tell you straight away – I understand that you are dissatisfied with the condition of your cottage – is that so?'

He was a County Councillor! That was it! – thought Packy. He'd come to make a report on the condition of the cottage. And to think that he had nearly run away from him!

'It's in a very bad state, sir,' he said. 'My mother is very anxious to get out of it.'

To a County Councillor that ought to be broad enough! Better however leave nothing to chance. 'Perhaps there is something you could do for us, sir,' he said. Throwing down his bundle of kindling he went nearer. What were a few bits of rotten branch to compare with the news he'd be bringing home if the gentleman promised him a Council cottage?

'Well, Packy, perhaps there may be something I can do for you!' said the gentleman. 'Sit down here beside me, and we'll discuss the matter, or better still, let us walk up and down; it gets so chilly out on the hillside at this hour of evening.'

And indeed it was more than chilly. The mist had started to rise. Already it roped the boles of the trees, and if it weren't for the little gentleman's company Packy would have been scared. As it was, he set about matching his pace to the pace of his friend, and stepped out boldly.

'I suppose you're a County Councillor, sir?' he asked, as they paced along.

'Eh? A County Councillor? What's that?' said the little man, and he stopped short in his stride, but the next minute he started off again. 'Don't let us delay,' he said. 'It's mortally cold out here.'

So he wasn't a County Councillor? He didn't even know what a Councillor was! Packy's heart sank. Where did he come from at all? And was it all for nothing he'd lost his time and his firewood. It was very tiring too, striding up and down on the top of the hill, because at every minute the little gentleman stepped out faster and faster, and where at first, when they passed them, the windflowers had shone out each single as a star, now they streamed past like ribbons of mist. Even the little man was out of breath. He was panting like the pinkeens that Packy and the Tubridys caught in the Boyne and put into jam-jars where they swam to the sides of the glass, their mouths gaping. Chancing to glance at him it seemed to Packy that the little man had got a lot older looking. His eyes looked very old!

'What's the matter, Packy?' asked the little man, just then, seeing him stare.

'Nothing, sir,' said Packy – 'I was just wondering if it is a thing that you are a foreigner?'

'Is it me?' cried the gentleman, 'a foreigner!' He stopped short in astonishment. 'I've been in this country a lot longer than you, Packy!' He paused, ' – about five thousand years longer, I should say.'

Packy too stopped short.

Was the little man cracked, he wondered? This, however, was a point he could not very well ask the gentleman to settle. He would have to decide for himself. So he said nothing. But he wasn't going to pace up and down the hill any more.

'I think I'd better be going home, sir,' he said politely, but decisively.

'Oh, but you can't go back to that wretched cottage,' cried the gentleman. 'Not till I see if I can do something for you!' he cried. 'Have you forgotten?'

Of course he hadn't forgotten. But if the gentleman was cracked, what use was there placing any hope in him?

'I've been thinking of your problem for some time past, Packy, as it happens,' he said, 'and it seems to me that there is very little use in trying to do anything to that old place of yours – '

That was sane enough, thought Packy.

'– and so,' he went on, 'what I have in mind is that you come and live with *me*!'

So he *was* cracked after all! Packy drew back. But the little man went on eagerly. 'I live right near here – yes – just down there – only a few paces,' he cried, pointing down the side of the hill towards the water's edge.

Now Packy wouldn't swear that he knew every single step of the ground at this point, because a great deal of it was covered with briar and scrub, but he'd be prepared to swear that there wasn't a house the size of a sixpence on the side of that hill!

'I see you don't believe me!' said the little man. 'Well – come and I'll show you!'

Now, the little man was so insistent, and Packy himself was so curious, that when the former set off down the slope, Packy set off after him, although it was by no means easy to follow him, for the undergrowth was dense, and the branches of the trees, that had never been cut back, or broken by cattle, hung down so low that in some places they touched the ground. To pass under them Packy had almost to go down on his knees. But the little fellow knew his way like a rabbit. He looped under the heavy boughs as easily as a bird, while Packy stumbled after, as often as not forgetting to lower his head, and getting a crack on the pate. 'Ouch!' he cried on one of these occasions.

'What's up?' asked the little man, looking irritably over his shoulder.

'I hit my head against a branch; that's all,' said Packy.

The little man looked crossly at him.

'That wasn't a branch you hit against,' he said sharply, 'it was a root!'

And indeed he was right. At that point, the hill sloped so steeply that the rain had washed the clay from the roots of the trees till you could walk under them in the same way as you'd walk through the eye of a bridge. It was just as he was about to duck under another of these big branching roots after the little man, that Packy noticed how dark it was on the other side, as if something had come up between them and the sky. He came to an abrupt stand. The little man, on the other hand, darted into the dimness.

'Mind your step there,' he cried, looking back over his shoulder. 'It's a bit dark, but you'll get used to it.' He fully expected Packy to follow him.

But Packy stuck his feet in the ground.

'Hold on a minute, sir,' he said. 'If it's a cave you live in, I'm not going a step further.'

He hadn't forgotten how, once, an uncle of his had come home from America, and hired a car and took him and his mother to New Grange to see the prehistoric caves. His mother couldn't be got to go into them, but he and his uncle crawled down a stone passage that was slimy and wet, and when they got to the caves they hardly had room to stand up. They could barely breathe either the air was so damp. And it had a smell like the smell that rises from a newly-made grave. All the time Packy kept thinking the earth would press down on the cave and crack it like an egg – and them along with it. No thank you! He had seen enough caves!

'You're not going to get me into any cave,' he said stoutly. The little man ran out into the light again.

'It's not a cave!' he cried. 'Do you think we had to scratch holes for ourselves like badgers or foxes? We may live inside the hill but we move around under the earth the same way that you move around over it. You've a lot to learn yet, Packy, you and your generation.'

'Is that so?' said Packy. 'Well, we can move in the air! And under the sea!'

'Bah!' said the little man. 'Not the way I meant! Not like the birds! Not like the fishes!'

'I suppose you're right there,' said Packy, but half-heartedly.

'What do you mean by supposing everything?' said the old man crossly. 'Don't you ever say yes or no? I hope you haven't a suspicious streak in you? Perhaps I should have known that when you kept running home all the week every time I tried to get your attention!'

'Oh, but that was different, sir,' said Packy. 'I thought then that you were one of the Shee!'

At this, however, the little man began to laugh.

'And who in the name of the Sod do you think I am *now*?' he said.

'I don't know, sir,' said Packy, 'but I'm not afraid of you anyway – a nice kind gentleman like you – why should I?'

'And if I were to tell you that I *am* one of the Shee,' said the little man, 'what would happen then?'

Packy pondered this.

'Perhaps you'd be only joking?' he said, but a doubtful look had come on his face.

'And if I wasn't joking,' said the little man, 'what then?'

'Well, sir,' said Packy, 'I suppose I'd be twice as glad then that I didn't go into the cave with you!'

'I tell you it's *not* a cave!' screamed the little man. 'And by the same token, will you stop calling us the Shee! What do they teach you in school at all, at all? Did you never hear tell of the Tuatha de Danaan? the noblest race that ever set foot in this isle? In five thousand years, no race has equalled us in skill or knowledge.'

Five thousand years! Packy started. Had he heard aright?

'Excuse me, sir,' he said then. 'Are you alive or dead?'

It seemed quite a natural question to ask, but it angered the little man.

'Do I look as if I was dead?' he cried. 'Wouldn't I be dust and ashes long ago if so?'

'Oh, I don't know about that,' said Packy. 'When my uncle hired the car that time – the time we went to New Grange – we passed

through Drogheda, and we went into the Cathedral to see Blessed
Oliver Plunkett's head. It's in a box on the altar. He's dead hundreds
of years: and he's not dust and ashes!'

But truth to tell, there was a big difference between the little
gentleman's head, and the head of the saint, because the venerable
bishop's head looked like an old football, nothing more, while the
little gentleman looked very much alive, especially at that moment,
because he was leaping with anger.

'Are you taught nothing at all nowadays?' he cried in disgust. 'Do
you not know anything about the history of your country? Were you
not taught that when we went into the hills we took with us the
secret that mankind has been seeking ever since – the secret of
eternal youth? But come! that's not the point. The point is – are you
coming any further, or are you not?'

Now there was no doubt about it, the situation had changed.
Packy stared past the little man, and although he could see nothing,
his curiosity undecided him. What a story he'd have for the
Tubridys if he'd once been inside that hill!

'Will you bring me back again, sir?' he asked, having in mind the
story about the changelings.

The little man looked at him.

'Well, Packy, I may as well be straight with you. An odd time –
now and again only – we take a notion for a human child and try to
lure him away to live with us forever under the hills, but we always
look for one who is dissatisfied with his lot in the world.'

'Oh, but I'm not dissatisfied with my lot,' cried Packy apprehensively.

'Oh come now!' said the little man, 'didn't I often overhear you
and your mother complaining about that wretched cottage of yours?'

'Oh, you might have heard us talking, sir, but it was my mother
that was discontented: not me. I was only agreeing to keep her in
good humour.'

'What's that?' said the little man sharply. 'Don't tell me I've got
the wrong end of the stick! Are you sure of what you're saying,
Packy? Because if that's the case I may as well stop wasting my
time.' He scowled very fiercely. After a minute though he seemed to
remember his manners. 'It's too bad,' he said, 'because you're the
sort of lad I like.'

'Thank you, sir,' said Packy. 'My mother will be pleased to hear
that.' Then as he made a move to go, upon an impulse he stopped. 'I
wonder, sir, if you'd mind my asking you a question before I go?'

'Why certainly not,' said the little man. 'But be quick, boy; it's very
cold out here on the hillside.'

'Well, sir,' said Packy, 'I'd like to know if it's true about Marty Tubridy – I mean – is he a changeling, sir?'

'Is it Marty Tubridy! Of course not!' said the old man. 'Your mother was right there,' he conceded. 'We have no use for weedy little creatures like the Tubridys: it isn't everyone we fancy, I can tell you.'

That was very gratifying to hear. His mother would be pleased at that too, thought Packy. Then he remembered that she would probably say it was all a likely story. He sighed.

The little man looked keenly at him.

'Are you changing your mind?'

Packy said nothing for a minute. Then he looked up.

'You didn't tell me whether I'd be able to get out again?' he asked.

'Really, Packy, you are an obstinate boy! I have no choice but to tell you the truth, which is that at the start I had no notion of letting you out again if I once got you inside, but as it's getting late, and I'm getting sick and tired arguing, I'm willing to make a bargain with you. I won't stop you from going home – if you want to go yourself, but don't blame me if you don't want to go!'

Well, that seemed fair enough.

'Oh, there's no fear of me wanting to stay!' he said confidently. 'Thank you kindly for asking me, sir. I'll go on for a short while. But wait a second while I take off my boots so I won't dirty the place: my feet are shocking muddy after slithering down that slope.'

For a minute the little gentleman looked oddly at him.

'Leave on your boots, Packy,' he said; then slowly and solemnly: 'Don't leave anything belonging to you outside. That's the very thing I'd have made you do, if I was not going to let you out again. I'd have had you leave some part of your clothing – your cap, or your scarf, or something, here on the outside of the hill – like a man would leave his clothes on the bank of the river if he was going to drown himself – so that people would find them and give up hopes of you. Because as long as there's anyone outside in the world still hoping a child will come back to them, it's nearly as hard for us to keep him inside as if he himself was still hoping to go back. Keep your boots on your feet, boy. You can't say I'm not being honest with you, can you?'

'I cannot, sir,' said Packy, 'but tell me, sir, those children you were telling me about – the ones that didn't want to go back to the world, did they always leave their shoes outside?'

'They did,' said the little man.

'Did they now?' said Packy reflectively. 'Wasn't that very foolish of them? How did they know they wouldn't be sorry when they got inside?'

The little man shrugged his shoulders.

'Ah sure don't we all have to take a chance some time or another in our lives?' he said. 'Look at us! Before we came to Erin we were endlessly sailing the seas looking for a land to our liking. And many a one we found. But it never satisfied us for long. No matter how often we beached our boats, we soon set sail again, till one day we saw *this* island rise up out of the seas and we put all our trust in the promise of her emerald shores. Before we went a foot inland do you know what we did? We set fire to our boats, down on the grey sands! That was taking a chance, wasn't it? So you can't expect me to have much sympathy with people that won't take a chance with their boots! Have you made up your mind about yours, by the way? You won't leave them? Very well then, lace them up again on you, and don't mind them being muddy. I'll get one of the women inside to give them a rub of a blacking brush. They're very muddy all right. Never mind that now though – follow me!' Then he turned around and ducking under the root of the tree again, he walked into what seemed to Packy to be a solid wall of earth.

But just as fog shrinks from light, or frost from fire, so, as they went inward, the earth seemed to give way before them. Nor was it the cold wet rock of New Grange either, but a warm dry clay in which, Packy noticed with interest as they went along, there were different layers of clay and sand and gravel and stone, just like he had seen in Swainstown Quarry when he went there once on a tipper-lorry. In fact he was so interested in the walls of clay that he hardly realized how deep into the hill they were going until the little man came to a stop.

'Well! Here we are!' he said, and Packy saw that they had arrived at what at first seemed to be a large room, but which he soon saw was merely a large space made by several people all gathered together.

But apparently these people rarely moved very far from where they were, for around them they had collected a variety of articles that suggested permanent habitation, in the way that furniture suggests habitation in a house. Not that the articles in the cave were furniture in any real sense of the word. Tables and chairs there were none. But in a corner a big harp gleamed, and randomly around about were strewn a number of vessels, basins and ewers and yes, a row of gleaming milking pails! With astonishment, Packy noticed that all these vessels, and the harp too, were as bright as if they were made of gold! He was staring at them when the little man shook him by the arm.

'Well, how do you like it down here?' he cried, and he was so feverishly excited he was dancing about on the tips of his toes.

Now, Packy didn't want to be rude, but the fact of the matter was that only for the gold basins and the gold pails, and the big gold harp, he didn't see anything very wonderful about the place. But of course, they would be something to tell the Tubridys about.

'They're not real gold, sure they're not?' he asked.

'Of course they are gold,' said the little man. And then, seeing that Packy seemed to doubt him, he frowned. 'In our day Ireland was the Eldorado of the world. I thought everyone knew that! Everything was made of gold. Even our buttons! Even the latchets of our shoes!' And he held out his foot to show that, sure enough, although Packy hadn't noticed it before, the latchets were solid gold. 'It was a good job for us that gold was plentiful,' he said irritably. 'I don't know what we'd do if we had to put up with some of the utensils you have today.'

'Oh, they're not too bad,' said Packy. 'There are grand enamel pails and basins in Leonards of Trim!'

'Is that so?' said the little man coldly. 'Perhaps it's a matter of taste. To be candid with you though, Packy, I wouldn't like to have to spend five thousand years looking at some of the delph on your kitchen-dresser!'

Packy laughed. 'There'd be no fear you'd have to look that long at them,' he said. 'They don't last any time. They's always getting broken.'

'Ah, that's not the way in here,' said the little man. 'Nothing ever gets cracked down here; nothing ever gets broken.'

Packy stared. 'You don't tell me!' he said. 'Do you never knock the handle off a cup, or a jug?' That was a thing he was always doing.

The little man shook his head.

'Oh, but I forgot,' said Packy, 'gold wouldn't break so easily.' Not that he thought it was such a good idea to have cups made of gold. When you'd pour your tea into them, wouldn't it get so hot it would scald the lip off you?

One day in the summer that was gone past, he and the Tubridys went fishing on the Boyne up beyond Rathnally, and they took a few grains of tea with them in case they got dry. They forgot to bring cups though, and they had to empty out their tin-cans of worms and use them for cups. But the metal rim of the can got red hot the minute the tea went into it, and they couldn't drink a drop. Gold would be just the same?

But in fact, there were no cups at all, it appeared.

'One no longer has any need for food, Packy,' said the little man, 'once one has learned the secret of eternal youth!'

'Do you mean you don't eat anything?' cried Packy, 'anything at all? Don't you ever feel hungry?'

'No, child,' said the little man sedately. 'Desire withers when perfection flowers. And if you stay here with us for long, you'll lose all desire too.'

'You're joking, sir!' said Packy, doubtful. At that very minute he had a powerful longing for a cut of bread and a swig of milk. Indeed he glanced involuntarily at the gold milking pails. The Tubridys said the Shee often stole into byres and stripped the cows' udders.

The little man had seen his glance and must have read his thoughts.

'A little harmless fun now and then,' he said, shamefacedly.

Had they been stripping cows lately? Packy wondered. Perhaps there might be a dreg in the bottom of one of the buckets? He craned his neck to see into them. They were all empty!

'I'm very dry, sir.' he said.

'That's only your imagination,' said the little man crossly. 'Stand there for a minute, like a good boy,' he said then, and he darted over to one of the women. 'There's something wrong somewhere,' he said to a woman that was sitting by the harp. And then he snapped his fingers. 'It's the boots,' he cried.

The young woman stood up. 'Give me your boots, son,' she said, 'and I'll get the mud off them.'

Now Packy was always shy of strange women, but this one spoke so like Mrs Tubridy that he felt at home with her at once. And indeed, just as Mrs Tubridy would have done, she caught the sleeve of his coat in her two fists and began to rub off the mud that was caked on it. It didn't brush off so easily though.

'I'll have to take a brush to it,' she said. 'Take your coat off, son, and I'll give it a rub too when I'm doing your boots.'

'That's very kind of you, ma'am,' said Packy, and he took off his coat. It was the coat of his good suit. His mother made him wear it that day so she'd get a chance to put a patch on the elbow of his old one. His vest was the vest belonging to the old suit.

'Is there mud on your vest as well?' asked the young woman.

'Oh no, ma'am,' said Packy. 'That's only splatters of pig-food and chicken-mash.'

'What matter! Give it to me,' she said. 'I may as well make the one job of it.'

But when he took off his vest his shirt was a show.

'That's only sweat-marks,' he protested, knowing she'd proffer to do the shirt as well. But there was no holding back from her any more than from his mother.

'Here, sonny,' she cried. 'Go behind that harp over there and take every stitch off you and we'll get them all cleaned and pressed for you. You can put this on while you're waiting,' she said, and she whipped a green dust-sheet off another harp.

It seemed to Packy that such courtesy was hardly necessary, but he went obediently behind the harp and stripped to the skin. Just as he reached out his hand, however, for the dust-sheet, the young woman came back with a big gold basin of water.

'What's that for?' cried Packy, drawing away from her.

She shoved a towel into his hands.

'Wrap that towel around you,' she said, 'while I try to get some of the dirt off you before you get back into your clean clothes.'

'Mud isn't dirt!' cried Packy indignantly. 'My mother washes me every Saturday night,' he cried, 'and this is only Tuesday.'

At this point the little man hurried over to them.

'It's not a question of cleanliness, Packy,' he said. 'It's a question of hospitality. Surely the ancient customs of the Gael have not fallen into such disuse in Ireland today? Does your mother not offer ablutions to those who cross your threshold?'

'What's that, sir?' said Packy, but he recollected that one day when his teacher called at the cottage, he slipped on the spud-stone at the gate and fell into a puddle, and that day his mother ran into the house and got out a big enamel basin and filled it with water for him to wash his hands. Then she got a towel and wiped the mud off the tail of his coat. She offered him an old pair of his father's pants too, but he wouldn't put them on. Oh, his mother wasn't far behind anyone, he thought, when it came to hospitality. And so, to show that he was very familiar with all such rites, he made an opening in the towel, and unbared first one hand, and then the other.

'That's a good boy,' she said. 'Now your foot. Now the other one!'

She didn't stop at his feet though, and before he knew where he was, there wasn't a cranny of him she hadn't scrubbed.

Never in his life had he been washed like that. It reminded him of the way Mrs Tubridy scoured old grandpa Tubridy's corpse the night he was waked.

He was especially struck with the way the black rims of his nails stood out against his bone-white hands. And he greatly regretted it when the young woman prised out the dirt with a little gold pin. And when she was done with his finger-nails, she began to prod at his toe-nails!

They must be terrible clean people altogether, he thought. His own mother was supposed to be the cleanest woman in the parish, yet she'd never dream of going that far. When his father died, and she was describing the kind of mortuary card she wanted to get for him, she held up her hand to the shopkeeper and showed him the rim of dirt under her nail.

'I want the border of the card as deep as that!' she said. Indeed she'd speak of the black of her nail as readily as another person would speak of the white of his eye!

These people must be terrible particular people, he thought. All those gold basins and gold ewers were for washing themselves, he supposed. And just then the young woman took out a comb and began to rake his hair so hard he felt like as if he'd been sculled. But the comb was solid gold too.

'Oh wait till the Tubridys hear about this,' he said ecstatically.

The young woman looked at him in a very peculiar way, and then she looked at the little man.

'There's something wrong still,' said the little man.

'Are you sure you washed every nook of him?' he asked. He'd got very cross again.

'I did,' said the young woman, and she was cross too.

I hope they're not going to start fighting, while I'm standing here in my skin, thought Packy, and he shivered. He ventured to pluck the little man by the sleeve.

'Excuse me, sir,' he said as politely as possible. 'Are my own clothes near ready do you think?'

But these innocent words seemed to infuriate the little man, and he turned on the young woman again.

'You missed some part of him!' he shouted. 'What about his ears? Did you take the wax out of them?'

'Oh, I forgot,' cried the young woman, and whipping the gold pin out of her bodice again she began to root in his ears.

There was such a lot of wax in his ears, Packy was shamed and he thought he'd better pass it off with a joke.

'I'll have no excuse now but to get up when my mother calls me in the morning,' he said.

But the little man seemed ready to dance with rage at that. 'What about his teeth?' he cried, ignoring him and calling to the young woman. 'Maybe there's a bit of food stuck between them?'

'That's it surely!' cried the young woman. 'Open your mouth, Packy,' she said, and she began to poke between his teeth with the needle, but to no avail. There was not a thing between his bright white teeth.

He had to laugh. 'That's the way the vet opens Bessie's mouth,' he said. 'Bessie is our cow.'

'Bother your cow Bessie,' said the little man, and he caught the young woman by the arm and shook her. 'Could there be a bit of grit in his eye?'

'I don't think so,' said the young woman, 'but we can try!' and she reached out and pushed up his eyelid. 'Nothing there,' she said. Then she looked into his other eye. 'Nothing there either.'

What was all this about? Packy wondered. What were they looking to find? And what about the milk? He thought they were going to try to get him a cup of milk after they'd washed him. He was still thirsty. But it was hardly worth while troubling them to get it for him, because he'd have to be going home. It would be getting very dark in the woods outside, he thought, and he looked around.

'Have you no windows?' he cried.

'What would we want with windows!' the little man exclaimed. 'If some people like to wake up and find the quilt all wet with rain, there are other people who don't,' he said venomously.

'Oh, but it isn't always raining!' cried Packy, knowing it was his own little window at home to which the little man was referring. And thinking of that small square window on a sunny morning his face lit up. There was something to be said for a broken pane at times. 'Once a swallow flew in my window – through the hole in the glass,' he said, and he gave a laugh of delight at the memory of it.

But the young woman made a face.

'Don't talk about birds!' she said. 'Dirty little things, always letting their droppings fall on everything.'

'It's great manure, though,' cried Packy. 'If you could get enough of it, you could make your fortune selling it to the people in the towns.'

At this however the little man shuddered violently.

'We may at times have vague regrets for the world outside, Packy,' he said in an admonitory tone, 'regrets for the stars, and the flowers, and the soft summer breezes, but we are certainly not sorry to have said farewell to the grosser side of life to which you have just now – somewhat indelicately – alluded.'

Packy stared, and there was a puzzled look on his face but suddenly it cleared and he nodded his head sagaciously. 'I suppose you were born in the town, sir?' he said. 'My mother says when people from the towns come out for a day in the country, they never stop talking about the smell of the flowers and the smell of the hay, but give them one smell of a cow shed and they're ready to run back to the town. But it's not a bad smell at all when you're used to it. I

suppose it makes a difference too when you have a cow of your own;
like us. I love the smell of the dung in Bessie's byre!'

'Indeed?' said the little man. 'You don't tell me!' He must have
been sarcastic though, because he turned to the young woman.
'That's the limit!' he said. 'I think we may give him up as a bad job.'
He turned back to Packy. 'Do you still feel the need of a cup of milk?'

'If it's not too much trouble, sir, please,' said Packy.

'I didn't say you were going to get it,' said the little man testily. 'I
asked if you felt the need of it.'

'I do, sir,' said Packy, 'but perhaps it's not worth while bothering
you. I ought to be thinking of getting home.'

'Did you hear that?' the little man cried, fairly screeching, as he
turned to the young woman. 'Oh, there is no doubt about it, there is
something wrong somewhere. We'd better let him go home.'

The young woman looked very sour. 'The sooner the better, if you
ask me,' she said. 'What kind of a child is he at all? Why didn't you
pick an ordinary one?'

'But he *is* an ordinary child,' screamed the little man. 'It's not my
fault, and it's certainly not his!' He turned to Packy. 'Don't mind
her, Packy. Women are all the same, under the hills, or over the
hills. You may as well go home. And you'd be advised to start off
soon, because it will be dark out on the hillside. Wait a minute till I
get your clothes!'

When they got the clothes, Packy couldn't help noticing that the
mud was still on them. And his boots were still in a shocking state.

'Tch, tch, tch!' said the little man. 'Women again! Try to overlook
it, Packy, as a favour to me. – Well? Are you ready? Better take my
hand: it's always easier to get in here than it is to get out!'

Yet a second later Packy saw a chink of light ahead, and it
widened and widened until suddenly he was at the opening of the
hill again, and above him was a great expanse of moonlit sky.

'I'm afraid there was a shower while we were inside,' said the little
man. 'I hope your twigs didn't get wet!'

'Oh, I may leave them till morning anyway,' said Packy. He had
been wondering how he'd carry them the way his finger had begun
to throb with the pain of the thorn in it.

'And why would you do that?' said the little man. 'Won't your
mother want them first thing in the morning?'

'She will,' said Packy, ' – but my finger is beginning to beal, I'm
afraid,' and he stuck it into his mouth again.

'What is the matter with it?' cried the little man. 'Show me!'

'Oh, it's nothing, sir,' said Packy. 'Only an old thorn I got when I
snatched up a bit of blackthorn.'

But the little man was beside himself.

'Show me! Show me!' he screeched. 'A thorn!' and he caught Packy's hand and tried to peer at it, but the moon had gone behind a cloud. He stamped his foot angrily. 'You don't mean to tell me it was there all the time! Oh, weren't we blind! It was *that* thorn kept pulling your mind back to the world. Oh, how was it we didn't see it?'

'How could you see it, sir?' said Packy. 'It's gone in deep. It'll have to have a poultice put on it.'

At that moment the moon sailed into a clearing in the clouds and shone down bright. The little man caught him by the sleeve.

'Will you come back for a minute and we'll take it out for you?' he cried. 'There's nothing safer than a gold pin when probing for a thorn.'

Packy held back. The little man meant well, he supposed, but God help him if he was depending on that same young woman who was supposed to have polished his boots and brushed his suit.

'I'd better go home and get my mother to do it,' he said.

The little man let go of his sleeve.

'All right, Packy,' he said. 'Go home to your mother. I can't blame you. I suppose you see through the whole thing anyway! As long as there was any particle of the earth still on you, you'd never lose your hankering for home. But I hope those women didn't handle you too roughly.'

'Oh not at all, sir,' said Packy politely.

His mother wouldn't have to wash him again for a year of Saturdays.

'Well I'm glad to think you bear no ill will,' said the little man. 'I wouldn't like you to have any hard feelings towards us.' Then he shook his head sadly. 'You must admit it was a bit unfortunate for me to be bested by a bit of a thorn. Ah well, it can't be helped now.'

He looked so sad Packy felt sad too.

'I suppose I'll see you around the woods some time, sir,' he said.

But the little man shook his head from side to side.

'I don't think you will,' he said.

There seemed no more to say.

'Well, I suppose I'd better be going,' said Packy. 'I hope I'll find my way.'

'Oh, you'll find your way all right,' said the little man. 'The moon is a fine big May moon. I'm sorry about your boots,' he added, calling after him, but he couldn't resist a last sly dig. 'Anyway you'd only destroy them again going in through the puddles around your door!'

'Oh, I don't mind the puddles,' said Packy. 'Only for the puddles we couldn't keep ducks; they'd be always straying down to the Boyne, and in the end they'd swim away from us altogether. Puddles have their uses.'

At that the little man laughed.

'I never met the like of you, Packy!' he said. 'Good-bye!'

'Good-bye sir,' said Packy.

And then he was alone.

Slowly he started up the hill until he came to the top where the windflowers were all closed up for the night. But on their shiny leaves the moon lay white. And there, a dark patch in the middle of the glade, was his bundle of twigs.

He gathered them up. His finger was still throbbing but he paid no heed to the pain. Only for that thorn he might never have got out of the cave. Because it wasn't much better than a cave, no matter what the little man said about it. He began to whistle. And when he came to the pathway leading to the gap in the demesne wall he ran down it full-tilt. In a minute he was out on the road again.

There had been a shower all right. All along the road there were puddles. But in every puddle there was a star. And when he got to the cottage the puddles around the door were as big as ever, but in them shone the whole glory of the heavens.

'Is that you, Packy?' cried the widow, running out to the door in a terrible state. 'What kept you so late, son?'

'Oh, wait till I tell you,' cried Packy, although he knew right well what she'd say:

A likely story!

The Patriot Son

It was a couple of years since Sean Mongon had set foot in Conerty's shop, so what did he want now?

From the window in the gable-end Matty saw him swinging down the street, and the next minute he walked in the doorway and up to the counter.

'Will you display this in your window, Matty, like a good chap?' he said casually, and he unrolled a cheaply-printed poster, the paper like a blotter, on which lettering had made a blurred impress.

As far as Matty could see it was a play-bill, with a crude picture of a woman in green in the middle of it, and the wording seemed to be in Gaelic, or in Gaelic letters. He partly guessed what it was, and he glanced uneasily across the shop to the haberdashery, where his mother was serving a customer. She never liked any of the Mongons. And although Matty could remember a time when their own shop was just as small as Mongon's, before the new barracks was built opposite them, yet his mother always referred to the Mongons' shop as poky and smelly, and she wondered how people could eat anything that came out of it.

But the Mongons did a good trade; particularly with the farmers from outside the town. Once when he was a child he had asked his mother why the country people did not tie up their traps and donkey-carts in their yard, like they did in Mongon's.

'Because we live opposite the barracks,' she said promptly, and pulling out the till from under the counter she ran the silver through her fingers like water. 'One R.I.C. man coming into the shop with his shilling in his hand is better than twenty traps tied in the yard and the ledgers swelling with debt! God bless the Constabulary!' she said.

And when, at that moment, through the window, they saw the Head Constable walking down the street, with his stomach out and his arms swinging, she shook her head.

'Isn't it a terrible thing to think a fine man like that would have enemies?' she cried.

For a minute he didn't know what she meant.

'Some people never can let bygones be bygones,' she went on. 'It's the Fenian bitterness. It's like a disease that's passed down from father to son. God protect us all!'

He knew then that she was having a dig at the Mongons, because Sean's grandfather had been a Fenian. The Mongons had his uniform in a box on top of the piano. Sean brought him in to see it one day after school. But he had been careful not to tell his mother about it. She was death on the Fenians.

'Oh, you know nothing of what people suffered in those days, son!' she said.

They were in the kitchen at the time of this conversation. He was sitting at the kitchen table doing his homework and she was standing stirring a pot on the range. But she was looking out of the window and after a few minutes she gave a big sigh.

'It would be a terrible thing if it were all to break out again,' she said softly, almost to herself, and the look on her face frightened the wits out of him.

'What do you mean, Mother?' he cried.

She turned to him.

'I'm afraid, son, there is some of the bad old seed still in the ground,' she said. 'The Head Constable was in the shop a while ago and he told me something: there are men drilling in the hills again!' She looked away for a minute, and then she turned and looked steadily at his face. 'Thank God you're only a child still,' she said.

Matty squirmed uncomfortably on his chair; he wasn't such a child at all: the following year he'd be leaving school.

It was just before the end of that year that the Gaelic classes were started. They were to be held at night in the school-house, and Master Cullen was giving his services free as teacher. Needless to say, Sean Mongon was the first to join them.

'Oh, come on, Matty,' he cried. 'Join up! We'll have great sport at them. And afterwards, to warm us up, the Master says he'll push back the benches and have a bit of a dance. It'll be great sport. The Master knows all the old jigs and reels, and the Walls of Limerick, and the Bridge of Athlone. We'll have the best of times!'

For his own part, Matty was inclined to go to the classes, just to be in the swim of things. But he was uneasy about what his mother would say. He knew her views on the Language Revival.

'What next?' she demanded, when she first read about the Gaelic League, and the language classes that were being held in Dublin. 'Do they want to drive the people backward instead of forward?'

He'd never have the face to tell her he was going to the classes.

'I'll have to ask my mother,' he said, shamefacedly.

Sean looked at him, at first incredulous, then contemptuous.

'Maybe you ought to ask leave of the R.I.C. as well!' he said. 'It wouldn't do to offend them, they're such good customers!'

Matty felt his face flush all over. And Sean saw it.

'Sorry!' he said, surprisingly, and his smile, that was always so winning, flashed across his face. 'I'm a bit on edge these days,' he said. 'No hard feelings, eh? It's just that we don't want the R.I.C. poking their noses into the classes. The next thing they'd be branding them as illegal organizations! They're terrible eejits in spite of everything.'

Did he fancy it, Matty wondered, or did Sean look at him slyly before he sauntered away. Anyway, he did not go to the classes that winter. And the next winter, although he had left school, he did not go to them either, in spite of the fact that by then the Gaelic League had got itself accepted all over the country, and had established centres in every town and village. As for Master Cullen's classes, they were held openly and boldly. Nearly all the young people in the town went to them, and some of the older people used to go down and stand at the door later in the evenings to look at the dancing. The R.I.C. themselves used to stroll down sometimes and stand in the doorway.

Matty's mother could hardly object to him joining the classes then, but she kept him so late in the shop, and he was so dog-tired when the shutters were put up at last, that by the time he got down to the school-house it wasn't worth while doing anything but hang about the door with the other onlookers. It all seemed very harmless; and he was aware only of the heat and the dust, the sweating faces of the men, the clapping of hands, and the stamping of feet.

But there were other nights when it was too late to go down at all, and then, looking out of the window as he was going to bed, the school-house lights, twinkling across the roofs of the other houses, troubled him, as he used to be troubled when he was a child by tales of faery lights that shone on the darksome bog to lure men to folly and destruction.

It was on those occasions that he was glad his mother had kept him from getting involved in what went on down there. He had begun to wonder if it was all as innocent as it seemed.

And now this play? Was it only what it purported to be; a little entertainment: or was there some undercurrent of intrigue? He looked dubiously at the play-bill he was being asked to display.

But Sean saw his hesitation, and he laughed.

'There are no flies on you, Matty, are there?' he said, and he winked, but affably, and not with any pronounced discretion. Suddenly he leant across the counter. 'It's supposed to be *The Colleen Bawn*,' he said, 'but we've doctored a good few of the lines. Do you get me? It's going a bit further than Irish classes, and jigs and reels, but it's time we showed more guts. Things have changed, haven't they?' he said, and he laughed, and jerked his head in the direction of the barracks across the street. 'We've moved forward since the time we were nervous about the classes at night in the school-house! They know all about them now; or at least they think they do: but they're afraid to take any action in case they might mistake the sheep for the goats. They don't know who to trust, and who to mistrust. And that's the way to have them. I hear they're even beginning to distrust each other. And so well they might. Did you see in the papers where an R.I.C. man down in – '

But at this moment, across the shop Matty caught his mother's baleful eye upon him, and he saw that outside the counter there was a small child with a halfpenny in its hand.

'Excuse me a minute, Sean,' he said awkwardly. 'I'll have to wait on this youngster.'

He hoped he'd go. But instead, Mongon took up the play-bill.

'I'll put this in the window for you. I think that's the best place for it, don't you?' he said, leaning into the window and draping it across the job lot of cups and saucers that were being offered that week at a special price.

When the youngster had gone he turned back to Matty.

'Do you know what I was thinking?' he said, and he chuckled. 'I was thinking that it's a picture of you we ought to have on the poster – a bloody little shopkeeper – and a banner around your arm to say that you were the Ireland of Today!'

Matty stared at him. Was he trying to be funny, he wondered. If so, it was a poor joke, specially when his mother could probably overhear everything that was said.

But Sean didn't seem to be joking, or at least he didn't look very light-hearted.

'Poor ignorant Ireland,' he said suddenly, in a low voice, as if to himself. 'Poor ignorant Ireland that doesn't want to be saved!'

Matty shrugged his shoulders. He must be cracked, he decided. And he wished harder than ever he would go about his business.

But still Sean stayed, leaning against the counter and looking around him.

'It's a long time since I was here, isn't it?' he said. 'But it's the same old place I see. You haven't made any changes, have you?' His eye strayed idly, it would seem, all over the shop and came to rest on the green baize door at the end. 'That door leads into the house, doesn't it?' he asked, pointing to it. 'Isn't that the way we used to run in and out the yard?'

'I suppose so,' said Matty flatly. He wanted to get rid of him. He could feel his mother's eyes boring holes in his head.

At long last Sean went.

'Well, so long!' he said inconsequentially, and sauntered out.

Partly drawn by the old fascination that the other always exerted on him, and partly to avoid meeting his mother's eyes, Matty went over to the gable window and looked up the street after him, but he could hear his mother crossing the shop and almost immediately she came and stood beside him looking out of the window.

'You ought to be more careful about who you're seen talking to nowadays, Matty,' she said, lowering her voice although they were alone. 'The Sergeant was telling me that several people in this town are under observation. I shouldn't be surprised if Sean Mongon was one of them. I hope he won't make a habit of coming down here. What did he want, anyway?'

Before he had time to tell her, however, she had seen the play-bill draped across the things in the window. Instantly she whipped it out of the window.

'So this is what brought him down here, is it?' she cried, and as she read it her eyes blazed. The next minute she tore it savagely in two bits. Matty was sure she was going to turn on him, but instead she spoke surprisingly gently, almost wheedlingly to him. 'I suppose you were right to let on we'd display it,' she said, 'but wouldn't it be an awful thing if you forgot to take it out of the window and the Head Constable passed and saw it?'

Matty looked at the torn poster. She had made it seem as if he would have torn it up if she hadn't done so.

It might be uncomfortable all right, he thought, to have had it in the window if the Head Constable came into the shop. But it would be ten times more uncomfortable if Sean came back and did not see it displayed anywhere.

What would he do then, he thought miserably? He wished she wouldn't interfere with everything he did. She was an interfering woman if ever there was one. Ever since he was a child. She had dictated to him in everything. Always the same, he thought bitterly. He'd never get a chance to say or do anything while she had her foot on his neck. And he'd never get away from her, because she'd never let him look at a girl, much less marry one, and bring her into the house. There wasn't a girl in the whole town that would have the courage to marry him, and come into the same house as her.

And then, freakishly, there flashed into his mind the image of the girl on the play-bill, and although he had only barely glimpsed her, it seemed as if she had some enormous strength or power that would vanquish any enemy – even his mother.

A paper woman! I must be cracked, he thought, and he set his mind to think of some excuse to make to Sean if he happened to find out they hadn't displayed the poster.

But it was to be three or four weeks before he met Sean again. And the circumstances of the meeting put the poster out of their minds.

One evening Matty had finished up earlier than usual and he had taken it into his head to stroll down to the school-house to watch the dancing. But when he turned into the school-yard to his surprise the school-house windows were dark and the building was empty. He went up to the door and rattled the handle. The door was locked. As he raised his head though, on the sweet spring air he got the faint smell of cigarette smoke, and looking down he saw that the gravel under his feet was marked with fresh footprints and the tyre-marks of bicycles. So they had been here! But why had they gone so early?

Uneasily he moved away from the black shadow of the building into the open moonlit yard. A ridiculous notion passed through his mind: the faery light! Had it lured them away – the gay throng – away from their warm habitations to the cold inhuman hills and the dark glensides?

A shiver ran over him, but he laughed at himself for his foolishness, and he went home to bed.

But he slept badly, disturbed by dreams of faery hosts and lonely glens, and woke when the dawn was coming up the sky. He got to his feet and went to the window.

There was nothing to be seen but the sight that had met his eyes every day since he was born, the ugly concrete walls of the new barracks, and the corrugated roofs of its sheds and out-houses.

Then, just as he was about to get back into bed, between the barracks and the corrugated sheds, he caught a glimpse of the green, dawn-lit fields beyond the town. And as they had never done in full daylight, those green fields called to him; a clear, sweet call. Unquestioningly he answered their call and in a few minutes he was stealing down the stairs so as not to waken his mother. In the street he paused too, and glanced uneasily at the windows of the barracks. The Constabulary, if they happened to see him, might think it odd of him to be out so early. For the rumours of men drilling were no longer so vague. All over the country men were drilling. And people who were not involved were careful to avoid doing anything irregular. But there was no one on foot in the barracks, and he passed unnoticed out of the town.

About two miles outside the town there was an old deserted castle sunk deep in the middle of a lush, waterlogged field. Sometimes in summer he used to cross the field and wander in its dark passages and vaulted arcades, but in winter it was a lonely place, and only served him as a landmark. At this point he usually turned homeward. This morning too, he was about to turn upon coming in sight of it, when his eye was caught by a thin feather of smoke wavering in the air from one of the thick buttressed chimneys. And almost at the same moment, on the other side of the hedge beside the road, he heard a sound of splashing in the little stream that had for some distance run along beneath the hedge.

Impulsively he called out and bent over the hedge.

To his astonishment it was Sean Mongon. For a minute it looked as if he was going to turn tail and run, until he saw it was Matty.

'Oh, it's only you!' he cried.

But Matty was stung to the quick by his tone.

'Who did you think it was?' he cried, nettled. 'Did you think it was the Constabulary?'

Still, he didn't expect Sean to take him up so sharply.

'How much do you know, Conerty?' he said.

Matty stared. There he was – Sean Mongon – whom he had known all his life; there he was – on the other side of the hedge too – a puny figure really, as slight as a girl, and looking – he noted – haggard and worn-out as if for want of sleep, and yet he was in some way a menacing, a dangerous figure.

But it was not fear that surged up in Matty, it was a grudging admiration.

'I don't know anything,' he said truthfully, even sadly. 'I wish I did!' he added with such fervour that Sean stared at him. 'Yes,' he cried recklessly, 'I wish I was in it – whatever it is, that is going on – I always did, but my mother came between me and it – the Movement, I mean,' he said out boldly.

Sean continued to stare at him.

'I wonder do you mean that,' he said soberly. 'I think you do. And I'm glad to hear you say it – at least. But it's too late now, Matty. You'll have to continue to be one of the onlookers.' He was making a reference to the Gaelic classes, thought Matty, and he felt ashamed of how early his caution had taken command of him. 'Go back to your shop, Matty,' said Sean then, gently, but with a tone of authority. 'The shopboys will soon be taking down the shutters and your mother will be wondering why you're not up and about your business. She'll be knocking at your door. Get back as fast as you can. You don't want her asking questions, do you? That wouldn't help us, you know!' He himself glanced to the east where the rapidly rising sun was striking through the trees as through a grille. 'I must be getting along,' he said in his casual way, and he began to stride back in the direction of the old castle, leaving Matty to stare disconsolately after him.

He was in his bare feet, Matty noticed, with his trousers rolled up, and the wet grass had stuck to his ankles, striping his white skin.

It was something that he had been trusted to keep silent, he thought bitterly, as he walked homeward in dejection.

In the town the shutters were still up on the shop-windows, and when he reached his own street he saw that even the barrack door was shut, and there was no smoke from its chimneys. Except for an old man pushing a handcart of straw in front of him, there was no sign of life in the whole street. And even the old man had a grotesque aspect, like a figure out of a dream, with his ragged clothes and his ramshackle handcart, one wheel of which was wobbling about as if at any moment it would roll from under the cart and let it down on the cobbles.

Amused, Matty followed the wobbly movement of the old man and his cart, and then, just as he was about to turn in to his own door, the wheel, with one last wobble, fell flat on the street, and the cart came down on its axle with a clatter, up-ending its load.

As the old fellow let out a loud volley of oaths, Matty laughed heartily. And from the barrack door which opened, one of the constables poked out his head and laughed also, and nodded across at Matty. There seemed no more to the incident, and Matty went into the shop to begin his day's work. Later in the morning, as he was lending a hand in taking down the shutters, he saw the old fellow trying to raise the wheel, but when he put his hand on it, the rotted wood came away from the rim and the whole thing fell flat again. So, after some words with the police, the old fellow shrugged his shoulders and went off up the street, presumably to find some means of putting his vehicle into motion again, or of getting some other conveyance to cart away the straw that, in the crisp breezes of the morning, was beginning to blow about the street. Already it had almost blocked up the mouth of the barracks.

But the police, as they came in and out of the shop during the day for their cigarettes and tobacco, took it in good part. It was his own mother who took it badly.

'A nice thing!' she cried, a score of times, or more, as she went to the window and looked out. 'A nice mess!'

It was when she was looking out on one of these occasions, late in the day, that Matty saw her frown, and looking over her shoulder he saw Sean coming down the street.

'What does this fellow want now?' she cried, and as if unable to endure the sight of him, she left the shop.

As for Matty, the incident of the upset cart in the street had taken his mind off the events of the earlier morning, but now, at the sight of Sean, his heart began to beat violently.

Had Sean come to look for him? He hurried forward to meet him. But Sean was calm and matter-of-fact.

'Hello, Matty,' he said easily, naturally. 'Can you spare me a few cans of paraffin oil?'

It was a bit of an anti-climax, and it made Matty cranky. He had only come on business. Ostentatiously, Sean threw down a pound note on the counter.

For a minute Matty hesitated. There was only a small profit on paraffin oil, and it was a troublesome commodity; it had to be kept outside the shop in the lobby near the yard door, and anyone handling it had to be careful not to contaminate anything else with the smell of it, and so it was usual only to supply it to regular customers.

'I'm sorry to bother you,' said Sean, as if he sensed Matty's reluctance. 'I'm not a customer, I know.' He paused. 'We usually get it in Flynn's, but – well, they didn't have any today,' he finished lamely.

'Oh, that's all right,' said Matty, and he began to take off his shop-coat. 'Have you got a can?' he asked, unable to resist making a compliment of giving it, but he regretted it next minute, as Sean began to make excuses. 'Oh, it doesn't matter, it's all right,' he said hastily. 'This way!' And he went out through the baize door into the little lobby where the big storage tank was kept. There he stooped down, and picked up a can. 'How much will I give you?' he asked.

But Sean was hardly heeding him as he stared around the lobby.

'Oh, fill it up,' he said casually, and going over to the door leading into the yard, he opened it and looked out. 'It's the same old place,' he said. 'I remember it well. I could make my way around here blindfold!' He stepped back and pointed to the other door, the house door, as it was called, that was opposite the baize door. 'That's the way into the front of the house, isn't it?' he asked. 'We used to go out into the street that way.'

But like the last time he heard them, these reminiscences of their boyish friendship sounded empty to Matty. He ignored them.

'It holds a gallon,' he said, putting a cap on the tin, and holding it out to him.

But Sean was peering into a dark corner behind the tank and the wall, and seeing a few old cans thrown together in a heap, he took up two with one hand and three with the other.

'Fill these up too, will you?' he said casually.

Matty was both irritated and surprised.

'Have you a car?' he asked, as he filled the fourth can.

'No,' said Sean shortly, 'but I'll manage them all right.' He took up two of the cans. 'I'll take these with me, and I'll call back for the rest. You can leave them somewhere convenient to the street. Better still, I'll leave them all and I'll get some kind of conveyance for them. But it may be late in the evening; the shop will probably be closed: you'd better leave them in the front hall, if you can manage it. Just inside the hall door would be the best place,' he said. Then he straightened up. 'Have you got that?' he said, in what Matty thought an impudent manner for one who was under a compliment to him. But evidently there was no offence meant, because Sean stooped and lifted two of the cans. 'I'll give you a hand,' he said. 'We may as well leave them out there now so there'll be no mistake.'

'Oh, there's no need,' said Matty.

He was wondering what his mother would say to cluttering up the front hall, but he decided that she seldom went into the hall anyway, and that it was so dark and dingy she might not see them even if she did go into it. He would prefer to put them there himself a little later. 'That'll be all right,' he repeated as he put the lid on the big drum of oil. Without waiting for him, Sean was about to go away, but on an impulse he turned around.

'Is there much left in the drum?' he asked.

Thinking he wanted more, Matty slapped the lid down ostentatiously.

'A few gallons,' he said, 'but I can't give you any more. I can't empty the tank for you. It wouldn't do to let our regular customers go short.'

'Oh, I don't want any more,' said Sean. 'I have more than enough. I just thought it might be no harm if that drum was empty tonight.'

Matty looked up. It was the kind of cryptic remark that lately he seemed to be hearing on all sides, and he was inclined to let it pass, but all at once a thought flashed into his mind – but it was too preposterous.

'You're not – you can't mean –?'

And then he remembered the cart-load of straw that still, at that late hour, stood outside the barracks. And without another word being spoken he knew all.

'You can't do it!' he cried. 'You'd be mad to try it!'

'Don't shout, you fool!' snapped Sean. Then, with less urgency, and speaking in a lower voice, he looked at Matty with something approximating to admiration. 'I didn't think you were so quick on the uptake,' he said, but he had moved nearer, and feeling him uncomfortably close in the small lobby, Matty looked down and saw that from his pocket there protruded the point of a gun. 'I only meant to do you a good turn, Matty,' said Sean, 'but take care you don't turn good into bad.'

Matty swallowed hard.

'I don't know what you mean!'

Immediately Sean stepped back from him.

'That's the right attitude to take!' he cried, slapping his thigh. 'I told you nothing. And you guessed nothing. See!'

Matty kept steady, although he was appalled.

'All right, Sean. You can trust me.'

Visibly, for a moment, the other relaxed.

'I know that,' he said. Then he got tense again. 'It's not only my own trust I'm putting in you,' he said savagely, 'but the trust of twenty or thirty men – perhaps even the trust of the whole Movement –'

Although he had begun to shudder violently, Matty's eyes did not falter.

'I know that,' he said steadily.

'I think you do,' said Sean soberly. Then suddenly he gave a kick to the cans. 'I won't wait to leave them out in the hall,' he said. 'You can do it for me.'

It was only an errand fit for a child, but it carried the implication of an enormous trust. Speechless, Matty nodded his head. His face was deadly white, and seeing that, perhaps, Sean put out a hand and rested it upon his shoulder.

'Look here,' he said, 'I told you nothing – we've agreed upon that – but there's no reason why you shouldn't empty that thing down the drain' – he nodded at the drum – 'and as a matter of fact, you might find some reason for being away from here tonight. Not that I think there'll be any danger, but I admit the street is narrow and a lot depends on the way the wind is blowing – you'd never know – you could take anything valuable with you – money or the like – nothing that would be remarkable, of course – nothing that would attract attention.'

The suggestion was meant to be friendly, Matty knew that. But at the same time he felt there was something belittling in the concession.

'Thanks, Sean,' he said quietly, 'but I think I'll stay here.' Then, with dismay, he remembered his mother. 'Oh, what about my mother?' he cried. 'I suppose she ought to be got out of here?'

Sean only shrugged his shoulders.

'If you can manage it without it appearing odd,' he said, 'to her, I mean.'

'You can leave it to me,' said Matty, wanting to reassure him. 'I won't make a false step.'

Like sunlight in the dingy lobby, Sean's smile broke over him.

'He that is not against me is with me, eh?' he said, and turning back towards the shop, he went out that way.

Picking up the cans in twos, Matty carried them into the hall.

It was dark there all right, and getting darker too, because already the day had begun to fade. With a little feeling of relief he realized that at least there would not be long hours of suspense. Whatever was to happen would be likely to commence soon enough. It was not yet time for the shop to close, but the shutters had already been brought in from the yard and stood against the wall. Once the shop was closed he need not worry if his mother found the tins. It would appear fairly reasonable then that they were left convenient to the hall door.

The shop was over an hour closed when she discovered them.

'Matty, what is all this paraffin doing here?' she cried.

Matty was at the back of the house, afraid that he might give anything away by looking out too often if he were in any of the front rooms. But just as he wondered what answer to give to her, with every nerve thrilling, his strained ears caught a sound in the street. Ignoring all but that sound, he stood transfixed.

His mother too heard something.

'Was that a shout?' she said, coming back from the hall, her face white. 'Listen!' she commanded. 'The Constabulary are challenging someone!'

But there was another sound, fainter than shout or challenge, which caught Matty's ear. It was a faint crackling sound, and the next minute he smelled something smouldering. Then his mother too got the smell.

'Oh, good God!' she cried. 'It's a fire – it's the barracks. The barracks is burning!' She made as if to rush out to the street, but he put out his arm. She strained to pass him. 'Will you let me pass?' she cried. 'What's the matter with you?'

It was something in the expression on his face that answered her.

'Oh, God!' she whispered, no longer straining against him. 'It's not malicious, is it?'

Malicious! It was a word out of the civilian life from which, without knowing it until that moment, he had already long since passed. Malicious: more than all the words that one by one had measured the difference between them since he was a child, this one word showed them to be sundered for ever. But he said nothing. Feverishly she was making the Sign of the Cross.

'Oh, God help them!' she whispered. 'Caught like rats in a trap.'

Then, suddenly, her thoughts veered. 'Which way is the wind?' she cried. 'Are the sparks flying this way?' She swung around towards the lobby. 'The oil drum,' she exclaimed. 'One spark would be enough –'

But before one thought was completed, another had taken its place.

'Those cans in the hall,' she cried. 'Get them out of there.' And when he didn't move, she darted towards the door. He caught her by the arm.

'Leave them there, Mother,' he said. 'They may be coming for them any minute.'

They? She turned around. And then the full enormity of the truth broke over her.

'Oh, God in Heaven!' she cried. 'It wasn't for that you sold the oil? You don't mean to say you knew all about it and you never told me – we could have warned them – we could have –' She wrung her hands. 'We could have done something,' she groaned. Then all at once she pulled herself together. 'Perhaps it's not too late yet. Those cans in the hall, you say they're coming back for them! I'll spoil their game there, anyway. Never mind about what's done: it can't be helped. Please God they'll never find out you had any hand in it –' She had broken away from him and reached the door, but at the door she couldn't help turning around. 'Oh, how could you do it?' she cried. 'Haven't I been all my life warning you against the like? Do you think a handful of fools are going to get the better of trained men like the R.I.C.? The constabulary will make bits of them, I tell you. And you along with them if they find out about these – but with God's help they won't find out. Here, give me a hand!'

As she caught up the cans, however, the voices in the street became louder, and there was a sound of running feet followed by a crash against the door behind which they stood, and then heavily, frantically, two fists beat against the panels.

'It's Sean! He wants the cans,' said Matty, 'and he's going to get them too,' he cried, as he tried to drag the cans out of her hand.

But the fists beat against the door again.

'Let me in, for Christ's sake,' said a voice. It was Sean all right. 'Don't mind the bloody cans but open the door.'

Both together, mother and son, let go the cans, and the oil spilled over the floor. In a second the hall was filled with the acrid smell. But they had both let go from different motives.

'Don't dare to open that door!' screamed the woman, and she threw herself forward.

But Matty had got there before her and the door was open.

Almost falling over them, Sean lurched forward.

'Why the hell didn't you open the door?' he rasped, as he stood panting and trying to get his breath. 'Close it now, you fool,' he cried, as hypnotized, Matty stood looking at him. 'Close it and lock it,' he cried. 'Put on those chains,' he cried, pointing to the rusty old chain that hung down inside it but was never used. 'The whole thing failed,' he said when he got his breath.

Matty looked up.

'I didn't –' he began.

'I know that,' said Sean, and he gave a bitter laugh. 'You'd be a dead bunny now if you did! No, it was the bloody straw let us down – it got damp, I suppose, out there in the street all evening; it wouldn't catch when we went to set fire to it – it only smouldered, and the beggars smelled the smoke. But we got away,' he cried. 'That's one good thing. And if we failed tonight, we won't fail the next time. Listen!' he said. 'They're searching the street, but I don't suppose they'll think of trying here.' He gave the dry laugh again. 'They'd never suspect you of being a patriot!' he said.

But there were sounds of someone approaching.

'What's that?' cried Sean, alert again.

'They're coming over here,' whispered Matty, the sweat pouring from him. 'Listen!'

Sean listened.

'I was expecting too much,' he said calmly. 'I'll have to get moving,' and he ran into the back lobby. But as he passed the oil vat he stopped. 'I'll throw this thing in here in the dark,' he said, and dragging off the old whitish trench-coat that was like a second skin to him, it was constantly on his back, he threw it behind the oil drum. 'I'll travel lighter without it,' he cried, 'and besides, it's too easily seen at night.'

They had forgotten the old woman, but as, at that moment, there was a violent knocking on the door, they became aware of her again. She was dragging at the chain and bolts.

'It's all right, constable,' she was shouting. 'I'm opening it as quick as I can. He's gone out the back way!'

Like a flame from the abortive fire, Matty felt shame run over him. But even in that preposterous moment, Sean put out a hand and laid it for an instant on his shoulder.

'It isn't your fault,' he said, and then as the yard door opened before him he prepared to plunge into the darkness. But on the brink he hesitated, and suddenly he turned back. 'Wait a minute! She may have done me more good than harm,' he cried. 'Prop open this door, like as if it was usually kept open – with that,' he cried, indicating with his foot an old iron weight on the floor. Then, with a last reckless laugh at Matty's stupefaction, he slipped behind the propped door.

It was so simple. Matty stared stupidly. He hardly understood, but it was a chance, he could see that; even if it was only a small one. As long as his mother hadn't seen them! But the oil drum was behind them, and the view from the front hall was broken by the cross-door that had almost closed after them. It might work out!

A tremendous excitement possessed him. If only there was something he could do! If he could put the police off the scent!

Suddenly, behind the big oil drum, he caught sight of the old trench-coat bundled into a ball. He rushed over and pulled it out.

The next minute he heard the front door crash open and the constabulary rushed into the hall.

Pulling the old trench-coat over him, Matty ran to the yard door, but on the threshold he waited for an instant till he heard the running feet reach the cross-door. They must catch a glimpse of him. The next minute he was racing across the yard.

What was it Sean planned to do? To get across the sheds and out into the next yard, and from there into the next, and the next?

As kids they used to scramble up on the sheds, but although he made for the lowest of them, the little pig-shed in the corner, he found he wasn't as agile as he used to be. Still he managed to grasp the ragged edge of the corrugated-iron roof and frantically he began to pull himself up on it. As his head came level with the tin he saw that although the yard was dark, it was dark from being overhung with buildings; above him the sky was brilliant with stars. And all at once, compounded out of the very stars it seemed, a spirit of elation flowed through him, such as he had never before experienced. And it seemed as if something that had eluded him all his life was all at once within his grasp.

Pushing his hands further forward on the rusty iron, and letting go his foothold, he exerted a tremendous pressure and heaved his body upward. But the next moment the house behind him was filled with shouts and then – as loud as if they had rained into his mouth, his eyes, his ears – the air was shattered with shots. And at the same moment he felt a ripping pain run like the jag of a knife down the side of his belly.

They got me, he thought, as he fell forward on his face. But the thought did nothing to dispel his elation which seemed only to grow greater, until in a kind of intoxication of excitement he lay there, feeling the hot blood trickling down inside his torn clothes.

It was a few minutes before it occurred to him that it was odd that they had not come looking for him. From where he lay, by raising his head, he could see the house, and the lighted door through which he had run out. No one had come through it! They were all still inside, the police, and – yes – his mother too. With difficulty he raised his head: they were bending over something. At first it looked like an old sack of potatoes, but as it twitched suddenly he saw it was a body: the body of Sean Mongon.

And at the same moment, the pain that had lacerated him tore again into his guts, and putting down his hand he felt the jagged fang of the rusted iron that had cut into him like a bullet.

Then his mother's voice came clear above the other voices that now were in the yard below him.

'He's up there on the top of the pig-shed!' she cried, and her voice was wheedling. 'He must have been frightened out of his wits!' she said.

And coming nearer, she called up to him:

'Come down out of that, you gom!'

The Great Wave

The Bishop was sitting in the stern of the boat. He was in his robes, with his black overcoat thrown across his shoulders for warmth, and over his arm he carried his vestments, turned inside out to protect them from the salt spray. The reason he was already robed was because the distance across to the island was only a few miles, and the island priest was spared the embarrassment of a long delay in his small damp sacristy.

The islanders had a visit from their Bishop only every four years at most, when he crossed over, as now, for the Confirmation cere-mony, and so to have His Grace arrive thus in his robes was only their due share: a proper prolongation of episcopal pomp. In his albe and amice he would easily be picked out by the small knot of islanders who would gather on the pier the moment the boat was sighted on the tops of the waves. Yes: it was right and proper for all that the Bishop be thus attired. His Grace approved. The Bishop had a reason of his own too, as it happened, but it was a small reason, and he was hardly aware of it anywhere but in his heart.

Now, as he sat in the boat, he wrapped his white skirts tighter around him, and looked to see that the cope and chasuble were well doubled over, so that the coloured silks would not be exposed when they got away from the lee of the land and the waves broke on the sides of the currach. The cope above all must not be tarnished. That was why he stubbornly carried it across his arm: the beautiful cope that came all the way from Stansstad, in Switzerland, and was so overworked with gilt thread that it shone like cloth of gold. The orphreys, depicting the birth and childhood of Christ, displayed the most elaborate work that His Grace had ever seen come from the Paramentenwerkstätte, and yet he was far from unfamiliar with the work of the Sisters there, in St Klara. Ever since he attained the bishopric he had commissioned many beautiful vestments and altar cloths for use throughout the diocese. He had once, at their instigation, broken a journey to Rome to visit them. And when he was there, he asked those brilliant women to explain to him the marvel, not of their skill, but of his discernment of it, telling them of his birth and early life as a simple boy, on this island towards which he was now faced.

'Mind out!' he said, sharply, as one of the men from the mainland who was pushing them out with the end of an oar, threw the oar into the boat, scattering the air with drops of water from its glossy blade. 'Could nothing be done about this?' he asked, seeing water under the bottom boards of the boat. It was only a small sup, but it rippled up and down with a little tide of its own, in time with the tide outside that was already carrying them swiftly out into the bay.

'Tch, tch, tch,' said the Bishop, for some of this water had saturated the hem of the albe, and he set about tucking it under him upon the seat. And then, to make doubly sure of it, he opened the knot of his cincture and re-tied it as tight about his middle as if it were long ago and he was tying up a sack of spuds at the neck. 'Tch, tch,' he repeated, but no one was unduly bothered by his ejaculations because of his soft and mild eyes, and, didn't they know him? They knew that in his complicated, episcopal life he had to contend with a lot, and it was known that he hated to give his old housekeeper undue thumping with her flat iron. But there was a thing would need to be kept dry – the crozier!

'You'd want to keep that yoke there from getting wet through, Your Grace,' said one of the men, indicating the crozier that had fallen on the boards. For all that they mightn't heed his little old-womanish ways, they had a proper sense of what was fitting for an episcopal appearance.

'I could hold the crozier perhaps,' said Father Kane, the Bishop's secretary, who was farther up the boat. 'I still think it would be more suitable for the children to be brought over to you on the mainland, than for you to be traipsing over here like this, and in those foreign vestments at that!'

He is thinking of the price that was paid for them, thought the Bishop, and not of their beauty or their workmanship. And yet, he reflected, Father Kane was supposed to be a highly-educated man, who would have gone on for a profession if he hadn't gone for the priesthood, and who would not have had to depend on the seminary to put the only bit of gloss on him he'd ever get – Like me – he thought! And he looked down at his beautiful vestments again. A marvel, no less, he thought, savouring again the miracle of his power to appreciate such things.

'It isn't as if *they'll* appreciate them over there,' said Father Kane, with sudden venom, looking towards the island, a thin line of green on the horizon.

'Ah, you can never say that for certain,' said the Bishop mildly, even indifferently. 'Take me, how did I come to appreciate such things?'

But he saw the answer in the secretary's hard eyes. He thinks it was parish funds that paid for my knowledge, and diocesan funds for putting it into practice! And maybe he's right! The Bishop smiled to himself. Who knows anything at all about how we're shaped, or where we're led, or how in the end we are ever brought to our rightful haven?

'How long more till we get there?' he asked, because the island was no longer a vague green mass. Its familiar shapes were coming into focus; the great high promontory throwing its purple shade over the shallow fields by the shore, the sparse white cottages, the cheap cement pier, constantly in need of repairs. And, higher up, on a ledge of the promontory itself there was the plain cement church, its spire only standing out against the sky, bleak as a crane's neck and head.

To think the full height of the promontory was four times the height of the steeple!

The Bishop gave a great shudder. One of the rowers was talking to him.

'Sure, Your Grace ought to know all about this bay. Ah, but I suppose you forget them days altogether now!'

'Not quite, not quite,' said the Bishop quickly. He slipped his hand inside his robes and rubbed his stomach that had begun already to roll after only a few minutes of the swell.

When he was a little lad, over there on the island, he used to think he'd run away, some day, and join the crew of one of the French fishing trawlers that were always moving backwards and forwards on the rim of the sky. He used to go to a quiet place in the shade of the Point, and settling into a crevice in the rocks, out of reach of the wind, he'd spend the day long staring at the horizon; now in the direction of Liverpool, now in the direction of the Norwegian fjords.

Yet, although he knew the trawlers went from one great port to another, and up even as far as Iceland, he did not really associate them with the sea. He never thought of them as at the mercy of it in the way the little currachs were that had made his mother a widow, and that were jottled by every wave. The trawlers used to seem out of reach of the waves, away out on the black rim of the horizon.

He had in those days a penny jotter in which he put down the day and hour a trawler passed, waiting precisely to mark it down until it passed level with the pier. He put down also other facts about it which he deduced from the small vague outline discernible at that distance. And he smiled to remember the sense of satisfaction and achievement he used to get from that old jotter, which his childish imagination allowed him to believe was a full and exhaustive report. He never thought of the long nights and the early dawns, the hours when he was in the schoolroom, or the many times he was kept in the cottage by his mother, who didn't hold with his hobby.

'Ah son, aren't you all I've got! Why wouldn't I fret about you?' she'd say to him, when he chafed under the yoke of her care.

That was the worst of being an only child, and the child of a sea widow into the bargain. God be good to her! He used to have to sneak off to his cranny in the rocks when he got her gone to the shop of a morning, or up to the chapel of an afternoon to say her beads. She was in sore dread of his even looking out to sea, it seemed! And as for going out in a currach! Hadn't she every currach-crew on the island warned against taking him out?

'Your mammy would be against me, son,' they'd say, when he'd plead with them, one after another on the shore, and they getting ready to shove their boats down the shingle and float them out on the tide.

'How will I ever get out to the trawlers if I'm not let out in the currachs?' he used to think. That was when he was a little fellow, of course, because when he got a bit older he stopped pestering them, and didn't go down near the shore at all when they were pulling out. They'd got sharp with him by then.

'We can't take any babbies out with us – a storm might come up. What would a babby like you do then?' And he couldn't blame them for their attitude because by this time he knew they could often have found a use for him out in the boats when there was a heavy catch.

'You'll never make a man of him hiding him in your petticoats,' they'd say to his mother, when they'd see him with her in the shop. And there was a special edge on the remark, because men were scarce, as could be seen anywhere on the island by the way the black frieze jackets of the men made only small patches in the big knots of women, with their flaming red petticoats.

His mother had a ready answer for them.

'And why are they scarce?' she'd cry.

'Ah, don't be bitter, Mary.'

'Well, leave me alone then. Won't he be time enough taking his life in his hands when there's more to be got for a netful of ling than there is this year!'

For the shop was always full of dried ling. When you thought to lean on the counter, it was on a long board of ling you leant. When you went to sit down on a box or a barrel it was on top of a bit of dried ling you'd be sitting. And right by the door, a greyhound bitch had dragged down a bit of ling from a hook on the wall and was chewing at it, not furtively, but to the unconcern of all, growling when it found it tough to chew, and attacking it with her back teeth and her head to one side, as she'd chew an old rind of hoof parings in the forge. The juice of it, and her own saliva mixed, was trickling out of her mouth onto the floor.

'There'll be a good price for the first mackerel,' said poor Maurya Keely, their near neighbour, whose husband was ailing, and whose son, Seoineen, was away in a seminary on the mainland studying to be a priest. 'The seed herring will be coming in any day now.'

'You'll have to let Jimeen out on that day if it looks to be a good catch,' she said, turning to his mother. 'We're having our currach tarred, so's to be all ready against the day.'

Everyone had sympathy with Maurya, knowing her man was nearly done, and that she was in great dread that he wouldn't be fit to go out and get their share of the new season's catch, and she counting on the money to pay for Seoineen's last year in the seminary. Seoineen wasn't only her pride, but the pride of the whole island as well, for, with the scarcity of menfolk, the island hadn't given a priest to the diocese in a decade.

'And how is Seoineen? When is he coming home at all?' another woman asked, as they crowded around Maurya. 'He'll soon be facing into the straight,' they said, meaning his ordination, and thinking, as they used the expression, of the way, when Seoineen was a young fellow, he used to be the wildest lad on the island, always winning the ass-race on the shore, the first to be seen flashing into sight around the Point, and he coming up the straight, keeping the lead easily to finish at the pier-head.

'He'll be home for a last leave before the end,' said his mother, and everyone understood the apprehension she tried to keep out of her voice, but which steals into the heart of every priest's mother thinking of the staying power a man needs to reach that end. 'I'm expecting him the week after next,' she said, then suddenly her joy in the thought of having him in the house again took over everything else.

'Ah, let's hope the mackerel will be in before then!' said several of the women at the one time, meaning there would be a jingle in everyone's pocket then, for Seoineen would have to call to every single cottage on the island, and every single cottage would want to have plenty of lemonade and shop-biscuits too, to put down before him.

Jimeen listened to this with interest and pleased anticipation.

Seoineen always took him around with him, and he got a share in all that was set down for the seminarian.

But that very evening Seoineen stepped on to the pier. There was an epidemic in the college and the seminarists that were in their last year, like him, were let home a whole week before their time.

'Sure, it's not for what I get to eat that I come home, Mother!' he cried, when Maurya began bewailing having no feasting for him. 'If there's anything astray with the life I've chosen it's not shortage of grub! And anyway, we won't have long to wait?' He went to the door and glanced up at the sky. 'The seed will be swimming inward tomorrow on the first tide!'

'Oh God forbid!' said Maurya. 'We don't want it that soon either, son, for our currach was only tarred this day!' and her face was torn with two worries now instead of one.

Jimeen had seen the twinkle in Seoineen's eye, and he thought he was only letting-on to know about such things, for how would he have any such knowledge at all, and he away at schools and colleges the best part of his life.

The seed was in on the first tide, though, the next day.

'Oh, they have curious ways of knowing things that you'd never expect them to know,' said Jimeen's own mother. It was taken all over the island to be a kind of prophecy.

'Ah, he was only letting-on, Mother,' said Jimeen, but he got a knock of her elbow over the ear.

'It's time you had more respect for him, son,' she said, as he ran out of the door for the shore.

Already most of the island boats were pulling hard out into the bay. And the others were being pushed out as fast as they could be dragged down the shingle.

But the Keely boat was still upscutted in the dune grass under the promontory, and the tar wetly gleaming on it. The other women were clustered around Maurya, giving her consolation.

'Ah sure, maybe it's God's will,' she said. 'Wasn't himself doubled up with pain in the early hours, and it's in a heavy sleep he is this minute – I wouldn't wake him up whether or no! – He didn't get much sleep last night. It was late when he got to his bed. Him and Seoineen stayed up talking by the fire. Seoineen was explaining to him all about the ordination, about the fasting they have to do beforehand, and the holy oils and the chrism and the laying-on of hands. It beat all to hear him! The creatureen, he didn't get much sleep himself either, but he's young and able, thank God. But I'll have to be going back now to call him for Mass.'

'You'll find you won't need to call Seoineen,' said one of the women. 'Hasn't him, and the like of him, got God's voice in their hearts all day and they ever and always listening to it. He'll wake of himself, you'll see. He'll need no calling!'

And sure enough, as they were speaking, who came running down the shingle but Seoineen.

'My father's not gone out without me, is he?' he cried, not seeing their own boat, or any sign of it on the shore, a cloud coming over his face that was all smiles and laughter when he was running down to them. He began to scan the bay that was blackened with boats by this time.

'He's not then,' said Maurya. 'He's above in his bed still, but leave him be, Seoineen – leave him be –' she nodded her head back towards the shade of the promontory. 'He tarred the boat yesterday, now knowing the seed 'ud be in so soon, and it would scald the heart out of him to be here and not able to take it out. But as I was saying to these good people, it's maybe God's will the way it's happened, because he's not fit to go out this day!'

'That's true for you, Mother,' said Seoineen, quietly. 'The poor man is nearly beat, I'm fearing.' But the next minute he threw back his head and looked around the shore. 'Maybe I'd get an oar in one of the other boats. There's surely a scarcity of men these days?'

'Is it you?' cried his mother, because it mortally offended her notion of the dignity due to him that he'd be seen with his coat off maybe – in his shirt sleeves maybe – red in the face maybe along with that and – God forbid – sweat maybe breaking out of him!

'To hear you, Mother, anyone would think I was a priest already. I wish you could get a look into the seminary and you'd see there's a big difference made there between the two sides of the fence!' It was clear from the light in his eyes as they swept the sea at that moment that it would take more than a suit of black clothes to stop him from having a bit of fun with an oar. He gave a sudden big laugh, but it fell away as sudden when he saw that all the boats had pulled out from the shore and he was alone with the women on the sand.

Then his face hardened.

'Tell me, Mother,' he cried. 'Is it the boat or my father that's the unfittest? For if it's only the boat then I'll make it fit! It would be going against God's plenitude to stay idle with the sea teeming like that – Look at it!'

For even from where they stood when the waves wheeled inward they could see the silver herring seed glistening in the curving wheels of water, and when those slow wheels broke on the shore they left behind them a spate of seed sticking to everything, even to people's shoes.

'And for that matter, wasn't Christ Himself a fisherman? Come, Mother – tell me the truth! Is the tar still wet or is it not?'

Maurya looked at him for a minute. She was no match for arguing with him in matters of theology, but she knew all about tarring a currach. 'Wasn't it only done yesterday, son,' she said. 'How could it be dry today?'

'We'll soon know that,' said Seoineen, and he ran over to the currach. Looking after him they saw him lay the palm of his hand flat on the upturned bottom of the boat, and then they heard him give a shout of exultation.

'It's not dry surely?' someone exclaimed, and you could tell by the faces that all were remembering the way he prophesied about the catch. Had the tar dried at the touch of his hands maybe?

But Seoineen was dragging the currach down the shingle.

'Why wouldn't it be dry?' he cried. 'Wasn't it a fine dry night. I remember going to the door after talking to my father into the small hours, and the sky was a mass of stars, and there was a fine, sharp wind blowing that you'd be in dread it would dry up the sea itself! Stand back there, Mother,' he cried, for her face was beseeching something of him, and he didn't want to be looking at it. But without looking he knew what it was trying to say. 'Isn't it towards my ordination the money is going? Isn't that argument enough for you?'

He had the boat nearly down to the water's edge. 'No, keep back there, young Jimeen,' he said. 'I'm able to manage it on my own, but let you get the nets and put them in and then be ready to skip in before I push out, because I'll need someone to help haul in the nets.'

'Is it Jimeen?' said one of the women, and she laughed, and then all the women laughed. 'Sure, he's more precious again nor you!' they said.

But they turned to his mother all the same.

'If you're ever going to let him go out at all, this is your one chance, surely? Isn't it like as if it was into the Hands of God Himself you were putting him, woman?'

'Will you let me, Ma?' It was the biggest moment in his life. He couldn't look at her for fear of a refusal.

'Come on, didn't you hear her saying yes – what are you waiting for?' cried Seoineen, giving him a push, and the next minute he was in the currach, and Seoineen had given it a great shove and he running out into the water in his fine shoes and all. He vaulted in across the keel. 'I'm destroyed already at the very start!' he cried, laughing down at his feet and trouser legs, and that itself seemed part of the sport for him. 'I'll take them off,' he cried, kicking the shoes off him, and pulling off his socks, till he was in his bare white feet. 'Give me the oars,' he cried, but as he gripped them he laughed again, and loosed his fingers for a minute, as one after the other he rubbed his hands on a bit of sacking on the seat beside him. For, like the marks left by the trawler men on the white bollard at the pier, the two bleached oars were marked with the track of his hands, palms, and fingers, in pitch black tar.

'The tar was wet!'

'And what of it?' cried Seoineen. 'Isn't it easy give it another lick of a brush?'

But he wasn't looking at Jimeen and he saying it, his eyes were lepping along the tops of the waves to see if they were pulling near the other currachs.

The other currachs were far out in the bay already: the sea was running strong. For all that, there was a strange still look about the water, unbroken by any spray. Jimeen sat still, exulting in his luck. The waves did not slap against the sides of the currach like he'd have thought they would do, and they didn't even break into spray where the oars split their surface. Instead, they seemed to go lolloping under the currach and lollop up again the far side, till it might have been on great glass rollers they were slipping along.

'God! Isn't it good to be out on the water!' cried Seoineen, and he stood up in the currach, nearly toppling them over in his exuberance, drawing in deep breaths, first with his nose, and then as if he were drinking it with his mouth, and his eyes at the same time taking big draughts of the coast-line that was getting farther and farther away. 'Ah, this is the life: this is the real life,' he cried again, but they had to look to the oars and look to the nets, then, for a while, and for a while they couldn't look up at sea or sky.

When Jimeen looked up at last, the shore was only a narrow line of green.

'There's a bit of a change, I think,' said Seoineen, and it was true.

The waves were no longer round and soft, like the little cnoceens in the fields back of the shore, but they had small sharp points on them now, like the rocks around the Point, that would rip the bottom out of a boat with one tip, the way a tip of a knife would slit the belly of a fish.

That was a venomous comparison though and for all their appearance, when they hit against the flank of the boat, it was only the waves themselves that broke and patterned the water with splotches of spray.

It was while he was looking down at these white splotches that Jimeen saw the fish.

'Oh look, Seoineen, look!' he cried, because never had he seen the like.

They were not swimming free, or separate, like you'd think they'd be, but a great mass of them together, till you'd think it was at the floor of the sea you were looking, only it nearer and shallower.

There must have been a million fish; a million, million, Jimeen reckoned wildly, and they pressed as close as the pebbles on the shore. And they might well have been motionless and only seeming to move like on a windy day you'd think the grass on the top of the promontory was running free like the waves, with the way it rippled and ran along a little with each breeze.

'Holy God, such a sight!' cried Seoineen. 'Look at them!'

But Jimeen was puzzled.

'How will we get them into the net?' he asked, because it didn't seem that there was any place for the net to slip down between them, but that it must lie on the top of that solid mass of fish, like on a floor.

'The nets: begod, I nearly forgot what we came out here for!' cried Seoineen, and at the same time they became aware of the activity in the other boats, which had drawn near without their knowing. He yelled at Jimeen. 'Catch hold of the nets there, you lazy good-for-nothing. What did I bring you with me for if it wasn't to put you to some use!' and he himself caught at a length of the brown mesh, thrown in the bottom of the boat, and began to haul it up with one hand, and with the other to feed it out over the side.

Jimeen, too, began to pull and haul, so that for a few minutes there was only a sound of the net swishing over the wood, and every now and then a bit of a curse, under his breath, from Seoineen as one of the cork floats caught in the thole pins.

At first it shocked Jimeen to hear Seoineen curse, but he reflected that Seoineen wasn't ordained yet, and that, even if he were, it must be a hard thing for a man to go against his nature.

'Come on, get it over the side, damn you,' cried Seoineen again, as Jimeen had slowed up a bit owing to thinking about the cursing. 'It isn't one netful but thirty could be filled this day! Sure you could fill the boat in fistfuls,' he cried, suddenly leaning down over the side, delving his bare hand into the water. With a shout, he brought up his hand with two fish, held one against the other in the same grip, so that they were as rigid as if they were dead. 'They're overlaying each other a foot deep,' he cried, and then he opened his fist and freed them. Immediately they writhed apart to either side of his hand in two bright arcs and then fell, both of them, into the bottom of the boat. But next moment they writhed into the air again, and flashed over the side of the currach.

'Ah begorras, you'll get less elbow-room there than here, my boys,' cried Seoineen, and he roared laughing, and he and Jimeen leant over the side, and saw that sure enough, the two mackerel were floundering for a place in the glut of fishes.

But a shout in one of the other currachs made them look up.

It was the same story all over the bay. The currachs were tossing tipsily in the water with the antics of the crews, that were standing up and shouting and feeding the nets ravenously over the sides. In some of the boats that had got away early, they were still more ravenously hauling them up, strained and swollen with the biggest catch they had ever held.

There was not time for Seoineen or Jimeen to look around either, for just then the keel of their own currach began to dip into the water.

'Look out! Pull it up – ! Catch a better grip than that, damn you. Do you want to be pulled into the sea. Pull, damn you, pull!' cried Seoineen.

Now every other word that broke from his throat was a curse, or what you'd call a curse if you heard them from another man, or in another place, but in this place, from this man, hearing them issue wild and free, Jimeen understood that they were a kind of psalm. They rang out over the sea in a kind of praise to God for all his plenitude.

'Up! Pull hard – up, now, up!' he cried, and he was pulling at his end like a madman.

Jimeen pulled too, till he thought his heart would crack, and then suddenly the big white belly of the loaded net came in sight over the water.

Jimeen gave a groan, though, when he saw it.

'Is it dead they are?' he cried, and there was anguish in his voice.

Up to this, the only live fish he had ever seen were the few fish tangled in the roomy nets, let down by the old men over the end of the pier, and *they* were always full of life, needling back and forth insanely in the spacious mesh till he used to swallow hard, and press his lips close together fearing one of them would dart down his gullet, and he'd have it ever after needling this way and that inside him! But there was no stir at all in the great white mass that had been hauled up now in the nets.

'Is it dead they are?' he cried again.

'Aahh, why would they be dead? It's suffocating they are, even below in the water, with the welter of them is in it,' cried Seoineen.

He dragged the net over the side where it emptied and spilled itself into the bottom of the boat. They came alive then all right! Flipping and floundering, and some of them flashing back into the sea. But it was only a few on the top that got away, the rest were kept down by the very weight and mass of them that was in it. And when, after a minute, Seoineen had freed the end of the net, he flailed them right and left till most of them fell back flat. Then, suddenly, he straightened up and swiped a hand across his face to clear it of the sweat that was pouring out of him.

'Ah sure, what harm if an odd one leps for it,' he cried. 'We'll deaden them under another netfall! Throw out your end,' he cried.

As Jimeen rose up to his full height to throw the net wide out, there was a sudden terrible sound in the sky over him, and the next minute a bolt of thunder went volleying overhead, and with it, in the same instant it seemed, the sky was knifed from end to end with a lightning flash.

Were they blinded by the flash? Or had it suddenly gone as black as night over the whole sea?

'Oh God's Cross!' cried Seoineen. 'What is coming? Why didn't someone give us a shout? Where are the others? Can you see them? Hoy there! Marteen! Seumas? Can you hear – ?'

For they could see nothing. And it was as if they were all alone in the whole world. Then, suddenly, they made out Marteen's currach near to them, so near that, but for Seoineen flinging himself forward and grabbing the oars, the two currachs would have knocked together. Yet no sooner had they been saved from knocking together than they suddenly seemed so far sundered again they could hardly hear each other when they called out.

'What's happening, in Christ's name?' bawled Seoineen, but he had to put up his hands to trumpet his voice, for the waves were now so steep and high that even one was enough to blot out the sight of Marteen. Angry white spume dashed in their faces.

'It's maybe the end of the world,' said Jimeen, terror-stricken.

'Shut up and let me hear Marteen!' said Seoineen, for Marteen was bawling at them again.

'Let go the nets,' Marteen was bawling – 'let go the nets or they'll drag you out of the boat.'

Under them then they could feel the big pull of the net that was filled up again in an instant with its dead weight of suffocating fish.

'Let it go, I tell you,' bawled Marteen.

'Did you hear? He's telling us to let it go,' piped Jimeen in terror, and he tried to free his own fingers of the brown mesh that had closed tight upon them with the increasing weight. 'I can't let go,' he cried, looking to Seoineen, but he shrank back from the strange wild look in Seoineen's eyes. 'Take care would you do anything of the kind!'

'It's cutting off my fingers!' he screamed.

Seoineen glared at him.

'A pity about them!' he cried, but when he darted a look at them, and saw them swelling and reddening, he cursed. 'Here – wait till I take it from you,' he cried, and he went to free his own right hand, but first he laced the laden fingers of his left hand into the mesh above the right hand, and even then, the blood spurted out in the air when he finally dragged it free of the mesh.

For a minute Seoineen shoved his bleeding fingers into his mouth and sucked them, then he reached out and caught the net below where Jimeen gripped it. As the weight slackened, the pain of the searing strings lessened, but next minute as the pull below got stronger, the pain tore into Jimeen's flesh again.

'Let go now, if you like, now I have a bit of a hold of it anyway – now I'm taking the weight of it off you,' said Seoineen.

Jimeen tried to drag free.

'I can't,' he screamed in terror, '– the strings are eating into my bones!'

Seoineen altered his balance and took more weight of the net at that place.

'Now!'

'I can't! I can't!' screamed Jimeen.

From far over the waves the voice of Marteen came to them again, faint, unreal, like the voices you'd hear in a shell if you held it to your ear.

'Cut free – cut free,' it cried, 'or else you'll be destroyed altogether.'

'Have they cut free themselves? That's what I'd like to know!' cried Seoineen.

'Oh, do as he says, Seoineen. Do as he says!' screamed Jimeen.

And then, as he saw a bit of ragged net, and then another and another rush past like the briery patches of foam on the water that was now almost level with the rowlocks, he knew that they had indeed all done what Marteen said; cut free.

'For the love of God, Seoineen,' he cried.

Seoineen hesitated for another instant. Then suddenly made up his mind and, reaching along the seat, he felt without looking for the knife that was kept there for slashing dogfish.

'Here goes,' he cried, and with one true cut of the knife he freed Jimeen's hands the two together at the same time, but, letting the knife drop into the water, he reached out wildly to catch the ends of the net before they slid into it, or shed any of their precious freight.

Not a single silver fish was lost.

'What a fool I'd be,' he gasped, 'to let go. They think because of the collar I haven't a man's strength about me any more. Then I'll show them. I'll not let go this net, not if it pull me down to hell.' And he gave another wild laugh. 'And you along with me!' he cried. 'Murder?' he asked then, as if he had picked up the word from a voice in the wind. 'Is it murder? Ah sure, I often think it's all one to God what a man's sin is, as long as it's sin at all. Isn't sin poison – any sin at all, even the smallest drop of it? Isn't it death to the soul that it touches at any time? Ah then! I'll not let go!' And even when, just then, the whole sea seemed littered with tattered threads of net, he still held tight to his hold. 'Is that the way? They've all let go! Well then, I'll show them one man will not be so easy beat! Can you hear me?' he cried, because it was hard to hear him with the crazy noise of the wind and the waves.

'Oh cut free, Seoineen,' Jimeen implored, although he remembered the knife was gone now to the bottom of the sea, and although the terrible swollen fingers were beyond help in the mangling ropes of the net.

'Cut free is it? Faith now! I'll show them all,' cried Seoineen. 'We'll be the only boat'll bring back a catch this night, and the sea seething with fish.' He gave a laugh. 'Sure that was the only thing that was spoiling my pleasure in the plenty, thinking that when the boats got back the whole island would be fuller of fish than the sea itself, and it all of no more value than if it was washed of its own accord on to the dirty counters of the shop! Sure it wouldn't be worth a farthing a barrel! But it will be a different story now, I'm thinking. Oh, but I'll have the laugh on them with their hollow boats, and their nets cut to flitters! I'll show them a man is a man, no matter what vows he takes, or what way he's called to deny his manhood! I'll show them! Where are they, anyway? Can you – see them – at all?' he cried, but he had begun to gasp worse than the fishes in the bottom of the boat. 'Can you – see them – at all? Damn you, don't sit there like that! Stand up – there – and tell me – can – you – see – them?'

It wasn't the others Jimeen saw though, when he raised his eyes from the torn hands in the meshes. All he saw was a great wall, a great green wall of water. No currachs anywhere. It was as if the whole sea had been stood up on its edge, like a plate on a dresser. And down that wall of water there slid a multitude of dead fish.

And then, down the same terrible wall, sliding like the dead fish, came an oar; a solitary oar. And a moment afterwards, but inside the glass wall, imprisoned, like under a glass dome, he saw – oh God! a face, looking out at him, staring out at him through a foot of clear green water. And he saw it was the face of Marteen. For a minute the eyes of the dead man stared into his eyes.

With a scream he threw himself against Seoineen, and clung to him tight as iron.

How many years ago was that? The Bishop opened his eyes. They were so near the shore he could pick out the people by name that stood on the pier-head. His stomach had stopped rolling. It was mostly psychological; that feeling of nausea. But he knew it would come back in an instant if he looked leftward from the shore, leftwards and upwards, where, over the little cement pier and over the crane-bill steeple of the church, the promontory that they called the Point rose up black with its own shadow.

For it was on that promontory – four times the height of the steeple – they had found themselves, he and Seoineen, in the white dawn of the day after the Wave, lying in a litter of dead fish, with the netful of fish like an anchor sunk into the green grass.

When he came to himself in that terrible dawn, and felt the slippy bellies of the fish all about him, he thought he was still in the boat, lying in the bottom among the mackerel, but when he opened his eyes and saw a darkness as of night, over his head, he thought it was still the darkness of the storm and he closed them again in terror.

Just before he closed them, though, he thought he saw a star, and he ventured to open them again, and then he saw that the dark sky over him was a sky of skin, stretched taught over timber laths, and the star was only a glint of light – and the blue light of day at that – coming through a split in the bottom of the currach. For the currach was on top of him! – Not he in the bottom of it.

Why then was he not falling down and down and down through the green waters? His hands rushed out to feel around him. But even then, the most miraculous thing he thought to grasp was a fistful of sand, the most miraculous thing he thought to have to believe was that they were cast up safe upon the shore.

Under his hands though, that groped through the fishes, he came, not on sand, but on grass, and not upon the coarse dune grass that grew back from the shore at the foot of the Point. It was soft, sweet little grass, that was like the grass he saw once when Seoineen and he had climbed up the face of the Point, and stood up there, in the sun, looking down at all below, the sea and the pier, and the shore and the fields, and the thatch of their own houses, and on a level with them, the grey spire of the chapel itself!

It was, when opening his eyes wide at last, he saw, out from him a bit, the black tip of that same chapel spire that he knew where he was.

Throwing the fish to left and right he struggled to get to his feet.

It was a miracle! And it must have been granted because Seoineen was in the boat. He remembered how he prophesied the seed would be on the tide, and in his mind he pictured their currach being lifted up in the air and flown, like a bird, to this grassy point.

But where was Seoineen?

'Oh Seoineen, Seoineen!' he cried, when he saw him standing on the edge of the Point looking downward, like they looked, that day, on all below. 'Oh Seoineen, was it a miracle?' he cried, and he didn't wait for an answer, but he began to shout and jump in the air.

'Quit, will you!' said Seoineen, and for a minute he thought it must be modesty on Seoineen's part, it being through him the miracle was granted, and then he thought it must be the pain in his hands that was at him, not letting him enjoy the miracle, because he had his two hands pressed under his armpits.

Then suddenly he remembered the face of Marteen he had seen under the wall of water, and his eyes flew out over the sea that was as flat and even now as the field of grass under their feet. Was Marteen's currach lost? And what of the others?

Craning over the edge of the promontory he tried to see what currachs were back in their places under the little wall dividing the sand from the dune, turned upside down and leaning a little to one side, so you could crawl under them if you were caught in a sudden shower.

There were no currachs under the wall: none at all.

There were no currachs on the sea.

Once, when he was still wearing a red petticoat like a girsha, there had been a terrible storm and half a score of currachs were lost. He remembered the night with all the women on the island down on the shore with storm lamps, swinging them and calling out over the noise of the waves. And the next day they were still there, only kneeling on the pier, praying and keening.

'Why aren't they praying and keening?' he cried then, for he knew at last the other currachs, all but theirs, were lost.

'God help them,' said Seoineen, 'at least they were spared that.'

And he pointed to where, stuck in the latticed shutters on the side of the steeple, there were bits of seaweed, and – yes – a bit of the brown mesh of a net.

'God help you,' he said then, 'how can your child's mind take in what a grown man's mind can hardly hold – but you'll have to know some time – we're all alone – the two of us – the whole island. All that was spared by that wall of water –'

'All that was on the sea, you mean?' he cried.

'And on the land too,' said Seoineen.

'Not my mother –?' he whimpered.

'Yes, and my poor mother,' said Seoineen. 'My poor mother that tried to stop us from going out with the rest.'

But it was a grief too great to grasp, and yet, yet even in face of it, Jimeen's mind was enslaved to the thought of their miraculous salvation.

'Was it a miracle, Seoineen?' he whispered. 'Was it a miracle we were spared?'

But Seoineen closed his eyes, and pushed his crossed arms deeper under his armpits. The grimace of pain he made was – even without words – a rebuke to Jimeen's exaltation. Then he opened his eyes again.

'It was my greed that was the cause of all,' he said, and there was such a terrible sorrow in his face that Jimeen, only then, began to cry. 'It has cost me my two living hands,' said Seoineen, and there was a terrible anguish in his voice.

'But it saved your life, Seoineen,' he cried, wanting to comfort him.

Never did he forget the face Seoineen turned to him.

'For what?' he asked. 'For what?'

And there was, in his voice, such despair, that Jimeen knew it wasn't a question but an answer; so he said no more for a few minutes. Then he raised his voice again, timidly.

'You saved my life too, Seoineen.'

Seoineen turned dully and looked at him.

'For what?'

But as he uttered them, those same words took on a change, and a change came over his face, too, and when he repeated them, the change was violent.

'For what?' he demanded. 'For what?'

Just then, on the flat sea below, Jimeen saw the boats, coming across from the mainland, not currachs like they had on the island, but boats of wood made inland, in Athlone, and brought down on lorries.

'Look at the boats,' he called out, four, five, six, any amount of them; they came rowing for the island.

Less than an hour later Seoineen was on his way to the hospital on the mainland, where he was to spend long months before he saw the island again. Jimeen was taken across a few hours later, but when he went it was to be for good. He was going to an aunt, far in from the sea, of whom he had never heard tell till that day.

Nor was he to see Seoineen again, in all the years that followed.

On the three occasions that he was over on the island he had not seen him. He had made enquiries, but all he could ever get out of people was that he was a bit odd.

'And why wouldn't he be?' they added.

But although he never came down to the pier to greet the Bishop like the rest of the islanders, it was said he used to slip into the church after it had filled up and he'd think he was unnoticed. And afterwards, although he never once would go down to the pier to see the boat off, he never went back into his little house until it was gone clear across to the other side of the bay. From some part of the island it was certain he'd be the last to take leave of the sight.

It had been the same on each visit the Bishop made, and it would be the same on this one.

When he would be leaving the island, there would be the same solicitous entreaties with him to put on his overcoat. Certainly he was always colder going back in the late day. But he'd never give in to do more than throw it over his shoulders, from which it would soon slip down on to the seat behind him.

'You'd do right to put it on like they told you,' said the secretary, buttoning up his own thick coat.

But there was no use trying to make him do a thing he was set against. He was a man had deep reasons for the least of his actions.

In the Middle of the Fields

Like a rock in the sea, she was islanded by fields, the heavy grass washing about the house, and the cattle wading in it as in water. Even their gentle stirrings were a loss when they moved away at evening to the shelter of the woods. A rainy day might strike a wet flash from a hay barn on the far side of the river – not even a habitation! And yet she was less lonely for him here in Meath than elsewhere. Anxieties by day, and cares, and at night vague, nameless fears – these were the stones across the mouth of the tomb. But who understood that? They thought she hugged tight every memory she had of him. What did they know about memory? What was it but another name for dry love and barren longing? They even tried to unload upon her their own small purposeless memories. 'I imagine I see him every time I look out there,' they would say as they glanced nervously over the darkening fields when they were leaving. 'I think I ought to see him coming through the trees.' Oh, for. God's sake! she'd think. I'd forgotten him for a minute!

It wasn't him *she* saw when she looked out at the fields. It was the ugly tufts of tow and scutch that whitened the tops of the grass and gave it the look of a sea in storm, spattered with broken foam. That grass would have to be topped. And how much would it cost?

At least Ned, the old herd, knew the man to do it for her. 'Bartley Crossen is your man, Ma'am. Your husband knew him well.'

She couldn't place him at first. Then she remembered. 'Oh, yes – that's his hay barn we see, isn't it? Why, of course! I know him well – by sight, I mean.' And so she did – splashing past on the road in a big muddy car, the wheels always caked with clay, and the wife in the front seat beside him.

'I'll get him to call around and have a word with you, Ma'am,' said the herd.

'Before dark!' she cautioned.

But there was no need to tell him. The old man knew how she always tried to be upstairs before it got dark, locking herself into her room, which opened off the room where the children slept, praying

devoutly that she wouldn't have to come down again for anything –
above all, not to answer the door. That was what in particular she
dreaded: a knock after dark.

'Ah, sure, who'd come near you, Ma'am, knowing you're a
woman alone with small children that might be wakened and set
crying? And, for that matter, where could you be safer than in the
middle of the fields, with the innocent beasts asleep around you?'

If he himself had to come to the house late at night for any reason
– to get hot water to stoup the foot of a beast, or to call the vet – he
took care to shout out long before he got to the gable. 'It's me,
Ma'am!' he'd shout. 'Coming! Coming!' she'd cry, gratefully, as
quick on his words as their echo. Unlocking her door, she'd run
down and throw open the hall door. No matter what the hour! No
matter how black the night! 'Go back to your bed now, you, Ma'am,'
he'd say from the darkness, where she could see the swinging yard
lamp coming nearer and nearer like the light of a little boat drawing
near to a jetty. 'I'll put out the lights and let myself out.' Relaxed by
the thought that there was someone in the house, she would indeed
scuttle back into bed, and, what was more, she'd be nearly asleep
before she'd hear the door slam. It used to sound like the slam of a
door a million miles away.

There was no need to worry. He'd see that Crossen came early.

It was well before dark when Crossen did drive up to the door.
The wife was with him, as usual, sitting up in the front seat the way
people sat up in the well of little tub traps long ago, their knees
pressed together, allowing no slump. The herd had come with
them, but only he and Crossen got out.

'Won't your wife come inside and wait, Mr Crossen?' she asked.

'Oh, not at all, Ma'am. She likes sitting in the car. Now, where's
this grass that's to be cut? Are there any stones lying about that
would blunt the blade?' Going around the gable of the house, he
looked out over the land.

'There's not a stone or a stump in it,' Ned said. 'You'd run your
blade over the whole of it while you'd be whetting it twenty times in
another place!'

'I can see that,' said Bartley Crossen, but absently, she thought.

He had walked across the lawn to the rickety wooden gate that led
into the pasture, and leaned on it. He didn't seem to be looking at
the fields at all, though, but at the small string of stunted thorns that
grew along the riverbank, their branches leaning so heavily out over
the water that their roots were almost dragged clear of the clay.

Suddenly he turned around and gave a sigh. 'Ah, sure, I didn't need to look! I know it well!' As she showed surprise, he gave a little laugh, like a young man. 'I courted a girl down there when I was a lad,' he said. 'That's a queer length of time ago now, I can tell you!' He turned to the old man. 'You might remember it.' Then he looked back at her. 'I don't suppose you were thought of at all in those days, Ma'am,' he said, and there was something kindly in his look and in his words. 'You'd like the mowing done soon, I suppose? How about first thing in the morning?'

Her face lit up. But there was the price to settle. 'It won't be as dear as cutting meadow, will it?'

'Ah, I won't be too hard on you, Ma'am,' he said. 'I can promise you that!'

'That's very kind of you,' she said, but a little doubtfully.

Behind Crossen's back, Ned nodded his head in approval. 'Let it go at that, Ma'am,' he whispered as they walked back towards the car. 'He's a man you can trust.'

And when Crossen and the wife had driven away, he reassured her again. 'A decent man,' he said. Then he gave a laugh – it, too, was a young kind of laugh for a man of his age; it was like a nudge. 'Did you hear what he said though – about the girl he courted down there? Do you know who that was? It was his first wife! You know he was twice married? Ah, well, it's so long ago I wouldn't wonder if you never heard it. Look at the way he spoke about her himself, as if she was some girl he'd all but forgotten! The thorn trees brought her to his mind! That's where they used to meet, being only youngsters, when they first took up with each other.

'Poor Bridie Logan – she was as wild as a hare. And she was mad with love, young as she was! They were company-keeping while they were still going to school. Only nobody took it seriously – him least of all, maybe – till the winter he went away to the agricultural college in Clonakilty. She started writing to him then. I used to see her running up to the postbox at the crossroads every other evening. And sure, the whole village knew where the letter was going. His people were fit to be tied when he came home in the summer and said he wasn't going back, but was going to marry Bridie. All the same, his father set them up in a cottage on his own land. It's the cottage that's used now for stall-feds – it's back of the new house. Oh, but you can't judge it now for what it was then! Giddy and all as she was – as lightheaded as a thistle – you should have seen the way she kept that cottage. She'd have had it scrubbed away if she didn't start having a baby. He wouldn't let her take the scrubbing brush into her hands after that!'

'But she wasn't delicate, was she?'

'Bridie? She was as strong as a kid goat, that one! But I told you she was mad about him, didn't I? Well, after she was married to him she was no better – worse, you'd say. She couldn't do enough for him! It was like as if she was driven on by some kind of a fever. You'd only to look in her eyes to see it. Do you know! From that day to this, I don't believe I ever saw a woman so full of going as that one! Did you ever happen to see little birds flying about in the air like they were flying for the divilment of it and nothing else? And did you ever see the way they give a sort of a little leap in the air, like they were forcing themselves to go a bit higher still – higher than they ought? Well, it struck me that was the way Bridie was acting, as she rushed about that cottage doing this and doing that to make him prouder and prouder of her. As if he could be any prouder than he was already and the child getting noticeable!'

'She didn't die in childbed?'

'No. Not in a manner of speaking, anyway. She had the child, nice and easy, and in their own cottage, too, only costing him a few shillings for one of those women that went in for that kind of job long ago. And all went well. It was no time till she was let up on her feet again. I was there the first morning she had the place to herself! She was up and dressed when I got there, just as he was going out to milk.

'"Oh, it's great to be able to go out again," she said, taking a great breath of the morning air as she stood at the door looking after him. "Wait! Why don't I come with you to milk!" she called out suddenly after him. Then she threw a glance back at the baby asleep in its crib by the window.

'"Oh, it's too far for you, Bridie!" he cried. The cows were down in the little field by the river – you know the field, alongside the road at the foot of the hill on this side of the village. And knowing she'd start coaxing him, he made out of the gate with the cans.

'"Good man!" I said to myself. But the next thing I knew, she'd darted across the yard.

'"I can go on the bike if it's too far to walk!" she said. And up she got on her old bike, and out she pedalled through the gate.

'"Bridie, are you out of your mind?" he shouted as she whizzed past him.

'"Arrah, what harm can it do me?" she shouted back.

'I went stiff with fright looking after her. And I thought it was the same with him, when he threw down the cans and started down the hill after her. But looking back on it, I think it was the same fever as always was raging in her that started raging in him, too. Mad with love, that's what they were, both of them – she only wanting to draw him on, and he only too willing!

'"Wait for me!" he shouted, but before she'd even got to the bottom she started to brake the bike, putting down her foot like you'd see a youngster do, and raising up such a cloud of dust we could hardly see her.'

'She braked too hard!'

'Not her! In the twinkle of an eye she'd stopped the bike, jumped off, turned it round, and was pedalling madly up the hill again, her head down on the handle-bars like a racing cyclist. But that was the finish of her!'

'Oh, no! What happened?'

'She stopped pedalling all of a sudden, and the bike half stopped, and then it started to go back down the hill a bit, as if it skidded on the loose gravel at the side of the road. That's what I thought happened, and him, too, I suppose, because we both began to run down the hill. She didn't get time to fall before we got to her. But what use was that? It was some kind of internal bleeding that took her. We got her into the bed, and the neighbours came running, but she was gone before the night.'

'Oh, such a thing to happen! And the baby?'

'Well, it was a strong child! And it grew into a fine lump of a lad. That's the fellow that drives the tractor for him now – the oldest son, Bartley.'

'Well, I suppose his second marriage had more to it, when all was said and done.'

'That's it. And she's a good woman – the second one. The way she brought up that child of Bridie's! And filled the cradle, year after year, with sons of her own. Ah sure, things always work out for the best in the end, no matter what!' he said, and he started to walk away.

'Wait a minute, Ned,' she said urgently. 'Do you really think he forgot about her – for years, I mean?'

'I'd swear it,' said the old man. And then he looked hard at her. 'It will be the same with you, too,' he added kindly. 'Take my word for it. Everything passes in time and is forgotten.'

As she shook her head doubtfully, he shook his emphatically. 'When the tree falls, how can the shadow stand?' he said. And he walked away.

I wonder! she thought as she walked back to the house, and she envied the practical country way that made good the defaults of nature as readily as the broken sod knits back into the sward.

Again that night, when she went up to her room, she looked down towards the river and she thought of Crossen. Had he really forgotten? It was hard for her to believe, and with a sigh she picked up her hairbrush and pulled it through her hair. Like everything else about her lately, her hair was sluggish and hung heavily down, but after a few minutes under the quickening strokes of the brush, it lightened and lifted, and soon it flew about her face like the spray above a weir. It had always been the same, even when she was a child. She had only to suffer the first painful drag of the bristles when her mother would cry out, 'Look! Look! That's electricity!' and a blue spark would shine for an instant like a star in the grey depths of the mirror.

That was all they knew of electricity in those dim-lit days when valleys of shadow lay deep between one piece of furniture and another. Was it because rooms were so badly lit then that they saw it so often, that little blue star? Suddenly she was overcome by longing to see it again, and, standing up impetuously, she switched off the light.

It was just then that, down below, the iron fist of the knocker was lifted and, with a loud, confident hand, brought down on the door.

It wasn't a furtive knock. She admitted that even as she sat stark with fright in the darkness. And then a voice that was vaguely familiar called out – and confidently – from below.

'It's me, Ma'am! I hope I'm not disturbing you!'

'Oh, Mr Crossen!' she cried out with relief, and, unlocking her door, she ran across the landing and threw up the window on that side of the house. 'I'll be right down!' she called.

'Oh, don't come down, Ma'am!' he shouted. 'I only want one word with you.'

'But of course I'll come down!' She went back to get her dressing-gown and pin up her hair, but as she did she heard him stomping his feet on the gravel. It had been a mild day, but with night a chill had come in the air, and, for all that it was late spring, there was a cutting east wind coming across the river. 'I'll run down and let you in from the cold,' she called, and, twisting up her hair, she held it against her head with her hand without waiting to pin it, and she ran down the stairs in her bare feet to unbolt the door.

'You were going to bed, Ma'am!' he said accusingly the minute she opened the door. And where he had been so impatient a minute beforehand, he stood stock-still in the open doorway. 'I saw the lights were out downstairs when I was coming up the drive,' he said contritely. 'But I didn't think you'd gone up for the night!'

'Neither had I!' she said lyingly, to put him at his ease. 'I was just upstairs brushing my hair. You must excuse me,' she added, because a breeze from the door was blowing her dressing-gown from her knees, and to pull it across she had to take her hand from her hair, so that the hair fell down about her shoulders. 'Would you mind closing the door for me?' she said, with some embarrassment, and she began to back up the stairs. 'Please go inside to the sitting-room, won't you?' she said, nodding towards the door of the small room off the hall. 'Put on the light. I'll be down in a minute.'

But although he had obediently stepped inside the door, and closed it, he stood stoutly in the middle of the hall. 'I shouldn't have come in at all,' he said. 'I know you were going to bed! Look at you!' he cried again in the same accusing voice, as if he dared her this time to deny it. He was looking at her hair. 'Excuse my saying so, Ma'am, but I never saw such a fine head of hair. God bless it!' he said quickly, as if afraid he had been rude. 'Doesn't a small thing make a big differ,' he said impulsively. 'You look like a young girl!'

In spite of herself, she smiled with pleasure. She wanted no more of it, all the same. 'Well, I don't feel like one!' she said sharply.

What was meant for a quite opposite effect, however, seemed to delight him and put him wonderfully at ease. 'Ah sure, you're a sensible woman! I can see that,' he said, and, coming to the foot of the stairs, he leaned comfortably across the newel post. 'Let you stay the way you are, Ma'am,' he said. 'I've only a word to say to you, and it's not worth your while going up them stairs. Let me have my say here and now and be off about my business! The wife will be waiting up for me, and I don't want that!'

She hesitated. Was the reference to his wife meant to put her at *her* ease? 'I think I ought to get my slippers,' she said cautiously. Her feet were cold.

'Oh, yes, put something on your feet!' he cried, only then seeing that she was in her bare feet. 'But as to the rest, I'm long gone beyond taking any account of what a woman has on her. I'm gone beyond taking notice of women at all.'

She had seen something to put on her feet. Under the table in the hall was a pair of old boots belonging to Richard, with fleece lining in them. She hadn't been able to make up her mind to give them away with the rest of his clothes, and although they were big and clumsy on her, she often stuck her feet into them when she came in from the fields with mud on her shoes. 'Well, come in where it's warm, so,' she said. She came back down the few steps and stuck her feet into the boots, and then she opened the door of the sitting-room.

She was glad she'd come down. He'd never have been able to put on the light. 'There's something wrong with the centre light,' she said as she groped along the wainscot to find the plug of the reading lamp. It was in an awkward place, behind the desk. She had to go down on her knees.

'What's wrong with it?' he asked, as, with a countryman's interest in practicalities, he clicked the switch up and down to no effect.

'Oh, nothing much, I'm sure,' she said absently. 'There!' She had found the plug, and the room was lit up with a bright white glow.

'Why don't you leave the plug in the socket, anyway?' he asked critically.

'I don't know,' she said. 'I think someone told me it's safer, with reading lamps, to pull them out at night. There might be a short circuit, or mice might nibble at the cord, or something – I forget what I was told. I got into the habit of doing it, and now I keep on.' She felt a bit silly.

But he was concerned about it. 'I don't think any harm could be done,' he said gravely. Then he turned away from the problem. 'About tomorrow, Ma'am!' he said, somewhat offhandedly, she thought. 'I was determined I'd see you tonight, because I'm not a man to break my word – above all, to a woman.'

What was he getting at?

'Let me put it this way,' he said quickly. 'You'll understand, Ma'am, that as far as I am concerned, topping land is the same as cutting hay. The same time. The same labour cost. And the same wear and tear on the blade. You understand that?'

On her guard, she nodded.

'Well now, Ma'am, I'd be the first to admit that it's not quite the same for you. For you, topping doesn't give the immediate return you'd get from hay –'

'There's no return from it!' she exclaimed crossly.

'Oh, come now, Ma'am, come! Good grassland pays as well as anything – you know you won't get nice sweet pickings for your beasts from neglected land, but only dirty old tow grass knotting under their feet. It's just that it's not a quick return, and so – as you know – I made a special price for you.'

'I do know!' she said impatiently. 'But I thought that part of it was settled and done.'

'Oh, I'm not going back on it, if that's what you think,' he said affably. 'I'm glad to do what I can for you, Ma'am, the more so seeing you have no man to attend to these things for you, but only yourself alone.'

'Oh, I'm well able to look after myself!' she said, raising her voice.

Once again her words had an opposite effect to what she intended. He laughed good-humouredly. 'That's what all women like to think!' he said. 'Well, now,' he said in a different tone of voice, and it annoyed her to see he seemed to think something had been settled between them, 'it would suit me – and I'm sure it's all the same with you – if we could leave your little job till later in the week, say till nearer to the time of the haymaking generally. Because by then I'd have the cutting bar in good order, sharpened and ready for use. Whereas now, while there's still a bit of ploughing to be done here and there, I'll have to be chopping and changing, between the plough and the mower, putting one on one minute and the other the next!'

'As if anyone is still ploughing this time of the year!' Her eyes hardened. 'Who are you putting before me?' she demanded.

'Now, take it easy, Ma'am. No one. Leastways, not without getting leave first from you.'

'Without telling me you're not coming, you mean!'

'Oh, now, Ma'am, don't get cross. I'm only trying to make matters easy for everyone.'

But she was very angry now. 'It's always the same story. I thought you'd treat me differently! I'm to wait till after this one, and after that one, and in the end my fields will go wild!'

He looked a bit shamefaced. 'Ah now, Ma'am, that's not going to be the case at all. Although, mind you, some people don't hold with topping, you know!'

'I hold with it!'

'Oh, I suppose there's something in it,' he said reluctantly. 'But the way I look at it, cutting the weeds in July is a kind of a topping.'

'Grass cut before it goes to seed gets so thick at the roots no weeds can come up!' she cried, so angry she didn't realize how authoritative she sounded.

'Faith, I never knew you were so well up, Ma'am!' he said, looking at her admiringly, but she saw he wasn't going to be put down by her. 'All the same now, Ma'am, you can't say a few days here or there could make any difference?'

'A few days could make all the difference! This farm has a gravelly bottom to it, for all it's so lush. A few days of drought could burn it to the butt. And how could I mow it then? What cover would there be for the "nice sweet pickings" you were talking about a minute ago?' Angrily, she mimicked his own accent without thinking.

He threw up his hands. 'Ah well, I suppose a man may as well admit when he's bested,' he said. 'Even by a woman. And you can't say I broke my promise.'

'I can't say but you tried hard enough,' she said grudgingly, although she was mollified that she was getting her way. 'Can I offer you anything?' she said then, anxious to convey an air of finality to their discussion.

'Oh, not at all, Ma'am! Nothing, thank you! I'll have to be getting home.' He stood up.

She stood up, too.

'I hope you won't think I was trying to take advantage of you,' he said as they went towards the door. 'It's just that we must all make out as best we can for ourselves – isn't that so? Not but you're well able to look after yourself, I must say. No one ever thought you'd stay on here after your husband died. I suppose it's for the children you did it?' He looked up the well of the stairs. 'Are they asleep?'

'Oh, long ago,' she said indifferently. She opened the hall door.

The night air swept in immediately, as it had earlier. But this time, from far away, it bore along on it the faint scent of new-mown hay. 'There's hay cut somewhere already!' she exclaimed in surprise. And she lifted her face to the sweetness of it.

For a minute, Crossen looked past her out into the darkness, then he looked back. 'Aren't you ever lonely here at night?' he asked suddenly.

'You mean frightened?' she corrected quickly and coldly.

'Yes! Yes, that's what I meant,' he said, taken aback. 'Ah, but why would you be frightened! What safer place could you be under the sky than right here with your own fields all about you!'

What he said was so true, and he himself as he stood there, with his hat in his hand, so normal and natural it was indeed absurd to think that he would no sooner have gone out the door than she would be scurrying up the stairs like a child! 'You may not believe it,' she said, 'but I am scared to death sometimes! I nearly died when I heard your knock on the door tonight. It's because I was scared that I was upstairs,' she said, in a further burst of confidence. 'I always go up the minute it gets dark. I don't feel so frightened up in my room.'

'Isn't that strange now?' he said, and she could see he found it an incomprehensibly womanly thing to do. He was sympathetic all the same. 'You shouldn't be alone! That's the truth of the matter,' he said. 'It's a shame!'

'Oh, it can't be helped,' she said. There was something she wanted to shrug off in his sympathy, while at the same time there was something in it she wanted to take. 'Would you like to do something for me?' she asked impulsively. 'Would you wait and put out the lights down here and let me get back upstairs before you go?'

After she had spoken, for a minute she felt foolish, but she saw at once that, if anything, he thought it only too little to do for her. He was genuinely troubled about her. And it wasn't only the present moment that concerned him; he seemed to be considering the whole problem of her isolation and loneliness. 'Is there nobody could stay here with you – at night even? It would have to be another woman, of course,' he added quickly, and her heart was warmed by the way – without a word from her – he rejected that solution out of hand. 'You don't want a woman about the place,' he said flatly.

'Oh, I'm all right, really. I'll get used to it,' she said.

'It's a shame, all the same,' he said. He said it helplessly, though, and he motioned her towards the stairs. 'You'll be all right for tonight, anyway,' he said. 'Go on up the stairs now, and I'll put out the lights.' He had already turned around to go back into the sitting – room.

Yet it wasn't quite as she intended for some reason, and it was somewhat reluctantly that she started up the stairs.

'Wait a minute! How do I put out this one?' he called out before she was halfway up.

'Oh, I'd better put out that one myself,' she said, thinking of the awkward position of the plug. She ran down again, and, going past him into the little room, she knelt and pulled at the cord. Instantly the room was deluged in darkness. And instantly she felt that she had done something stupid. It was not like turning out a light by a switch at the door and being able to step back at once into the lighted hall. She got to her feet as quickly as she could, but as she did, she saw that Crossen had come to the doorway. His bulk was blocked out against the light beyond. 'I'll leave the rest to you,' she said, in order to break the peculiar silence that had come down on the house.

But he didn't move. He stood there, the full of the doorway.

'The other switches are over there by the hall door,' she said, unwilling to brush past him. Why didn't he move? 'Over there,' she repeated, stretching out her arm and pointing, but instead of moving he caught at her outstretched arm, and, putting out his other hand, he pressed his palm against the door-jamb, barring the way.

'Tell me,' he whispered, his words falling over each other, 'are you never lonely – at all?'

'What did you say?' she said in a clear voice, because the thickness of his voice sickened her. She had hardly heard what he said. Her one thought was to get past him.

He leaned forward. 'What about a little kiss?' he whispered, and to get a better hold on her he let go the hand he had pressed against the wall, but before he caught at her with both hands she had wrenched her arm free of him, and, ignominiously ducking under his armpit, she was out next minute in the lighted hall.

Out there – because light was all the protection she needed from him, the old fool – she began to laugh. She had only to wait for him to come sheepishly out.

But there was something she hadn't counted on; she hadn't counted on there being anything pathetic in his sheepishness. There was something actually pitiful in the way he shambled into the light, not raising his eyes. And she was so surprisingly touched by him that before he had time to utter a word she put out her hand. 'Don't feel too bad,' she said. 'I didn't mind.'

Even then, he didn't look at her. He just took her hand and pressed it gratefully, his face still turned away. And to her dismay she saw that his nose was running water. Like a small boy, he wiped it with the back of his fist, streaking his face. 'I don't know what came over me,' he said slowly. 'I'm getting on to be an old man now. I thought I was beyond all that.' He wiped his face again. 'Beyond letting myself go, anyway,' he amended miserably.

'Oh, it was nothing,' she said.

He shook his head. 'It wasn't as if I had cause for what I did.'

'But you did nothing,' she protested.

'It wasn't nothing to me,' he said dejectedly.

For a minute, they stood there silent. The hall door was still ajar, but she didn't dare to close it. What am I going to do with him now, she thought. I'll have him here all night if I'm not careful. What time was it, anyway? All scale and proportion seemed to have gone from the night. 'Well, I'll see you in the morning, Mr Crossen!' she said, as matter-of-factly as possible.

He nodded, but made no move. 'You know I meant no disrespect to you, Ma'am, don't you?' he said then, looking imploringly at her. 'I always had a great regard for you. And for your husband, too. I was thinking of him this very night when I was coming up to the house. And I thought of him again when you came to the door looking like a young girl. I thought what a pity it was him to be taken from you, and you both so young! Oh, what came over me at all? And what would Mona say if she knew?'

'But you wouldn't tell her, I hope!' she cried. What sort of a figure would she cut if he told about her coming down in her bare feet with her hair down her back! 'Take care would you tell her!' she warned.

'I don't suppose I ought,' he said, but he said it uncertainly and morosely, and he leaned back against the wall. 'She's been a good woman, Mona. I wouldn't want anyone to think different. Even the boys could tell you. She's been a good mother to them all these years. She never made a bit of difference between them. Some say she was better to Bartley than to any of them! She reared him from a week old. She was living next door to us, you see, at the time –' He hesitated. 'At the time I was left with him,' he finished in a flat voice. 'She came in that first night and took him home to her own bed – and, mind you, that wasn't a small thing for a woman who knew nothing about children, not being what you'd call a young girl at the time, in spite of the big family she gave me afterwards. She took him home that night, and she looked after him. It isn't every woman would care to be responsible for a newborn baby. That's a thing a man doesn't forget easy! There's many I know would say that if she hadn't taken him someone else would have, but no one only her would have done it the way she did.

'She used to have him all day in her own cottage, feeding him and the rest of it. But at night, when I'd be back from the fields, she'd bring him home and leave him down in his little crib by the fire alongside of me. She used to let on she had things to do in her own place, and she'd slip away and leave us alone, but that wasn't her real reason for leaving him. She knew the way I'd be sitting looking into the fire, wondering how I'd face the long years ahead, and she left the child there with me to break my thoughts. And she was right. I never got long to brood. The child would give a cry, or a whinge, and I'd have to run out and fetch her to him. Or else she'd hear him herself maybe, and run in without me having to call her at all. I used often think she must have kept every window and door in her place open, for fear she'd lose a sound from either of us. And so, bit by bit, I was knit back into a living man. I often wondered what would have become of me if it wasn't for her. There are men and when the bright way closes to them there's no knowing but they'll take a dark way. And I was that class of man.

'I told you she used to take the little fellow away in the day and bring him back at night? Well, of course, she used to take him away again coming on to the real dark of night. She'd take him away to her own bed. But as the months went on and he got bigger, I could see she hated taking him away from me at all. He was beginning to smile and play with his fists and be real company. "I wonder ought I leave him with you tonight," she'd say then, night after night. And sometimes she'd run in and dump him down in the middle of the big double bed in the room off the kitchen, but the next minute she'd snatch him up again. "I'd be afraid you'd overlie him! You might only smother him, God between us and all harm!" "You'd better take him," I'd say, I used to hate to see him go myself by this time. All the same, I was afraid he'd start crying in the night, and what would I do then? If I had to go out for her in the middle of the night, it could cause a lot of talk. There was talk enough as things were, I can tell you, although there was no grounds for it. I had no more notion of her than if she wasn't a woman at all – would you believe that? But one night when she took him up and put him down, and put him down and took him up, and went on and went on about leaving him or taking him, I had to laugh. "It's a pity you can't stay along with him, and that would settle all," I said. I was only joking her, but she got as red as fire, and next thing she burst out crying! But not before she'd caught up the child and wrapped her coat around him. Then, after giving me a terrible look, she ran out of the door with him.

'Well, that was the beginning of it. I'd no idea she had any feelings for me. I thought it was only for the child. But men are fools, as women well know, and she knew before me what was right and proper for us both. And for the child, too. Some women have great insight into these things! And God opened my own eyes then to the woman I had in her, and I saw it was better I took her than wasted away after the one that was gone. And wasn't I right?'

'Of course you were right,' she said quickly.

But he slumped back against the wall, and the abject look came back into his eyes.

I'll never get rid of him, she thought desperately. 'Ah, what ails you!' she cried impatiently. 'Forget it, can't you?'

'I can't,' he said simply. 'And it's not only me – it's the wife I'm thinking about. I've shamed her!'

'Ah, for heaven's sake. It's nothing got to do with her at all.'

Surprised, he looked up at her. 'You're not blaming yourself, surely?' he asked.

She'd have laughed at that if she hadn't seen she was making headway – another stroke and she'd be rid of him. 'Arrah, what are you blaming any of us for!' she cried. 'It's got nothing to do with any of us – with you, or me, or the woman at home waiting for you. It was the other one! That girl – your first wife – Bridie! It was her! Blame her! She's the one did it!' The words had broken from her. For a moment, she thought she was hysterical and that she could not stop. 'You thought you could forget her,' she said, 'but see what she did to you when she got the chance!' She stopped and looked at him.

He was standing at the open door. He didn't look back. 'God rest her soul,' he said, and he stepped into the night.

Happiness

Mother had a lot to say. This does not mean she was always talking but that we children felt the wells she drew upon were deep, deep, deep. Her theme was happiness: what it was, what it was not; where we might find it, where not; and how, if found, it must be guarded. Never must we confound it with pleasure. Nor think sorrow its exact opposite.

'Take Father Hugh,' Mother's eyes flashed as she looked at him. 'According to him, sorrow is an ingredient of happiness – a *necessary* ingredient, if you please!' And when he tried to protest she put up her hand. 'There may be a freakish truth in the theory – for some people. But not for me. And not, I hope, for my children.' She looked severely at us three girls. We laughed. None of us had had much experience with sorrow. Bea and I were children and Linda only a year old when our father died suddenly after a short illness that had not at first seemed serious. 'I've known people to make sorrow a *substitute* for happiness,' Mother said.

Father Hugh protested again. 'You're not putting me in that class, I hope?'

Father Hugh, ever since our father died, had been the closest of anyone to us as a family, without being close to any one of us in particular – even to Mother. He lived in a monastery near our farm in County Meath, and he had been one of the celebrants at the Requiem High Mass our father's political importance had demanded. He met us that day for the first time, but he took to dropping in to see us, with the idea of filling the crater of loneliness left at our centre. He did not know that there was a cavity in his own life, much less that we would fill it. He and Mother were both young in those days, and perhaps it gave scandal to some that he was so often in our house, staying till late into the night and, indeed, thinking nothing of stopping all night if there was any special reason, such as one of us being sick. He had even on occasion slept there if the night was too wet for tramping home across the fields.

When we girls were young, we were so used to having Father

Hugh around that we never stood on ceremony with him but in his presence dried our hair and pared our nails and never minded what garments were strewn about. As for Mother – she thought nothing of running out of the bathroom in her slip, brushing her teeth or combing her hair, if she wanted to tell him something she might otherwise forget. And she brooked no criticism of her behaviour. 'Celibacy was never meant to take all the warmth and homeliness out of their lives,' she said.

On this point, too, Bea was adamant. Bea, the middle sister, was our oracle. 'I'm so glad he *has* Mother,' she said, 'as well as her having him, because it must be awful the way most women treat them – priests, I mean – as if they were pariahs. Mother treats him like a human being – that's all.'

And when it came to Mother's ears that there had been gossip about her making free with Father Hugh, she opened her eyes wide in astonishment. 'But he's only a priest!' she said.

Bea giggled. 'It's a good job he didn't hear *that*,' she said to me afterwards. 'It would undo the good she's done him. You'd think he was a eunuch.'

'Bea!' I said. 'Do you think he's in love with her?'

'If so, he doesn't know it,' Bea said firmly. 'It's her soul he's after! Maybe he wants to make sure of her in the next world!'

But thoughts of the world to come never troubled Mother. 'If anything ever happens to me, children,' she said, 'suddenly, I mean, or when you are not near me, or I cannot speak to you, I want you to promise you won't feel bad. There's no need! Just remember that I had a happy life – and that if I had to choose my kind of heaven I'd take it on this earth with you again, no matter how much you might annoy me!'

You see, annoyance and fatigue, according to Mother, and even illness and pain, could coexist with happiness. She had a habit of asking people if they were happy at times and in places that – to say the least of it – seemed to us inappropriate. 'But are you happy?' she'd probe as one lay sick and bathed in sweat, or in the throes of a jumping toothache. And once in our presence she made the inquiry of an old friend as he lay upon his deathbed.

'Why not?' she said when we took her to task for it later. 'Isn't it more important than ever to be happy when you're dying? Take my own father! You know what he said in his last moments? On his deathbed, he defied me to name a man who had enjoyed a better life. In spite of dreadful pain, his face *radiated* happiness!' Mother nodded her head comfortably. 'Happiness drives out pain, as fire burns out fire.'

Having no knowledge of our own to pit against hers, we thirstily drank in her rhetoric. Only Bea was sceptical. 'Perhaps you *got* it from him, like spots, or fever,' she said. 'Or something that could at least be slipped from hand to hand.'

'Do you think I'd have taken it if that were the case!' Mother cried. 'Then, when he needed it most?'

'Not there and then!' Bea said stubbornly. 'I meant as a sort of legacy.'

'Don't you think in *that* case,' Mother said, exasperated, 'he would have felt obliged to leave it to your grandmother?'

Certainly we knew that in spite of his lavish heart our grandfather had failed to provide our grandmother with enduring happiness. He had passed that job on to Mother. And Mother had not made too good a fist of it, even when Father was living and she had him – and later, us children – to help.

As for Father Hugh, he had given our grandmother up early in the game. 'God Almighty couldn't make that woman happy,' he said one day, seeing Mother's face, drawn and pale with fatigue, preparing for the nightly run over to her own mother's flat that would exhaust her utterly.

There were evenings after she came home from the library where she worked when we saw her stand with the car keys in her hand, trying to think which would be worse – to slog over there on foot, or take out the car again. And yet the distance was short. It was Mother's day that had been too long.

'Weren't you over to see her this morning?' Father Hugh demanded.

'No matter!' said Mother. She was no doubt thinking of the forlorn face our grandmother always put on when she was leaving. ('Don't say good night, Vera,' Grandmother would plead. 'It makes me feel too lonely. And you never can tell – you might slip over again before you go to bed!')

'Do you know the time?' Bea would say impatiently, if she happened to be with Mother. Not indeed that the lateness of the hour counted for anything, because in all likelihood Mother *would* go back, if only to pass by under the window and see that the lights were out, or stand and listen and make sure that as far as she could tell all was well.

'I wouldn't mind if she was happy,' Mother said.

'And how do you know she's not?' we'd ask.

'When people are happy, I can feel it. Can't you?'

We were not sure. Most people thought our grandmother was a gay creature, a small birdy being who even at a great age laughed like a girl, and – more remarkably – sang like one, as she went about her day. But beak and claw were of steel. She'd think nothing of sending Mother back to a shop three times if her errands were not exactly right. 'Not sugar like that – that's *too* fine; it's not castor sugar I want. But *not* as coarse as *that*, either. I want an in-between kind.'

Provoked one day, my youngest sister, Linda, turned and gave battle. 'You're mean!' she cried. 'You love ordering people about!'

Grandmother preened, as if Linda had acclaimed an attribute. 'I was always hard to please,' she said. 'As a girl, I used to be called Miss Imperious.'

And Miss Imperious she remained as long as she lived, even when she was a great age. Her orders were then given a wry twist by the fact that as she advanced in age she took to calling her daughter Mother, as we did.

There was one great phrase with which our grandmother opened every sentence: 'if only'. 'If only,' she'd say, when we came to visit her – 'if only you'd come earlier, before I was worn out expecting you!' Or if we were early, then if only it was later, after she'd had a rest and could enjoy us, be *able* for us. And if we brought her flowers, she'd sigh to think that if only we'd brought them the previous day she'd have had a visitor to appreciate them, or say it was a pity the stems weren't longer. If only we'd picked a few green leaves, or included some buds, because, she said disparagingly, the poor flowers we'd brought were already wilting. We might just as well not have brought them! As the years went on, Grandmother had a new bead to add to her rosary: if only her friends were not all dead! By their absence, they reduced to nil all *real* enjoyment in anything. Our own father – her son-in-law – was the one person who had ever gone close to pleasing her. But even here there had been a snag. 'If only he was my real son!' she used to say with a sigh.

Mother's mother lived on through our childhood and into our early maturity (though she outlived the money our grandfather left her), and in our minds she was a complicated mixture of valiance and defeat. Courageous and generous within the limits of her own life, her simplest demand was yet enormous in the larger frame of Mother's life, and so we never could see her with the same clarity of vision with which we saw our grandfather, or our own father. Them we saw only through Mother's eyes.

'Take your grandfather!' she'd cry, and instantly we'd see him, his eyes burning upon us – yes, upon *us*, although in his day only one of us had been born: me. At another time, Mother would cry, 'Take your own father!' and instantly we'd see *him* – tall, handsome, young, and much more suited to marry one of us than poor bedraggled Mother.

Most fascinating of all were the times Mother would say 'Take

me!' By magic then, staring down the years, we'd see blazingly clear
a small girl with black hair and buttoned boots, who, though plain
and pouting, burned bright, like a star. 'I was happy, you see,'
Mother said. And we'd strain hard to try and understand the
mystery of the light that still radiated from her. 'I used to lean along
a tree that grew out over the river,' she said, 'and look down
through the grey leaves at the water flowing past below, and I used
to think it was not the stream that flowed but me, spread-eagled
over it, who flew through the air! Like a bird! That I'd found the
secret!' She made it seem there might *be* such a secret, just waiting to
be found. Another time she'd dream that she'd be a great singer.

'We didn't know you sang, Mother!'

She had to laugh. 'Like a crow,' she said.

Sometimes she used to think she'd swim the Channel.

'Did you swim *that* well, Mother?'

'Oh, not really – just the breast stroke,' she said. 'And then only
by the aid of two pig bladders blown up by my father and tied
around my middle. But I used to throb – yes, throb – with
happiness.'

Behind Mother's back, Bea raised her eyebrows.

What was it, we used to ask ourselves – that quality that she, we
felt sure, misnamed? Was it courage? Was it strength, health, or
high spirits? Something you could not give or take – a conundrum?
A game of catch-as-you-can?

'I know,' cried Bea. 'A sham!'

Whatever it was, we knew that Mother would let no wind of
violence from within or without tear it from her. Although, one
evening when Father Hugh was with us, our astonished ears heard
her proclaim that there might be a time when one had to slacken
hold on it – let go – to catch at it again with a surer hand. In the way,
we supposed, that the high-wire walker up among the painted stars
of his canvas sky must wait to fling himself through the air until the
bar he catches at has started to sway perversely from him. Oh no,
no! That downward drag at our innards we could not bear, the belly
swelling to the shape of a pear. Let happiness go by the board. 'After
all, lots of people seem to make out without it,' Bea cried. It was too
tricky a business. And might it not be that one had to be born with a
flair for it?

'A flair would not be enough,' Mother answered. 'Take Father
Hugh. He, if anyone, had a flair for it – a natural capacity! You've
only to look at him when he's off guard, with you children, or
helping me in the garden. But he rejects happiness! He casts it from
him.'

'That is simply not true, Vera,' cried Father Hugh, overhearing her. 'It's just that I don't place an inordinate value on it like you. I don't think it's enough to carry one all the way. To the end, I mean – and after.'

'Oh, don't talk about the end when we're only in the middle,' cried Mother. And, indeed, at that moment her own face shone with such happiness it was hard to believe that earth was not her heaven. Certainly it was her constant contention that of happiness she had had a lion's share. This, however, we, in private, doubted. Perhaps there were times when she had had a surplus of it – when she was young, say, with her redoubtable father, whose love blazed circles around her, making winter into summer and ice into fire. Perhaps she did have a brimming measure in her early married years. By straining hard, we could find traces left in our minds from those days of milk and honey. Our father, while he lived, had cast a magic over everything, for us as well as for her. He held his love up over us like an umbrella and kept off the troubles that afterwards came down on us, pouring cats and dogs!

But if she did have more than the common lot of happiness in those early days, what use was that when we could remember so clearly how our father's death had ravaged her? And how could we forget the distress it brought on us when, afraid to let her out of our sight, Bea and I stumbled after her everywhere, through the woods and along the bank of the river, where, in the weeks that followed, she tried vainly to find peace.

The summer after Father died, we were invited to France to stay with friends, and when she went walking on the cliffs at Fécamp our fears for her grew frenzied, so that we hung on to her arm and dragged at her skirt, hoping that like leaded weights we'd pin her down if she went too near to the edge. But at night we had to abandon our watch, being forced to follow the conventions of a family still whole – a home still intact – and go to bed at the same time as the other children. It was at that hour, when the coast guard was gone from his rowing boat offshore and the sand was as cold and grey as the sea, that Mother liked to swim. And when she had washed, kissed, and left us, our hearts almost died inside us and we'd creep out of bed again to stand in our bare feet at the mansard and watch as she ran down the shingle, striking out when she reached the water where, far out, wave and sky and mist were one, and the greyness closed over her. If we took our eyes off her for an instant, it was impossible to find her again.

'Oh, make her turn back, God, please!' I prayed out loud one night.

Startled, Bea turned away from the window. 'She'll *have* to turn back sometime, won't she? Unless . . . ?'

Locking our damp hands together, we stared out again. 'She wouldn't!' I whispered. 'It would be a sin!'

Secure in the deterring power of sin, we let out our breath. Then Bea's breath caught again. 'What if she went out so far she used up all her strength? She couldn't swim back! It wouldn't be a sin then!'

'It's the intention that counts,' I whispered.

A second later, we could see an arm lift heavily up and wearily cleave down, and at last Mother was in the shallows, wading back to shore.

'Don't let her see us!' cried Bea. As if our chattering teeth would not give us away when she looked in at us before she went to her own room on the other side of the corridor, where, later in the night, sometimes the sound of crying would reach us.

What was it worth – a happiness bought that dearly.

Mother had never questioned it. And once she told us, 'On a wintry day, I brought my own mother a snowdrop. It was the first one of the year – a bleak bud that had come up stunted before its time – and I meant it for a sign. But do you know what your grandmother said? "What good are snowdrops to me now?" Such a thing to say! What good is a snowdrop at all if it doesn't hold its value always, and never lose it! Isn't that the whole point of a snowdrop? And that is the whole point of happiness, too! What good would it be if it could be erased without trace? Take me and those daffodils!' Stooping, she buried her face in a bunch that lay on the table waiting to be put in vases. 'If they didn't hold their beauty absolute and inviolable, do you think I could bear the sight of them after what happened when your father was in hospital?'

It was a fair question. When Father went to hospital, Mother went with him and stayed in a small hotel across the street so she could be with him all day from early to late. 'Because it was so awful for him – being in Dublin!' she said. 'You have no idea how he hated it.'

That he was dying neither of them realized. How could they know, as it rushed through the sky, that their star was a falling star! But one evening when she'd left him asleep Mother came home for a few hours to see how we were faring, and it broke her heart to see the daffodils out all over the place – in the woods, under the trees, and along the sides of the avenue. There had never been so many, and she thought how awful it was that Father was missing them. 'You sent up little bunches to him, you poor dears!' she said. 'Sweet little bunches, too – squeezed tight as posies by your little fists! But stuffed into vases they couldn't really make up to him for not being able to see them growing!'

So on the way back to the hospital she stopped her car and pulled a great bunch – the full of her arms. 'They took up the whole back seat,' she said, 'and I was so excited at the thought of walking into his room and dumping them on his bed – you know – just plomping them down so he could smell them, and feel them, and look and look! I didn't mean them to be put in vases, or anything ridiculous like that – it would have taken a rainwater barrel to hold them. Why, I could hardly see over them as I came up the steps; I kept tripping. But when I came into the hall, that nun – I told you about her – that nun came up to me, sprang out of nowhere it seemed, although I know now that she was waiting for me, knowing that somebody had to bring me to my senses. But the way she did it! Reached out and grabbed the flowers, letting lots of them fall – I remember them getting stood on. "Where are you going with those foolish flowers, you foolish woman?" she said. "Don't you know your husband is dying? Your prayers are all you can give him now!"

'She was right. I *was* foolish. But I wasn't cured. Afterwards, it was nothing but foolishness the way I dragged you children after me all over Europe. As if any one place was going to be different from another, any better, any less desolate. But there was great satisfaction in bringing you places your father and I had planned to bring you – although in fairness to him I must say that he would not perhaps have brought you so young. And he would not have had an ulterior motive. But above all, he would not have attempted those trips in such a dilapidated car.'

Oh, that car! It was a battered and dilapidated red sports car, so depleted of accessories that when, eventually, we got a new car Mother still stuck out her hand on bends, and in wet weather jumped out to wipe the windscreen with her sleeve. And if fussed, she'd let down the window and shout at people, forgetting she now had a horn. How we had ever fitted into it with all our luggage was a miracle.

'You were never lumpish – any of you!' Mother said proudly. 'But you were very healthy and very strong.' She turned to me. 'Think of how you got that car up the hill in Switzerland!'

'The Alps are not hills, Mother!' I pointed out coldly, as I had done at the time, when, as actually happened, the car failed to make it on one of the inclines. Mother let it run back until it wedged against the rock face, and I had to get out and push till she got going again in first gear. But when it got started it couldn't be stopped to pick me up until it got to the top, where they had to wait for me, and for a very long time.

'Ah, well,' she said, sighing wistfully at the thought of those trips. 'You got something out of them, I hope. All that travelling must have helped you with your geography and your history.'

We looked at each other and smiled, and then Mother herself laughed. 'Remember the time,' she said, 'when we were in Italy, and it was Easter, and all the shops were chock-full of food? The butchers' shops had poultry and game hanging up outside the doors, fully feathered, and with their poor heads dripping blood, and in the windows they had poor little lambs and suckling pigs and young goats, all skinned and hanging by their hindfeet.' Mother shuddered. 'They think so much about food. I found it revolting. I had to hurry past. But Linda, who must have been only four then, dragged at me and stared and stared. You know how children are at that age; they have a morbid fascination for what is cruel and bloody. Her face was flushed and her eyes were wide. I hurried her back to the hotel. But next morning she crept into my room. She crept up to me and pressed against me. "Can't we go back, just once, and look again at that shop?" she whispered. "The shop where they have the little children hanging up for Easter!" It was the young goats, of course, but I'd said "kids", I suppose. How we laughed.' But her face was grave. 'You were *so* good on those trips, all of you,' she said. 'You were really very good children in general. Otherwise I would never have put so much effort into rearing you, because I wasn't a bit maternal. You brought out the best in me! I put an unnatural effort into you, of course, because I was taking my standards from your father, forgetting that his might not have remained so inflexible if he had lived to middle age and was beset by life, like other parents.'

'Well, the job is nearly over now, Vera,' said Father Hugh. 'And you didn't do so badly.'

'That's right, Hugh,' said Mother, and she straightened up, and put her hand to her back the way she sometimes did in the garden when she got up from her knees after weeding. 'I didn't go over to the enemy anyway! We survived!' Then a flash of defiance came into her eyes. 'And we were happy. That's the main thing!'

Father Hugh frowned. 'There you go again!' he said.

Mother turned on him. 'I don't think you realize the onslaughts that were made upon our happiness! The minute Robert died, they came down on me – cohorts of relatives, friends, even strangers, all draped in black, opening their arms like bats to let me pass into their company. "Life is a vale of tears," they said. "You are privileged to find it out so young!" Ugh! After I staggered on to my feet and began to take hold of life once more, they fell back defeated. And the first day I gave a laugh – pouff, they were blown out like candles. They weren't living in a real world at all; they belonged to a ghostly world where life was easy: all one had to do was sit and weep. It takes effort to push back the stone from the mouth of the tomb and walk out.'

Effort. Effort. Ah, but that strange-sounding word could invoke little sympathy from those who had not learned yet what it meant. Life must have been hardest for Mother in those years when we older ones were at college – no longer children, and still dependent on her. Indeed, we made more demands on her than ever then, having moved into new areas of activity and emotion. And our friends! Our friends came and went as freely as we did ourselves, so that the house was often like a café – and one where pets were not prohibited but took their places on our chairs and beds, as regardless as the people. And anyway it was hard to have sympathy for someone who got things into such a state as Mother. All over the house there was clutter. Her study was like the returned-letter department of a post-office, with stacks of paper everywhere, bills paid and unpaid, letters answered and unanswered, tax returns, pamphlets, leaflets. If by mistake we left the door open on a windy day, we came back to find papers flapping through the air like frightened birds. Efficient only in that she managed eventually to conclude every task she began, it never seemed possible to outsiders that by Mother's methods anything whatever could be accomplished. In an attempt to keep order elsewhere, she made her own room the clearing house into which the rest of us put everything: things to be given away, things to be mended, things to be stored, things to be treasured, things to be returned – even things to be thrown out! By the end of the year, the room resembled an obsolescence dump. And no one could help her; the chaos of her life was as personal as an act of creation – one might as well try to finish another person's poem.

As the years passed, Mother rushed around more hectically. And although Bea and I had married and were not at home any more, except at holiday time and for occasional weekends, Linda was noisier than the two of us put together had been, and for every follower we had brought home she brought twenty. The house was never still. Now that we were reduced to being visitors, we watched Mother's tension mount to vertigo, knowing that, like a spinning top, she could not rest till she fell. But now at the smallest pretext Father Hugh would call in the doctor and Mother would be put on the mail boat and dispatched for London. For it was essential that she get far enough away to make phoning home every night prohibitively costly.

Unfortunately, the thought of departure often drove a spur into her and she redoubled her effort to achieve order in her affairs. She would be up until the early hours ransacking her desk. To her, as always, the shortest parting entailed a preparation as for death. And as if it were her end that was at hand, we would all be summoned, although she had no time to speak a word to us, because five minutes before departure she would still be attempting to reply to letters that were the acquisition of weeks and would have taken whole days to dispatch.

'Don't you know the taxi is at the door, Vera?' Father Hugh would say, running his hand through his grey hair and looking very dishevelled himself. She had him at times as distracted as herself. 'You can't do any more. You'll have to leave the rest till you come back.'

'I can't, I can't!' Mother would cry. 'I'll have to cancel my plans.'

One day, Father Hugh opened the lid of her case, which was strapped up in the hall, and with a swipe of his arm he cleared all the papers on the top of the desk pell-mell into the suitcase. 'You can sort them on the boat,' he said, 'or the train to London!'

Thereafter, Mother's luggage always included an empty case to hold the unfinished papers on her desk. And years afterwards a steward on the Irish Mail told us she was a familiar figure, working away at letters and bills nearly all the way from Holyhead to Euston. 'She gave it up about Rugby or Crewe,' he said. 'She'd get talking to someone in the compartment.' He smiled. 'There was one time coming down the train I was just in time to see her close up the window with a guilty look. I didn't say anything, but I think she'd emptied those paper of hers out the window!'

Quite likely. When we were children, even a few hours away from us gave her composure. And in two weeks or less, when she'd come home, the well of her spirit would be freshened. We'd hardly know her – her step so light, her eye so bright, and her love and patience once more freely flowing. But in no time at all the house would fill up once more with the noise and confusion of too many people and too many animals, and again we'd be fighting our corner with cats and dogs, bats, mice, bees and even wasps. 'Don't kill it!' Mother would cry if we raised a hand to an angry wasp. 'Just catch it, dear, and put it outside. Open the window and let it fly away!' But even this treatment could at times be deemed too harsh. 'Wait a minute.

Close the window!' she'd cry. 'It's too cold outside. It will die. That's why it came in, I suppose! Oh dear, what will we do?' Life would be going full blast again.

There was only one place Mother found rest. When she was at breaking point and fit to fall, she'd go out into the garden – not to sit or stroll around but to dig, to drag up weeds, to move great clumps of corms or rhizomes, or indeed quite frequently to haul huge rocks from one place to another. She was always laying down a path, building a dry wall, or making compost heaps as high as hills. However jaded she might be going out, when dark forced her in at last her step had the spring of a daisy. So if she did not succeed in defining happiness to our understanding, we could see that whatever it was, she possessed it to the full when she was in her garden.

One of us said as much one Sunday when Bea and I had dropped round for the afternoon. Father Hugh was with us again. 'It's an unthinking happiness, though,' he cavilled. We were standing at the drawing-room window, looking out to where in the fading light we could see Mother on her knees weeding, in the long border that stretched from the house right down to the woods. 'I wonder how she'd take it if she were stricken down and had to give up that heavy work!' he said. Was he perhaps a little jealous of how she could stoop and bend? He himself had begun to use a stick. I was often a little jealous of her myself, because although I was married and had children of my own, I had married young and felt the weight of living as heavy as a weight of years. 'She doesn't take enough care of herself,' Father Hugh said sadly. 'Look at her out there with nothing under her knees to protect her from the damp ground.' It was almost too dim for us to see her, but even in the drawing-room it was chilly. 'She should not be let stay out there after the sun goes down.'

'Just you try to get her in then!' said Linda, who had come into the room in time to hear him. 'Don't you know by now anyway that what would kill another person only seems to make Mother thrive?'

Father Hugh shook his head again. 'You seem to forget it's not younger she's getting!' He fidgeted and fussed, and several times went to the window to stare out apprehensively. He was really getting quite elderly.

'Come and sit down, Father Hugh,' Bea said, and to take his mind off Mother she turned on the light and blotted out the garden. Instead of seeing through the window, we saw into it as into a mirror, and there between the flower-laden tables and lamps it was ourselves we saw moving vaguely. Like Father Hugh, we, too, were waiting for her to come in before we called an end to the day.

'Oh, this is ridiculous!' Father Hugh cried at last. 'She'll have to listen to reason.' And going back to the window he threw it open.

'Vera!' he called. 'Vera!' – sternly, so sternly that, more intimate than an endearment, his tone shocked us. 'She didn't hear me,' he said, turning back blinking at us in the lighted room. 'I'm going out to get her.' And in a minute he was gone from the room. As he ran down the garden path, we stared at each other, astonished; his step, like his voice, was the step of a lover. 'I'm coming, Vera!' he cried.

Although she was never stubborn except in things that mattered, Mother had not moved. In the wholehearted way she did every-thing, she was bent down close to the ground. It wasn't the light only that was dimming; her eyesight also was failing, I thought, as instinctively I followed Father Hugh.

But halfway down the path I stopped. I had seen something he had not: Mother's hand that appeared to support itself in a forked branch of an old tree peony she had planted as a bride was not in fact gripping it but impaled upon it. And the hand that appeared to be grubbing in the clay in fact was sunk into the soft mould. 'Mother!' I screamed, and I ran forward, but when I reached her I covered my face with my hands. 'Oh Father Hugh!' I cried. 'Is she dead?'

It was Bea who answered, hysterical. 'She is! She is!' she cried, and she began to pound Father Hugh on the back with her fists, as if his pessimistic words had made this happen.

But Mother was not dead. And at first the doctor even offered hope of her pulling through. But from the moment Father Hugh lifted her up to carry her into the house we ourselves had no hope, seeing how effortlessly he, who was not strong, could carry her. When he put her down on her bed, her head hardly creased the pillow. Mother lived for four more hours.

Like the days of her life, those four hours that Mother lived were packed tight with concern and anxiety. Partly conscious, partly delirious, she seemed to think the counterpane was her desk, and she scrabbled her fingers upon it as if trying to sort out a muddle of bills and correspondence. No longer indifferent now, we listened, anguished, to the distracted cries that had for all our lifetime been so familiar to us. 'Oh, where is it? Where is it? I had it a minute ago! Where on earth did I put it?'

'Vera, Vera, stop worrying,' Father Hugh pleaded, but she waved him away and went on sifting though the sheets as if they were sheets of paper. 'Oh, Vera!' he begged. 'Listen to me. Do you not know –'

Bea pushed between them. 'You're not to tell her!' she comman-ded. 'Why frighten her?'

'But it ought not to frighten her,' said Father Hugh. 'This is what I was always afraid would happen – that she'd be frightened when it came to the end.'

At that moment, as if to vindicate him, Mother's hands fell idle on the coverlet, palm upward and empty. And turning her head she stared at each of us in turn, beseechingly. 'I cannot face it,' she whispered. 'I can't! I can't! I can't!'

'Oh, my God!' Bea said, and she started to cry.

'Vera. For God's sake listen to me,' Father Hugh cried, and pressing his face to hers, as close as a kiss, he kept whispering to her, trying to cast into the dark tunnel before her the light of his own faith.

But it seemed to us that Mother must already be looking into God's exigent eyes. 'I can't!' she cried. 'I can't!'

Then her mind came back from the stark world of the spirit to the world where her body was still detained, but even that world was now a whirling kaleidoscope of things which only she could see. Suddenly her eyes focussed, and, catching at Father Hugh, she pulled herself up a little and pointed to something we could not see. 'What will be done with them?' Her voice was anxious. 'They ought to be put in water anyway,' she said, and leaning over the edge of the bed, she pointed to the floor. 'Don't step on that one!' she said sharply. Then more sharply still, she addressed us all. 'Have them sent to the public ward,' she said peremptorily. 'Don't let that nun take them; she'll only put them on the altar. And God doesn't want them! He made them for *us* – not for Himself!'

It was the familiar rhetoric that all her life had characterized her utterances. For a moment we were mystified. Then Bea gasped. 'The daffodils!' she cried. 'The day Father died!' And over her face came the light that had so often blazed over Mother's. Leaning across the bed, she pushed Father Hugh aside. And, putting out her hands, she held Mother's face between her palms as tenderly as if it were the face of a child. 'It's all right, Mother. You don't *have* to face it! It's over!' Then she who had so fiercely forbade Father Hugh to do so blurted out the truth. 'You've finished with this world, Mother,' she said, and, confident that her tidings were joyous, her voice was strong.

Mother made the last effort of her life and grasped at Bea's meaning. She let out a sigh, and, closing her eyes, she sank back, and this time her head sank so deep into the pillow that it would have been dented had it been a pillow of stone.

A Memory

James did all right for a man on his own. An old woman from the village came in for a few hours a day and gave him a hot meal before she went home. She also got ready an evening meal needing only to be heated up. As well, she put his breakfast egg in a saucepan of water beside the paraffin stove, with a box of matches beside it in case he mislaid his own. She took care of all but one of the menial jobs of living. The one she couldn't do for him was one James hated most – cleaning out ashes from the grate in his study and lighting up the new fire for the day.

James was an early riser and firmly believed in giving the best of his brain to his work. So, the minute he was dressed he went out to the kitchen and lit the stove under the coffee pot. Then he got the ash bucket and went at the grate. When the ashes were out the rest wasn't too bad. There was kindling in the hot press and the old woman left a few split logs for getting up a quick blaze. He had the room well warmed by the time he had eaten his breakfast. His main objection to doing the grate was that he got his suit covered with ashes. He knew he ought to wear tweeds now that he was living full-time at the cottage, but he stuck obstinately to his dark suit and white collar, feeling as committed to this attire as to his single state. Both were part and parcel of his academic dedication. His work filled his life as it filled his day. He seldom had occasion to go up to the University. When he went up it was to see Myra, and then only on impulse if for some reason work went against him. This did happen periodically in spite of his devotion to it. Without warning a day would come when he'd wake up in a queer, unsettled mood that would send him prowling around the cottage, lighting up cigarette after cigarette and looking out of the window until he'd have to face the fact that he was not going to do a stroke. Inevitably the afternoon would see him with his hat and coat on, going down the road to catch the bus for Dublin – and an evening with Myra.

This morning he was in fine fettle though, when he dug the shovel into the mound of grey ash. But he was annoyed to see a volley of sparks go up the black chimney. The hearth would be hot, and the paper would catch fire before he'd have time to build his little pyre. There was more kindling in the kitchen press, but he'd have felt guilty using more than the allotted amount, thinking of the poor old creature wielding that heavy axe. He really ought to split those logs himself.

When he first got the cottage he used to enjoy that kind of thing. But after he'd been made a research professor and able to live down there all year round he came to have less and less zest for manual work. He sort of lost the knack of it. Ah well, his energies were totally expended in mental work. It would not be surprising if muscularly he got a bit soft.

James got up off his knees and brushed himself down. The fire was taking hold. The nimble flames played in and out through the dead twigs as sunlight must once have done when the sap was green. Standing watching them, James flexed his fingers. He wouldn't like to think he was no longer fit. Could his increasing aversion to physical labour be a sign of decreasing vigour? He frowned. He would not consider himself a vain man, it was simply that he'd got used to the look of himself; was accustomed to his slight, spare figure. But surely by mental activity he burned up as much fuel as any navvy or stevedore? Lunatics never had to worry about exercise either! Who ever saw a corpulent madman? He smiled. He must remember to tell that to Myra. Her laugh was always so quick and responsive although even if a second or two later she might seize on some inherently serious point in what had at first amused her. It was Myra who had first drawn his attention to this curious transference – this drawing off of energies – from the body to the brain. She herself had lost a lot of the skill in her fingers. When she was younger – or so she claimed – she'd been quite a good cook, and could sew, and that kind of thing, although frankly James couldn't imagine her being much good about the house. But when she gave up teaching and went into free-lance translation her work began to make heavy demands on her, and she too, like him, lost all inclination for physical chores. Now – or so she said – she could not bake a cake to save her life. As for sewing – well here again frankly – to him the sight of a needle in her hand would be ludicrous. In fact he knew – they both knew – that when they first met, it was her lack of domesticity that had been the essence of her appeal for him. For a woman, it was quite remarkable how strong was the intellectual climate of thought in which she lived. She had concocted a sort of cocoon of thought and wrapped herself up in it. One became aware of it immediately one stepped inside her little flat. There was another thing! The way she used the word flat to designate what was really a charming little mews house. It was behind one of the Georgian squares, and it had a beautiful little garden at the back and courtyard in front. He hadn't been calling there for very long until he understood why she referred to it as her flat. It was a word that did not have unpleasant connotations of domesticity.

Her little place had a marvellously masculine air, and yet, miraculously, Myra herself remained very feminine. She was, of course, a pretty woman, although she hated him to say this – and she didn't smoke, or drink more than a dutiful pre-dinner sherry with him, which she often forgot to finish. And there was a nice scent from her clothes, a scent at times quite disturbing. It often bothered him and was occasionally the cause of giving her the victory in one of the really brilliant arguments that erupted so spontaneously the moment he stepped inside the door.

Yes, it was hard to believe Myra could ever have been a homebody. But if she said it was so, then it *was* so. Truth could have been her second name. With regard to her domestic failure, she had recently told him a most amusing story. He couldn't recall the actual incident, but it had certainly corroborated her theory of the transference of skill. It was – she said – as if part of her had become palsied, although at the time her choice of that word had made him wince, it was so altogether unsuitable for a woman like her, obviously now in her real prime. He'd pulled her up on that. Verbal exactitude was something they both knew to be of the utmost importance, although admittedly rarer to find in a woman than a man.

'It is a quality I'd never have looked to find in a woman, Myra,' he'd said to her on one of his first visits to the flat – perhaps his very first.

He never forgot her answer.

'It's not something I'd ever expect a man to look for in a woman,' she said. 'Thank you, James, for not jumping to the conclusion that I could not possibly possess it.'

Yes – that must have been on his first visit because he'd been startled by such quick-fire volley in reply to what had been only a casual compliment. No wonder their friendship got off to a flying start!

Thinking of the solid phalanx of years that had been built up since that evening, James felt a glow of satisfaction, and for a moment he didn't realize that the fire he was supposed to be tending had got off to a good start, and part at least of his sense of well-being was coming from its warmth stealing over him.

The flames were going up the chimney with soft nervous rushes and the edges of the logs were deckled with small sharp flames, like the teeth of a saw. He could safely leave it now and have breakfast.

But just then he did remember what it was Myra had been good at when she was young. Embroidery! She had once made herself an evening dress with the bodice embroidered all over in beads. And she'd worn it! So it must have been well made. Even his sister Kay, who disliked Myra, had to concede she dressed well. Yes, she must indeed have been fairly good at sewing in her young days. Yet one day recently when she ripped her skirt in the National Library she hadn't been able to mend it.

'It wasn't funny, James,' she chided when he laughed. 'The whole front pleat was ripped. I had to borrow a needle and thread from the lavatory attendant. Fortunately I had plenty of time – so when I'd taken it off and sewed it up I decided to give it a professional touch – a finish – with a tailor's arrow. It took time but it was well done and the lavatory attendant was very impressed when I held the skirt up! But next minute when I tried to step into it I found I'd sewn the back to the front. I'd formed a sort of gusset. Can you picture it. I'd turned it into trousers!'

Poor Myra! He laughed still more.

'I tell you, it's not funny, James. And it's the same with cooking. I used at least to be able to boil an egg, whereas now – ' she shrugged her shoulders. 'You know how useless I am in the kitchen.'

She had certainly never attempted to cook a meal for him. They always went out to eat. There was a small café near the flat and they ate there. Or at least they did at the start. But when one evening they decided they didn't really want to go out – perhaps he'd had a headache, or perhaps it was a really wet night, but anyway whatever it was, Myra made no effort to – as she put it – slop up some unappetizing smather. Instead she lifted the phone, and got on to the proprietor of their little café and – as she put it – administered such a dose of coaxy-orum – she really had very amusing ways of expressing herself – that he sent around two trays of food. Two trays, mind you. That was so like her – so quick, so clever. And tactful, too. That night marked a new stage in their relationship.

They'd been seeing a lot of each other by then. He'd been calling to the flat pretty frequently and when they went out for a meal, although the little café was always nearly empty, he had naturally paid the bill each time.

'We couldn't go on like that though, James!' she'd said firmly when he'd tried to pay for the trays of food that night. And she did finally succeed in making him see that if he were to come to the flat as often as she hoped he would – and as he himself certainly hoped – it would put her under too great an obligation to have him pay for the food every time.

'Another woman would be able to run up some tasty little dish that wouldn't cost tuppence,' she said, 'but – ' she made a face ' – that's out. All the same I can't let you put me under too great a compliment to you. Not every time.'

In the end they'd settled on a good compromise. They each paid for a tray.

He had had misgivings, but she rid him of them.

'What would you eat if I wasn't here, Myra?' he'd asked.

'I wouldn't have *cooked* anything, that's certain,' she said, and he didn't pursue the topic, permitting himself just one other brief inquiry.

'What do other people do, I wonder?'

This Myra dismissed with a deprecating laugh.

'I'm afraid I don't know,' she said. 'Or care! Do you?'

'Oh Myra!' In that moment he felt she elevated them both to such pure heights of integrity. 'You know I don't,' he said, and he'd laid his hand over hers as she sat beside him on the sofa.

'That makes two of us!' she said, and she drew a deep breath of contentment.

It was a rich moment. It was probably at that moment he first realized the uniquely undemanding quality of her feeling for him.

But now James saw that the fire was blazing madly. He had to put on another log or it would burn out too fast. He threw on a log and was about to leave the study when, as he passed his desk, a nervous impulse made him look to see that his papers were not disarranged, although there was no one to disturb them.

The papers, of course, were as he had left them. But then the same diabolical nervousness made him go over and pick up the manuscript. Why? He couldn't explain, except that he'd worked late the previous night and, when he did that, he was always idiotically nervous next day, as if he half expected to find the words had been mysteriously erased during the night. That had happened once! He'd got up one morning as usual, full of eagerness to take up where he thought he'd left off only to find he'd stopped in the middle of a sentence – had gone to bed defeated, leaving a most involved and complicated sentence unfinished. He'd only dreamed that he'd finished it off.

This morning, thank heavens, it was no dream. He'd finished the sentence – the whole chapter. It was the last chapter too. A little rephrasing, perhaps some rewording, and the whole thing would be ready for the typist.

Standing in the warm study with the pages of his manuscript in his hand James was further warmed by a self-congratulatory glow. This was the most ambitious thing he'd attempted so far – it was no less than an effort to trace the creative process itself back, as it were, to its source-bed. How glad he was that he'd stuck at it last night. He'd paid heavily for it by tossing around in the sheets until nearly morning. But it was worth it. His intuitions had never yielded up their meanings so fast or so easily. But suddenly his nervousness returned. He hoped to God his writing wasn't illegible? No. It was readable. And although his eye did not immediately pick up any of the particularly lucid – even felicitous – phrases that he vaguely remembered having hit upon, he'd come on them later when he was re-reading more carefully.

Pleased, James was putting down the manuscript, but on an impulse he took up the last section again. He'd bring it out to the kitchen and begin his re-reading of it while he was having his breakfast, something he never did, having a horror of foodstains on paper. It might, as it were, recharge his batteries, because in spite of his satisfaction with the way the work was going, he had to admit to a certain amount of physical lethargy, due to having gone to bed so late.

It was probably wiser in the long run to do like Myra and confine oneself to a fixed amount of work per day. Nothing would induce Myra to go beyond her pre-determined limit of two thousand words a day. Even when things were going well! It was when they were going well that paradoxically she often stopped work. Really her method of working amazed him. When she encountered difficulty she went doggedly on, worrying at a word like a dog with a bone – as she put it – in order, she explained, to avoid carrying over her frustration with it to the next day. On the other hand, when things were going well and her mind was leaping forward like a flat stone skimming the surface of a lake (her image again, not his, but good, good) *then* sometimes she stopped.

'Because then, James, I have a residue of enthusiasm to start me off next day! I'm not really a dedicated scholar like you – I need stimulus.'

She had a point. But her method wouldn't work for him. It would be mental suicide for him to tear himself away when he was excited. It was only when things got sticky he stopped. When an idea sort of seized up in his mind and he couldn't go on.

There was nothing sticky about last night though. Last night his brain buzzed with ideas. Yet now, sitting down to his egg, the page in his hand seemed oddly dull – a great hunk of abstraction. He took the top off the egg before reading on. But after a few paragraphs he looked at the numbering of the pages. Had the pages got mixed up? Here was a sentence that seemed to be in the wrong place. The whole passage made no impact. And what was this? He'd come on a line that was meaningless, absolutely meaningless – gibberish. With a sickening feeling James put down the manuscript and took a gulp of coffee. Then, by concentrating hard he could perceive – could at least form a vague idea of – what he'd been trying to get at in this clumsy passage. At one point indeed he had more or less got it, but the chapter as a whole – ? He sat there stunned.

What had happened? Could it be that what he'd taken for creative intensity had been only nervous exhaustion? Was that it? Was Myra right? Should he have stopped earlier? Out of the question. In the excited state he'd been in, he wouldn't have slept a wink at all – even in the early hours. And what else could he have done but go to bed? A walk, perhaps? At that time of night? On a country road in the pitch dark? It was all very well for Myra – the city streets were full of people at all hours, brightly lit, and safe underfoot.

Anyway Myra probably did most of her work in the morning. He didn't really know for sure of course, except that whenever he turned up at the flat there was never any sign of papers about the place. The thought of that neat and orderly flat made him look around the cottage and suddenly he felt depressed. The old woman did her best, but she wasn't up to very much. The place could do with a rub of paint, the woodwork at least, but he certainly wasn't going to do it. He wouldn't be able. James frowned again. Why was his mind harping on this theme of fitness? He straightened up as if in protest at some accusation, but almost at once he slumped down, not caring.

He got his exercise enough on the days he went to Dublin. First the walk to the bus. Then the walk at the other end, because no matter what the weather, he always walked from the bus to the flat. It was a good distance too, but it prolonged his anticipation of the evening ahead.

Ah well! He wouldn't be going today. That was certain. He gathered up his pages. He'd have to slog at this thing till he got it right. He swallowed down the last of his coffee. Back to work.

The fire at any rate was going well. It was roaring up the chimney. The sun too was pouring into the room. Away across the river in a far field cattle were lying down: a sign of good weather it was said.

Hastily, James stepped back from the window and sat down at his desk. It augured badly for his work when he was aware of the weather. Normally he couldn't have told if the day was wet or fine.

That was the odd thing about Dublin. There, the weather did matter. There he was aware of every fickle change in the sky, especially on a day like today that began with rain and later gave way to sunshine. The changes came so quick in the city. They took one by surprise, although one was alerted by a thousand small signs, whereas the sodden fields were slow to recover after the smallest shower. In Dublin the instant there was a break in the clouds, the pavements gave back an answering glint. And after that came a strange white light mingling water and sun, a light that could be perceived in the reflections under foot without raising one's eyes to the sky at all. And how fast then the paving stones dried out into pale patches. Like stepping stones, these patches acted strangely on him, putting a skip into his otherwise sober step!

Talk of the poetry of Spring. The earth's rebirth! Where was it more intoxicating than in the city, the cheeky city birds filling the air with song, and green buds breaking out on branches so black with grime it was as if iron bars had sprouted. Thinking of the city streets his feet ached to be pacing them. James glanced out again at the fields with hatred.

Damn, damn, damn. The damage was done. He'd let himself get unsettled. It would be Dublin for him today. He looked at the clock. He might even go on the early bus. Only what would he do up there all day? His interest in Dublin had dwindled to its core, and the core was Myra.

All the same, he decided to go on the early bus. 'Come on, James! Be a gay dog for once. Get the early bus. You'll find plenty to do. The bookshops! The National Library! Maybe a film? Come on. You're going whether you like it or not, old fellow.'

Catching up the poker James turned the blazing logs over to smother their flames. A pity he'd lit the fire, or rather it was a pity it couldn't be kept in till he got back. It would be nice to return to a warm house. But old Mrs Nully had a mortal dread of the cottage taking fire in his absence. James smiled thinking how she had recently asked why he didn't install central heating. In a three-roomed cottage! Now where on earth had she got that notion, he wondered, as he closed the door and put the key under the mat for her. Then, as he strode off down to the road, he remembered that a son of hers had been taken on as houseman in Asigh House, and the son's wife gave a hand there at weekends. The old woman had probably been shown over the house by them before the Balfes moved into it.

The Balfes! James was nearly at the road, and involuntarily he glanced back across the river to where a fringe of fir trees in the distance marked out the small estate of Asigh. Strange to think – laughable really – that Emmy, who once had filled every cranny of his mind, should only come to mind now in a train of thought that had its starting point in a plumbing appliance!

Here James called himself to order. It was a gross exaggeration to have said – even to himself – that Emmy had ever entirely filled his mind. He'd only known her for a year, and that was the year he finished his Ph.D. He submitted the thesis at the end of the year, and his marks, plus the winning of the travelling scholarship, surely spoke for a certain detachment of mind even when he was most obsessed by her?

He glanced back again at the fir trees. Emmy only stood out in his life because of the violence of his feeling for her. It was something he had never permitted himself before; and never would again. When the affair ended, it ended as completely as if she had been a little skiff upon a swiftly flowing river, which, when he'd cut the painter, was carried instantly away. For a time he'd no way of knowing whether it had capsized or foundered. As it happened, Emmy had righted herself and come to no harm.

Again, James had to call himself to order. How cruel he made himself seem by that metaphor. Yet for years that was how he'd felt obliged to put it to himself. That was how he'd put it to Myra when he first told her about Emmy. But Myra was quick to defend him, quick to see, and quick to show him how he had acted in self-defence. His career would have been wrecked, because of course with a girl like Emmy marriage would have become inescapable. And, of course, then as now, marriage for him was out. It was never really in the picture.

Later, after Myra appeared on the scene, he came to believe that a man and woman could enter into a marriage of minds.

'But when one is young, James,' Myra said, 'one can't be expected to be both wise and foolish at the same time.'

A good saying. He'd noticed, and appreciated, the little sigh with which she accompanied her words, as if she didn't just feel *for* him but *with* him. Then she asked the question that a man might have asked.

'She married eventually I take it, this Emmy?'

'Oh good lord, yes.' How happy he was to be able to answer in the affirmative. If Emmy had not married it would have worried him all his life. But she did. And, all things considered, surprisingly soon.

'Young enough to have a family?' Myra probed, but kindly, kindly. He nodded. 'I take it,' she said then, more easily, 'I take it she married that student who – '

James interrupted ' – the one she was knocking around with when I first noticed her?'

'Yes, the one that was wrestling with that window when you had to step down from the rostrum and yank it open yourself?'

Really Myra was unique. Her grasp of the smallest details of that incident, even then so far back in time, was very gratifying.

He had been conducting a tutorial and the lecture room got so stuffy he'd asked if someone would open a window? But when a big burly fellow – the footballer type – tried with no success, James strode down the classroom himself, irritably, because he half thought the fellow might be having him on to create a diversion. And when he had to lean in across a student whose chair was right under the window, he was hardly aware it was a girl, as he exerted all his strength to bring down the heavy sash. Only when the sash came down and the fresh air rushed in overhead did he find he was looking straight into the eyes of a girl – Emmy.

That was all. But during the rest of the class their eyes kept meeting. And the next day it was the same. Then he began to notice her everywhere, in the corridors, in the Main Hall, and once across the Aula Maxima at an inaugural ceremony. And she'd seen him too. He knew it. But for a long time, several weeks, there was nothing between them except this game of catch-catch with their eyes. And always, no matter how far apart they were, it was as if they had touched.

James soon found himself trembling all over when her eyes touched him. Then one day in the library she passed by his desk and he saw that a paper in her hand was shaking as if there was a breeze in the air. But there was no breeze. Still, deliberately, he delayed the moment of speaking to her because there was a kind of joy in waiting. And funnily enough when they did finally speak neither of them could afterwards remember what their first spoken words had been. They had already said so much with their eyes.

Myra's comment on this, though, was very shrewd. 'You had probably said all there was to say, James.' Again she gave that small sigh of hers that seemed to put things in proportion: to place him, and Emmy too, on the map of disenchantment where all mankind, it seems, must sojourn for a time. And indeed it was sad to think that out of the hundreds of hours that he and Emmy had spent together, wandering along the damp paths of Stephen's Green, sitting in little cafés, and standing under the lamps of Leeson Street where he was in lodgings, he could recall nothing of what was said. 'You probably spent most evenings trying out ideas for your thesis on her, poor girl.' Myra had a dry humour at times, but he had to acknowledge it was likely enough, although if so, Emmy used to listen as if she were drinking in every word.

When he'd got down at last to the actual writing of the thesis they did not meet so often. In fact he could never quite remember their last meeting either. Not even what they had said to each other at parting. Of course long before that they must have faced up to his situation. He'd been pretty sure of getting the travelling scholarship, so it must have been an understood thing that he'd be going away for at least two years. And in the end, he left a month sooner than he'd intended. They never actually did say good-bye. He'd gone without seeing her – just left a note at her digs. And for a while he wasn't even sure if she'd got it. She'd got it all right. She wrote and thanked him. How that smarted! *Thanked* him for breaking it off with her. Years later, telling Myra, he still felt the sting of that.

Myra was marvellous though.

'Hurt pride, my dear James. Nothing more, don't let it spoil what is probably the sweetest thing in life – for all of us, men or women – our first shy, timid love.' There was a tenderness in her voice. Was she remembering some girlish experience of her own? The pang of jealousy that went through him showed how little Emmy had come to mean to him.

Myra put him at ease.

'We all go through it, James, it's only puppy love.'

'Puppy love! I was twenty-six, Myra!'

'Dear, dear James.' She smiled. 'Don't get huffy. I know quite well what age you were. You were completing your Ph.D., and you were old enough to conduct tutorials. You were not at the top of the tree, but you had begun the ascent!'

It was so exactly how he'd seen himself in those days, that he laughed. And with that laugh the pain went out of the past.

'Dear James,' she said again, 'anyone who knows you – and loves you,' she added quickly, because they tried never to skirt away from that word love, although they gave it a connotation all their own, 'anyone who loves you, James, would know that even then, where women were concerned, you'd be nothing but a lanky, bashful boy. Wait a minute!' She sprang up from the sofa. 'I'll show you what I mean.' She took down the studio photograph she'd made him get taken the day of his honorary doctorate. 'Here!' She shoved the silver frame into his hands, and going into the room where she slept, she came back with another photograph. 'You didn't know I had this one?' He saw with some chagrin that it was a blow-up from a group photograph taken on the steps of his old school at the end of his last year. 'See!' she said. 'It's the same face in both, the same ascetical features, the same look of dedication.' Then she pressed the frame end face inward, against her breast. 'Oh James, I bet Emmy was the first girl you ever looked at! My dear, it was not so much the girl as the experience itself that bowled you over.'

Emmy was not the first girl he'd looked at. In those days he was always looking at girls, but looking at them from an unbridgeable distance. When he looked at Emmy the space between them seemed to be instantly obliterated. Emmy had felt the same. That day in class her mind had been a million miles away. She was trying to make up her mind about getting engaged to the big burly fellow, the one who couldn't open the window; James could not remember his name, but he was a type that could be attractive to women. The fellow was pestering her to marry him, and the attentions of a fellow like that could have been very flattering to a girl like Emmy. She was so young. Yet, after she met *him* it was as if a fiery circle had been blazed around them, allowing no way out for either until he, James, in the end had to close his eyes and break through, not caring about the pain as long as he got outside again.

Because Myra was right. Marriage would have put an end to his academic career. For a man like him it would have been suffocating.

'Even now!' Myra said, and there was a humorous expression on her face, because of course, in their own way, he and Myra *were* married. Then, in a business-like way, as if she were filling up a form for filing away, she asked him another question. 'What family did they have?'

'She had five or six children, I think, although she must have been about thirty by the time she married.' James couldn't help throwing his eyes up to heaven at the thought of such a household. Myra too raised her eyebrows.

'You're joking?' she said. 'Good old Balfe!' But James was staring at her, hardly able to credit she had picked up Emmy's married name. He himself had hardly registered it, the first time *he'd* heard it, so that when last summer Asigh House had been bought by people named Balfe, it simply hadn't occurred to him that it could have been Emmy and her husband until one day on the road a car passed him and the woman beside the driver reminded him oddly of her. The woman in the car was softer and plumper and her hair was looser and more untidy – well fluffier anyway – than Emmy's used to be, or so he thought, until suddenly he realized it *was* her. Emmy! She didn't recognize him though. But then she wasn't looking his way. She was looking out over the countryside through which she was passing. It was only when the car turned left at the crossroad the thought hit him, that she had married a man named Balfe, and that Balfe was the name of the people who'd bought Asigh. It was a shock. Not only because of past associations, but more because he had never expected any invasion of his privacy down here. It was his retreat, from everything and everyone. Myra – even Myra – had never been down there. She was too sensible to suggest such a thing. And he wouldn't want her to come either.

Once when he'd fallen ill he'd lost his head and sent her a

telegram, but even then she'd exercised extreme discrimination. She despatched a nurse to take care of him, arranging with the woman to phone her each evening from the village. Without once coming down, she had overseen his illness – which fortunately was not of long duration. She had of course ascertained to her satisfaction that his condition was not serious. The main thing was that she set a firm precedent for them both. It was different when he was convalescing. Then she insisted that he come up to town and stay in a small hotel near the flat, taking his evening meal with her, as on ordinary visits except – James smiled – except that she sent a taxi to fetch him, and carry him back, although the distance involved was negligible, only a block or two.

Remembering her concern for him on that occasion, James told himself that he could never thank her enough. He resolved to let her see he did not take her goodness for granted. Few women could be as self-effacing.

Yet, in all fairness to Emmy, she had certainly effaced herself fast. One might say drastically. After that one note of thanks – it jarred again that she had put it like that – he had never once heard or seen her until that day she passed him here on the road in her car. So much for his fears for his privacy. Unfounded! For days he'd half expected a courtesy call from them, but after a time he began to wonder if they were aware at all that he lived in the neighbourhood? After all, their property was three or four miles away, and the river ran between. It was just possible Emmy knew nothing of his existence. Yet somehow, he doubted it. As the crow flies he was less than two miles away. He could see their wood. And was it likely the local people would have made no mention of him? No, it was hard to escape the conclusion that Emmy might be avoiding him. Although Myra – who was never afraid of the truth – had not hesitated to say that Emmy might have forgotten him altogether!

'Somehow I find that hard to believe, Myra,' he'd said, although after he'd made the break, there had been nothing. Nothing, nothing, nothing.

But Myra was relentless.

'You may not like to believe it, James, but it could be true all the same,' she said. Then she tried to take the hurt out of her words by confessing that she herself found it dispiriting to think a relationship that had gone so deep, could be erased completely. 'I myself can't bear to think she did not recognize you that day she passed you on the road. *She* may have changed – you said she'd got stouter –' That wasn't the word he'd used, but he'd let it pass – 'whereas you, James, can hardly have changed at all, in essentials, I mean. Your figure must be the same as when you were a young man. I can't bear to think she didn't even *know* you.'

'She wasn't looking straight at me, Myra.'

'No matter! You'd think there'd have been some telepathy between you; some force that would *make* her turn. Oh, I can't bear it!'

She was so earnest he had to laugh.

'It is a good job she didn't see me,' he said. Emmy being nothing to him then, it was just as well there should be no threat to his peace and quiet.

Such peace; such quiet. James looked around at the sleepy countryside. The bus was very late though! What was keeping it?

Ah, here it came. Signalling to the driver, James stepped up quickly on to the running board so the man had hardly to do more than go down into first gear before starting off again. In spite of how few passengers there were, the windows were fogged up and James had to clear a space on the glass with his hand to see out. It was always a pleasant run through the rich Meath fields, but soon the unruly countryside gave way to neatly squared-off fields with pens and wooden palings, where cattle were put in for the night before being driven to the slaughter-house.

James shuddered. He was no country-man. Not by nature anyway. He valued the country solely for the protection it gave him from people. When he lived in Dublin he used to work in the National Library, but as he got older he began to feel that in the eyes of the students and the desk-messengers, he could have appeared eccentric. Not objectionably so, just rustling his papers too much, and clearing his throat too loudly; that kind of thing. He'd have been the first to find that annoying in others when he was young. The cottage was much better. It also served to put that little bit of distance between him and Myra which they both agreed was essential.

'If I lived in Dublin I'd be here at the flat every night of the week,' he'd once said to her. 'I'm better off down there – I suppose – stuck in the mud!'

That was an inaccurate – and unfair – description of his little retreat, but the words had come involuntarily to his lips which showed how he felt about the country in general. The city streets of Dublin were so full of life, and the people were so dapper and alert compared with the slow-moving country people. Every time he went up there he felt like an old fogy – that was until he got to Myra's – because Myra immediately gave him back a sense of being alive. Mentally at least Myra made him feel more alive than twenty men.

The bus had now reached O'Connell Bridge, where James usually descended, so he got out. He ought to have got out sooner and walked along the Quays. One could kill a whole morning looking over the book barrows. Now he would have to walk back to them.

Perhaps he ought not to have come on the early bus? It might not be so easy to pass the time. And after browsing to his heart's content and leaning for a while looking over the parapet on to the Liffey, it was still only a little after 1 o'clock when he strolled back to the centre of the city. He'd have to eat something and that would use up another hour or more. He'd buy a paper and sit on over his coffee.

James hadn't bargained on the lunchtime crowds though. All the popular places were crowded, and in a few of the better places, one look inside was enough to send him off! These places too were invaded by the lunchtime hordes, and the menu would cater for these barbarians. If there should by chance happen to be a continental dish on the menu – a goulash or pasta – it would nauseate him to see the little clerks attacking it with knife and fork as if it was a mutton chop.

At this late hour how about missing out on lunch altogether? It never hurt to skip a meal, although, mind you, he was peckish. How about a film? He hadn't been in a cinema for years. And just then, as if to settle the matter – James saw he was passing a cinema. It was exceptionally small for a city cinema, but without another thought he bolted inside.

Once inside, he regretted that he hadn't checked the time of the showings. He didn't fancy sitting through a newsreel, to say nothing of a cartoon. He had come in just in the middle of a particularly silly cartoon. He sat in the dark fuming. To think he'd let himself in for this stuff. It was at least a quarter of an hour before he realized with rage that he must have strayed into one of the new-fangled newsreel cinemas about which Myra had told him. For another minute he sat staring at the screen, trying to credit the mentality of people who voluntarily subjected themselves to this kind of stuff. He was about to leave and make for the street, when without warning his eyes closed. He didn't know for how long he had dozed off, but on waking he was really ravenous. But wouldn't it be crazy to eat at this hour and spoil his appetite for the meal with Myra? He could, he supposed, go around to the flat earlier – now – immediately? Why wait any longer? But he didn't know at what hour Myra herself got there. All he knew was that she was always there after seven, the time he normally arrived.

But wasn't it remarkable now he came to think of it, that she *was* always there when he called. Very occasionally at the start she had let drop dates on which she had to go to some meeting or other, and he'd made a mental note of them, but as time went on she gave up these time-wasting occupations. There had been one or two occasions she had been going out, but had cancelled her arrangements immediately he came on the scene. He had protested of course, but lamely, because quite frankly it would have been frightfully disappointing to have come so far and found she really had to go out.

Good God – supposing that were to happen now? James was so scared at the possibility of such a catastrophe he determined to lose no more time but get around there quick. Just in case. He stepped out briskly.

The lane at the back of Fitzwilliam Square, where Myra had her mews, was by day a hive of small enterprises. A smell of cellulosing and sounds of welding filled the air. In one courtyard there was a little fellow who dealt in scrap-iron and he made a great din. But by early evening, the big gates closed on these businesses, the high walls made the lane a very private place, and the mews-dwellers were disturbed by no sound harsher than the late song of the birds nesting in the trees of the doctors' gardens.

Walking down the lane and listening to those sleepy bird-notes gave James greater pleasure than walking on any country road. His feet echoed so loudly in the stillness that sometimes before he rapped on her gate at all, Myra would come running out across the courtyard to admit him. A good thing that! Because otherwise he'd have had to rap with his bare knuckles; Myra had no knocker.

'You know I don't encourage callers, James,' she'd said once smiling. 'Few people ferret me out here – except you; and, of course, the tradesmen. And I know their step too! It's nearly as quiet here as in your cottage.'

'Quiet?' He'd raised his eyebrows. 'Listen to those birds; I never heard such a din!'

Liking a compliment to be oblique, she'd squeezed his arm as she drew him inside.

This evening however James was less than halfway down the lane when at the other end he saw Myra appear at the wicket gate. If she hadn't been bareheaded he'd have thought she was going out!

'Myra?' he called in some dismay.

She laughed as she came to meet him. 'I heard your footsteps,' she said. 'I told you! I always do.'

'From this distance?'

She took his arm and smiled up at him. 'That's nothing! It's a wonder I don't hear you walking down the country road to get the bus.' She matched her step with his. Normally he hated to be linked, but with Myra it seemed to denote equality, not dependence.

Suddenly she unlinked her arm. 'Well, I may as well confess something,' she said more seriously. 'This evening I was listening for you. I was expecting you.'

They had reached the big wooden gate of the mews and James, glancing in through the open wicket across the courtyard, was startled to see, through the enormous window by which she had replaced the doors of the coach-house, that the little table at which they ate was indeed set up, and with places laid for two! She wasn't joking then? An unpleasant thought crossed his mind – was she expecting someone else? But reading his mind, Myra shook her head.

'Only you, James.'

'I don't understand – '

'Neither do I!' she said quickly. 'I *was* expecting you though. And I ordered our trays!' Here she wrinkled her nose in a funny way she had. 'I made the order a bit more conservative than usual. No prawns!' He understood at once. He loved prawns. 'So you see,' she continued, 'if my oracle failed, and you didn't come, the food would do for sandwiches tomorrow. As you know, I'm no use at hotting up left-overs. It smacks too much of – '

He knew. He knew.

'Too wifey,' he smiled. And she smiled. This was the word they'd ear-marked to describe a certain type of woman they both abhorred.

'You could always have fed the prawns to the cat next door,' James said. 'Whenever I'm coming he's sitting on the wall smacking his lips.'

'But James,' she said, and suddenly she stopped smiling, 'he doesn't know when you're coming – any more than me!'

'Touché,' James admitted to being caught out there. He wasn't really good at smart remarks. 'Ah well, it's a lucky cat who knows there's an even chance of a few prawns once or twice a month. That's more than most cats can count on.' Bending his head he followed her in through the wicket. 'Some cats have to put up with a steady diet of shepherd's pie and meat loaf.'

They were inside now, and he sank down on the sofa. Myra, who was still standing, shuddered.

'What would I do if you were the kind of man who *did* like shepherd's pie?' she said. 'I'm sure there are such men.' But she couldn't keep up the silly chaff. 'I think maybe I'd love you enough to try and make it – ' she laughed, ' – if I could. I don't honestly think I'd be able. The main thing is that you are *not* that type. Let's stop fooling. Here, allow me to give you a kiss of gratitude – for being you.'

Lightly she laid her cheek against his, while he for his part took her hand and stroked it.

It was one of the more exquisite pleasures she gave him, the touch of her cool skin. His own hands had a tendency to get hot although he constantly wiped them with his handkerchief. He had always preferred being too cold to being too hot. Once or twice when he had a headache – which was not often – Myra had only to place her hand on his forehead for an instant and the throbbing ceased. This evening he didn't have a headache but all the same he liked the feel of her hand on his face.

'Do that again,' he said.

'How about fixing the drinks first?' she said.

That was his job. But he did not want to release her hand, and he made no attempt to stand up. Unfortunately just then there was a rap on the gate.

'Oh bother,' he said.

'It's only the Catering Service,' Myra said, and for a minute he didn't get the joke. She laughed then and he noticed she meant the grubby little pot-boy who brought the trays around from the café.

'Let me get them,' he said, but she had jumped up and in a minute she was back with them.

'I must tell you,' she said. 'You know the man who owns the cafe? Well, he gave me such a dressing-down this morning when I was ordering these.' James raised his eyebrows as he held open the door of the kitchenette to let her through. 'Just bring me the warming plate, will you please, James,' she said interrupting herself. 'I'll pop the food on it for a second while we have our little drink.' She glanced at her watch. 'Oh, it's quite early still.' She looked back at him. 'But you were a little later than usual, I think, weren't you?'

'I don't think so,' he said vaguely, as he fitted the plug of the food-warmer into the socket. 'If anything, I think I was a bit earlier. But I could be wrong. When one has time to kill it's odd how often one ends up being late in the end!'

'Time to kill?'

She looked puzzled. Then she seemed to understand. 'Oh James. You make me tired. You're so punctilious. Haven't I told you a thousand times that you don't have to be polite with me? If your bus got in early you should have come straight to the flat. Killing time indeed. Standing on ceremony, eh?'

He handed her her drink.

'You were telling me something about the proprietor of the café – that he was unpleasant about something? You weren't serious?'

'Oh that! Of course not.'

Yet for some reason he was uneasy. 'Tell me,' he said authoritatively.

Naturally, she complied. 'He was really very nice,' she said. 'He
intended phoning me. He just wanted to say there was no need to
wash the plates before sending them back. I'm to hand them to the
messenger in the morning just as they are – and not *attempt* to wash
them.' Knowing how fastidious she was, James was about to
pooh-pooh the suggestion, but she forestalled him. 'I can wrap them
up in the napkins, and then I won't be affronted by the sight. And I
need feel under no compliment to the café – it's in their own
interests as much as in mine. They have a big washing machine – I've
seen it – with a special compartment like a dentist's sterilization
cabinet, and of course they couldn't be sure that a customer would
wash them properly. You can imagine the cat's lick some women
would give them!'

James could well imagine it. He shuddered. Myra might hate
housework, but anything she undertook she did to perfection.
Unexpectedly she held out her glass.

'Let's have another drink,' she said. They seldom took more than
one. 'Sit down,' she commanded. 'Let's be devils for once.' This
time though she sat on the sofa and swung her feet up on it so he
had to sit in the chair opposite. 'There's nothing that makes the
ankles ache like thinking too hard,' she said.

James didn't really understand what she meant but he laughed
happily.

'Seriously!' she said. 'I am feeling tired this evening. I'm so glad
you came. I think maybe I worked extra hard this morning because I
was looking forward to seeing you later. Oh, I'm so glad you came,
James. I would have been bitterly disappointed if you hadn't
showed up.'

James felt a return of his earlier uneasiness.

'I'm afraid that premonition of yours is more than I can understand,' he said, but he spoke patiently, because she was not a
woman who had to be humoured. 'As a matter of fact I never had
less intention of coming to town. I'd already lit the fire in my study
when I suddenly took the notion. I had to put the fire out!'

At that, Myra left down her glass and swung her feet back on to
the floor.

'What time did you leave?' she asked, and an unusually crisp note
in her voice took him unawares.

'I thought I told you,' he said apologetically, although there was
nothing for which to apologize. 'I came on the morning bus.'

'Oh!' It was only one word, but it fell oddly on his ears. She
reached for her drink again then, and swallowed it down. Somehow

that too bothered him. 'Is that what you meant by having to kill time?' she asked.

'Well – ' he began, not quite knowing what to say. He took up his own drink and let it down fairly fast for him.

'Oh, don't bother to explain,' she said. 'I think you will agree though it would have been a nice gesture to have lifted a phone and let me know you were in town and coming here tonight.'

'But – '

'No buts about it. You knew I'd be here waiting whether you came or not. Isn't that it?'

'Myra!'

He hardly recognized her in this new mood. Fortunately the next moment she was her old self again.

'Oh James, forgive me. It's just that you've *no* idea – simply *no* idea how much it meant to me tonight to know in advance – ' She stopped and carefully corrected herself ' – to have had that curious feeling – call it instinct if you like – that you were coming. It made such a difference to my whole day. But now – ' Her face clouded over, ' – to think that instead of just having had a hunch about it, I could have known for certain. Oh, if only you'd been more thoughtful, James.' Sitting up straighter she looked him squarely in the eye. 'Or were you going somewhere else and changed your mind?'

What a foolish question.

'As if I ever go anywhere else!'

Her face brightened a bit at that, but not much.

'You'll hardly believe it,' she said after a minute, 'but I could have forgiven you more easily if you had been going somewhere else, and coming here *was* an afterthought. It would have excused you more.'

Excused? What was all this about? He must have looked absolutely bewildered, because she pulled herself up.

'Oh James, please don't mind me.' She leant forward and laid a hand on his knee. 'Your visits give me such joy – I don't need to tell you that – I ought to be content with what I have. Not knowing in advance is one of the little deprivations that I just have to put up with, I suppose.'

But now James was beginning to object strongly to the way she was putting everything. He stood up. As if his doing so unnerved her, she stood up too.

'It may seem a small thing to ask from you, James, but I repeat what I said – you could have phoned me.' Then, as if that wasn't bad enough, she put it into the future tense. 'If you would only try, once in a while, to give me a ring, even from the bus depot, so I could – '

' – could what?' James couldn't help the coldness in his voice, although considering the food that was ready on the food-warmer, his question, he knew, was ungenerous. On the other hand he felt it was absolutely necessary to keep himself detached, if the evening was not to be spoiled. He forced himself to speak sternly. 'Much as I enjoy our little meals together, it's not for the food I come here, Myra. You must know that.' He very, very nearly added that in any case he paid for his own tray, but when he looked at her he saw she had read these unsaid words from his eyes. He reddened. There was an awkward silence. Yet when she spoke she ignored everything he had said and harked back to what she herself had said.

'Wouldn't it be a very small sacrifice to make, James, when one thinks of all the sacrifices I've made for you? And over so many years?' Her words, which to him were exasperating beyond belief, seemed to drown her in a torrent of self-pity. 'So many, many years,' she whispered.

It was only ten.

'You'd think it was a lifetime,' he said irritably. Her face flushed.

'What is a lifetime, James?' she asked, and when he made no reply she helped him out. 'Remember it is not the same for a woman as for a man. *You* may think of yourself as a young blade, but I . . .'

She faltered again, as well she might, and bit her lip. She wasn't going to cry, was she? James was appalled. Nothing had ever before happened that could conceivably have given rise to tears, but it was an unspoken law with them that a woman should never shed tears in public. Not just unspoken either. On one occasion years ago she herself had been quite explicit about it.

'We do cry sometimes, we women, poor weaklings that we are. But I hope I would never be foolish enough to cry in the presence of a man. And to do it to you of all people, James, would be despicable.' At the time he'd wondered why she singled him out. Did she think him more sensitive than most? He'd been about to ask when she'd given one of her witty twists to things. 'If I did, I'd have you snivelling too in no time,' she said.

Yet here she was now, for no reason at all, on the brink of tears, and apparently making no effort to fight them back.

Myra was making no effort to stem her tears because she did not know she was crying. She really did despise tears. But now it seemed to her that perhaps she'd been wrong in always hiding her feelings. Other women had the courage to cry. Even in public too. She'd seen them at parties. And recently she'd seen a woman walking along the street in broad daylight with tears running down her cheeks, not bothering to wipe them away. Thinking of such women, she wondered if she perhaps had sort of – she paused to find the right word – sort of denatured herself for James?

Denatured: it was an excellent word. She'd have liked to use it then and there but she had just enough sense left to keep it to herself for the moment. Some other time when they were talking about someone else, she would bring it out and impress him. She must not forget the word.

When Myra's thoughts returned to James she felt calmer about him. He was not unkind. He was not cruel – the opposite in fact. What had gone wrong this evening was more her fault than his. When they'd first met she had sensed deep down in him a capacity for the normal feelings of friendship and love. Yet throughout the years she had consistently deflected his feelings away from herself and consistently encouraged him to seal them off. Tonight it seemed that his emotional capacity was completely dried up. Despair overcame her. She'd never change him now. He was fixed in his faults, cemented into his barren way of life. Tears gushed into her eyes again but this time she leant her head back quickly to try and prevent them rolling down, but they brimmed over and splashed down on her hands.

'Oh James, I'm sorry,' she whispered, but she saw her apology was useless; the damage was done. Then her heart hardened. What harm? She wasn't really sorry. Not for him anyway. Oh, not for him. It was for herself she was sorry.

Grasping at a straw, then, she tried to tell herself, nothing was ever too late. Perhaps tonight some lucky star had stood still in the sky over her head and forced her to be true to herself for once. James would see the real woman for a change. Oh, surely he would? And surely he would come over and put his arm around her. He would: he would. She waited.

When he did not move, and did not utter a single word, she had to look up.

'Oh no!' she cried. For what she saw in his eyes was ice. 'Oh James, have you no heart? What you have done to me is unspeakable! Yet you can't even pity me!'

James spoke at last. 'And what, Myra, what, may I ask, have I done to you?'

'You have – ' She stopped, and for one second she thought she'd have control enough to bite back the word, but she hadn't. 'You have denatured me,' she said.

Oh God, what had she done *now*? Clapping her hands over her mouth too late, she wondered if she could pretend to some other meaning in the words. Instead, other words gushed out, words worse and more hideous. Hearing them she herself could not understand where they came from. It was as if, out of the corners of the room, she was being prompted by the voices of all the women in the world who'd ever been let down, or fancied themselves badly treated. The room vibrated with their whispers. Go on, they prompted. Tell him what you think of him. Don't let him get away with it. He has got off long enough. To stop the voices she stuck her fingers into her ears, but the voices only got louder. She had to shout them down. She saw James's lips were moving, trying to say something, but she could not hear him with all the shouting. When she finally caught a word or two of what he said she herself stopped trying to penetrate the noise. Silence fell. She saw James go limp with relief.

'What did you say? I – I didn't hear you,' she gulped.

'I said that if that's the way you feel, Myra, there's nothing for me to do but to leave.'

She stared at him. He was going over to the clothes' rack and was taking down his coat. What had got into them? How had they become involved in this vulgar scene? She had to stop him. If he went away like this would he ever come back? A man of his disposition? Could she take him back? Neither of them was of a kind to gloss over things and leave them unexplained knowing that unexplained they could erupt again – and again. Something had been brought to light that could never be forced back underground. Better all the same to let their happiness dry up if it must, than be blasted out of existence like this in one evening. Throwing out her arms she ran blindly towards him.

'James, I implore you. James! James! Don't let this happen to us.' She tried to enclose him with her arms, but somehow he evaded her and reached to take his gloves from the lid of the gramophone. Next thing she knew he'd be at the door.

'Do you realize what you're doing?' She pushed past him and ran to the door pressing her back against it, and throwing out her arms to either side. It was an outrageous gesture of crucifixion, and she knew she was acting out of character. She was making another and more frightful mistake. 'If you walk out this door, you'll never come through it again, James.'

All he did was try to push her to one side, not roughly, but gently.

'James! Look at me!'

But what he said then was so humiliating she wanted to die.

'I am looking, Myra,' he said.

There seemed nothing left to do but hit him. She thumped at his chest with her closed fists. That made him stand back all right. She had achieved that at least! If she was not going to get a chance to undo the harm she'd done, then she'd go the whole hog and let him think the worst of her. She was ashamed to think she had been about to renege on herself. She flung out her arms again, not hysterically this time, but with passion, real, real passion. Let him see what he was up against. But whatever he thought, James said nothing. And he'd have to be the one to speak first. Myra couldn't trust herself any more.

In the end, she did have to speak. 'Say something, James,' she pleaded.

'All right,' he said then. 'Be so kind, Myra, as to tell me what you think you're gaining by this performance?' he nodded at her outstretched arms. 'This nailing of yourself to the door like a stoat!'

The look in his eyes was ugly. She let her arms fall at once and running back to the sofa flung herself face down upon it screaming and kicking her feet.

She didn't even hear the door bang after him, or the gate slam.

Outside in the air James regretted that he had not shut the door more gently, but after the coarse and brutal words he had just used it was inconsistent to worry about the small niceties of the miserable business. His ugly words echoed in his mind, and he felt defiled by them. He had an impulse to go back and apologize, if only for his language. Nothing justified that kind of thing from a man. He actually raised his hand to rap on the gate, but he let it fall, overcome by a stronger impulse – to make good his escape. But as he hurried up the lane his unuttered words too seemed base and unworthy – a mean-minded figure of speech – that could only be condoned by the fact that he had been so grievously provoked, and by the over-whelming desire that had been engendered in him to get out in the air. If Myra had not stood aside and let him pass, he'd have used brute force. All the same nothing justified the inference that he was imprisoned. Never, never had she done anything to hold him. Never had he been made captive except perhaps by the pull of her mind upon his mind. He'd always been free to come or go as he chose. If in the flat they had become somewhat closed in of late it was from expediency – from not wanting to run into stupid people. If they had gone out to restaurants or cafés nowadays some fool would be sure to blunder over and join them, reducing their evening to the series of banalities that passed for conversation with most people. No, no, the flat was never a prison. Never. It was their nest. And now he'd fallen out of the nest. Or worse still been pushed out. All of a sudden James felt frightened. Was it possible she had meant what she said? Could it be that he would never again be able to go back there? Nonsense. She was hysterical.

He stood for a minute considering again whether he should not perhaps go back? Not that he'd relish it. But perhaps he ought to do so – in the interests of the future. No, he decided. Better give her time to calm down. Another evening would be preferable. If necessary he'd be prepared to come up again tomorrow evening. Or later this same evening? That would be more sensible. He looked back. She must be in a bad state when she hadn't run out after him. Normally she'd come to the gate and stay standing in the lane until he was out of sight. Even in the rain.

James shook his head. What a pity. If she'd come to the gate he could have raised his hands or something, given some sign – there merest indication would be enough – of his forgiveness. He could have let her see he bore no rancour. But the gesture would not want to be ambiguous. Not a wave; that would be over-cordial, and he didn't want her stumbling up the lane after him. No more fireworks thank you! But it would not want to appear final either. A raised hand would have been the best he could do at that time. He was going to walk on again when it occurred to him that if he'd gone back he need not have gone inside. Just a few words at the gate, but on the whole it was probably better to wait till she'd calmed down. Then he could safely take some of the blame, and help her to save face. Fortunately he did not have the vanity that, in another man, might make such a course impossible. It was good for the soul sometimes to assume blame – even wrongly. James immediately felt better, less bottled up. He walked on. But he could not rid his thoughts of the ugly business. He ought to have known that no woman on earth but was capable, at some time or another, of a lapse like Myra's. And Myra, of course, was a woman. How lacking he'd been in foresight. He'd have to go more carefully with her in future. Next time they met, although he would not try to exonerate himself from the part he'd played in the regrettable scene, at the same time it would not be right to rob her of the therapeutic effects of taking her share of the blame. He felt sure that, being fair-minded people, both of them, they would properly apportion the blame.

Anyway he resolved to put the whole thing out of his mind until after he'd eaten. To think he'd eaten nothing since morning! After he'd had some food he'd be better able to handle the situation.

James had reached the other end of the lane now and gone out under the arch into Baggot Street again. Where would he eat? He'd better head towards the centre of the city. It ought not to be as difficult as it had been at midday, although an evening meal in town could be quite expensive. He didn't want a gala-type dinner, but not

some awful slop either that would sicken him. He was feeling bad.
The tension had upset his stomach and he was not sure whether he
was experiencing hunger pangs or physical pain. Damn Myra. If
she'd been spoiling for a fight, why the devil hadn't she waited till
after their meal? She'd say this was more of his male selfishness, but
if they had eaten they'd have been better balanced and might not
have had a row at all. What a distasteful word – the word row! Yet,
that's what it was – a common row. James came to a stand again. He
wouldn't think twice of marching back and banging on the gate and
telling her to stop her nonsense and put the food on the table. She
was probably heartbroken. But if that was the case she'd have to
come to the door with her face flushed and her hair in disorder.
Sobered by such a distasteful picture he walked on. He could not
possibly subject her to humiliation like that. It would be his duty to
protect her from exposing herself further. Perhaps he'd write her a
note and post it in the late-fee box at the G.P.O. before he got the
bus for home. She'd have it first thing in the morning, and after a
good night's sleep she might be better able to take what he had to
say. He began to compose the letter.

'*Dear Myra* – ' But he'd skip the beginning: that might be sticky.
He'd have to give that careful thought. The rest was easy. Bits and
pieces of sentences came readily to his mind – '*We must see to it that,
like the accord that has always existed between us, discord too, if it should
arise, must be* – '

That was the note to sound. He was beginning to feel his old self
again. He probably ought to make reference to their next meeting?
Not too soon – this to strike a cautionary note – but it might not be
wise to let too much time pass either –

'*because, Myra, the most precious element of our friendship* – '

No, that didn't sound right. After tonight's scene, friendship
didn't appear quite the right word. A new colouring had been given
to their relationship by their tiff. But here James cursed under his
breath. Tiff. Such a word! What next? Where were these trite words
coming from? She'd rattled him all right. Damn it. Oh damn it.

James abandoned the letter for a moment when he realized he had
been plunging along without regard to where he was headed.
Where would he eat? There used to be a nice quiet little place in
Molesworth Street, nearly opposite the National Library. It was
always very crowded but with quite acceptable sorts from the library
or the Arts School. He made off down Kildare Street.

When James reached the café in Molesworth Street however and
saw the padlock on the area railings, he belatedly remembered it
was just a coffee-shop, run by voluntary aid for some charitable
organization, and only open mornings. He stood, stupidly staring at

the padlock. Where would he go now? He didn't feel like traipsing all over the city. Hadn't there been talk some time ago about starting a canteen in the National Library! Had that got under way? He looked across the street. An old gentleman was waddling in the Library gate with his brief case under his arm. James strode after him.

But just as he'd got to the entrance, the blasted porter slammed the big iron gate – almost in his face. He might have had his nose broken.

'Sorry, sir. The Library is closed. Summer holidays, sir.'

'But you just let in someone! I saw that man – '

James glared after the old man who was now ambling up the steps to the reading room.

'The gentleman had a pass, sir,' the porter said. 'There's a skeleton staff on duty in the stacks and the Director always gives out a few permits to people doing important research.' The fellow was more civil now. 'It's only fair, sir. It wouldn't do, sir, would it, to refuse people whose work is – ' But here he looked closer at James and, recognizing him, his civility changed into servility. 'I beg your pardon, Professor,' he said. 'I didn't recognize you, sir. I would have thought you'd have applied for a permit. Oh dear, oh dear!' The man actually wrung his hands – 'if it was even yesterday, I could have got hold of the Director on the phone, but he's gone away – out of the country too I understand.'

'Oh, that's all right,' James said, somewhat mollified by being recognized and remembered. He was sorry that he, in turn, could not recall the porter's name. 'That's all right,' he repeated. 'I wasn't going to use the library anyway. I thought they might have opened that canteen they were talking about some time back – ?'

'Canteen, sir? When was that?' The fellow had clearly never heard of the project. He was looking at James as if he was Lazarus come out of the tomb.

'No matter. Good evening!' James said curtly, and he walked away. Then, although he had never before in his life succumbed to the temptation of talking to himself, now, because it was so important, he put himself a question out loud.

'Have I lost touch with Dublin?' he asked. And he had to answer simply and honestly. 'I have.' He should have known the library was always closed this month. If only there was a friend on whom he could call. But he'd lost touch with his friends too.

He looked around. There used to be a few eating places in this vicinity, or rather he could have sworn there were. It hardly seemed possible they were *all* closed down. Where on earth did people eat in

Dublin nowadays? They surely didn't go to the hotels? In his day the small hotels were always given over at night to political rallies or football clubs. And the big hotels were out of the question. Not that he'd look into the cost at this stage. He stopped. If it was anywhere near time for his bus he wouldn't think twice of going straight back without eating at all.

It was all very well for Myra. She ate hardly anything anyway. He often felt that as far as food went, their meal together meant nothing to her. Setting up that damned unsteady card-table, and laying out those silly plates of hers shaped like vine leaves and too small to hold enough for a bird. They reminded him of when his sisters used to make him play babby-house.

Passing Trinity College, James saw there was still two hours to go before his bus, but it was just on the hour. There might be a bus going to Cavan? The Cavan bus passed through Garlow Cross, only a few miles from the cottage. How about taking that? He'd taken it once years ago, and although he was younger and fitter in those days, he was tempted to do it. His stomach was so empty it was almost caving in, but he doubted if he could eat anything now. He felt sickish. He might feel better after sitting in the bus. And better anything than hanging about the city.

At that moment on Aston Quay James saw the Cavan bus. It was filling up with passengers, and the conductor and driver, leaning on the parapet of the Liffey, were taking a last smoke. James was about to dash across the street, but first he dashed into a sweet shop to buy a bar of chocolate, or an apple. The sensation in his insides was like something gnawing at his guts. He got an apple and a bar of chocolate as well, but he nearly missed the bus. Very nearly. The driver was at the wheel and the engine was running. James had to put on a sprint to get across the street, and even then the driver was pulling on the big steering wheel and swivelling the huge wheels outward into the traffic before putting the bus in motion. James jumped on the step.

'Dangerous that, sir,' said the young conductor.

'You hadn't begun to move!' James replied testily, while he stood on the platform getting his breath back.

'Could have jerked forward, sir. Just as you were stepping up!'

'You think a toss would finish me off, eh?' James said. He meant the words to be ironical, but his voice hadn't been lighthearted enough to carry off the joke.

The conductor didn't smile. 'Never does any of us any good, sir, at any age.'

James looked at him with hatred. The fellow was thin and

spectacled. Probably the over-conscientious sort. Feeling no inclination to make small talk he lurched into the body of the bus, and sat down on the nearest seat. He was certainly glad to be off his feet. He hadn't noticed until now how they ached. Such a day. Little did he think setting off that it would be a case of About Turn and Quick March.

James slumped down in his seat, but when he felt the bulge of the apple in his pocket he brightened up, and was about to take it out when he was overcome by a curious awkwardness with regard to the conductor. Instead, keeping his hand buried in his pocket he broke off a piece of the chocolate and surreptitiously put it into his mouth. He would nearly have been too tired to chew the apple. He settled back on the seat and tried to doze. But now Myra's words kept coming back. They were repeating on him, like indigestion.

To think she should taunt him with how long they'd known each other? Wasn't it a good thing they'd been able to put up with each other for so long? What else but time had cemented their relationship? As she herself had once put it, very aptly, they'd invested a lot in each other. Well, as far as he was concerned she could have counted on *her* investment to the end. Wasn't it their credo that it didn't take marriage lines to bind together people of their integrity. He had not told her, not in so many words – from delicacy – but he had made provision for her in his will. He'd been rather proud of the way he'd worded the bequest too, putting in a few lines of appreciation that were, he thought, gracefully, but more important, tactfully expressed.

Oh, why had she doubted him? Few wives could be as sure of their husbands as she of him – but he had to amend this – as she *ought* to be, because clearly she had set no value on his loyalty. What was that she'd said about the deprivations she'd suffered? '*One of the many deprivations*'! Those might not have been her exact words, but that was more or less what she'd implied. What had come over her? He shook his head. Had they not agreed that theirs was the perfect solution for facing into the drearier years of ageing and decay? That dreary time was not imminent, of course, but alas it would inevitably come. The process of ageing was not attractive, and they both agreed that if they were continually together – well, really married for instance – the afflictions of age would be doubled for them. On the other hand, with the system they'd worked out, neither saw anything but what was best, and best preserved, in the other. As the grosser aspects of age became discernible, if they could not conceal them from themselves, at least they could conceal them from each other. To put it flatly, if they had been married a dozen times over, that would still be the way he'd want things to be at the end. It was disillusioning now to find she had not seen eye to eye with him on this. Worse still, she'd gone along with him and paid lip-service to his ideals while underneath she must all the time have dissented.

Suddenly James sat bolt upright. That word she used: deprivation. She couldn't have meant that he'd done her out of children? What a thought! Surely it was unlikely that she could have had a child even when they first met? What age was she then? Well, perhaps not too old but surely to God she was at an age when she couldn't have fancied putting herself in *that* condition? And what about all the cautions that were given now on the danger of late conception? How would *she* like to be saddled with a retarded child? Why, it was her who first told him about recent medical findings! And – wait a minute – that was early in their acquaintance too, if he remembered rightly. He could recall certain particulars of the conversation. They had been discussing her work, and the demands it made on her. She was, of course, aware from the first that *he* never wanted children, that he abhorred the thought of a houseful of brats, crawling everywhere, and dribbling and spitting out food. They overran a place. As for the smell of wet diapers about a house, it nauseated him. She'd pulled him up on that though.

'Not soiled diapers, James. The most slovenly woman in the world has more self-respect than to leave dirty diapers lying about. But I grant you there often is a certain odour – I've found it myself at times in the homes of my friends, and it has surprised me, I must say – but it comes from *clean* diapers hanging about to air. At worst it's the smell of steam. They have to be boiled you know.' She made a face. 'I agree with you, though. It's not my favourite brand of perfume.'

Those were her very words. If he were to be put in the dock at this moment he could swear to it. Did that sound like a woman who wanted a family? Yet tonight she had insinuated – James was so furious he clenched his hands and dug his feet into the floorboards as if the bus were about to hurtle over the edge of an abyss and he could put a brake on it.

Then he thought of something else: something his sister Kay had said.

It was the time Myra had had to go into hospital for a few weeks. Nothing serious, she'd said. Nothing to worry about, or so she'd told him. Just a routine tidying up job that most people – presumably she meant women – thought advisable. Naturally he'd encouraged her to get it over and done with: not to put it on the long finger. The shocking thing was how badly it had shaken her. He was appalled at how frightful she'd looked for months afterwards.

Finally the doctors ordered her to take a good holiday, although it hadn't been long since her summer holidays. She hadn't gone away that summer, except for one long week-end in London, but she'd packed up her work and he'd gone up more often. But the doctor was insistent that this time she was to go away. Oddly enough, her going away had hit him harder than her going into hospital. If they could have gone away together it would have been different. That, of course, was impossible. There was no longer a spot on the globe where one mightn't run the risk of bumping into some busybody from Dublin.

'What will I do while you're away?' he'd asked.

'Why don't you come up here as usual,' she suggested, 'except you need order only one tray.'

But she over-estimated the charm of the flat for its own sake. And he told her so.

'Nonsense,' she said. 'Men are like cats and dogs; it's their habitat they value, not the occupants.'

'I'll tell you what I'll do,' he said finally. 'I'll come up the day you're coming back and I'll have a fire lit – how about that?'

'Oh James, you are a dear. It would make me so glad to be coming back.'

'I should hope you'd be glad to be coming back anyway?'

'Oh yes, but you must admit it would be extra special to be coming back to find you here – in our little nest.'

There! James slapped his knee. *That* was where he'd got the word nest. He had to hand it to her; she was very ingenious in avoiding the word 'home'. She was at her best when it came to these small subtleties other people overlooked. And the day she was due back he had fully intended to be in the flat before her, were it not for a chance encounter with his sister Kay and a remark of hers that upset him.

Kay knew all about Myra. Whether she approved of her or not James did not know: Kay and himself were too much alike to embarrass each other by confidences. That was why he found what she said that day so extraordinary.

'Very sensible of her to go away,' Kay had said, 'otherwise it takes a long time, I believe, to recover from that beastly business.' Beastly business? What did she mean? Unlike herself, Kay had gone on and on. 'Much messier than childbirth I understand. Also, I've heard, James, that it's worse for an unmarried woman – ' she paused – 'I mean a childless woman.' Then feeling – as well she might – that she'd overstepped herself, she looked at her watch. 'I'll have to fly,' she said. And perhaps to try and excuse her indiscretion she resorted to something else that was rare for Kay – banality. 'It's sort of the end of the road for them, I suppose,' she said, before she hurried away leaving him confused and dismayed.

He had never bothered to ask Myra what her operation had been. He didn't see that it concerned him. At any age there were certain danger zones for a woman that had to be kept under observation. But what if it had been a hysterectomy! Was that any business of his? Medically speaking, it wasn't all that different from any other ectomy – tonsillectomy, appendectomy. What was so beastly about it? If it came to that, the most frightful mess of all was getting one's antrums cleaned out. He knew all about *that*. Anyway the whole business was outside his province. Or at least he had thought so then.

Then, then, then. But now, now it was as if he'd been asked to stand up and testify to something. It was most unfair. Myra herself had never arraigned him. Neither before nor after. Admittedly he had not given her much encouragement. But he could have sworn that she herself hadn't given a damn at the time. Ah, but – and this was the rub, the whole business could have bred resentment, could have rankled within her and gone foetid. Considered in this new light the taunts she had flung at him tonight could no longer be put down to hysteria and written off – something long festering had suppurated. He put his hand to his head. Dear God, to think she had allowed him to bask all those years in a fool's paradise!

He closed his eyes. Thank heavens he hadn't demeaned himself by going back to try and patch things up. He'd left the way open should he decide to sever the bond completely. Perhaps he ought to sever it, if only on the principle that if a person once tells you a lie, that puts an end to truth between you forever. A lie always made him feel positively sick. And God knows he felt sick enough as it was. There was a definite burning sensation now in his chest as well as his stomach. He looked around the steamy bus. Could it be the fumes of the engine that were affecting him? He'd have liked to go and stand on the platform to get some fresh air, but he hated to make himself noticeable, although the bus was now nearly empty. He stole a look at the other passengers to see if anyone was watching him. He might have been muttering to himself, or making peculiar faces. Just to see if anyone would notice he stealthily, but deliberately, made a face into the window, on which the steam acted like a backing of mercury. And sure enough the damn conductor was looking straight at him. James felt he had to give the fellow a propitiating grin, which the impudent fellow took advantage of immediately.

'Not yet, sir,' he said. 'I'll tell you when you're there!'

Officious again. Well, smart as he was, he didn't know his countryside. Clearing a space on the foggy glass, James looked out. It was getting dark outside now but the shape of the trees could still be seen against the last light in the west. The conductor was wrong! They *were* there! He jumped to his feet.

'Not yet, sir,' the blasted fellow called out again, and loudly this time for all to hear.

Ignoring him, James staggered down the bus to the boarding-platform, where, without waiting for the conductor to do it, he defiantly hit the bell to bring the bus to a stop. The fellow merely shrugged his shoulders. James threw an angry glance at him, and then, although the bus had not quite stopped, deliberately and only taking care to face the way the bus was travelling so that if he did fall it would be less dangerous, he jumped off.

Luckily he did not fall. He felt a bit shaken, as he regained his balance precariously on the dark road. He was glad to think he had spiked that conductor. He could tell he had by the smart way the fellow hit the bell again and set the bus once more in motion, that for all his solicitude on the Quays, he'd hardly have noticed if one had fallen on one's face on the road: or cared.

And Myra? If Myra were to read a report of the accident in the newspaper tomorrow, how would *she* feel? More interesting still – what would she tell her friends? Secretive as their relationship was supposed to be, James couldn't help wondering if she might not have let the truth leak out to some people. Indeed, this suspicion had lurked in his mind for some time, but he only fully faced it now.

What about those phone calls she sometimes got? Those times when she felt it necessary to plug out the phone and carry it into her bedroom? Or else talk in a lowered voice, very different from the normal way in which she'd call out 'wrong number' and bang down the receiver? Now that he thought about it, the worst give-away was when she'd let the phone ring and ring without answering it at all. It nearly drove him mad listening to that ringing.

'What will they think, Myra?' he'd cry. When she used to say the caller would think she was out, he nearly went demented altogether at her lack of logic.

'They wouldn't keep on ringing if they didn't suspect you were here,' he exploded once.

Ah! The insidiousness of her answer hadn't fully registered at the time. *Now* it did though.

'Oh, they'll understand.' That was what she'd said.

Understand what? He could only suppose she had given her friends some garbled explanation of things.

'Oh damn her! Damn her!' he said out loud again. There was no reason now why he shouldn't talk out loud or shout if he liked here on the lonely country road. 'Damn, damn,' he shouted. 'Damn, damn, damn!'

Immediately James felt uncomfortable. What if there was someone listening? A few yards ahead, to the left, there was a lighted window. But suddenly he was alerted to something odd. There should not be a light on the left. The shop at the crossroads should be on the other side. He looked around. Could that rotten little conductor have been right? Had he got off too soon? Perhaps that was why the fellow had hit that bell so smartly? To give him no time to discover his mistake?

For clearly he *had* made a mistake, and a bloody great one. He peered into the darkness. But the night was too black, he could see nothing. He had no choice but to walk on.

By the time James had passed the cottage with the lighted window, his eyes were getting more used to the dark. All the same when a rick of hay reared up to one side of the road it might have been a mountain! Where was he at all? And a few seconds later when unexpectedly the moon slipped out from behind the clouds and glinted on the tin roof of a shed in the distance it might have been the sheen of a lake for all he recognized of his whereabouts. Just then, however, he caught sight of the red tail light of the bus again. It had only disappeared because the bus had dipped into a valley. It was now climbing out of the dip again, and going up a steep hill. Ah! he knew that hill. He wasn't as far off his track as he thought. Only a quarter of a mile or so, but he shook his head. In his present state that was about enough to finish him. Still, things could have been worse.

Meanwhile a wisp of vapoury cloud had come between the moon and the earth and in a few minutes it was followed by a great black bank of cloud. Only for a thin green streak in the west it would have been pitch dark again. This streak shed no light on his way but it acted on James like a sign, an omen.

He passed the hayrick. He passed the tin shed. But now another mass of blackness rose up to the left and came between him and the sky. It even hid the green streak this time though he was able to tell by a sudden resinous scent in the air and a curious warmth that the road was passing through a small wood. His spirits rose at once. These were the trees he could see from his cottage. Immediately, his mistake less disastrous, the distance lessened. If only that conductor could know how quickly he had got his bearings! The impudent fellow probably thought he'd left him properly stranded. And perhaps as much to spite the impudent fellow as anything else, when at that instant a daring thought entered his mind and he gave it heed. What if he were to cut diagonally across this wood? It could save him half a mile. It would actually be putting his mistake to work for him.

'What about it, James? Come on. Be a sport,' he jovially exhorted himself.

And seeing that his green banner was again faintly discernible through the dark trees, he called on it to be his lodestar, and scrambled up on the grass bank that separated the road from the wood.

James was in the wood before it came home to him that of course this must be Asigh wood – it must belong to the Balfes! No matter. Why should he let that bother him? The wood was nowhere near their house as far as he remembered its position by daylight. It was composed mostly of neglected, self-seeded trees, more scrub than timber – almost waste ground – ground that had probably deteriorated into commonage.

As he advanced into the little copse – wood was too grand a designation for it – James saw it was not as dense as it seemed from the road, or else at this point there was a pathway through it. Probably it was a short cut well known to the locals, because even in the dark he thought he saw sodden cigarette packets on the ground, and there were toffee wrappers and orange peels lodged in the bushes. Good signs.

Further in, however, his path was unexpectedly blocked by a fallen tree. It must have been a long time lying on the ground because when he put his hand on it to climb over, it was wet and slimy. He quickly withdrew his hand in disgust. He'd have to make his way round it.

The path was not very well defined on the other side of the log. It looked as if people did not after all penetrate this far. The litter at the edge of the wood had probably been left by children. Or by lovers who only wanted to get out of sight of the road? Deeper in, the scrub was thicker, and in one place he mistook a strand of briar for barbed wire it was so tough and hard to cut through. You'd need wire clippers!

James stopped. Was it foolhardy to go on? He'd already ripped the sleeve of his suit. However, the pain in his stomach gave him his answer. Nothing that would get him home quicker was foolish.

'Onward, James,' he said wearily.

And then, damn it, he came to another fallen tree. Again he had to work his way around it. Mind you, he hadn't counted on this kind of thing. The upper branches of this tree spread out over an incredibly wide area. From having to look down, instead of up, he found that –

momentarily of course – he'd lost his sense of direction. Fortunately, through the trees, he could take direction from his green banner. Fixing on it, he forged ahead.

But now there were new hazards. At least twice, tree stumps nearly tripped him, and there were now dried ruts that must have been made by timber lorries at some distant date. Lucky he didn't sprain his ankle. He took out his handkerchief and wiped his forehead. At this rate he wouldn't make very quick progress. He was beginning to ache in every limb, and when he drew a breath, a sharp pain ran through him. The pains in his stomach were indistinguishable now from all the other pains in his body. It was like the way a toothache could turn the whole of one's face into one great ache. The thought of turning back plagued him too at every step. Stubbornly, though, he resisted the thought of turning. To go on could hardly be much worse than to go back through those briars?

A second later James got a fall, a nasty fall. Without warning, a crater opened up in front of him and he went head-first into it. Another fallen tree, blown over in a storm evidently, because the great root that had been ripped out of the ground had taken clay and all with it, leaving this gaping black hole. Oh God! He picked himself up and mopped his forehead with his sleeves.

This time he had to make a wide detour. Luckily after that the wood seemed to be thinning out. He was able to walk a bit faster, and so it seemed reasonable to deduce that he might be getting near to the road at the other end. His relief was so great that perhaps that was why he did not pause to take his bearings again, and when he did look up he was shocked to see the green streak in the sky was gone. Or was it? He swung around. No, it was there, but it seemed to have veered around and was now behind him. Did that mean he was going in the wrong direction? Appalled, he leant back against a tree. His legs were giving way under him. He would not be able to go another step without a rest. And now a new pain had struck him between the shoulders. He felt around with his foot in the darkness looking for somewhere to sit, but all he could feel were wads of soggy leaves from summers dead and gone.

Perhaps it was just as well – if he sat down he might not be able to get up again. Then the matter was taken out of his hands. He was attacked by a fit of dizziness, and his head began to reel. To save himself from falling he dropped down on one knee and braced himself with the palms of his hands against the ground. Bad as he was, the irony of his posture struck him – the sprinter, tensed for the starter's pistol! Afraid of cramp he cautiously got to his feet. And he thought of the times when, as a youngster playing hide and seek, a rag would be tied over his eyes and he would be spun around like a top, so that when the blindfold was removed, he wouldn't know which way to run.

Ah, there was the green light! But how it had narrowed! It was only a thin line now. Still, James lurched towards it. The bushes had got dense again and he was throwing himself against them, as against a crashing wave, while they for their part seemed to thrust him back. Coming to a really thick clump he gathered up enough strength to hurl himself against it, only to find that he went through it as if it was a bank of fog, and sprawled out into another clearing.

Was it the road at last? No. It would have been lighter overhead. Instead a solid mass of blackness towered over him, high as the sky. Were it not for his lifeline of light he would have despaired. As if it too might quench he feverishly fastened his eyes on it. It was not a single line any more. There were three or four lines. Oh God, no? It was a window, a window with a green blind drawn down, that let out only the outline of its light. A house? Oh God, not Balfe's? In absolute panic James turned and with the vigour of frenzy crashed back through the undergrowth in the way he had come. This time the bushes gave way freely before him, but the silence that had pressed so dank upon him was shattered at every step and he was betrayed by the snapping and breaking of twigs. When a briar caught on his sleeve it gave out a deafening rasp. Pricks from a gorse bush bit into his flesh like sparks of fire, but worse still was the prickly heat of shame that ran over his whole body.

'Damn, damn, damn,' he cried, not caring suddenly what noise he made. Why had he run like that? – Like a madman? – Using up his last store of strength? What did he care about anyone or anything if only he could get out of this place? What if it was Balfe's? It was hardly the house? Probably an outbuilding? Or the quarters of a hired hand? Why hadn't he called out?

Sweat was breaking out all over him now and he had to exert a superhuman strength not to let himself fall spent, on the ground, because if he did he'd stay there. He wouldn't be able to get up. To rest for a minute he dropped on one knee again. The pose of the athlete again! Oh, it was a pity Myra couldn't see him, he thought bitterly, but then for a moment he had a crazy feeling that the pose was for real. He found himself tensing the muscles of his face, as if at any minute a real shot would blast-off and he would spring up and dash madly down a grassy sprint-track.

It was then that a new, a terrible, an utterly unendurable pain exploded in his chest.

'God, God!' he cried. His hands under him were riveted to the ground. Had he been standing he would have been thrown. 'What is the matter with me?' he cried. And the question rang out over all the wood. Then, as another spasm went through him other questions were torn from him. Was it a heart attack? A stroke? – In abject terror, not daring to stir, he stayed crouched. 'Ah, Ah, Ahh . . . ' The pain again. The pain, the pain, the pain.

'Am I dying?' he gasped, but this time it was the pain that answered, and answered so strangely James didn't understand because it did what he did not think possible: it catapulted him to his feet, and filled him with a strength that never, never in his life had he possessed. It ran through him like a bar of iron – a stanchion that held his ribs together. He was turned into a man of iron! If he raised his arms now and thrashed about, whole trees would give way before him, and their branches, brittle as glass, would clatter to the ground. 'See Myra! See!' he cried out. So he had lost his vigour? He'd show her! But he had taken his eyes off the light. Where was it? Had it gone out? 'I told you not to go out,' he yelled at it, and lifting his iron feet he went crashing towards where he had seen it last.

But the next minute he knew there was something wrong. Against his face he felt something wet and cold, and he was almost overpowered by the smell of rank earth and rotting leaves. If he'd fallen he hadn't felt the fall. Was he numbed? He raised his head. He'd have to get help. But when he tried to cry out no sound came.

The light? Where was it. 'Oh, don't go out,' he pleaded to it, as if it was the light of life itself, and to propitiate it, he gave it a name. 'Don't go out, Emmy,' he prayed. Then came the last and most anguished question of all. Was he raving? No, no. It was only a window. But in his head there seemed to be a dialogue of two voices, his own and another that answered derisively. 'What window?' James tried to explain that it was the window in the classroom. Hadn't he opened it when the big footballer wasn't able to pull down the sash? He, James, had leant across the desk and brought it down with one strong pull. But where was the rush of sweet summer air? There was only a deathly chill. And where was Emmy?

With a last desperate effort James tried to stop his mind from stumbling and tried to fasten it on Myra. Where was *she*? She wouldn't have failed him. But she *had* failed him. Both of them had failed him. Under a weight of bitterness too great to be borne his face was pressed into the wet leaves, and when he gulped for breath, the rotted leaves were sucked into his mouth.

The Shrine

Next morning the Canon's housekeeper brought Mary her breakfast in bed and, much as she hated to think of the old woman lumbering up the stairs with the heavy tray, Mary was glad not to have to face her uncle until later in the morning. By then, if her fiancé did as he intended, he would have gone traipsing off over the countryside. And, left alone with the Canon, she could try to patch up last night's unfortunate quarrel. She had heard the Canon going out to say early Mass and she'd heard his car crunching the gravel under her window on his return. But she had not heard Don go down. Had he given up his plan? She half hoped he had. She was afraid to think what her uncle would say if he found out what was in Don's mind.

Then, as she was pouring a second cup of tea, Mary heard voices below raised in a brief but sharp exchange. Next minute the front door closed. Springing out of bed and going to the window, she was in time to see Don hitting out across the fields in the direction of the Shrine. She sighed. If the two men had continued their argument this morning nothing would save the weekend. Damn the Shrine anyway, she thought. If only she hadn't let her uncle inveigle them into going there last night when Don and she were both tired after the long drive from Dublin.

The meal old Ellen had prepared for them was very good, and while they were eating it the two men seemed to be getting on famously. If they'd sat on at the table a little longer, even the Canon himself might have been unwilling to stir out. But she herself had been anxious to get the visit to the Shrine over and done with, and it seemed a good idea to go down at that hour when the booths and stalls would, she thought, be closed up and shuttered for the night. She hadn't realized that it was Lady Day, and that business would be going full blast until the final busload of pilgrims left with the traders' touts running alongside the departing coaches in a frantic effort to sell one more statue, one more holy-water font, one more medal.

When they arrived at the Shrine it was blazing with candles, and the yard around the relatively inoffensive church had the festive air of a bazaar. She'd seen Don staring with disgust at one booth where gigantic bunches of rosary beads hung down between brown scapulars. 'Like overripe berries,' she whispered, hoping to make light of the vulgarity. But Don didn't laugh. 'Poisonous berries,' he retorted. And Mary glanced nervously at her uncle in case the old man might have overheard. At the time she couldn't have said whether it was fortunate or unfortunate when Mullins came running across from his new shop and started slobbering all over them. To her surprise the Canon, usually unsociable, accepted the fellow's invitation to go inside and have a glass of sherry – which was of course undrinkable – and she saw Don look at his glass as if he expected to see an engraving of the Virgin on it.

All the same, things might not have been too bad if Don had not already known about Mullins. To while away the time on the drive down from Dublin, she had told him how Mullins had been the first to set up a stall at the church gate after the Apparition, and how he had made so much money that he'd built his present premises opposite the grotto. Unfortunately she had also told Don about the other woman – the woman who had ousted his wife, who was now in a mental home.

'Is that the slut?' Don asked, quite audibly, as they passed through the shop on their way upstairs and saw the creature queening it behind the counter.

They only stayed a short while in Mullins's. Even the Canon couldn't stomach Mullins's sycophancy. Indeed the shopkeeper's eulogies of the proposed new basilica may well have been what triggered off their row later that evening. Mullins had a plaster-of-paris model of the proposed, and monstrously ugly, basilica on the counter of his shop with a money box in front of it. Needless to say he was chairman of the fund-raising committee.

And, when they were back in the parlour of the parochial house and Don asked the Canon innocently enough what he estimated the cost would be, Mary herself was staggered by the figure her uncle mentioned, but Don was fit to be tied.

'And where are you going to raise a sum like that?' Don cried. 'You're surely not going to dun it out of your poverty-stricken parishioners?'

'Not at all,' said the Canon airily. 'We're raising money all over Ireland, all over the world in fact. You'd be surprised how much is pouring in from England and America – even Australia.' He looked quite pleased with himself until he remembered the word Don had used and his face went purple. 'Did you say "dun it out of people"?' After that the full fury of the row broke over her.

Oh, why did she bring Don down here in the first place? Why didn't she wait and let her uncle meet him on the day of the wedding? The old man was probably lonely enough at the thought of her marriage without being led to think, as he probably did now, that she was marrying an atheist. But her uncle's wedding present had been so generous she'd felt that the least she could do was to bring Don down and introduce him in advance. Not that she should have been surprised by his present, considering the long unbroken history of his generosity towards her ever since she was a child. Her mother was the Canon's only sister whom he had almost idolized, and, since her mother was a widow, he'd insisted on paying Mary's school fees and buying her books and her clothes. Indeed he used to buy her lots of little odds and ends that her mother could never have afforded. And when her mother died he virtually became her guardian. She had to be sent away to boarding school, of course, but she came to stay in the parochial house for all her school holidays. How he used to fuss about her! He was like a hen with one chick, making her change her clothes if she was out in the rain for a minute, and often insisting on drying her hair himself with a huge, and not always clean, towel of his own. As for the meals he provided! The fact that he was an ascetic himself did not prevent him from feeding her like a prize bantam. It was not only her physical welfare that concerned him, of course. He used to talk continually about modesty and purity, thinking that at her age she was too young to be embarrassed or to embarrass him. He probably thought that although she would not fully comprehend his veiled remarks, all the same something of his meaning would seep into her subconscious and when she was older his words might come back to her and be an armour against temptation – a breastplate to protect her from sin.

Poor Uncle! He must have been scared stiff when she'd first gone up to Dublin to the university, thinking she'd surely lose her virginity there. On the occasional week-end when she'd come down to visit him he always managed to drag a reference to the flesh into his sermon, making it clear that the Faith was the only prop that could be relied upon to keep the moral structure from collapse. And, as time went on, whenever she was in the congregation his sermon would be directed at her, as she sat where she'd always done, in the front pew, right under the pulpit.

'Innocence is like the bloom on a peach,' he'd intone, looking impersonally up at the organ loft. 'And when a rot sets in, it sets in at the core and works outward, slowly, so it is often a long time before the damage shows. This of course is part of the devil's clever plan. That gentleman always takes a private and personal delight in making his latest victim do his evil work for him. It is a common practice with him to see to it that the seduced becomes in turn the seducer.'

His sermons were mainly meant to be preventative, however, and if he found that one of his female parishioners had succumbed to a sin of the flesh he dropped his flowery talk pretty quickly and moved in decisively with great common sense to take action to prevent the girl from being what he referred to as 'pulped'. That crude word had always made Mary shudder. And what a sharp ear the old man had for discovering illicit pregnancies. In a matter of hours he'd have nipped the scandal in the bud and, with alarming dispatch, married off the offending girl. Whenever possible he married her to the father of the child, but if for any reason that was not possible, he'd unload her on to some ageing but compliant bachelor. At first Mary used to be shocked at the latter stratagem, but she was forced to admit the victims themselves usually thrived on his treatment. As well as providing a solution for the girls' problems, the marriages generally acted like a tonic on the old fellows and gave them a new lease of life. Frequently, girls thus hastened into wedlock ripened into pious matrons upon whom the Canon could later count for help in handling similar cases as they cropped up.

Mary had to smile as she reflected that there would have been no fear of her uncle's quarrelling with her fiancé if for one moment he'd thought there had been any hanky-panky, as he'd put it, between them. If he'd thought that was the case, he wouldn't have let any obstacle – not even Don's criticism of the Shrine – come between him and the speedy celebration of their nuptials. He would have seen to it that their plans were put forward and that they were married post-haste. Well, she had never given him grounds to worry about her on that score. She had never betrayed his trust in her. And, to give him his due, of late years he had never, or at least never before last night, shown the slightest anxiety about her in that respect. In her last year at college he had not only allowed her to go hitch-hiking on the Continent, knowing she'd be staying in youth hostels or cheap hotels, but had financed her trips, seeming as it were to participate in them vicariously by making out itineraries and route maps. His display of distrust last night was just an attempt to insult Don, albeit a well-calculated insult. When he and Don finally stopped arguing, long past midnight, and then only because they were all three exhausted as well as miserably unhappy, the old man stumped up the stairs in front of them and, after showing Don to his room, waited ostentatiously until the door closed on him before escorting her to her room. Outside her room, too, he stood waiting for her to close her door before trundling off to his own bed. As if she needed to be shown the way to the little room where she'd spent so many nights of her life. So many happy nights at that. But she forgave him. And, indeed, feeling certain Don would sneak down the corridor to say a private good-night to her, she stealthily opened her door again, just a crack, so there would be no need for him to knock. When she did hear him creeping along the landing she jumped out of bed and went to the door with her finger to her lips.

'Don't come in Don, please,' she begged.

'Why not?' Don asked roughly, but he glanced nervously at the Canon's door. 'He wouldn't come out, would he?' He seemed shaken at the thought.

'No, of course not. He wouldn't stoop to tactics like that, but we've upset him enough for one night,' she said. She was already afraid she would not sleep a wink for wondering whether the old man was lying awake in his uncomfortable bed, on the other side of the wall, castigating himself for imaginary failures on his part. 'Go back to your own room, Don, please,' she begged. All the same, catching him by the sleeve, she held him back for a second to ask if he still intended to go poking around the countryside. For he had managed as they came up the stairs to convey that he was going to do this; he had a hunch there could be mineral deposits in the area. Even though he was no expert, he wanted to poke around to see if there would be any justification for setting up further tests later. 'I hope my uncle doesn't know what you have in mind?' she asked anxiously.

'I don't care whether he knows or not,' Don said. 'Anyway, it's only a hunch. And if there should turn out to be minerals here, the old man couldn't but be pleased at the possibilities of prosperity there would be for his people.' She said nothing and Don's face hardened. 'Unless he thinks that every acre in the parish is sacred,' he said.

She and Don then began to quarrel between themselves, a silly hissing quarrel conducted in whispers and raised eyebrows. She was entirely on her fiancé's side, but for her uncle's sake she couldn't help protesting that a large-scale development in the area could threaten the Shrine – if only by taking from its dignity.

'Its dignity?' Don gave her a contemptuous look.

'I mean its importance.'

'That's more like it,' Don said, and he turned and went back to his own room, cross now with her as well as with the Canon. Was he only bluffing, she wondered, as she closed the door and went over to the window to stare out into the darkness. Could there be any real possibility that the impoverished earth out there could yield a proper livelihood for the people and free them from the ignominy of selling cheap religious objects to the sick and dying? It was hours before she went to sleep.

And now, this morning, as she lay sipping her tea, Mary looked out again at the bare and desolate land that even by day was dark or else lit fitfully by a harsh, glaring light falling on it in shafts between rain-laden clouds. When she was up and dressed, and as she ran down the stairs to the little parlour, she deliberately forced herself to appear gay and friendly.

The parlour was frightfully hot and stuffy, and the Canon was sitting in his battered armchair reading his Office, in front of a fire which had obviously been burning for several hours. It was roaring up the chimney. Although the door was open, the heat was stifling, and yet the old man had dragged the chair closer to the fire. His dog-eared breviary had been familiar to Mary since she was a child. As always when she appeared, he took up the burnt-out pipe that rested on the arm of his chair and put it between the pages to mark the place. But this morning he did not greet her. Instead he glanced at the delicately constructed glass-and-brass carriage clock that stood to one side of the mantelshelf in a clutter of odds and ends, among which pride of place was shared by a photograph of her mother and a framed photograph of the Shrine.

'I was going to get Ellen to give you a call,' he said. 'We'd want to start soon if we're going to pick up that fellow of yours in time for his lunch.'

Mary's heart lifted. If her uncle was going to fetch Don himself in his own car, he must have made up with him this morning, after all. 'He ought to have had his fill by now of plodding around in the mud,' he said. 'And we don't want the meal to be dried up and not worth eating.'

'Thank you, Uncle,' Mary said, but she glanced at the clock. In doing so she had to put her hand up to shield her face from the heat. The room was positively suffocating, and the smell of roasting meat coming up from the kitchen made it seem hotter still. 'It's a bit early yet to go for him, Uncle,' she said gently, and she sat down on the other side of the fire. 'You've no idea how carried away he gets when he's doing this sort of field work.'

'I can imagine! I can imagine!' the Canon said, but he looked across at her oddly. 'What is the purpose behind this foolish expedition?' he asked. To her relief, she saw by the expression on his face that this was less a question than a sneer. Not prepared to cross swords with him, she thought she'd jolly him into a better humour by taking a bantering tone.

'If anyone has to wait about in the cold, better him than us, Uncle!' she said. 'He never knows when to stop on these forages. He'll be laden down like a packhorse when we find him, his pockets full of sand and rocks and lumps of clay. Wait till you see!'

Not knowing that the slightly derogatory tone in her voice was intentional, the old man chuckled.

'In that case he might be glad enough to see us arrive ahead of time,' he said drily, but he settled back into his chair. A moment later he looked across at her sharply. 'He wore his good suit, did you know that?' It seems a bit odd he didn't bring a pair of old trousers if he intended grubbing around in the clay.'

'Oh, he probably only took the notion when he got here,' she said cautiously. As far as she could see the Canon was not really suspicious, just sceptical about Don's abilities. He leant forward. 'No matter what you may think to the contrary, my dear, your young man is no different from all the other engineers in Ireland today. From Fair Head to Mizzen Head there isn't an engineer in the country that hasn't had his head turned by the tall stories that are going the rounds about the mining up in the midlands, the sinking of oil wells and all that. They're puffed up to the gills with nonsense. They all think they'll make themselves into millionaires overnight.'

'I don't think you're right there,' Mary said evenly. 'It's only the politicians and the foreign investors that are getting anything out of the mining in Meath. The people who owned the land originally got very little. I understand most of them were bought out early in the game. As for the engineers, they are foreigners for the most part. I can assure you, Uncle, the whole operation didn't bring much prosperity to the local people, unless maybe to the shopkeepers and the common labourers.'

The Canon pressed his lips together. 'I'm glad to hear that at least. I've no sympathy with the Meath people. Why weren't they content with what was to be got off the top of the ground, in God's good sunlight, without burrowing into the bowels of the earth? The land around Trim, Navan, and Kells is the richest land in Ireland. Every blade of grass up there would have been a stalk of pure gold to the poor people down here. People with large families of children at that! Not the withered old bachelors that own all the land up there. But no! No! The people up in the fat grassland weren't satisfied with God's plenty! They had to try and lay their hands on lazy money, get-rich-quick-money. Mark my words, Mary, those people won't be satisfied until they've turned Ireland into another Lancashire. They won't stop until we have slag heaps as high as Aberfan, where we once had the greenest fields in the world.'

He was so incensed that Mary felt she had better try and calm him down. 'To give them their due, Uncle, I believe the mining companies themselves are making great efforts to preserve the amenities. They remove the topsoil and set it aside with the intention of putting it back after they've sunk the shafts and got the underground structure ready for work. The landscape will be completely restored in a few years' time.'

'Is that so?' She couldn't be sure if he believed her or if he was being sarcastic. In any event his eyes had suddenly been drawn, as by a magnet, to the photograph of the Shrine and dwelt lovingly on it. 'Thanks to the good God, our little Shrine is bringing more prosperity to the people hereabout with every year that passes. It's not only providing them with their daily bread but giving them spiritual food as well.' Mary could only stare at him in amazement. It was Don's contention, and the start of the quarrel, that the local people were being destroyed by what Don called trading in the Temple. She looked sharply at the old man. He was no fool. He could not have forgotten Don's words. His own words must have had some obscure intent. He stood up. 'What puzzles me, Mary, is why, after the views he expressed last night, your young man should want to subject himself again to a sight apparently as objectionable to him as our blessed grotto.' Did she fancy it, Mary wondered, or was there anger still smouldering behind his eyes? 'What's this his words were?' he asked. ' "Commercial exploitation. Trading on the frailty of the sick and infirm." ' Mary winced. It was a pity Don had used such strong words. Her uncle had mimicked him to the life. Then, lapsing back into his own voice he uttered one single word. 'Guff!' he said. 'Guff!'

'Oh, Uncle, Don didn't mean you to take things up the way you did!' she cried. 'He was really and truly concerned about the poverty down here. He'd never seen anything like it!'

'Well, why then can't he appreciate the money the Shrine is raking in for these poor people. They are making more money every year. Wait till we implement our plans, and have a new car park and a decent hotel, then you'll see!' he said. 'Tell your young man that, Mary! Make him see it.' It was almost as if he was trying to win her as an ally. 'Do you know, Mary, it's my belief that under cover of pretending to make this survey, or whatever it is he's up to, your young man may have had it in mind to go down to the Shrine again, behind backs as it were, and take another look at it, and maybe revise his opinions in the light of how I presented the facts to him this morning, when he blustered out a lot more of his silly socialist nonsense and tried to be blasé. I'm pretty sure he was only trying to save face, and give himself time to think over my words.'

Mary couldn't believe her ears. How could a man like him – she glanced around the parlour so crowded with books and prints, paintings and maps – how could a man who had devoted a lifetime to study, a man who read in four or five languages, how could he delude himself to this extent? Her uncle, however, was going from strength to strength in his delusion. 'Between ourselves, my dear, we may have converted the fellow! God works in mysterious ways, you know.'

Suddenly Mary became more alert. Was it possible this last idiotic remark was a sly probe.

'Don is not going anywhere near the Shrine, Uncle,' she said assertively. 'Not until he has finished his survey. He's only meeting us there because it's a convenient place to meet, an easy landmark.'

Her uncle merely smiled indulgently. 'Ah, well. One way or another I suppose we may as well humour him. Let him rootle away to his heart's content if it makes him happy. The worst that can happen to him is catch a cold in the head.' He winked at her. 'Not that we'd want him laid up now that he's got his new job.'

Mary would have been only too glad to change the subject and talk about her fiancé's prospects were it not that she was now worried on another score. 'The appointment isn't absolutely certain yet, Uncle,' she said. 'I thought you understood that? That's why we're not putting our engagement in the paper just yet. Of course we'll get married whether he gets the job or not, but things won't be so smooth for us if he doesn't get it.'

'They certainly won't. It's preposterous to think of it.' It was touching to see how concerned he was about her future. 'I thought he was dead certain to get that job? Why didn't you tell me there was doubt about it? I don't know that I could have done much. If it were in my own diocese I might have had some influence, but all the same there's never any knowing what a few words mightn't do if whispered into the right ear.' He frowned. 'Is it too late now to make a few inquiries?'

'Oh yes, I think so, Uncle,' she said, but lightly, because although there was undoubtedly still a small uncertainty about the appointment, Don felt fairly confident of getting it all the same.

'Well remember, you've only to say the word,' said the Canon, and he winked at her again. Then, looking away once more, he said an extraordinary thing. 'You're sure of the other thing? I mean to say I hope he's the right man for you and all that?'

She was very much annoyed. 'Uncle! How can you ask such a thing? I wouldn't have brought him all the way down here to see you if I wasn't certain about that.'

The old man sighed. 'Don't be cross with me, my dear. You must know I don't like losing you. Things will never be the same again when there's somebody with us all the time.'

Mary jumped up and gave him a light kiss on the cheek. 'Silly-billy! Don isn't just "somebody". You'll find he's the most marvellous, marvellous person. Just because you had a little disagreement with him –'

That was a mistake.

'Did you say a little disagreement?'

Mary gave him another quick kiss. 'Don't be so touchy, Uncle.' She looked down at him. He had put on the scowl by which he used to try to intimidate her when she was small, but which generally just made her laugh. Remembering those days, she looked at him pertly. 'You've got to like him,' she said, stamping her foot like a child.

The Canon softened. 'Ah well,' he said. 'I've no doubt you'll get your own way in this as in everything else, my dear. I've spoiled you for too long to expect matters to be mended now.'

'People are never spoiled by love, Uncle, and you know that,' Mary said soberly. 'One day you'll love Don just as much as you love me.' Ignoring his raised eyebrows she went on, 'Did I ever tell you he was going to do geology, but his family felt that engineering was more practical?'

'Good for them,' he said. 'They were quite right.'

She was glad to see she'd succeeded in distracting him by this piece of information. 'I'm afraid, Uncle, he wasn't really reconciled to it until he and I began to think of marriage.'

'Don't worry. Engineering is a better bet any day,' said the Canon. 'A county engineer gets a fairly decent salary – and that's the main thing, isn't it?'

'I suppose so,' Mary said, doubtfully. 'All the same, I can't help feeling he's clipping his wings for my sake.' Seeing the scowl come back on his face, she hurried to make her point clear before he interrupted her again. 'I think he'd like to put his gifts to work in some way that would bring him more personal fulfilment.'

'Nonsense!' The Canon positively glared at her. 'Personal fulfilment indeed! What does that mean in the name of God? There's only one form of fulfilment for any man in this, his one and only earthly life, and that is – ' He broke off suddenly and Mary was frightened for a minute by a fiery glint that came into his eyes, until she realized it was only a reflection from the flames, into which he was staring.

In any case, a second later he seemed to have forgotten what he had been saying. 'Well, he's young, he'll learn, like the rest of us,' he said. 'But you must be his helpmate, Mary – in this, as in all else. You must be God's voice from now on, speaking quietly but clearly in his ear, day and night.' He fixed her with a fierce gaze. 'That's why I'm not really worried about last night's diatribe against the Shrine. I know when you're married you'll knock sense into him. I'll admit it upset me, at the time, to see you so spineless, but I hope I am able to make allowances.'

In spite of the heat of the fire, Mary, on impulse, knelt down beside him. 'Uncle, you must know, you must have seen, that the views Don expressed were not just his own. You must have realized I share them. If anything, they originated with me.'

To her amazement he didn't seem angered.

'Ah, that's only natural,' he said, and he chuckled. 'The male makes the nest but the female has to lure him into it, so she may sometimes have to change her colours for a short time in the courting season, like the birds and the beasts, but when she finally settles down, she shows her true colours and rules the roost. I have no fears about you. If God sends you children I know you'll bring them up in the way our Holy Mother the Church has ordained.' He nodded his head in agreement with himself. 'I suppose I may take it for granted that this fellow of yours hasn't altogether lost the Faith in spite of his spouting last night?'

'Of course not,' Mary said crisply. 'He goes to Mass and so on, if that's what you mean. Most Sundays anyway.'

But her uncle's face darkened again and he grabbed the sides of the chair as if he found it hard to control himself. 'Mary!' He was outraged. 'Mary! That's no way to speak of Holy Mass.' But his outrage was centred less on her than on Don. 'So he goes "most Sundays"! How condescending! I hope his Maker appreciates his graciousness!'

'Don't worry! I'd say his Maker has more appreciation of him than you have!' Mary said hotly. 'But please let's not quarrel about him, Uncle. No matter what you think of him, surely you're glad he's not taking me out of Ireland altogether, in which case you and I might never see each other again? It looked at one time as if we might have to emigrate.'

With relief, she saw she had struck the right note at last. He was visibly touched.

'I didn't know there was ever any question of that.' The Canon seemed stunned by the mere idea. 'Where would you have gone?' he asked dully.

'Oh, I don't know,' Mary said carelessly. 'Things didn't come to that. I suppose it would probably have been Africa, or somewhere like that.'

'Preposterous!' The Canon's exclamation was as vehement as if their going was still a possibility. He actually shook his fist in the air. 'I can tell you I'd never let that happen. Not without putting up a struggle.' He sat forward. 'Are you sure you're telling me the truth, Mary? Are you sure there's no danger of his being turned down for this job even yet? Perhaps I ought to telephone one or two people – just to be on the safe side. Oh, Mary, Mary,' he cried, and his anxiety now had a pathetic quality: 'Apart from not wanting you to go far away, I couldn't bear to think of you living anywhere else in the world, even after I'm dead, except in our own safe little island – God bless it.'

For the first time since her arrival the evening before something of his old affection for her showed in his eyes, and Mary was saddened when she noticed a scattering of large flaky freckles that she hadn't seen before on the backs of his hands. A sign of age? The big brown blotches were disfiguring on his otherwise fine thin hands, with the fingertips slightly bent back. Wasn't that, too, a sign of something – generosity?

Then, as she was staring at his hands, the Canon raised them and clawed at the arms of his chair, trying to drag it still nearer the fire. When he failed, because of the heavy iron fender that was in the way, he heaved himself forward and held his hands almost on top of the flames. Surely he couldn't be cold? Mary had already pushed her own chair as far back as it would go against the bookcase behind her, and yet she was still uncomfortably hot. But although her uncle's forehead was glistening with sweat, she saw that his bony hands were white and bloodless. She was stabbed with pity for him, and it occurred to her that it was as if face and hands did not belong to the same man, just as this parlour where they sat, with the accumulated treasures of a lifetime, did not seem to belong under the same roof with the bleak bedrooms overhead, furnished with ugly outsized furniture, the relics of former priests of the parish. The Canon's own bedroom was particularly cold and uninviting, and it was always pervaded by a sour odour that made Mary shudder on the few occasions in recent years when she had gone in there to help the old housekeeper turn his lumpy mattress.

The room he had appointed to her, years before, when she'd come on her first visit – it was the Easter holidays – was, then as now, bleak enough too, God knows, but he had allowed her to paste up gaily coloured pictures cut out of magazines, and they partly hid the hideous yellow wallpaper. Now mildew from raindown had worked its way through these glossy pictures, and some of them were peeling off the walls, but Mary's heart melted to think how she had grown to love the dark ugly room. Compared with the clinical bareness of her cubicle in the convent, this room had a power to tug at her heart. Even last night its charm was not quite eclipsed. And no wonder! It was the only real home she'd ever known, because however tightly the Canon clung to the belief that she remembered the home her poor mother had tried to hold together after the death of her husband, Mary had in fact almost forgotten that former existence. She had even forgotten what her mother looked like, but, knowing that her uncle could not bear to think that all memory of his beloved sister had been totally obliterated from her mind, she used to nod in agreement with him when he'd extol the dead woman's hair, her eyes, her classic profile. After all, the photograph on his mantelpiece was always there to vouch for her beauty. Mary looked up at it now, but seeing her look up, the Canon thought she was looking at the clock.

'Is it time to go, do you think?' he asked.

'Let's give him another few minutes,' she said.

'Well, then – ' The Canon went back to his breviary.

Mary smiled. The daily reading of his Office always seemed a heavy burden on him. He certainly seized every odd minute to get it over and done with. It was a wonder he didn't know it by heart. Surely some priests did? While he was reading it, she gave herself up to the quietness that had fallen over the room, broken only by the fall of a coal from the fire. She would let him finish, and after that they'd go and fetch Don.

The old man was a long time reading his Office. Mary may even have dozed off, because she started violently when her uncle placed his breviary on the arm of his chair and stood up. 'Where is your coat?' he asked. His own was always thrown across a chair near the door in case he got an urgent sick call.

'It's on the hall rack, I think,' Mary said, getting to her feet and going towards the door, but there she stopped in surprise and peered into the semi-dark behind it. 'That's not another new painting, Uncle? Not another Jack Yeats?' It was an unnecessary question. There could be no mistaking the glory of colour in sea and sky, and although she hadn't seen it till then, the small painting, once seen, dominated the room. 'How much did you pay for it?' she asked, off guard in her excitement. Yeats's prices had been rising steeply.

The Canon glanced nervously down the hallway before answering, and then, to her amusement, he raised his voice. 'I got it cheap,' he said loudly. 'For nothing!' Then he lowered his voice again. 'It's important, Mary, to keep these things from going out of the country, no matter what one has to pay for them,' he said.

'No excuses needed, Uncle,' Mary said, laughing, but she felt she had blundered badly. 'Why hide it away behind the door though?' she asked after a minute.

The Canon looked at his painting with a mixture of pride and embarrassment. 'It's a good enough place for it when the door is shut,' he said sheepishly.

'And when is this door ever closed?' Mary asked slyly. 'You can never close it because the room is always at oven temperature.'

But looking around the room she saw there was not much room for the painting anywhere on the crowded walls. Nor was it a bad idea to place it at a distance from the two large Yeatses on the opposite wall, particularly since they belonged to the painter's early period. She went closer to the little painting, and for a moment let its beauty stream into her soul. Then she turned teasingly towards the old man. 'I suppose there is no trying to wheedle you into leaving me this in your will?' she asked with mock seriousness. 'I suppose you'll be leaving it to the Church with the rest of your treasures?'

'We'll see. We'll see, my dear,' the Canon said. She saw she had made him very happy by her approval of his purchase. 'Mind your p's and q's and you never know what you might get!'

Uncle and niece smiled into each other's eyes. They were on familiar ground now. This was the kind of playful dialogue that used to give them such fun when she was a small girl. One day she had artlessly disclosed that she thought all his possessions would some day belong to her. 'When you are dead, Uncle, I mean,' she'd added, with a child's idea of tact. But young as she'd been, she was quick-witted enough to stand rebuked by her uncle's answer. He'd gone over to the mantelpiece and taken down the photograph of the Shrine with the church in the background. 'And the Shrine as well?' he'd said. She'd bitten her lip in shame and snuggled against his frowzy soutane to hide her blushes. So now, remembering the sweetness of their relationship in those days, and grateful for all he had done for her, she grew serious.

'Oh, Uncle, you've given me so much! Don't ever think I took it for granted. Thank you. Thank you.'

The Canon too grew serious, even harsh, 'Don't make me regret it, that's all. Let's have no more performances like last night,' he said.

And, believing her promise could be kept, she held out her hand.

'No more, I promise,' she said.

'Come on then,' he said. 'Get your coat and let's be off.'

Before the Shrine was built, and before the new trunk road was constructed, the church was seven miles from the parochial house. This was an unusually long distance between a priest and his church, but in the impoverished countryside there was no nearer place of a standard to accommodate a priest. And at first the Canon had not complained of the long drive, even in the cold of winter. But after the Apparition, and especially after the erection of the grotto on the site where the Blessed Mother and the holy saints had appeared, he changed and now could scarcely hide how sorely it chafed him to be so far from the sanctified spot. One of his long-term plans was to build a new parochial house nearer to the centre of activity. Meanwhile he had to be content with the new road which cut a mile and a half off the distance between him and the Shrine. Now, as they drove off, Mary wondered if he had had a hand in getting the new road built. A word in the right ear? She smiled indulgently at him.

They had only gone a few yards along the new road when they came to the place where the old road ran off it. This old road had had to be left for the convenience of a few cottages which would otherwise have been isolated, but it was not maintained and was in a poor state of repair. Yet, when they came to it, Mary impulsively put her hand on her uncle's sleeve.

'Oh, Uncle, would you mind if we went by the old road?' She was not really clear why she made the suggestion, but it did not seem too preposterous considering that the abandoned road looped back again to rejoin the trunk road a few miles further along. She saw at once from the Canon's face that she'd dampened his spirits, which had been rising steadily since they left the house. He resented anything that would delay the joyful moment when he'd catch his first sight of the church spire. Although disgruntled, he dropped into a lower gear and turned on to the small dirt road, but when after a few minutes the curve brought them around again to face in the direction of the Shrine, his good spirits were restored. It was as if the compass needle of his heart had swung around with the steering wheel. And when the spire of the church eventually appeared Mary knew that he would be the first to see it, not because his eyesight was better than hers, but because it was with the eye of love he'd pick it out.

Love, she thought sadly; it was love that was at the root of all the contradictions in him. He thought he had cut out all need for it from his body, and although for a time his natural feelings for her mother, and later for herself, had seemed to fill the vacancy, it was not enough. The vacuum had to be filled and he had filled it with devotion to the Shrine.

She glanced at him as he strained over the wheel, staring straight in front of him. Of course, she thought, of course his eyes of flesh could not but see the tawdriness and vulgarity of the traders' booths at the entrance to the grotto, but the inner eye of love looked through them to the spot on which he believed the Virgin had appeared, and in time the whole place became transfigured for him. Mary sighed, and she too looked ahead, but she was looking only at the road which was more rutted and riddled with potholes than she'd realized. And when, just then, they came to a bad patch and she joggled against the old man, he started.

'Move over, Mary,' he said sharply. 'You're in the way of the gears.'

Like a scalded cat Mary edged as far over on the seat as she could. She'd forgotten how sensitive he was to being seen in public with her. Even when she was a small girl he was always constrained in her company if they were out anywhere in public. He never, then, permitted himself the simple signs of affection he'd show her when they were at home. On the rare visits he'd made to Dublin he seldom took her out for a meal to a restaurant or hotel. Instead, he'd buy delicacies and bring them to her flat and have her prepare a feast for herself there. He was especially ill at ease whenever she had to travel in the car with him. Broadminded as she hoped she was, Mary had a certain sympathy with his dread of giving rise to scandal. She had seen people looking at them oddly on occasion. Worse still, she had found herself looking with curiosity at other priests she saw in the company of women, although in those cases, too, there was most likely a blood relationship. Sometimes even here in his own parish, where he was well known, she knew he was uneasy in her company, thinking that strangers – visitors to the Shrine for instance – would not know she was his niece. Yes, there was some sense in the old man's scruples. It would be a sorry thing if, having unfailingly honoured his vow all his life, he should be misjudged at any time, but sorrier still if, when he was old, he were thought in the end to have succumbed to lust. Poor dear! Her heart melted and, seeing a pile of booklets on the tray under the dashboard, and taking them for new hymn books, she pulled one out, intending to compliment him on it. When his face lit up she realized with a sinking heart that the booklets were about the Shrine.

'Oh, I forgot to show you those, Mary,' he said. 'Ignore the cover, my dear, it's not meant to be a work of art, you know – it's intended to sell for sixpence, which will barely cover the cost of publication. We'll only break even after we sell three thousand.' His face clouded over, but only for a moment. 'We're hopeful the whole edition may be sold out after next summer's pilgrimage, and we've already planned some important changes in the second edition. Open it, open it,' he prompted as Mary sat apathetically with the booklet unopened on her lap, dazed by the realization that a simple mistake had brought them back to the dangerous topic. 'The print is bad, I know that,' he said. 'And there may be printer's errors in spite of my having read the proofs myself – ' He had slowed down the car in order to see her reaction. 'Go on, look through it! I'd be glad of any criticism you have to make. You can't study it carefully now, I know, but I'll give you a copy to take back with you. I'll give you several copies so you can distribute them among your friends. Your young man might even like to have one – after he's been down at the Shrine for a second time.' Here the old man nudged her, and Mary could hardly suppress a shiver of apprehension. She opened the booklet but immediately her attention was arrested by a line on the first page.

'Oh Uncle! I didn't know the Shrine was not recognized by the Church,' she cried.

'Read on,' the Canon said, complacently. 'There was a misunderstanding at the beginning. That's all. It has been recognized now – more or less.' He paused and cleared his throat, and then to her consternation broke into such a pat defence of the Shrine that she felt he must have recited it so many times that he had it off by heart. 'The Church is, at all times, reluctant to guarantee the authenticity of any apparition – except, of course, those recorded in Holy Scripture – but, after proper investigation, the bishop of any diocese can declare that, as far as human testimony can be relied upon, a given apparition may be said to have taken place – or to have given the appearance of having done so. This declaration does not imply a binding obligation to believe on the part of the faithful, but it is recognized practice to regard such a place as sanctified.' There was an almost hypnotic quality in the old man's voice, but as he neared the end of the peroration he sounded a bit rattled. 'It was a destructive element in this country that put out the story that our Shrine had not been granted full recognition.' He turned accusingly towards her. 'You as a Catholic, Mary, ought to know that there is not such a vast difference between proven authenticity and a pious recommendation to the faithful of such devotions as arise out of custom. Read on. Read on. You'll see that the Holy See was pleased to grant many liturgical privileges to our Shrine.'

Mary no longer needed to be urged to read. She was devouring the cheap print. In spite of having been familiar with the Shrine since she was a child, she was astonished to see how little she knew about the actual Apparition.

'I never knew all this about its being such a wet night, such an awful night – '

'Torrential rain,' the Canon confirmed, nodding his head vigorously. 'You don't mean to say you didn't know that! Now you see the need for my little publication. The parish priest at the time had just come from a sick call and was drying his clothes by the fire.'

'That's such a personal detail it makes the whole story come to life,' Mary said, genuinely amazed. 'Don must read this.'

'Of course he must,' said the Canon. 'It's extraordinary how many people are ignorant of what happened here, although if they'd put their pride in their pockets, and come down here, they'd see that the same glow of sanctity that emanated from those heavenly figures still shines down on us today and on all who come to us.'

Mary was scarcely listening. Indeed she felt obliged to offer an apology, an explanation, for her absorption. 'It's not so much the supernatural aspect that fascinates me, Uncle,' she said, 'it's the ordinariness of it all. Those people who first saw the strange light at the church and thought nothing of it – that's so human, isn't it? And then, the others, who actually saw the figures, but thought they were only statues! Can't you imagine thinking that yourself?' She laughed. Then she stopped laughing. 'Oh, but there's something that doesn't ring true. When they saw that the feet of the statues were not touching the ground they fell down on their knees and started to say the rosary. Yet in the middle of the rosary they jumped up and ran around the town to tell everyone a miracle had taken place, and work up a crowd. Now that was a bit hasty, don't you think? That smacks to me of the fake miracle at Templemore, a bit claptrap –'

'Claptrap?' With a jerk the Canon braked the car and brought it to a standstill. 'You missed the real reason for their conviction,' he said sternly. He leaned across her and leafed through the thin pages. 'They saw that the ground was dry under the feet of the Virgin. You must have missed that, Mary.'

'Yes, I did, but all the same that seems to me to be a bit –' She hesitated.

' – a bit what?'

'Well, a bit small-minded, Uncle, if you don't mind my saying so, a bit petty in the middle of all the marvels, for the Blessed to keep themselves dry when everyone else must have been soaked to the skin.'

Her uncle looked flustered. 'Well, what would you have had them do, hold umbrellas over their heads – the Virgin, I mean, and the Blessed Saints?'

Mary laughed half-heartedly. 'No. I didn't expect that, but why couldn't they have picked a fine night to appear?' She looked back at the booklet. 'One of those poor people kneeling there in the rain was over seventy. It's almost as bad as if they – the Virgin and the others – *did* have their umbrellas with them!'

'Mary! Watch your words, please. I'm used to irreverence, but blasphemy is another matter.'

'Sorry, Uncle.' Mary patted his knee. 'But you asked for my opinion – about the booklet, I mean,' she added tactfully. 'And something about the way this is put makes it hard, for me anyway, to swallow.'

The Canon started up the car again. 'All miracles are,' he said succinctly.

Mary had to agree with that. 'I suppose so,' she said. Then she gave an exclamation. 'Wait! Here's something I consider downright unedifying. When one family ran out they forgot all about a poor old woman who was dying and whom they were meant to be minding. They left her all alone.'

The Canon gripped the wheel tightly and began to go faster. 'She didn't die, though. Did you see that? That you might say in itself was a kind of miracle within a miracle. The old woman struggled out of her bed and tried to follow them, a woman who was at death's door.'

Mary said nothing to that. What was there to say? She had to admit to herself that the Church had in general examined the case very thoroughly. On the other hand, the case for authenticity seemed to have at least one weakness, a flaw, in fact.

'It says here that those who testified to having seen the Apparition were afterwards said to have been drunk at the time.'

The Canon, however, seemed to exult in this charge. 'Agreed!' he cried. 'That is an accusation commonly made by enemies of the Church. But I am happy to say it is an accusation that is easy to refute in our case.'

'But one of those who saw the Virgin was a boy of twelve,' Mary cried. 'Another was only five! What need was there to prove those children were not drunk?' She laid down the book and turned and looked steadily at the old man. 'I repeat, Uncle – you asked my opinion and here it is. It seems to me that it's easier to believe in the Apparition than it is to believe in this promotion of it. It's all this promotion that seems fishy, especially years afterwards when the evidence, even at the time, was scanty.' Putting the booklet back where she got it, she made up her mind that Don must not see it. 'As for the Vatican's affiliating the Shrine with the basilicas in Lourdes and Lisieux, and granting facilities for pilgrimages – well, quite frankly – ' She was going to say, irreverently, that this piece of propaganda stuck in her gizzard, but they had come to the place where the old road joined the new, and the Canon was sitting bolt upright, getting ready for his first glimpse of the church spire. He'd only got a vague drift of what she'd just said.

'Lourdes and Lisieux, did you say?' he asked, absently. 'They'll only be in the halfpenny place in five or six years from now. The fame of this place is growing by leaps and bounds, and when the new basilica goes up and we have a car park and public conveniences – ' He stopped. 'The expansion will be such that there won't be a shop site to be had within a three-mile radius. There will be shops stretching out as far as this junction! And they'll all do a good business, too. People may not stop on the way into the town – they're always too eager to reach the Shrine – but on their way out, even when they're anxious to get home, either because of small children being jaded and cross, or because of some poor invalid in the back seat of the car who is dreading a long return journey, you'll find there will still be plenty of people stopping.' He seemed to brood for a minute on what he'd said and then nodded his head emphatically in confirmation of its truth. 'In their eagerness to get to the grotto people often forget to buy a souvenir, a rosary or a crucifix, to take back to some old person, a relative, or a neighbour maybe who was good to them in former times, and although they couldn't be expected to turn around and go back, they mightn't grudge the time it would take to stop at a shop along the route.' He turned earnestly to Mary. 'I don't think it would be asking too much of anyone to hop out of his car and snatch up a scapular or an *agnus dei* if he thought it might solace some poor soul, do you?' Mercifully, Mary was spared from giving an answer because the Canon had caught sight of the spire. 'I see it!' he cried, triumphantly, although it was a few seconds before Mary herself could discern against the dark rain-laden clouds the slightly less dark steeple. Within a few minutes they drew up outside the church, standing in its shamble of wooden stalls, with the enormous granite grotto, so grotesquely disproportionate to it, at its gable.

The grotto was unusually empty of people for the time of day. There was no sign of life except for a fat pigeon pecking at the litter in the gutter.

There was certainly no sign at all of Don.

'I knew he'd keep us waiting,' Mary said, just to humour her uncle, but as she spoke, the door of Mullins's shop opened and Mullins ran out in his shirt sleeves hastily swallowing down the food in his mouth as if he'd been at table when he spotted them.

'Good day, Canon. Good day, miss,' he gushed. 'Are you looking for the young gentleman?' To Mary's disgust, he ogled her. 'I recognized him as he was passing here about an hour ago, and I ran out. He was glad to see me, and he gave me a message for you, Canon. He said not to wait your meal for him and that he'd make his own way back.' Then he turned to Mary. 'He had a message for you too, miss. He told me to tell you he had hopes – whatever he meant by that!' The disgusting fellow leered again, having evidently put some interpretation of his own on what might be those hopes.

'Thank you,' Mary said coldly.

The Canon was more cordial. 'Good man, good man!' he said, and without going into the church he pulled up for a minute at the grotto and looked appraisingly at it.

'We need more litter containers,' he said, clapping his hands to shoo away the pigeons. As the Canon turned the car, Mary saw with some amusement that there were splatters of bird droppings on the heads of the Blessed. Then as they drove past the open door of the church she saw the red glow of the sanctuary lamp and bowed her head from force of habit. The Canon, however, bent over the steering wheel, was heading out of the place at a speed unusual for him. Mary looked in surprise at his face. It was suffused with a dark red flush. And when he spoke his voice had a savage intensity.

'What was behind that message Mullins gave you?' he demanded. For a moment she thought that having seen Mullins's leer, her uncle, too, had read something ugly into it. Next minute she realized he had read the message rightly. 'So that's it!' he cried. 'I was slow for once in my life.' He brought the car to an abrupt stop. 'Tell me the truth! What tomfoolery is that fellow going on with?'

'Oh, Uncle. Let's not go into it now,' Mary said desperately.

'Explain yourself, miss!' said the Canon, and although his form of address harked back again to her childhood, this time it had, as it was intended to have, an adverse effect on her.

'This is neither the time nor the place to discuss the matter,' she said coldly.

'You're right there. That's certain,' the Canon snapped back. 'And let me tell you this, miss, the right time will never come. Whatever that fool of a fellow may have in mind, he doesn't know that backing is needed for a scheme of any kind, whether it's sound or not. Not only here but in every country in the world. And I can assure you here and now that in Holy Ireland there wouldn't be one solitary soul who'd back up a scheme that would – ' he paused ' – would interfere with a place sanctified by tradition, and hallowed by the presence of so many sick and suffering human beings.'

'But, Uncle,' Mary cried, 'Don doesn't necessarily envisage development of any kind in the immediate vicinity of the grotto.'

'Bah!' said the Canon. 'Didn't I tell you our own enterprise will spread over a radius of three or four miles from the present centre.' His face was now so inflamed by fury that Mary was frightened for him. He was actually shaking his fist at her. 'Do you think if those developers were once given their head there'd be any controlling them? Do you never read a newspaper? The gang that's mining up in the County Meath are planning to re-route the road from Naval to Kells. Did you hear that? You didn't? Well, that shows the lengths they're prepared to go to accommodate their own interests. And there's talk of altering the course of the Boyne, the most historic river in Ireland, or in Europe for that matter. Those fellows wouldn't think twice of shifting a whole town if it got in their way – ' Suddenly, the old man seemed to lose himself in thoughts of his own. 'Heathens and infidels,' he muttered. Then he swung around to face her again. 'It's a pity your fine fiancé didn't take himself off to hell or to Africa or wherever it was you said he was going. A great lob he'd be for the country that would get him.'

Mary was absolutely staggered. She wouldn't stoop to remind him that she would have been going with Don. 'If that's the way you feel about him, Uncle,' she said with as much calm as she could command, 'the best thing I can do for both of you is prevent you from meeting again.' She opened the car door. 'I'll get out here if you don't mind.'

The Canon was greatly taken aback. 'How do you think you'll get back to the parochial house?' he blustered. 'You're not as fit as that footballer of yours.'

If he meant to mend matters by drollery, he was making a big error. 'I'll manage,' Mary said. 'If he should happen to arrive back, perhaps you'd have Ellen ask him to take our car and come to meet me.' Seeing he only partly got her meaning, she looked straight in his face. 'Perhaps I could trouble you to put my overnight case in the back seat.'

'You're not coming into the house at all?' His bluster was gone, but he still didn't believe she was in earnest. 'What about the meal? What about all the trouble Ellen has taken over it?'

'I'm sorry,' Mary said. 'Truly I am. But you must make what excuses you can.'

She got out of the car.

Going back along the trunk road the Canon drove fast, and when he arrived at the parochial house he went straight into the parlour and threw a few logs on the still fiercely burning fire. Then he called down the passage to Ellen.

'I'll be eating alone, Ellen. They had to go back,' he said to her, giving no explanation. He frowned when the old woman pattered up and stood in the doorway with a bewildered look on her face.

'You didn't let them go back without anything to eat, did you?' she asked. 'Not all the way to Dublin?'

'What's that?' The Canon seemed surprised at the mention of Dublin, as if his thoughts were elsewhere. He recollected himself. 'Yes, to Dublin,' he said, but he smiled enigmatically, and when Ellen sloped away he closed the parlour door. A plan had already formed in his mind and was acting as ballast to keep him steady. All the same, to fortify himself further, after he'd shut the door, he stood still and took a look at his little painting. But with the door closed the lighting on it was wrong, and the glass reflected back the white glare from the window, obliterating the glorious colours. To have had it glassed was a mistake. He shouldn't have listened to the gallery-owner who had insisted that due to its rough texture, the paint would get damaged if it wasn't given protection. He bent and peered into the emerald whorls of the shore grasses and indigo deeps of the sea. He wasn't at all sure that the paint hadn't already been damaged even before the glass was put over it. For that matter, now that he studied it closely, he wasn't sure he approved of Yeats's over-liberal use of the palette knife. That was a fad Yeats got talked into when he was old and sick. He bent closer still and opened the door a fraction to put the painting once more into shadow. Yes. He could see it better now. The heavily laid-on paint in sea, sky, and shore certainly gave dimension to the solitary human figure in the foreground. But the figure itself was not much more than a conglomeration of blobs, swirls, and coagulated lumps of crude paint. The Canon felt that if he stuck his finger into one of those blobs it would burst and turpentine or linseed would ooze out from the canvas. The over-use of the palette knife might yet bring down the prices Yeats was fetching, he mused, turning away in irritation from the picture. It had not calmed him. Stalking into the hall he yelled out once more to Ellen. 'Don't bring in my food till I tell you, I want to make a phone call.' Going back into his den and closing the door, he lifted the telephone receiver and, lowering his voice, gave the operator a name and a number and asked her to put through a personal call.

A few minutes later there was the crackle of a voice at the other end of the line.

'Ah, Tim? Is that you?' said the Canon, his temper enormously improved. 'It is? Good! How are you? Same here! Same here, thank God. Well, look Tim, I won't hold you up with preambles. I'll be seeing you next month anyway at the Priests' Retreat, but look here! Do you happen to recall a fellow who was in the seminary with us, a fellow that cracked up badly and was sent home? Wasn't his name Gargan? Yes, that's the fellow. Yes. Yes, he got over it fairly well and married and reared a family. Yes, yes. I know that. That's right. That's the very fellow. Well, what I wanted to know was whether I'm right in thinking that although the story given out to us in the seminary was that he was being sent home, he was really being sent – as we guessed at the time – to the other place? That's right. That's what I thought. Could you tell me something else, Tim? How long was he in that place? Oh! is that so? You don't say? He must have been a fairly bad case. Anyway, be that as it may, thank you, Tim, for the information, but let me ask you something else before I let you go. Would you say it ran in the family? Ah well, I know all that. Times have changed and so on. Thanks be to God they have good doctors there, now at any rate. They can work wonders with electric shock and insulin. I was listening to a programme about that on the radio only the other day, but I think they still have reservations in some cases. Apparently there are cases where it is what you might call congenital, and then – Yes. Yes? I'm listening. I agree. I agree entirely. That's what I thought. And that's why I'm phoning you. You know, I suppose, there's a job coming up in your diocese – ah, don't worry, Tim, just a run-of-the-mill job – district engineer. There must be hundreds of suitable applicants. Well, I understand the decision is more or less made, and it's being given to a young fellow who – what's that, Tim? Oh!' Here, although he was alone in the parlour, the Canon chuckled. 'Ah, you read me,' he said. 'That's the very man, a son of our other man. Oh, this young fellow – what's that? Yes. Yes, I've met him. Yes, I agree he seems to have all his marbles – more than his share would be more like – that's not my objection to him, although it might be thought a district engineer ought to be fairly responsible – cambering roads and building bridges and that kind of thing. By the way, did you read in the papers about that terrible business in America recently, where forty or fifty poor souls went to their death when a bridge collapsed. And hundreds were injured. It was way out in Ohio, or somewhere like that, but people are people the world over. Well, as I was saying, I wouldn't like to be whoever was responsible for appointing the district engineer in that case, would you? I think I'd sooner be one of the poor unfortunates that plunged to their death in the river. I'd even go so far as to say I'd rather be the man that made the miscalculation, than a member of the selection committee that didn't vet the applicants properly. Ah yes, yes. I know that only too well, Tim. All the same, we can't neglect to do our homework, can we, when it comes to matters like this?'

Here, the Canon began to tap his foot impatiently on the linoleum. 'Yes, yes, Tim. I hear you. I know what you're trying to get across to me, but let me ask you another question. Did you ever read a book called *The Bridge of San Luis Rey*? You didn't? Ah, what's the matter with you? Are you going to seed up there in the fat land? Look, I'll bring it to the retreat and let you have a loan of it. Don't forget to give it back, that's all. There's a powerful description in it of a bridge collapsing. It will interest you, apropos of this matter we're discussing.' Here, however, the Canon seemed to suffer a loss of memory. 'What's this we were talking about anyway?' he asked. 'Oh, yes, about that job – ' There was a brief pause while the Canon listened to the voice at the other end of the line. 'No, that would be far too late. You'll have to act at once,' he said emphatically. Then he put his hand over the mouthpiece of the phone. 'Excuse me a minute, Tim,' he said, and raised his head to listen to the sound of a car starting up outside, followed a few seconds later by the sound of a car driving away. 'Nothing wrong, nothing at all,' he reassured his listener. 'But, with regard to this job, Tim, I know what I'm talking about. There's more to this than meets the eye. There are more reasons than one why we don't want this type of fellow in a key position. Do you get me? You do. Well, I'll see you at the retreat. And I won't forget to bring you that book.'

The Canon's face had resumed a normal expression, and he seemed about to hang up the receiver when there was another crackle on the line. His expression changed slightly. 'Yes, I know he is engaged, which makes it more awkward, I admit. In fact there's something I'm not sure I ought to mention. I think I'd better though, since you'd find out anyway, you old fox! And I hope when I tell you, you'll see how concerned I am for the public good. You see, it's to a relative of my own the fellow's engaged. Yes. Oh, you knew, did you? Well, all I can say is, I'm sure that like myself you must have thought she'd have done better for herself, a pretty girl like her, and clever as well. Diabolically clever, you might say. You might even go so far as to say that in many ways, as God made them, he matched them. But let me make one thing plain. You're not to let yourself be concerned over my niece. I can't afford to be concerned about her myself in a situation so grave. The fellow may be all right – who knows – but that's not to say that we can let him be placed in a position where even the slightest weakness could result in calamity for untold numbers of people. Don't be concerned about Mary, Tim. A bit of experience outside Ireland never hurt anyone, and she's no more of an exception to that rule than he is. Never fear, they'll be back home in a few years, and if he stands up to the test of time we might be able to do something for him then, eh? I may be on the blower to you if that time comes, Tim! We might fix them up with something similiar to what they're aspiring to now – if we're both in the land of the living, which I hope, God willing, we will be. By the way, while we're on the subject, I didn't ask about the old lumbago? Ah, good! Good. That's about the way I feel myself.' A thin trickle of laughter came down the wire and was echoed by a loud confident laugh from the Canon. Then apparently he had cause to give his friend further reassurance. 'Oh, stop worrying about the girl, Tim. Women are only interested in making a home. It doesn't matter a damn to them where it is – Dublin or – ' He frowned. 'Or Africa, or wherever.' Since the last word seemed a weak one on which to end, or wanting perhaps to give a professional touch to the conversation – the Canon's voice took on an unctuous tone.

'God bless, Tim,' he said.

'God bless,' the answer crackled back. 'God bless.'